PENGUIN CLASSICS

THE PENGUIN BOOK OF GHOST STORIES

MICHAEL NEWTON was both an undergraduate and postgraduate at University College London. He is the author of *Savage Girls and Wild Boys: A History of Feral Children* (Faber & Faber, 2002) and of a book on *Kind Hearts and Coronets* for the British Film Institute's Film Classics series (2003). He has also edited Edmund Gosse's *Father and Son* for Oxford World's Classics and Joseph Conrad's *The Secret Agent* for Penguin. He has taught at UCL, Central Saint Martins College of Art and Design and Princeton University, and currently works at the University of Leiden. At present he is completing a book on the history of assassination and political violence.

T0176152

The Penguin Book of Ghost Stories

From Elizabeth Gaskell to Ambrose Bierce

Edited with an Introduction by
MICHAEL NEWTON

PENGUIN BOOKS

PENGUIN CLASSICS

Published by the Penguin Group
Penguin Books Ltd, 80 Strand, London WC2R 0RL, England
Penguin Group (USA) Inc., 375 Hudson Street, New York, New York 10014, USA
Penguin Group (Canada), 90 Eglinton Avenue East, Suite 700, Toronto, Ontario, Canada M4P 2Y3
(a division of Pearson Penguin Canada Inc.)
Penguin Ireland, 25 St Stephen's Green, Dublin 2, Ireland
(a division of Penguin Books Ltd)
Penguin Group (Australia), 250 Camberwell Road, Camberwell, Victoria 3124, Australia
(a division of Pearson Australia Group Pty Ltd)
Penguin Books India Pvt Ltd, 11 Community Centre, Panchsheel Park, New Delhi – 110 017, India
Penguin Group (NZ), 67 Apollo Drive, Rosedale, North Shore 0632, New Zealand
(a division of Pearson New Zealand Ltd)
Penguin Books (South Africa) (Pty) Ltd, 24 Sturdee Avenue, Rosebank, Johannesburg 2196, South Africa

Penguin Books Ltd, Registered Offices: 80 Strand, London WC2R 0RL, England

www.penguin.com

This selection first published in Penguin Classics 2010

027

Selection and editorial material copyright © Michael Newton, 2010

The Acknowledgements on page ix constitute an extension of this page

The moral right of the editor has been asserted

Set in 10.25/12.25 pt PostScript Adobe Sabon
Typeset by Rowland Phototypesetting Ltd, Bury St Edmunds, Suffolk
Printed in England by Clays Ltd, Elcograf S.p.A.

ISBN: 978-0-141-44236-5

www.greenpenguin.co.uk

To Lena Müller

Contents

Acknowledgements

For their support, patience and encouragement and ghostly advice, I thank my editors at Penguin, Marcella Edwards, Mariateresa Boffo and Rachel Love. For help with the text, I am grateful to Elisabeth Merriman and to Kate Parker for her invaluable attentiveness, her thoughtfulness and diligence. Thanks to Professor Dafydd Johnson and to Michiel de Vaan for their generous help with the Welsh language. I am similarly indebted to Evert-Jan van Leeuwen for help from the other side.

For permission to reprint W. W. Jacobs's 'The Monkey's Paw', I am grateful to the Society of Authors as the Literary Representative of the Estate of W. W. Jacobs.

Chronology of the Ghost Story
1820–1914

As well as ghost stories, this chronology includes significant critical and other non-fiction works on the supernatural.

1820   Washington Irving, 'The Legend of Sleepy Hollow' (collected in *The Sketch Book of Geoffrey Crayon, Gent*)

1823   Charles Lamb, 'Witches and Other Night-Fears' (from *Essays of Elia*)

1824   Translation into English of Ernest Theodor Wilhelm Hoffmann, *The Devil's Elixir* (*Die Elixiere des Teufels*); Mary Shelley, 'On Ghosts' (published in the *London Magazine*); Sir Walter Scott, 'Wandering Willie's Tale' (from the novel *Redgauntlet*)

1827   Sir Walter Scott, 'On the Supernatural in Fictitious Composition' (published in the *Foreign Quarterly Review*)

1830   James Hogg, 'The Mysterious Bride' (published in *Blackwood's Magazine*); Robert MacNish, *The Philosophy of Sleep*, including an account of a woman who haunted herself; Sir Walter Scott, *Letters on Demonology and Witchcraft*

1836–7 Charles Dickens, 'The Story of the Goblins who Stole a Sexton' (from the novel *Pickwick Papers*)

1837   Nathaniel Hawthorne, *Twice-Told Tales*

1838   Sheridan Le Fanu, 'The Ghost and the Bone-setter' (published in *Dublin University Magazine*)

1839   Edgar Allan Poe, *Tales of the Grotesque and Arabesque*

1840   Robert Barham, 'The Spectre of Tappington' and 'The Leech of Folkestone' (collected in *The Ingoldsby Legends*)

1842   Edward Bulwer Lytton, *Zanoni*

1843   Charles Dickens, *A Christmas Carol*

1845   Edgar Allan Poe, 'The Facts in the Case of M. Valdemar' (published in the *American Review*)

1846   Nathaniel Hawthorne, *Mosses from an Old Manse*

1847   Emily Brontë, *Wuthering Heights*

1848   Catherine Crowe, *The Night-Side of Nature*

1851   Sheridan Le Fanu, *Ghost Stories and Tales of Mystery*

1852   Elizabeth Gaskell, 'The Old Nurse's Story' (published in *Household Words*)

1855   Wilkie Collins, 'Mad Monkton' (published in *Fraser's Magazine*); Elizabeth Gaskell, *Lizzie Leigh; and Other Tales*

1857   Dinah Maria Mulock (Mrs Craik), 'M. Anastatius' and 'The Last House in C— Street' (collected in *Nothing New*)

1858   Fitz-James O'Brien, 'The Diamond Lens' (published in the *Atlantic Monthly*)

1859   Fitz-James O'Brien, 'What Was It?' (published in *Harper's New Monthly Magazine*) and 'The Wondersmith' (*Atlantic Monthly*); Edward Bulwer Lytton, 'The Haunted and the Haunters' (*Blackwood's Magazine*); Catherine Crowe, *Ghosts and Family Legends*

1860   Mary Elizabeth Braddon, 'The Cold Embrace' (published in *Welcome Guest*)

1861   Edward Bulwer Lytton, *A Strange Story*; Sheridan Le Fanu, *The House by the Churchyard* (1861–3)

1862   Mary Elizabeth Braddon, *Ralph the Bailiff and Other Tales* (including 'Eveline's Visitant' and 'The Cold Embrace')

1864   Daniel Dunglas Home, *Incidents in My Life*; Robert Browning, 'Mr Sludge, "The Medium"' (collected in *Dramatis Personae*)

1865   Amelia B. Edwards, 'The North Mail' (collected in *Miss Carew*); Charles Dickens and Charles Allston Collins, 'The Trial for Murder' (published in *All the Year Round*)

1866   Alfred Russel Wallace, *The Scientific Aspect of the Supernatural*; Charles Dickens, 'No. 1 Branch Line: The Signal-man' (published in the Christmas number of *All the Year Round*)

1868   Henry James, 'The Romance of Certain Old Clothes' (published in the *Atlantic Monthly*)

1869   Sheridan Le Fanu, 'Green Tea' (published in *All the Year Round*)

1871   Harriet Beecher Stowe, 'The Ghost in the Mill' and 'The Ghost in the Cap'n Brown House' (collected in *Oldtown Fireside Stories*)

1872   Sheridan Le Fanu, *In a Glass Darkly* (including 'Green Tea')

1873   Amelia B. Edwards, *Monsieur Maurice*; Rhoda Broughton, *Tales for Christmas Eve*

1875   W. H. Mumler, *Personal Experiences of William H. Mumler in Spirit Photography*; foundation in New York of the Theosophical Society by Helena Blavatsky

1879   Margaret Oliphant, *A Beleaguered City*

1880   William Crookes, *Experiments with Psychical Phenomena*; Sheridan Le Fanu, *The Purcell Papers*

1881   Fitz-James O'Brien, *The Poems and Stories of Fitz-James O'Brien*; Robert Louis Stevenson, 'Thrawn Janet' (published in the *Cornhill Magazine*)

1882   Margaret Oliphant, 'The Open Door' (published in *Blackwood's Magazine*); Mrs J. H. (Charlotte) Riddell, *Weird Stories*; foundation in London of the Society for Psychical Research by Frederic William Henry Myers, Henry Sidgwick, Edmund Gurney and others

1884   Grant Allen, 'Our Scientific Observances of a Ghost' (collected in *Strange Stories*)

1885   Margaret Oliphant, *Two Tales of the Seen and Unseen* (including 'The Open Door')

1887   Robert Louis Stevenson, *The Merry Men and Other Tales and Fables*; Lafcadio Hearn, *Some Chinese Ghosts*; Oscar Wilde, 'The Canterville Ghost' (published in the *Court and Society Review*); Mrs J. H. Riddell, *Idle Tales*

1888   Mary Louisa Molesworth, *Four Ghost Stories*

1889   Mrs J. H. Riddell, 'A Terrible Vengeance' (collected in *Princess Sunshine*)

1890   Vernon Lee, *Hauntings*; Mrs Henry Wood, 'A Curious Experience' (collected in *Johnny Ludlow*); Rudyard Kipling, 'At the End of the Passage' (published in the *Boston Herald*) and *The Phantom Rickshaw, and Other Tales*

1891   Rudyard Kipling, *Life's Handicap* (including 'At the End of the Passage'); Ambrose Bierce, 'An Occurrence at Owl Creek Bridge' (collected in *Tales of Soldiers and Civilians*);

Henry James, 'Sir Edmund Orme' (published in *Black and White*)

1892 Helena Petrovna Blavatsky, *Nightmare Tales*; Henry James, 'Owen Wingrave' (published in the *Graphic*)

1893 Ambrose Bierce, *Can Such Things Be?*; E. Nesbit, *Grim Tales*; B. M. Croker, *To Let*

1894 Sheridan Le Fanu, *The Watcher and Other Weird Stories*; Arthur Machen, *The Great God Pan* and *The Inmost Light*; F. Marion Crawford, *The Upper Berth*

1895 M. R. James, 'Canon Alberic's Scrap-Book' (published in *National Review*) and 'Lost Hearts' (*Pall Mall Magazine*); Arthur Machen, *The Three Impostors*

1896 Mary Louisa Molesworth, *Uncanny Tales*

1898 Joseph Conrad, 'The Idiots' (collected in *Tales of Unrest*); Henry James, *The Turn of the Screw*

1899 Henry James, 'The Real Right Thing' (published in *Colliers Weekly*); Arthur Machen, 'The White People'; Vernon Lee, 'The Doll' (collected in *For Maurice: Five Unlikely Stories*)

1900 Lafcadio Hearn, 'Nightmare-Touch' (collected in *Shadowings*); Robert Hichens, 'How Love Came to Professor Guildea' (collected in *Tongues of Conscience*); Richard Marsh, *The Seen and the Unseen*

1901 Barry Pain, *Stories in the Dark* (including 'The Undying Thing')

1902 H. G. Wells, 'The Story of the Inexperienced Ghost' (published in *Strand Magazine*); Frank Norris, 'The Ship That Saw a Ghost' (published in *Overland Monthly*); W. W. Jacobs, 'The Monkey's Paw' (first published in *Harper's New Monthly Magazine* and collected in *The Lady of the Barge*); Frank Podmore, *Modern Spiritualism: A History and a Criticism*

1903 Mary E. Wilkins Freeman, *The Wind in the Rose-Bush, and Other Stories of the Supernatural*; William Dean Howells, 'His Apparition' (collected in *Questionable Shapes*); Mark Twain, 'A Ghost Story' (collected in *Sketches New and Old*); Robert Hugh Benson, *The Light Invisible*; Arthur Christopher Benson, *The Hill of Trouble and Other Stories*; F. W. H. Myers, *Human Personality and Its Survival After Death*

1904   M. R. James, *Ghost Stories of an Antiquary* (including
" "Oh, Whistle, and I'll Come to You, My Lad" "); William
James, *Varieties of Religious Experience*; Lafcadio Hearn,
Kwaidan; Rudyard Kipling, 'They' (collected in *Actions and
Reactions*)

1905   Arthur Christopher Benson, *The Isles of Sunset*

1906   Algernon Blackwood, *The Empty House and Other
Ghost Stories*; O. Henry, 'The Furnished Room' (collected in
The Four Million)

1907   Ambrose Bierce, 'The Moonlit Road' (published in
Cosmopolitan); Robert Hugh Benson, *A Mirror of Shalott*;
Algernon Blackwood, *The Listener, and Other Stories*

1908   Algernon Blackwood, *John Silence, Physician Extraordinary*; William Hope Hodgson, *The House on the Borderland*; Perceval Landon, 'Thurnley Abbey' (collected in *Raw
Edges*); Henry James, 'The Jolly Corner' (published in the
English Review)

1909   Mary Austin, 'The Readjustment' (collected in *Lost
Borders*); William Hope Hodgson, *The Ghost Pirates*

1910   Edith Wharton, 'Afterward' (published in *Century
Magazine*) and *Tales of Men and Ghosts* (including 'The
Eyes' and 'Afterward'); Sir William Barrett, *Automatic
Writing*; Algernon Blackwood, 'The Wendigo' (collected in
The Lost Valley and Other Stories); Walter de la Mare, *The
Return*; Ambrose Bierce, reissue of *Can Such Things Be?*
(including 'The Moonlit Road') as vol. 3 of *The Collected
Works of Ambrose Bierce*

1911   Oliver Onions, *Widdershins* (including 'The Beckoning
Fair One'); F. Marion Crawford, *The Screaming Skull*; M. R.
James, *More Ghost Stories of an Antiquary*

1912   E. F. Benson, *The Room in the Tower and Other Stories*

1913   William Hope Hodgson, *Carnacki the Ghost Finder*

Introduction

The ghost is the most enduring figure in supernatural fiction.
He is absolutely indestructible . . . He changes with the styles
in fiction but he never goes out of fashion. He is the really
permanent citizen of the earth, for mortals, at best, are but
transients.   Dorothy Scarborough,
The Supernatural in Modern English Fiction

GHOST, *n.* The outward and visible sign of an inward fear.
                              Ambrose Bierce, *The Devil's Dictionary*

It is the haunted who haunt.
                         Elizabeth Bowen, 'The Happy Autumn Fields'

GHOST WORDS

Someone is afraid. In a dark house or on an empty railway
platform, at the foot of the staircase or there on a lonely beach.
When critics discuss the ghost story, they often pay no more
than lip-service to the intended impact of the tale itself. The
critics' words remove us from the place where the story's words
first took us. In the ghost story, through the representation of
another's fear, we become afraid. We take on the sensation of
terror, the alert uneasiness that translates random sounds into
intentions, a room's chill into watchfulness, and leaves us with
the anxious apprehension of an other's presence. The stories
fix images of profound uneasiness in our minds. These images
remain and act afterwards, when the story is over, as paths to
renewed anxiety. From the stories in this collection, memories
rise up of Thrawn Janet's crooked walk, like a rag doll that has
been hanged; the bereaved mother desperately reaching for the
bolt to the door in 'The Monkey's Paw', with the visitor outside;
or in M. R. James's tale, on a sunless day, in a dream, a

man running along the sands, breathless, worn out, pursued inexorably by a blind, muffled figure.

The ghost story aims at the retention of such pictures; it intends the production of such fears. It wants sympathetic shudders. There is undoubtedly something disreputable about that intention. Certainly M. R. James, a Cambridge don and the greatest writer of ghost stories, was made to feel so. Like pornography, or the 'weepie', ghost stories are meant to evoke a physical reaction. Their art mobilizes emotion; it organizes feeling. In recent years, the figure of the ghost has been rehabilitated by theorists, taken as a symbol for almost any kind of cultural or philosophical haunting. In the process, the ghost has been taken seriously, made into a matter for the intellect. Ghosts are no longer dreamt, no longer felt, no longer feared, but rather played with and thought through.

Yet such theorizing surely obscures the main point. In pornography, we are aroused by another's arousal; in a 'weepie', we shed tears for another's sadness; in a ghost story, we are frightened by another's fear. Imaginative sympathy lies at the centre of this art form. Exchange is the key; all the stories turn on this idea of correspondence. Yet it is curious how regularly such identifications falter at the figure of the ghost. The spectre is that with which, in most cases, we cannot identify. We see the ghost, we hear it, but we can rarely place ourselves in its position. The ghost acts as the limit of our compassion. Only those tales, such as Margaret Oliphant's 'The Open Door' (1882), that can see the human in the spirit, allow pity for the ghost. More usually, it is precisely the sense that the ghost is not human at all, but somehow anti-human, that prevents our acknowledgement of kinship. Instead, we side with the haunted, not the haunters; with the terrified, and not the menacing. This may be because ultimately the haunters are the texts themselves, and the haunted their readers.

There have of course always been stories about ghosts; however, the 'ghost story' itself, as understood by literary critics, is a Romantic invention. Its prime begins, tentatively, in the 1820s, hits its stride in the 1850s, reaches its zenith between the 1880s and the outbreak of the First World War, and peters out in the 1950s, as its last great exponents, Elizabeth Bowen and Walter de la Mare, end their careers as short-story writers. Naturally, however, there are great ghost stories written after that period, notably Kingsley Amis's *The Green Man* (1969), and the genre continues to enjoy great success in film and also on stage in the excellent plays of Conor MacPherson and in the highly popular stage adaptation of Susan Hill's *The Woman in Black* (1983).

It is an interesting, but unanswerable, question as to why the ghost story should have flourished then, and why, in particular, in the British Isles and America. Some tentative explanations may be given, though ultimately they leave the central mystery unexplained. One reason for its sudden rise lies in the peculiar talents and interests of a few individuals. The fact that Walter Scott, Edgar Allan Poe, Charles Dickens, Elizabeth Gaskell and Henry James embraced the genre of the supernatural tale undoubtedly influenced their contemporaries and later followers. The sheer genius displayed in their tales exposed the possibilities of the form. These talented writers required – and found – equally talented readers. Such stories as Edith Wharton and others were writing presuppose a frightened reader, but also one who is peculiarly attentive, responding to events, creating meaning and weighing evidence.

Although he frequently voiced scepticism about spiritualism and spectral materializations, Charles Dickens was nonetheless an enthusiast for ghost stories. While the link is at least as old as William Shakespeare's *Hamlet* (*c.* 1599–1601), it was very likely Dickens who established for Victorians the connection between Christmas and ghost stories, through the inset narrative of 'The Story of the Goblins who Stole a Sexton' in the Christmas celebrations in *Pickwick Papers* (1836–7) and, of course, through *A Christmas Carol* (1843). The festive ghost is a curious conjunction, though one that expresses the central paradox of the genre: that is, the intertwining of cosiness and terror. The bond between Christmas and ghost stories would in time become a cultural cliché: as a character in Elizabeth Bowen's 1920s story 'The Back Drawing-Room' cynically remarks: ' "Bring in the Yule log, this is a Dickens Christmas. We're going to tell ghost stories." '[1] As well as his contribution to the genre as writer, Dickens encouraged ghost-story writing in others and his taste for such tales influenced his practice as editor: notable ghost stories by Elizabeth Gaskell, Wilkie Collins, Sheridan Le Fanu and others appeared in magazines he edited.

There was also, for later practitioners, the legitimating influence of Henry James. If the form could seem to some inherently vulgar, James's fascination with 'the fantastic-gruesome, the supernatural thrilling' raised its status.[2] Clearly James recognized the possible embarrassment aroused by such a predilection – he commented that 'one man's amusement is at the best ... another's desolation'.[3] For James the ghost story represented the limit of his feeling comfortable with the tale of adventure; on the other side of the boundary lay the impossible pirates and detectives of Robert Louis Stevenson and Joseph Conrad. The ghost was somehow finer, deeper, more subtle, better attuned to James's interest in the drama of consciousness. When someone as fastidious as he could approve, an element of refinement could elevate the form.

For writers, too, there was the appeal of genre fiction. The form itself with its loose set of rules enabled the talented writer to offer variations on the spectral theme. Exploiting the familiarity of the form's repeated situations, the writers could allow the genre to do some of the work for them, using the frame to create their own peculiar effects. The ghost story could therefore at once be a rigidly limited genre and a form of striking variety.

As M. R. James pointed out, the ghost story is after all only a particular kind of short story.[4] The history of the short story is therefore necessarily entwined with that of the ghost. The reasons why the short story flourished as it did in the late nineteenth and early twentieth centuries are clear to see. In the British context, although its effects can be exaggerated, the expansion of an educated reading public following W. E. Forster's Elementary Education Act of 1870 led to a significant increase in demand for good literary material. New printing technologies (linotype, rotary printers and so on) fostered the mass production of books; a new raft of publishing houses entered the business. Though still in relative terms prohibitively expensive for most, book prices nonetheless had fallen significantly by the end of the century. The gradual demise of the three-volume Victorian novel and the rise of interest in briefer forms also contributed. Partly, the desire for the succinct was provoked by the proliferation of periodicals, many of which (from socialist bulletins to society journals, from children's papers to cycling magazines) required fiction to fill their pages. Though novels continued to be serialized, short stories were increasingly seen as the ideal fictional form for magazine readers. For writers, short stories paid more for less work; hence the production of short fiction was an excellent way to remain solvent. Editors were eager for stories, and writers were keen to provide them.

Alongside such material concerns there lies an increasing critical interest in the short story as a literary kind. The form itself was rather fluid, its chief characteristic being the indeterminate matter of its length. It was the American critic Brander Matthews who coined the term 'short-story' in 1884; in theorizing about such texts, he borrowed much from Edgar Allan Poe, the first great theorist of the short story and also its first great practitioner. Poe's idea that the story aimed at unity of effect achieved through concision became central to the understanding of the form. Compression brought greater impact.

When Brander Matthews published a book on the subject, he entitled it *The Philosophy of the Short-story* (1901). That 'philosophy' looked to many to be a matter of fragmentation, as though the story, through 'unity of effect', expressed the multiplicity, the contradictions of life. This interest in the broken was supposed by many to echo the disruptions of modern existence. Critics remarked that the very brevity of the form suited the short-winded modern mind, which could not attend to things for long, and was perpetually hurried from event to event.

At its most literary, the short story could be provocative, enigmatic. By contrast, some of the most popular forms of the short story were far from open-ended. The comic yarn that moved to a punchline, the tale that turned finally on some twist, the detective story that made for the unmasking of a crime, all enacted closure, a self-contained expression of finality. By rigorous critics such stories would be faintly damned as mere

'anecdotes', opposed to the uncertain glance, the subtle epi-
phany of the true 'short story'. The ghost story itself would
combine both options uneasily; a genre tale, certainly, but one
where endings were troubling, unsettled, sometimes painfully
unresolved. Ghost stories must need be brief, because their
effect is so tentative, so tenuous, their enchantment so fragile.

Robert Louis Stevenson asserted that the end of a tale should
be 'bone of the bone and blood of the blood of the beginning'.[5]
However, the question of how best to end a ghost story remained open. There was no compulsion to end with marriage,
or detection; and if the end were death, it was always only a
repetition of the original death that permitted the haunting in
the first place. The *telos* of the ghost story remained unresolved,
because in the nineteenth century the ghost no longer had a
stock purpose to fulfil within the tale. In the early modern
period (1500–1800), the ghost had appeared as minister of
justice, engaged still with the business of life. It returned from
the dead to settle wills and inheritances, or was engaged with
matters of revenge, or busy with requests for burial. (The belief
that the righteous laying of the body will end the walking of
the spirit remains a theme in later ghost stories too.) The ghost
was occupied with disturbances in the family (or in religious
practice); it would set about putting these right, and as such
was a figure on the side of law, of religion, of order.

In the late nineteenth/early twentieth century, the ghost sometimes also has such a purpose – the spectres of Mary Austin's
'The Readjustment' (1909) or Edith Wharton's 'Afterward'
(1910) come to mind, or the guardian ghost in M. R. James's
'A Warning to the Curious' (1925). In different circumstances,
the ghost could seem a mere spirit of place, tied meaninglessly
to one location. Oscar Wilde's 'The Canterville Ghost' (1887)
parodies the righteous spirit in a tale where haunting becomes
a pointless and self-imposed duty. The question of motivation
therefore time and again rebounds on to the haunted, who seem
now, in a turning of the tables, to be the active agent in the
tale.

The ghost story depends upon anticipation touched with reti-
cence. Forebodings reach us; a potentially unnoticed strangeness
is there to catch the eye. Such stories most often avoid outrage-

ous violence; they make us think horrors, not minutely witness them. From their beginnings, what might come lies hidden in the visible world of the story, itself so like the real world we live and die in. As with the detective story, a genre closely related, the reader must look for clues.[6] These are rarely hard to discern. That is because the ghost story is not about guessing an ending, it's about dreading its inevitable arrival. The indications of the ghost's coming are therefore not so much clues as forebodings and portents. Stories are based on hints, deferrals, postponements, while heading towards a dénouement that is a confrontation with the thing itself; the end of the tale is often merely the moment when the ghost comes into sight.

THE HAUNTERS

What is a ghost? It is a figure that remains at once interpretable and evading, exceeding interpretation. All in the self that cannot be understood stands personified in the ghost.

Therefore, perhaps above anything else, the ghost is a way of engaging with our mystification about death. It survives with the belief that there is something left over when the human body becomes a corpse, that there is a residue, or remnant, that does not cease in the moment of dying. Some ghosts exude the horrors of the charnel house; others remain imperturbably decorous. Freed from the necessities of life, these ghosts neither eat nor drink, breathe nor excrete; they do not rot or putrefy, processes that somehow shame our bodies, but remain always cool, dignified and therefore inhuman.

The ghost can also seem something of a performer. This was one of the jokes of Oscar Wilde's 'The Canterville Ghost', where the spook busies himself impersonating an entire gallery of housebound spectres. In Henry James's 'The Jolly Corner' (1908), the ghost resembles a figure in a pantomime, a madcap Harlequin mocking the elderly Pantaloon that is the haunted man.

Such theatricality calls to mind the thought that the ghost (or the ghost-story writer) might, like an actor, be a professional deceiver. The modern ghost exists in the gaps caused by the fallibility of our perceptions. It occupies a world of doubt, where the senses can deceive. When A. E. Housman wrote to M. R. James regarding the haunted telescope in 'A View from a Hill' (1925), he observed coolly that something seemed to be wrong with the optics.[7] In the ghost story, there are many such faulty instruments and organs of sense. Repeatedly we follow the rapid correction of a mistake in perception; or just the opposite – the mind's doubt that what we are perceiving can in fact be there. There is a ghost, we know it, but the seer cannot accept the fact. In any case, from the writer's viewpoint, a ghost is an object best left vague. Appearance can produce bathos, and so humour.

Humour is rather awkwardly present in Grant Allen's 'Our Scientific Observances of a Ghost' (collected in *Strange Stories*, 1884). Here the narrator and his accomplices subject a poor phantom to meticulous physical examination. Such thorough scrutiny had its real-life counterpart in the period, as the vogue for spiritualism (beginning in the 1840s) led to the scientific study of 'supernatural' phenomena. The key event – and very likely the subject satirized in Allen's tale – was the foundation in 1882 of the Society for Psychical Research (SPR). Ghosts were seen by many at the time as the limiting border to scientific study, a subject on which science would necessarily have nothing to say. For others, the ghost, as a phenomenon within the real world, was a justifiable object for investigation. If supernatural incidents occurred within the physical realm, they could be enquired into and understood like any other. The ghost therefore existed on an uneasy boundary between the material and the immaterial, life and death, the analysable and the ineffable.

One means by which the ghost story could explore scientific investigation of spiritual phenomena was through the figure of the psychic doctor or private investigator. Sheridan Le Fanu's Martin Hesselius, the fictional collector of the uncanny tales of *In a Glass Darkly* (1872), is the ancestor of such types. A practitioner of metaphysical medicine, Hesselius is also a kind of detective, one who sees what others miss. (This might also be said, in a darker key, of the Rev. Mr Jennings, the victim in one of Le Fanu's tales, 'Green Tea'.) Later examples of this type would include Algernon Blackwood's John Silence or William Hope Hodgson's Thomas Carnacki.

This technical approach to the ghost seemed to some a sad demystification. While Henry James knew and liked F. W. H. Myers, one of the central figures in the SPR, he also fretted that the Society might strip away the sacred horror from a ghost. In fact, James need not have worried. Myers himself enjoyed such a supernatural tale as Robert Louis Stevenson's *The Strange Case of Dr Jekyll and Mr Hyde* (1886). Moreover some of the SPR's treatises could read uncannily like fictional ghost stories.

The division between feigning and truth was in any case necessarily evoked in documentary accounts of the 'supernatural'. Issues of belief lay at the heart of both the SPR's activities and the form of the ghost story itself. In both cases, the reader was to be persuaded of something that the rational mind hesitated to accept. As George Bernard Shaw once wrote to Henry James: 'No man who doesn't believe in a ghost ever sees one.'[8] The fear in a ghost story is the fear of what we imagine: that is, of what we might fantasize and believe about others, about the world, about our houses, about ourselves. The ghost story is a literary form that invites us to imagine horrors. It operates in that realm where magic and science become confused, and where dreams and reality merge.

HAUNTINGS

The essential structure of the ghost story, from the 1840s onwards, can be read as the account of an intrusion into a space. As such, one of the first questions it raises is that of social roles and proprieties: who here is the intruder, the haunted or the haunter?

The ghost's intrusion brings the unassimilable, the fact of death, abruptly into view. Yet perhaps 'intrusion' is the wrong word. Rather in the ghost's haunting something suddenly appears in correspondence with something else. It is an unexpected and unsettling connection that shocks us.

These correspondences derive from the classic ghost story's leaning on the deviation from the accustomed world. The ghost brings to light interference from elsewhere, the unwarranted entry of a disrupting element – one that is uncannily at home there. The familiar unveils its association with the unfamiliar. M. R. James argued that the rooting of a story in the common world of habits and timetables would aid the process of sympathetic identification between the reader and the haunted one. This rapport was one more of the genre's correlations, and the key to its power to frighten.

The territory of the ghost story itself operates within the quotidian world and obeys, except for the ghost, the rules of realism. In particular, the American ghost story gives us a neighbourhood ghost, tied to the literary regionalism of the period, as in 'The Ghost in the Cap'n Brown House' (1871) and 'The Wind in the Rose-Bush' (1903). British ghosts figure likewise in specific environments, including a surprisingly high count of stories in border districts, Elizabeth Gaskell's 'The Old Nurse's Story' (1852) exemplifying this tendency.

This interruption of the credible by the fantastic places the ghost story within the late nineteenth-century questioning of the facility of 'realism' to describe the world. In that sense, ghost stories were proto-modernist texts. In another, the genre was a parasite living off the realistic mode, an infringement of a literary convention on the basis of style. That violation itself becomes entirely acceptable, conventional and comprehensible in terms of genre. We just have to remember that it's 'only a ghost story'. Seen in these terms, the contravention of literary realism, its penetration by the fantastic, becomes safe, cosy and unthreatening.

Within the ghost story, there are many forms of similar encroachment. The spiritual intrudes on the physical, and in so doing becomes correspondingly physical itself. The most feared property of the ghost is its ability to touch you. As the American critic Dorothy Scarborough (1878–1935) put it: 'it is through the sense of touch that the worst form of haunting comes. Seeing a supernatural visitant is terrible, hearing him is direful, smelling him is loathsome, but having him touch you is the climax of horror.'[9] Yet can one be touched by the disembodied?

The other great fear evoked by the ghost story is that we will be dragged off from our own space, and taken to the place where the ghost comes from. That might be imagined as some intangible locale, a pocket in reality, another dimension. It may belong to some distant elsewhere, or be thought of as overlapping, a place jointly 'owned' by the haunter and the haunted, a coincidental time.

In another instance of such correspondences and invasions, the historical past can breach the present. During the late nineteenth century, some saw fear itself as atavistic, a return to archetypal primal panic. Yet rather the ghost story shows that fear is always new; it occurred before, it occurs now, and the past fear becomes a present one – much as the fictional character's terror may be re-evoked in the reader. In M. R. James's stories, this particular theme is exhibited through the discovery and handling of some antiquarian object: a book, a mezzotint, a whistle.

This historical interpenetration surfaces in many guises. The ghost's return may signal a lingering form of pagan malevolence. Elsewhere, as in Margaret Oliphant's 'The Open Door', the haunting may seem a mechanical repetition of the past, in which the ghost duplicates over and over some lost original action. The past stays on, but as a disturbance within the present. In other tales, the ghost symbolizes the enduring, while the living human stands for the transient.

The ghost may act as a symbol of the lost past, but it manifests itself in modern conditions. Newfangled electric lights do not dispel its presence; it haunts railways, modern flats, houses withdrawn from bustling streets. Within the city, the ghost is that which cannot be absorbed rationally, which cannot be taken by the blasé. Confronted with unavoidable presence (or its trace), the self is shocked into feeling, and out of logical thought.

Parallel to the haunting of the historical past is the idea that the ghost reveals adult life as suddenly being in correspondence with childhood fears. The theme is strong in Rudyard Kipling's 'At the End of the Passage' (1890), where the company of male colleagues staves off a horrifying return to infantile dread in sleep. As the Irish writer Frank O'Connor (1903–1966) put it, talking more generally of Kipling's work, but clearly evoking this particular tale: 'If one were left alone, nightmare succeeded.'[10] This was a further way in which ghostly horrors might seem atavistic. Lafcadio Hearn's 'Nightmare-Touch' (1900) draws together the dread felt by primitive man and the night-fears of children. The dream itself, the night-terror, might similarly encroach, as in childhood, on the real world. M. R. James's '"Oh, Whistle, and I'll Come To You, My Lad"' (1904) informs us that for the storyteller the haunting here was brought to mind by a childhood memory; the narrator's *'Experto crede'* (see p. 270) intimates a personal involvement in the tale.

There are purely literary forms of the ghost story's characteristic intrusions, in which the genre elements themselves might seem to be interventions. The reader may also become aware of the incursion of extraneous texts in the form of quotation and allusion. The key example of this would be that moment in Sheridan Le Fanu's 'Green Tea' (1869) where Dr Hesselius pauses to read passage after passage from Emanuel Swedenborg's *Arcana Coelestia*, on the correspondence between the spiritual and material world, and for a moment one work haunts another.

Politically speaking, as has been often observed, the ghost story mirrors the imperial expansionism of the period and hence denotes the intrusion of the disturbingly 'foreign' into the comfortably domestic, hinting, as elsewhere, at their tacit interconnection. In the work of Kipling, and others, the colonized world was in any case imagined as the site for mystic horrors. For example, India could seem an uncanny place, replete with hidden secrets, dark beliefs and murky possibilities. The plot of W. W. Jacobs's 'The Monkey's Paw' turns on the arrival in Britain of an imperial property, one linked to fakirs and *The Arabian Nights*; the heroes' family name of 'White' is perhaps a significant choice in this connection. Even in Henry James's 'The Jolly Corner' there are such *arrivistes*: the gloom of *'ombres chinoises'* (see p. 304) falls upon the domestic world.

Finally, the ghost raids our privacy. The haunting is a foray into the domestic realm. The very coldness of the ghost signals this; it enters like air from outside, and occupies that place in the house where the warmth of home falters. Ghosts are the intrusion – the link – between the private and the public. Their haunting demonstrates that this secure place is not sealed off, but lies open to others, to previous inhabitants, to strangers. In this sense, the ghost is a figure equivocally connected or contrasted with the domestic servant, also a sharer of the home who may or may not be counted as a part of the family. Certainly ghost stories frequently show an interest in such borderline figures, as in Elizabeth Gaskell's 'The Old Nurse's Story', Henry James's *The Turn of the Screw* (1898) and Edith Wharton's 'Afterward', or the dependable or unreliable servants in tales by Robert Hichens, Edward Bulwer Lytton and Margaret Oliphant.

Most often, therefore, the intruded-on space is a house. There are of course many outdoors ghost stories – Algernon Blackwood specialized in them. Margaret Oliphant's 'The Open Door' occupies a transitional place, the haunted site being a now disused boundary between inside and outside. The haunted house nevertheless stands at the centre of the genre. There may be psychological reasons for this: after all, the house is a convenient symbol for the human mind, spatially imagined.

Curiously, such spooky residences also evoke other more social concerns. Very often, temporary residents occupy the haunted house, moving in and moving on, as in Bulwer Lytton's 'The Haunted and the Haunters' (1859), while the ghost itself – a more established tenant – stays put. In part, this follows from purely literary concerns: as ghost stories depend on shock, the ghost must be a discovery, just such a surprise as a new tenant might stumble on. However, such tales also fitted changing patterns of property ownership. A shifting population, estranged from lasting connection to place, could thrill themselves with tales where their own evanescence was displayed. It was not merely the increasing urbanization of Britain and America that provided the background for these spectral anxieties. It is notable that the haunted tenant is often someone returning from Britain's colonies, a person displaced from 'home' by the processes of imperial expansion. Such fleeting inhabitants fitted the American situation too, as Fitz-James O'Brien's 'What Was It?' (1859) or O. Henry's 'The Furnished Room' (1906) demonstrate. The house in Henry James's 'The Jolly Corner' itself has its double, being one of two houses that Spencer Brydon, the tale's hero, owns in downtown Manhattan:

one a long-unvisited family home, filled with memories; the other, a place for rent.

The transient tenant discovers his rooms to be already furnished with a ghost. In such a circumstance, the renter finds himself the trespasser. As casual references in 'The Open Door' and 'Afterward' clarify, the ghost could also be seen as a charming and even fashionable form of fixture and fitting: nothing else than a ghost is wanted to make a property perfect. This modish response to the supernatural rubs up against the fact that the tenants – particularly Wharton's (and, in 'The Canterville Ghost', Oscar Wilde's) American leaseholders – are contemporary intrusions into the 'long, long story' of a British house's past. In this way, the ghost tale brings into connection the modern, brief, fragmented forms of the present (exemplified in the short story itself) and lingering, haunted history.

As the nineteenth century progresses, the old Gothic properties, the abbeys, the ruins, the graveyards, the castles, are slowly replaced by modern scenes. Often the haunting takes place in anonymous, shabby, unspectacular neighbourhoods. The old settings represent the abiding: such ruins are places of rest and stasis, symbols of durability too, for all their being wrecked. The modern environment seems essentially temporary. If the haunted do occupy some ancient house, they do so as passing tenants, fixed-term renters. The new haunted houses are provisional, merely passing estates. The building boom of the 1890s flooded the great cities with new – and often empty – houses. In 1917, Dorothy Scarborough noted: 'But as houses are so much less permanent now than formerly, ghosts would be at a terrible disadvantage if they had to be evicted every time a building was torn down.'[11] In these transitory cities the ghosts resided as paradoxical manifestations of solidity.

THE HAUNTED

Who typically were the haunted? Callous lovers, governesses and lost travellers, certainly, but beyond those traditional groups, within the mass of stories from the late nineteenth and early twentieth centuries, two new kinds of victim emerge: the bachelor and the troubled family. Both are seen as abortive examples of domesticity. Into their compromised worlds the ghost comes, an undead symbol of their failures.

In the case of the committed bachelor, the ghost stands for his inability to connect with others. The heroes of tales by Sheridan Le Fanu, Henry James, Robert Hichens, M. R. James and Oliver Onions all endure a version of this fate. Hichens's 'How Love Came to Professor Guildea' (1900) stands as the archetypal account of such hauntings, where the ghost avenges a refusal to love. Such stories re-imagine the ghost as stalker, even as unrequited lover, as in Mary Elizabeth Braddon's 'The Cold Embrace' (1860). Some of these bachelor ghost stories were written by men who were most likely themselves hiddenly homosexual. Perhaps in this group of tales the fears of men threatened by the social conformity of marriage could find a fitting symbol for their ambivalence.

For the bachelor, the ghost marks an end to privacy. Haunting is an incursion into the private zone, the home that defines itself by the absence of others, by the rejection of unwanted sharers of the space. Yet the haunting too is a private experience, located within the prison-cage of consciousness, where the spirit is only visible, touchable, audible to the haunted one. It is an invasion within the sense of the self. Only the reader shares that experience.

The alternative sets of modern victims are unhappy couples and beleaguered families. These haunted tend to appear in tales authored by women. Examples would include: Margaret Oliphant's 'The Open Door', Mary Wilkins Freeman's 'The Wind in the Rose-Bush', Mary Austin's 'The Readjustment' or Edith Wharton's 'Afterward'. Here the ghost points to the failure within a relationship. In Wharton's tale, the wife discovers that in two senses she is domesticated with a horror: both the ghost that is only recognized as such afterwards, and the guilty, greedy husband she does not really know. Like most wives, Wharton tells us, the heroine of this tale never looked into what her husband does for a living. This willed blindness to the public life casts a spectral shadow over the private (rented) home.

For bachelors or confused relatives and spouses, being

haunted offers a challenge to one's ability to take in the finer elements of the situation. In the case of Henry James, the haunted one must needs be especially sensitive, an alert and perceptive observer, a 'poor [pitiable, sensitive] gentleman', as he puts it.[12] The experience of the ghost was to be, after all, a dilemma for consciousness, for our faculty of interpretation.

This view of the ingredients necessary for a good ghost story would not be shared by all the writers in this volume. There is an 'extrovert' as well as an 'introvert' version of the form. For Edward Bulwer Lytton, for instance, the supernatural story is not about the numinous, it is about a struggle. Such tales present fear through a depiction of the resistance to it. Bulwer Lytton's hero in 'The Haunted and the Haunters' takes pistols and knives when he goes to encounter his ghosts. Such virile boldness tends to be a feature of the earlier nineteenth-century tales. By the end of the century, Henry James's version of the form was triumphant. In the hands of Henry James and his fellow practitioners, the ghost story explored psychological complexity. These interests operated variously, offering diverse routes into the hinterland of consciousness.

For instance, in tales of madness such as Sheridan Le Fanu's 'Green Tea', the ultimate fear is that we are haunting ourselves. As Dorothy Scarborough remarks of ghosts: 'We'd rather see than be one.'[13] Entrapped in a peculiar vision of the world, Mr Jennings cannot flee from the evil familiar that dogs his steps, and that is either an objective spirit or his private hallucination. He is imprisoned with another; but what if that other is himself? That this ghost story, like so many, ends with self-murder should not surprise us. For in suicide the self treats itself as though it were another. Henry James's 'The Jolly Corner' presents an analogous doubled self, and if the self here is so split, then by definition it is not single or coherent, and above all not limited to the present body. That of course is the central fear – and consolation – of the ghost story: the idea that we are not limited to the physical. The resistance to the spectral therefore acts as a clinging to earthly life and to the possession of our single body.

The self may also come under threat from the removal of its will. Sleepwalkers, the hypnotized and entranced are all recurrent figures in the period's literature of terror. This absence of will also appears in some ghosts, when they are automatic figures, locked within recurrent action and appearance. Bulwer Lytton remarks of such ghosts that they give the impression of being 'soul-less'. (Of course, the most terrifying ghosts are precisely those who do manifest a will, and one attuned to malevolence.) Elsewhere, in this regard, the reflex movements of the ghost are strangely paralleled in the haunted. Frequently in the ghost story the haunted one becomes a mere spectator of events. Such tales present merely a reaction to something seen or heard. But such reaction need not be passive. Much as the ghost story looked to a speculative and astute reader, so the tales themselves posited a rational hero and heroine, alive to the nuance of what they witness. They are busy with the task of understanding.

However, within the ghost story could be found other kinds of observer, whose astuteness was certainly not of a kind to impress Henry James. It is a feature of the genre that beasts should be particularly alive to the presence of a ghost. But why should animals be able to detect ghosts where we cannot? The belief forges a link between the bestial and the spiritual, one that bypasses the human that connects the two. Moreover, this link brings up the definition of the human by being on either side of the necessary limits that allow that definition: we are not animals; nor are we ghosts. In this sense, both animal and ghost (and monster) possess one thing in common: they are generally without language. It is startling how rarely in these stories we encounter a conversable spook. The silent ghost appears to have lost its words in the act of dying.

In Ambrose Bierce's 'The Moonlit Road' (1907), the ghost of Julia Hetman apparently talks, but her voice is channelled through the fictional medium Bayrolles. She speaks, but through another; the ghost's words are sounded in another person's mouth, possessing but not encompassing another's voice. If Bayrolles is indeed some kind of pun on the French *paroles* or 'words' (as in the character Parolles in Shakespeare's *All's Well That Ends Well*), then this may also be taken as Bierce alluding to the fact of speech, and its simultaneous presence within and radical alienation from the speaker (as *paroles* both loiter about and are not found in Bayrolles). Other stories play similar games. In 'Green Tea', we hear of the monkey's voice, which interrupts Mr Jennings with dreadful blasphemies; yet this is a voice that cannot be quoted; it is in the tale, but never heard, never given the form of words.

If the ghost story does concern itself with the question as to what is a human being, it must do so primarily through an assertion that we, uniquely on this planet, are supposed to possess immortal souls. Some have described the monkey in 'Green Tea' as a Darwinian emanation, a symbol of our anxiety that no such distinguishing soul exists. It is surprising to discover how many ghost-story writers were Christians: Sheridan Le Fanu, Margaret Oliphant, Arthur Machen, M. R. James and R. H. Benson, to name only the most obvious examples. Yet no simple theological point of view adheres to the genre. The stories can suggest order, but also chaos; they can depict, as in incarnation, the interpenetration of the spiritual and physical worlds, but also a malignant and hostile universe. As many atheists, occultists and agnostics as Christians contributed to the form. However, questions of religious faith cling to such stories as Harriet Beecher Stowe's 'The Ghost in the Cap'n Brown House' or Robert Louis Stevenson's 'Thrawn Janet' (1881). Enlightened deists and modern agnostics come in for a tough time in some of the stories in this volume. The religious sceptic, or Sadducee, makes a good victim, since his scepticism rules out the idea that he might be just imagining his persecution. There were other ways to set out the tension between faith and doubt. Bulwer Lytton focuses on the relation between scientific belief and occult phenomena, describing scientific processes of investigation directed towards the metaphysical. As these two discourses grow confused and intertwined, a productive tension arises; we are in a region between two forms of understanding. Here, as in other stories, the conviction persists that science has not covered all the ground; a residue of inexplicability remains.

LAYING THE GHOST

M. R. James declared that the aim of his stories was to make the reader 'pleasantly uncomfortable'.[14] The comfort may come from the fact that the ghost story evades far worse fears: the horrors, the losses, the wars and tortures of the material world. Kipling really did see 'shadows and things that were not there', as he puts it in his autobiography, *Something of Myself* (1936), but these were induced by the childhood breakdown brought on by the abuse visited upon him by his guardians at his foster-home in Southsea.[15] His hallucinations were put down as 'showing off', and, as a further punishment, he was separated from his sister. Here was a darkness deeper than that of a mere spook. In that sense, the ghost story might be a way of talking about our confrontation with such actual nightmares, a getting around the censor by evoking instead the supplemental fear of other worlds.

Nonetheless in the strongest ghost stories a highly uncomforting sense of life itself as essentially nightmarish is plainly there. It is curious that such darkness should be triggered by such odd elements. The ghost story relies on associations, on a bag of tricks, a strange assembly of tropes, objects and atmospheres, of narrative twists and unaccountable turns. Such things would elicit fear in life, just as they do in fiction. These might include: disembodied sounds, scents without objects, a touch without a person; the muffled, the hidden, the obscure; someone staring at us from a long way off; the emaciated and the small; a mirror in the dark; a cellar chill; a shadow in an upstairs window; children and the accoutrements of childhood – clowns, dolls or puppets; the melancholy of dusk; bat-squeaks and beetles humming; footsteps behind; lonely places – woods or bare platforms; invisibility and darkness; the feeling of being watched; a thing unexpectedly there.

It would be a hard task to account for the reasons why such haunted properties should still terrify us. If listing them makes the ghost story seem a perfunctory or automatic affair, then nothing could be further from the truth. It is the diversity and plenitude of the form that stays with the reader, the fact that it so often and so brilliantly works. The range of great and talented writers attracted to the form is likewise staggering. If the great Gothic sin is curiosity, then that fault remains intimately entangled with the Romantic virtue of wonder. For Henry James, it was the fact that such stories both touched on 'the blest faculty of wonder' and also endowed wonder with a motive that formed the chief enticements of such tales. They permitted a perilous foray into enchantment; they were, and remain, the 'most possible form of fairy tale'.[16] They are expressions of pure art, and paths to a pure, if complicated, pleasure.

NOTES

1. Elizabeth Bowen, *The Collected Stories of Elizabeth Bowen* (London: Vintage, 1999), p. 203.
2. From a letter to Frederick A. Duneka, editor of *Harper's New Monthly Magazine*, in Philip Horne (ed.), *Henry James: A Life in Letters* (London: Penguin, 1999), p. 437.
3. Henry James, Preface to *The Altar of the Dead, The Beast in the Jungle, The Birthplace and Other Tales*, vol. 17 of the *New York Edition* (London: Macmillan and Co., 1909), p. xvii.
4. M. R. James, from the Introduction to *Ghosts and Marvels: A Selection of Uncanny Tales from Daniel Defoe to Algernon Blackwood*, ed. V. H. Collins (Oxford: Oxford University Press, 1924), p. v.
5. Robert Louis Stevenson, from *The Letters of Robert Louis Stevenson*, ed. Bradford A. Booth and Ernest Mehew, vol. 7 (New Haven and London: Yale University Press, 1995), p. 155.
6. In an article, 'Ghosts – Treat Them Gently!', printed in the *Evening News* (17 April 1931), M. R. James writes: 'The recrudescence of ghost stories in recent years is notable: it corresponds, of course, with the vogue of the detective tale.'
7. Quoted in Michael Cox, *M. R. James: An Informal Portrait* (Oxford: Oxford University Press, 1983), p. 145.
8. Quoted in Leon Edel (ed.), *Henry James: Stories of the Supernatural* (London: Barrie & Jenkins, 1971), p. 314.
9. Dorothy Scarborough, *The Supernatural in Modern English Fiction* (New York and London: G. P. Putnam's Sons, 1917), p. 101.

10. Frank O'Connor, *The Lonely Voice: A Study of the Short Story* (London: Macmillan, 1963), p. 110.
11. Scarborough, *The Supernatural*, p. 106.
12. Henry James, Preface to *The Altar of the Dead*, p. xx.
13. Scarborough, *The Supernatural*, p. 81.
14. M. R. James, *Ghost Stories of an Antiquary* (London: Edward Arnold, 1904), p. viii.
15. Rudyard Kipling, *Something of Myself*, ed. Robert Hampson (London: Penguin Books, 1987), p. 42.
16. Henry James, Preface to *The Altar of the Dead*, p. xvi.

Further Reading

In the 1970s and 1980s, it was customary to preface any consideration of the ghost story by remarking on the fact that very little critical attention had been paid to the genre. No one need make such a lament now. There now follows a select list of books that can deepen your understanding of the ghost story, and of the tales in this book.

Bibliographical Studies

Bleiler, Everett F., *The Guide to Supernatural Fiction* (Kent, OH: Kent State University Press, 1983).

Wilson, Neil, *Shadows in the Attic: A Guide to British Supernatural Fiction*, with an Introduction by Ramsey Campbell (Boston Spa and London: the British Library, 2000).

Books and Essays on Ghost Stories and the Supernatural by Contemporary Practitioners

Dickens, Charles, 'On Ghosts' (1848), reprinted as 'Dickens on Ghosts: An Uncollected Article', *The Dickensian*, vol. 59, no. 339 (1963), pp. 5–14.

—— 'Review: *The Night Side of Nature; or, Ghosts and Ghost Seers* by Catherine Crowe', *The Examiner* (26 February 1848), reprinted in *'The Amusements of the People' and Other Papers: Reports, Essays and Reviews 1834–51*, vol. 2 of *The Dent Uniform Edition of Dickens' Journalism*, ed. Michael Slater (London: J. M. Dent, 1996), pp. 80–91.

—— 'Rather a Strong Dose', *All the Year Round* (4 April 1863), pp. 133–6.

James, Henry, Preface to *The Altar of the Dead, The Beast in the Jungle, The Birthplace and Other Tales*, vol. 17 of the *New York Edition* (London: Macmillan and Co., 1909), pp. v–xxix.

James, M. R., Introduction to *Ghosts and Marvels: A Selection of Uncanny Tales from Daniel Defoe to Algernon Blackwood*, ed. V. H. Collins (Oxford: Oxford University Press, 1924), pp. v–xiii.

—— 'Stories I Have Tried to Write', *The Touchstone*, vol. 2 (30 November 1929), pp. 46–7.

—— 'Some Remarks on Ghost Stories', *The Bookman* (December 1929), pp. 169–172.

Lamb, Charles, 'Witches, and Other Night-Fears', *Essays of Elia* (1823) (London: Everyman's Library, 1962), pp. 76–82.

Lang, Andrew, 'The Comparative Study of Ghost Stories', *Nineteenth Century*, vol. 17 (1885), pp. 623–32.

—— 'Ghosts Up to Date', *Blackwood's Magazine*, vol. 155 (1894), pp. 47–58.

Lovecraft, Howard Phillips, *Supernatural Horror in Literature* (New York: B. Abramson, 1945).

Scott, Sir Walter, 'On the Supernatural in Fictitious Composition; and particularly on the Works of Ernest William Hoffmann', *Foreign Quarterly Review*, vol. 1 (1827), pp. 312–15, 325–6.

—— *Letters on Demonology and Witchcraft. Addressed to J. G. Lockhart, Esq.* (London: John Murray, 1830).

Shelley, Mary, 'On Ghosts', *The London Magazine*, vol. 9 (1824), pp. 253–4.

Literary Criticism on the Ghost Story

Botting, Fred, *Gothic* (London: Routledge, 1995).

Bowen, Elizabeth, 'The Second Ghost Book', *After-Thought: Pieces About Writing* (London: Longman, 1962), pp. 101–104.

Bown, Nicola, Burdett, Carolyn, and Thurschwell, Pamela (eds.), *The Victorian Supernatural* (Cambridge: Cambridge University Press, 2004).

Briggs, Julia, *Night Visitors: The Rise and Fall of the English Ghost Story* (London: Faber & Faber, 1977).

——'The Ghost Story' in David Punter (ed.), *A Companion to the Gothic* (Oxford: Blackwell, 2000), pp. 122–131.

Dickerson, Virginia, *Victorian Ghosts in the Noontide: Women Writers and the Supernatural* (Columbia, OH, and London: University of Missouri Press, 1996).

Mighall, Robert, *A Geography of Victorian Gothic Fiction: Mapping History's Nightmares* (Oxford: Oxford University Press, 1999).

Penzoldt, Peter, *The English Short Story of the Supernatural* (London: Peter Nevill, 1952).

Scarborough, Dorothy, *The Supernatural in Modern English Fiction* (New York and London: G. P. Putnam's Sons, 1917).

Sullivan, Jack, *Elegant Nightmares: The English Ghost Story from Le Fanu to Blackwood* (Athens, OH: Ohio University Press, 1978).

Weinstock, Jeffrey Andrew (ed.), *Spectral America: Phantoms and the National Imagination* (Madison, WI: University of Wisconsin Press, 2004).

Wolfreys, Julian, *Victorian Hauntings: Spectrality, Gothic, the Uncanny, and Literature* (Basingstoke: Palgrave Macmillan, 2001).

Woolf, Virginia, 'Henry James's Ghost Stories', *The Times Literary Supplement* (22 December 1921), reprinted in *Granite and Rainbow* (London: Hogarth Press, 1958), pp. 65–72.

Literary Theory and the Figure of 'the Ghost'

Buse, Peter, and Stott, Andrew (eds.), *Ghosts: Deconstruction, Psychoanalysis, History* (London: Macmillan, 1999).

Davis, Colin, *Haunted Subjects: Deconstruction, Psychoanalysis and the Return of the Dead* (London: Palgrave Macmillan, 2007).

Derrida, Jacques, *Specters of Marx: The State of the Debt, the Work of Mourning and the New International*, trans. Peggy Kamuf (London and New York: Routledge, 1994).

Todorov, Tzvetan, *The Fantastic: A Structural Approach to a Literary Genre* (1970), trans. Richard Howard (Ithaca, NY: Cornell University Press, 1975).

Some Histories of Ghosts

Davies, Owen, *The Haunted: A Social History of Ghosts* (Basingstoke: Palgrave Macmillan, 2007).

——(ed.), *Ghosts: A Social History* (collection of primary material relating to ghosts), 5 vols. (London: Pickering & Chatto, 2009).

Handley, Sasha, *Visions of an Unseen World: Ghost Beliefs and Ghost Stories in Eighteenth-Century England* (London: Pickering & Chatto, 2007).

Maxwell-Stuart, P. G., *Ghosts: A History of Phantoms, Ghouls & Other Spirits of the Dead* (Stroud: Tempus, 2006).

Thomas, Keith, *Religion and the Decline of Magic* (London: Weidenfeld & Nicolson, 1971).

Studies in the History of Spiritualism

Brandon, Ruth, *The Spiritualists: The Passion for the Occult in the Nineteenth and Twentieth Centuries* (London: Weidenfeld & Nicolson, 1983).

Darnton, Robert, *Mesmerism and the End of the Enlightenment in France* (Cambridge, MA: Harvard University Press, 1968).

Oppenheim, Janet, *The Other World: Spiritualism and Psychical Research in England, 1850–1914* (Cambridge: Cambridge University Press, 1985).

Owen, Alex, *The Darkened Room: Women, Power and Spiritualism in Late Victorian England* (London: Virago, 1989).

Winter, Alison, *Mesmerized: Powers of Mind in Victorian Britain* (Chicago: University of Chicago Press, 1998).

Some Useful Biographical Works

Calder, Jenni, *RLS: A Life Story* (biography of Robert Louis Stevenson) (London: Hamish Hamilton, 1980).

Carrington, Charles, *Rudyard Kipling: His Life and Work* (London: Macmillan, 1955).

Cott, Jonathan, *Wandering Ghost: The Odyssey of Lafcadio Hearn* (New York: Knopf, 1991).

FURTHER READING

Cox, Michael, *M. R. James: An Informal Portrait* (Oxford: Oxford University Press, 1983).

Glasser, Leah Blatt, *In a Closet Hidden: The Life and Work of Mary E. Wilkins Freeman* (Amherst, MA: University of Massachusetts Press, 1996).

Hedrick, Joan D., *Harriet Beecher Stowe: A Life* (Oxford: Oxford University Press, 1994).

James, Anthony, *W. W. Jacobs: A Biography* (Knebworth: Able Publishing, 1999).

James, M. R., *Eton and King's* (London: Williams & Norgate, 1926).

Jay, Elisabeth, *Mrs Oliphant: 'A Fiction to Herself'* (Oxford: Clarendon Press, 1995).

Johnson, Edgar, *Charles Dickens: His Tragedy and Triumph*, 2 vols. (London: Gollancz, 1953).

Kipling, Rudyard, *Something of Myself* (London: Macmillan, 1937).

Lewis, R. W. B., *Edith Wharton: A Biography* (New York: Harper & Row, 1975).

McCormack, W. J., *Sheridan Le Fanu and Victorian Ireland* (Oxford: Clarendon Press, 1980).

Mitchell, Leslie George, *Bulwer Lytton: The Rise and Fall of a Victorian Man of Letters* (London: Hambledon and London, 2003).

Morris, Roy, *Ambrose Bierce: Alone in Bad Company* (New York and Oxford: Oxford University Press, 1998).

Oliphant, Margaret, *The Autobiography of Margaret Oliphant*, ed. Elisabeth Jay (Oxford: Oxford University Press, 1990).

Pfaff, Richard William, *Montague Rhodes James* (London: Scolar Press, 1980).

Rees, Joan, *Amelia Edwards: Traveller, Novelist and Egyptologist* (London: Rubicon Press, 1998).

Stineman, Esther Lanigan, *Mary Austin: Song of a Maverick* (New Haven, CT, and London: Yale University Press, 1989).

Uglow, Jenny, *Elizabeth Gaskell: A Habit of Stories* (London: Faber & Faber, 1993).

Wharton, Edith, *A Backward Glance* (New York and London: D. Appleton-Century Co., 1934).

Wolff, Robert, *Sensational Victorian: The Life and Fiction of*

Mary Elizabeth Braddon (New York: Garland Publishing, 1979).
Woole, Francis, *Fitz-James O'Brien: A Literary Bohemian of the Eighteen-Fifties* (Boulder, CO: University of Colorado Press, 1944).

A Note on the Texts

In choosing the texts for this anthology, I worked on the principle that a story should be good in itself: that is, well written, sophisticated and (if possible) frightening. This means that I felt it best not to shy away from some obvious choices. In my view, some very good anthologies of ghost stories are weakened by a desire to pick surprising, neglected or substandard stories by the best writers in the genre, or second-rank stories by largely forgotten writers. As a result, the editors produce anthologies for people who collect such anthologies and who already own the classic tales. While this book intends to provide something for such readers, it aims more at the person who will buy only one such book for private reading or for study, and for those who want one volume that brings together the very best examples of the genre. For this reason, many familiar undisputed classics have been included, especially with a sense of what will work in private reading and in the seminar room. The aim of the anthology is therefore primarily just to gather the finest ghost stories of the period 1848–1914.

The decision to include American, English, Scottish and Irish works was intended for reasons of variety, to demonstrate how interdependent these various local traditions were, and to get away from the narrowly nationalist (and nostalgic) practice of labelling all ghost stories of this period as 'English'. The only constraints on inclusion in the volume were those of length and copyright. The first meant the omission of such wonderful writers as Vernon Lee and Rhoda Broughton; the second accounts for the absence of Algernon Blackwood, Walter de la Mare, Arthur Machen, Robert Hichens, Oliver Onions and E. F. Benson. I am in no doubt that in this instance, as presumably in others, the extension of copyright in the UK to seventy years is depriving certain great writers of readers, and damaging their literary reputations.

Details of the copy-text for each story collected here are given in the Biographical and Explanatory Notes. There would be strong arguments for choosing the first magazine publication as the basis for the copy-texts, as this presents the stories in their original form. Magazine publication was also the medium by which such stories reached their widest audience, as well as being more lucrative for authors. The more ephemeral periodical form was the more vital. Initially, publishing short stories in volume form meant a little prestige, and a little more money, but not much more. Traditionally, it was supposed (and is still now believed) that volumes of short stories sell poorly. However, as the nineteenth century reached its close, this situation subtly changed. This was in part a response to a shift towards the sense that the short story was a particularly vigorous and significant form, one closely allied to the breathlessness, the speed and the fragmentation of modern life. Artistic ambition and a greater sense of the professionalism of the artist led to a wish to see stories collected together in volume form. The collection offered distinction, bolstered an author's reputation, suggested the permanency of literary regard (in opposition to the short story's supposed embracing of the ephemeral), provided an opportunity for revision and, most importantly, allowed for a coherent and attractively readable printed form. For all these reasons, volume publication began, despite economic considerations, to vie with magazine and periodical publication, and it is from their first publication in book form that the copy-texts of the stories in this collection nearly always derive. While, in some instances, as with Bulwer Lytton's 'The Haunted and the Haunters', the book version of a story is certainly the more authoritative one, this policy chiefly reflects the difficulty of obtaining some of the periodical versions of the stories and the fact that a number of these are too fragile to copy. Despite this, the order of the stories follows the chronology of their first publication.

The copy-texts have been reproduced largely in the form in which they originally appeared. A few basic aspects of house style, mostly typographic, have been applied and American spellings (where these differ from British spellings of the period) have been anglicized. Obvious printer's errors have been emended; otherwise spelling and punctuation have not been altered and, in most cases, any inconsistencies and oddities have been retained. Sometimes the grammar may appear to be slightly awkward as a result, but this is a feature of the original texts. Any footnotes (marked with an asterisk in this edition) are also part of the original texts.

THE PENGUIN BOOK OF
GHOST STORIES

*From Elizabeth Gaskell
to Ambrose Bierce*

ELIZABETH GASKELL

The Old Nurse's Story

You know, my dears, that your mother was an orphan, and an only child; and I dare say you have heard that your grandfather was a clergyman up in Westmoreland, where I come from.[1] I was just a girl in the village school, when, one day, your grandmother came in to ask the mistress if there was any scholar there who would do for a nurse-maid; and mighty proud I was, I can tell ye, when the mistress called me up, and spoke to my being a good girl at my needle, and a steady honest girl, and one whose parents were very respectable, though they might be poor. I thought I should like nothing better than to serve the pretty young lady, who was blushing as deep as I was, as she spoke of the coming baby, and what I should have to do with it. However, I see you don't care so much for this part of my story, as for what you think is to come, so I'll tell you at once. I was engaged and settled at the parsonage before Miss Rosamond (that was the baby, who is now your mother) was born. To be sure, I had little enough to do with her when she came, for she was never out of her mother's arms, and slept by her all night long; and proud enough was I sometimes when missis trusted her to me. There never was such a baby before or since, though you've all of you been fine enough in your turns; but for sweet, winning ways, you've none of you come up to your mother. She took after her mother, who was a real lady born; a Miss Furnivall, a grand-daughter of Lord Furnivall's, in Northumberland.[2] I believe she had neither brother nor sister, and had been brought up in my lord's family till she had married your grandfather, who was just a curate, son to a shopkeeper in Carlisle – but a clever, fine gentleman as ever was – and one who was a right-down hard worker in his parish, which was very wide, and scattered all abroad over the Westmoreland Fells.[3] When your mother, little Miss Rosamond, was about four or five years old, both her parents died in a fortnight – one after the other. Ah! that was a sad time. My pretty young mistress and me was looking for another baby, when my master came home from one of his long rides, wet, and tired, and took the fever he died of; and then she never held up her head again, but just lived to see her dead baby, and have it laid on her breast before she sighed away her life. My mistress had asked me, on her death-bed, never to leave Miss Rosamond; but if she had never spoken a word, I would have gone with the little child to the end of the world.

The next thing, and before we had well stilled our sobs, the executors and guardians came to settle the affairs. They were my poor young mistress's own cousin, Lord Furnivall, and Mr Esthwaite, my master's brother, a shopkeeper in Manchester; not so well to do then, as he was afterwards, and with a large family rising about him. Well! I don't know if it were their settling, or because of a letter my mistress wrote on her death-bed to her cousin, my lord; but somehow it was settled that Miss Rosamond and me were to go to Furnivall Manor House, in Northumberland, and my lord spoke as if it had been her mother's wish that she should live with his family, and as if he had no objections, for that one or two more or less could make no difference in so grand a household. So, though that was not the way in which I should have wished the coming of my bright and pretty pet to have been looked at – who was like a sunbeam in any family, be it never so grand – I was well pleased that all the folks in the Dale should stare and admire, when they heard I was going to be young lady's maid at my Lord Furnivall's at Furnivall Manor.

But I made a mistake in thinking we were to go and live where my lord did. It turned out that the family had left Furnivall Manor House fifty years or more. I could not hear that my poor young mistress had ever been there, though she had been brought up in the family; and I was sorry for that, for I should have liked Miss Rosamond's youth to have passed where her mother's had been.

My lord's gentleman, from whom I asked as many questions

as I durst, said that the Manor House was at the foot of the
Cumberland Fells, and a very grand place; that an old Miss
Furnivall, a great-aunt of my lord's, lived there, with only a
few servants; but that it was a very healthy place, and my lord
had thought that it would suit Miss Rosamond very well for a
few years, and that her being there might perhaps amuse his
old aunt.

I was bidden by my lord to have Miss Rosamond's things
ready by a certain day. He was a stern proud man, as they say
all the Lords Furnivall were; and he never spoke a word more
than was necessary. Folk did say he had loved my young mistress; but that, because she knew that his father would object,
she would never listen to him, and married Mr Esthwaite; but
I don't know. He never married at any rate. But he never took
much notice of Miss Rosamond; which I thought he might have
done if he had cared for her dead mother. He sent his gentleman
with us to the Manor House, telling him to join him at Newcastle that same evening;[4] so there was no great length of time
for him to make us known to all the strangers before he, too,
shook us off; and we were left, two lonely young things (I was
not eighteen), in the great old Manor House. It seems like
yesterday that we drove there. We had left our own dear parsonage very early, and we had both cried as if our hearts would
break, though we were travelling in my lord's carriage, which
I thought so much of once. And now it was long past noon on
a September day, and we stopped to change horses for the last
time at a little smoky town, all full of colliers and miners. Miss
Rosamond had fallen asleep, but Mr Henry told me to waken
her, that she might see the park and the Manor House as we
drove up. I thought it rather a pity; but I did what he bade me,
for fear he should complain of me to my lord. We had left all
signs of a town, or even a village, and were then inside the gates
of a large wild park – not like the parks here in the south,
but with rocks, and the noise of running water, and gnarled
thorn-trees, and old oaks, all white and peeled with age.

The road went up about two miles, and then we saw a great
and stately house, with many trees close around it, so close that
in some places their branches dragged against the walls when
the wind blew; and some hung broken down; for no one seemed

to take much charge of the place; – to lop the wood, or to keep the moss-covered carriage-way in order. Only in front of the house all was clear. The great oval drive was without a weed; and neither tree nor creeper was allowed to grow over the long, many-windowed front; at both sides of which a wing projected, which were each the ends of other side fronts; for the house, although it was so desolate, was even grander than I expected. Behind it rose the Fells, which seemed unenclosed and bare enough; and on the left hand of the house, as you stood facing it, was a little, old-fashioned flower-garden, as I found out afterwards. A door opened out upon it from the west front; it had been scooped out of the thick dark wood for some old Lady Furnivall; but the branches of the great forest trees had grown and overshadowed it again, and there were very few flowers that would live there at that time.

When we drove up to the great front entrance, and went into the hall I thought we should be lost – it was so large, and vast, and grand. There was a chandelier all of bronze, hung down from the middle of the ceiling; and I had never seen one before, and looked at it all in amaze. Then, at one end of the hall, was a great fire-place, as large as the sides of the houses in my country, with massy andirons and dogs to hold the wood; and by it were heavy old-fashioned sofas.[5] At the opposite end of the hall, to the left as you went in – on the western side – was an organ built into the wall, and so large that it filled up the best part of that end. Beyond it, on the same side, was a door; and opposite, on each side of the fire-place, were also doors leading to the east front; but those I never went through as long as I stayed in the house, so I can't tell you what lay beyond.

The afternoon was closing in and the hall, which had no fire lighted in it, looked dark and gloomy, but we did not stay there a moment. The old servant, who had opened the door for us bowed to Mr Henry, and took us in through the door at the further side of the great organ, and led us through several smaller halls and passages into the west drawing-room, where he said that Miss Furnivall was sitting. Poor little Miss Rosamond held very tight to me, as if she were scared and lost in that great place, and as for myself, I was not much better. The west drawing-room was very cheerful-looking, with a warm fire in it, and plenty of good, comfortable furniture about. Miss Furnivall was an old lady not far from eighty, I should think, but I do not know. She was thin and tall, and had a face as full of fine wrinkles as if they had been drawn all over it with a needle's point. Her eyes were very watchful to make up, I suppose, for her being so deaf as to be obliged to use a trumpet. Sitting with her, working at the same great piece of tapestry, was Mrs Stark, her maid and companion, and almost as old as she was. She had lived with Miss Furnivall ever since they both were young, and now she seemed more like a friend than a servant; she looked so cold and grey, and stony, as if she had never loved or cared for any one; and I don't suppose she did care for any one, except her mistress; and, owing to the great deafness of the latter, Mrs Stark treated her very much as if she were a child. Mr Henry gave some message from my lord, and then he bowed good-bye to us all, – taking no notice of my sweet little Miss Rosamond's out-stretched hand – and left us standing there, being looked at by the two old ladies through their spectacles.

I was right glad when they rung for the old footman who had shown us in at first, and told him to take us to our rooms. So we went out of that great drawing-room, and into another sitting-room, and out of that, and then up a great flight of stairs, and along a broad gallery – which was something like a library, having books all down one side, and windows and writing-tables all down the other – till we came to our rooms, which I was not sorry to hear were just over the kitchens; for I began to think I should be lost in that wilderness of a house. There was an old nursery, that had been used for all the little lords and ladies long ago, with a pleasant fire burning in the grate, and the kettle boiling on the hob, and tea things spread out on the table; and out of that room was the night-nursery, with a little crib for Miss Rosamond close to my bed. And old James called up Dorothy, his wife, to bid us welcome; and both he and she were so hospitable and kind, that by and by Miss Rosamond and me felt quite at home; and by the time tea was over, she was sitting on Dorothy's knee, and chattering away as fast as her little tongue could go. I soon found out that Dorothy was from Westmoreland, and that bound her and me together, as it were; and I would never wish to meet with kinder people than were old James and his wife. James had lived pretty nearly all his life in my lord's family, and thought there was no one so grand as they. He even looked down a little on his wife; because, till he had married her, she had never lived in any but a farmer's household. But he was very fond of her, as well he might be. They had one servant under them, to do all the rough work. Agnes they called her; and she and me, and James and Dorothy, with Miss Furnivall and Mrs Stark, made up the family; always remembering my sweet little Miss Rosamond! I used to wonder what they had done before she came, they thought so much of her now. Kitchen and drawing-room, it was all the same. The hard, sad Miss Furnivall, and the cold Mrs Stark, looked pleased when she came fluttering in like a bird, playing and pranking hither and thither, with a continual murmur, and pretty prattle of gladness. I am sure, they were sorry many a time when she flitted away into the kitchen, though they were too proud to ask her to stay with them, and were a little surprised at her taste; though to be sure, as Mrs Stark said, it was not to be wondered at, remembering what stock her father had come of. The great, old rambling house was a famous place for little Miss Rosamond. She made expeditions all over it, with me at her heels; all, except the east wing, which was never opened, and whither we never thought of going. But in the western and northern part was many a pleasant room; full of things that were curiosities to us, though they might not have been to people who had seen more. The windows were darkened by the sweeping boughs of the trees, and the ivy which had overgrown them: but, in the green gloom, we could manage to see old China jars and carved ivory boxes, and great heavy books, and, above all, the old pictures!

Once, I remember, my darling would have Dorothy go with us to tell us who they all were; for they were all portraits of some of my lord's family, though Dorothy could not tell us the names of every one. We had gone through most of the rooms, when we came to the old state drawing-room over the hall, and there was a picture of Miss Furnivall; or, as she was called in those days, Miss Grace, for she was the younger sister. Such a beauty she must have been! but with such a set, proud look, and such scorn looking out of her handsome eyes, with her eyebrows just a little raised, as if she wondered how any one could have the impertinence to look at her; and her lip curled at us, as we stood there gazing. She had a dress on, the like of which I had never seen before, but it was all the fashion when she was young: a hat of some soft white stuff like beaver, pulled a little over her brows, and a beautiful plume of feathers sweeping round it on one side; and her gown of blue satin was open in front to a quilted white stomacher.[6]

'Well, to be sure!' said I, when I had gazed my fill. 'Flesh is grass, they do say; but who would have thought that Miss Furnivall had been such an out-and-out beauty, to see her now?'[7]

'Yes,' said Dorothy. 'Folks change sadly. But if what my master's father used to say was true, Miss Furnivall, the elder sister, was handsomer than Miss Grace. Her picture is here somewhere; but, if I show it you, you must never let on, even to James, that you have seen it. Can the little lady hold her tongue, think you?' asked she.

I was not so sure, for she was such a little sweet, bold, open-spoken child, so I set her to hide herself; and then I helped Dorothy to turn a great picture, that leaned with its face towards the wall, and was not hung up as the others were. To be sure, it beat Miss Grace for beauty; and, I think, for scornful pride, too, though in that matter it might be hard to choose. I could have looked at it an hour, but Dorothy seemed half frightened at having shown it to me, and hurried it back again, and bade me run and find Miss Rosamond, for that there were some ugly places about the house, where she should like ill for the child to go. I was a brave, high-spirited girl, and thought little of what the old woman said, for I liked hide-and-seek as well as any child in the parish; so off I ran to find my little one.

As winter drew on, and the days grew shorter, I was sometimes almost certain that I heard a noise as if some one was playing on the great organ in the hall. I did not hear it every evening; but, certainly, I did very often; usually when I was sitting with Miss Rosamond, after I had put her to bed, and keeping quite still and silent in the bed-room. Then I used to hear it booming and swelling away in the distance. The first night, when I went down to my supper, I asked Dorothy who had been playing music, and James said very shortly that I was a gowk to take the wind soughing among the trees for music: but I saw Dorothy look at him very fearfully, and Bessy, the kitchen-maid, said something beneath her breath, and went quite white. I saw they did not like my question, so I held my peace till I was with Dorothy alone, when I knew I could get a good deal out of her. So, the next day, I watched my time, and I coaxed and asked her who it was that played the organ; for I knew that it was the organ and not the wind well enough, for all I had kept silence before James. But Dorothy had had her lesson I'll warrant, and never a word could I get from her. So then I tried Bessy, though I had always held my head rather above her, as I was evened to James and Dorothy, and she was little better than their servant. So she said I must never, never tell; and if I ever told, I was never to say *she* had told me; but it was a very strange noise, and she had heard it many a time, but most of all on winter nights, and before storms; and folks did say, it was the old lord playing on the great organ in the hall, just as he used to do when he was alive; but who the old lord was, or why he played, and why he played on stormy winter evenings in particular, she either could not or would not tell me. Well! I told you I had a brave heart; and I thought it was rather pleasant to have that grand music rolling about the house, let who would be the player; for now it rose above the great gusts of wind, and wailed and triumphed just like a living creature, and then it fell to a softness most complete; only it was always music, and tunes, so it was nonsense to call it the wind. I thought at first, that it might be Miss Furnivall who played, unknown to Bessy; but, one day when I was in the hall by myself, I opened the organ and peeped all about it and around it, as I had done to the organ in Crosthwaite Church once before, and I saw it was all broken and destroyed inside, though it looked so brave and fine;[8] and then, though it was noon-day, my flesh began to creep a little, and I shut it up, and run away pretty quickly to my own bright nursery; and I did not like hearing the music for some time after that, any more than James and Dorothy did. All this time Miss Rosamond was making herself more, and more beloved. The old ladies liked her to dine with them at their early dinner; James stood behind

Miss Furnivall's chair, and I behind Miss Rosamond's all in state; and, after dinner, she would play about in a corner of the great drawing-room, as still as any mouse, while Miss Furnivall slept, and I had my dinner in the kitchen. But she was glad enough to come to me in the nursery afterwards; for, as she said, Miss Furnivall was so sad, and Mrs Stark so dull; but she and I were merry enough; and, by-and-by, I got not to care for that weird rolling music, which did one no harm, if we did not know where it came from.

That winter was very cold. In the middle of October the frosts began, and lasted many, many weeks. I remember, one day at dinner, Miss Furnivall lifted up her sad, heavy eyes, and said to Mrs Stark, 'I am afraid we shall have a terrible winter,' in a strange kind of meaning way. But Mrs Stark pretended not to hear, and talked very loud of something else. My little lady, and I did not care for the frost; not we! As long as it was dry we climbed up the steep brows, behind the house, and went up on the Fells, which were bleak, and bare enough, and there we ran races in the fresh, sharp air; and once we came down by a new path that took us past the two old gnarled holly-trees, which grew about half-way down by the east side of the house. But the days grew shorter, and shorter; and the old lord, if it was he, played away more, and more stormily and sadly on the great organ. One Sunday afternoon, – it must have been towards the end of November – I asked Dorothy to take charge of little Missey when she came out of the drawing-room, after Miss Furnivall had had her nap; for it was too cold to take her with me to church, and yet I wanted to go. And Dorothy was glad enough to promise, and was so fond of the child that all seemed well; and Bessy and I set off very briskly, though the sky hung heavy and black over the white earth, as if the night had never fully gone away; and the air, though still, was very biting and keen.

'We shall have a fall of snow,' said Bessy to me. And sure enough, even while we were in church, it came down thick, in great large flakes, so thick it almost darkened the windows. It had stopped snowing before we came out, but it lay soft, thick and deep beneath our feet, as we tramped home. Before we got to the hall the moon rose, and I think it was lighter then, –

what with the moon, and what with the white dazzling snow –
than it had been when we went to church, between two and
three o'clock. I have not told you that Miss Furnivall and Mrs
Stark never went to church: they used to read the prayers
together, in their quiet gloomy way; they seemed to feel the
Sunday very long without their tapestry-work to be busy at. So
when I went to Dorothy in the kitchen, to fetch Miss Rosamond
and take her up-stairs with me, I did not much wonder when
the old woman told me that the ladies had kept the child with
them, and that she had never come to the kitchen, as I
had bidden her, when she was tired of behaving pretty in the
drawing-room. So I took off my things and went to find her,
and bring her to her supper in the nursery. But when I went
into the best drawing-room, there sat the two old ladies, very
still and quiet, dropping out a word now and then, but looking
as if nothing so bright and merry as Miss Rosamond had ever
been near them. Still I thought she might be hiding from me; it
was one of her pretty ways; and that she had persuaded them
to look as if they knew nothing about her; so I went softly
peeping under this sofa, and behind that chair, making believe
I was sadly frightened at not finding her.

'What's the matter, Hester?' said Mrs Stark sharply. I don't
know if Miss Furnivall had seen me, for, as I told you, she was
very deaf, and she sat quite still, idly staring into the fire, with
her hopeless face. 'I'm only looking for my little Rosy-Posy,'
replied I, still thinking that the child was there, and near me,
though I could not see her.

'Miss Rosamond is not here,' said Mrs Stark. 'She went away
more than an hour ago to find Dorothy.' And she too turned
and went on looking into the fire.

My heart sank at this, and I began to wish I had never left
my darling. I went back to Dorothy and told her. James was
gone out for the day, but she and me and Bessy took lights and
went up into the nursery first, and then we roamed over the
great large house, calling and entreating Miss Rosamond to
come out of her hiding place, and not frighten us to death in
that way. But there was no answer; no sound.

'Oh!' said I at last, 'can she have got into the east wing and
hidden there?'

But Dorothy said it was not possible, for that she herself had never been in there; that the doors were always locked, and my lord's steward had the keys, she believed; at any rate, neither she nor James had ever seen them: so, I said I would go back, and see if, after all, she was not hidden in the drawing-room, unknown to the old ladies; and if I found her there, I said, I would whip her well for the fright she had given me; but I never meant to do it. Well, I went back to the west drawing-room, and I told Mrs Stark we could not find her anywhere, and asked for leave to look all about the furniture there, for I thought now, that she might have fallen asleep in some warm hidden corner; but no! we looked, Miss Furnivall got up and looked, trembling all over, and she was no where there; then we set off again, every one in the house, and looked in all the places we had searched before, but we could not find her. Miss Furnivall shivered and shook so much, that Mrs Stark took her back into the warm drawing-room; but not before they had made me promise to bring her to them when she was found. Well-a-day! I began to think she never would be found, when I bethought me to look out into the great front court, all covered with snow. I was up-stairs when I looked out; but, it was such clear moonlight, I could see quite plain two little footprints, which might be traced from the hall door, and round the corner of the east wing. I don't know how I got down, but I tugged open the great, stiff hall door; and, throwing the skirt of my gown over my head for a cloak, I ran out. I turned the east corner, and there a black shadow fell on the snow; but when I came again into the moonlight, there were the little footmarks going up – up to the Fells. It was bitter cold; so cold that the air almost took the skin off my face as I ran, but I ran on, crying to think how my poor little darling must be perished, and frightened.[9] I was within sight of the holly-trees, when I saw a shepherd coming down the hill, bearing something in his arms wrapped in his maud. He shouted to me, and asked me if I had lost a bairn; and, when I could not speak for crying, he bore towards me, and I saw my wee bairnie lying still, and white, and stiff, in his arms, as if she had been dead. He told me he had been up the Fells to gather in his sheep, before the deep cold of night came on, and that under the holly-trees (black marks on the hill-side, where no other bush was for miles around) he had found my little lady – my lamb – my queen – my darling – stiff, and cold, in the terrible sleep which is frost-begotten. Oh! the joy, and the tears of having her in my arms once again! for I would not let him carry her; but took her, maud and all, into my own arms, and held her near my own warm neck, and heart, and felt the life stealing slowly back again into her little gentle limbs. But she was still insensible when we reached the hall, and I had no breath for speech. We went in by the kitchen door.

'Bring the warming-pan,' said I; and I carried her up-stairs and began undressing her by the nursery fire, which Bessy had kept up. I called my little lammie all the sweet and playful names I could think of, – even while my eyes were blinded by my tears; and at last, oh! at length she opened her large blue eyes. Then I put her into her warm bed, and sent Dorothy down to tell Miss Furnivall that all was well; and I made up my mind to sit by my darling's bedside the live-long night. She fell away into a soft sleep as soon as her pretty head had touched the pillow, and I watched by her till morning light; when she wakened up bright and clear – or so I thought at first – and, my dears, so I think now.

She said, that she had fancied that she should like to go to Dorothy, for that both the old ladies were asleep, and it was very dull in the drawing-room; and that, as she was going through the west lobby, she saw the snow through the high window falling – falling – soft and steady; but she wanted to see it lying pretty and white on the ground; so she made her way into the great hall; and then, going to the window, she saw it bright and soft upon the drive; but while she stood there, she saw a little girl, not so old as she was, 'but so pretty,' said my darling, 'and this little girl beckoned to me to come out; and oh, she was so pretty and so sweet, I could not choose but go.' And then this other little girl had taken her by the hand, and side by side the two had gone round the east corner.

'Now you are a naughty little girl, and telling stories,' said I. 'What would your good mamma, that is in heaven, and never told a story in her life, say to her little Rosamond, if she heard her – and I dare say she does – telling stories!'

'Indeed, Hester,' sobbed out my child, 'I'm telling you true. Indeed I am.'

'Don't tell me!' said I, very stern. 'I tracked you by your foot-marks through the snow; there were only yours to be seen: and if you had had a little girl to go hand-in-hand with you up the hill, don't you think the foot-prints would have gone along with yours?'

'I can't help it, dear, dear Hester,' said she, crying, 'if they did not; I never looked at her feet, but she held my hand fast and tight in her little one, and it was very, very cold. She took me up the Fell-path, up to the holly trees; and there I saw a lady weeping and crying; but when she saw me, she hushed her weeping, and smiled very proud and grand, and took me on her knee, and began to lull me to sleep; and that's all, Hester – but that is true; and my dear mamma knows it is,' said she, crying. So I thought the child was in a fever, and pretended to believe her, as she went over her story – over and over again, and always the same. At last Dorothy knocked at the door with Miss Rosamond's breakfast; and she told me the old ladies were down in the eating parlour, and that they wanted to speak to me. They had both been into the night-nursery the evening before, but it was after Miss Rosamond was asleep; so they had only looked at her – not asked me any questions.

'I shall catch it,' thought I to myself, as I went along the north gallery. 'And yet,' I thought, taking courage, 'it was in their charge I left her; and it's they that's to blame for letting her steal away unknown and unwatched.' So I went in boldly, and told my story. I told it all to Miss Furnivall, shouting it close to her ear; but when I came to the mention of the other little girl out in the snow, coaxing and tempting her out, and wiling her up to the grand and beautiful lady by the holly-tree, she threw her arms up – her old and withered arms – and cried aloud, 'Oh! Heaven, forgive! Have mercy!'

Mrs Stark took hold of her; roughly enough, I thought; but she was past Mrs Stark's management, and spoke to me, in a kind of wild warning and authority.

'Hester! keep her from that child! It will lure her to her death! That evil child! Tell her it is a wicked, naughty child.' Then, Mrs Stark hurried me out of the room; where, indeed, I was glad enough to go; but Miss Furnivall kept shrieking out, 'Oh! have mercy! Wilt Thou never forgive! It is many a long year ago –'

I was very uneasy in my mind after that. I durst never leave Miss Rosamond, night or day, for fear lest she might slip off again, after some fancy or other; and all the more, because I thought I could make out that Miss Furnivall was crazy, from their odd ways about her; and I was afraid lest something of the same kind (which might be in the family, you know) hung over my darling. And the great frost never ceased all this time; and, whenever it was a more stormy night than usual, between the gusts, and through the wind, we heard the old lord playing on the great organ. But, old lord, or not, wherever Miss Rosamond went, there I followed; for my love for her, pretty helpless orphan, was stronger than my fear for the grand and terrible sound. Besides, it rested with me to keep her cheerful and merry, as beseemed her age. So we played together, and wandered together, here and there, and everywhere; for I never dared to lose sight of her again in that large and rambling house. And so it happened, that one afternoon, not long before Christmas day, we were playing together on the billiard-table in the great hall (not that we knew the right way of playing, but she liked to roll the smooth ivory balls with her pretty hands, and I liked to do whatever she did); and, by-and-by, without our noticing it, it grew dusk indoors, though it was still light in the open air, and I was thinking of taking her back into the nursery, when, all of a sudden, she cried out:

'Look, Hester! look! there is my poor little girl out in the snow!'

I turned towards the long narrow windows, and there, sure enough, I saw a little girl, less than my Miss Rosamond – dressed all unfit to be out-of-doors such a bitter night – crying, and beating against the window-panes, as if she wanted to be let in. She seemed to sob and wail, till Miss Rosamond could bear it no longer, and was flying to the door to open it, when, all of a sudden, and close upon us, the great organ pealed out so loud and thundering, it fairly made me tremble; and all the more, when I remembered me that, even in the stillness of that dead-cold weather, I had heard no sound of little battering hands upon the window-glass, although the Phantom Child had seemed to put forth all its force; and, although I had seen it wail and cry, no faintest touch of sound had fallen upon my ears. Whether I remembered all this at the very moment, I do not know; the great organ sound had so stunned me into terror; but this I know, I caught up Miss Rosamond before she got the hall-door opened, and clutched her, and carried her away, kicking and screaming, into the large bright kitchen, where Dorothy and Agnes were busy with their mince-pies.

'What is the matter with my sweet one?' cried Dorothy, as I bore in Miss Rosamond, who was sobbing as if her heart would break.

'She won't let me open the door for my little girl to come in; and she'll die if she is out on the Fells all night. Cruel, naughty Hester,' she said, slapping me; but she might have struck harder, for I had seen a look of ghastly terror on Dorothy's face, which made my very blood run cold.

'Shut the back kitchen door fast, and bolt it well,' said she to Agnes. She said no more; she gave me raisins and almonds to quiet Miss Rosamond: but she sobbed about the little girl in the snow, and would not touch any of the good things. I was thankful when she cried herself to sleep in bed. Then I stole down to the kitchen, and told Dorothy I had made up my mind. I would carry my darling back to my father's house in Applethwaite; where, if we lived humbly, we lived at peace. I said I had been frightened enough with the old lord's organ-playing; but now, that I had seen for myself this little moaning child, all decked out as no child in the neighbourhood could be, beating and battering to get in, yet always without any sound or noise – with the dark wound on its right shoulder; and that Miss Rosamond had known it again for the phantom that had nearly lured her to her death (which Dorothy knew was true); I would stand it no longer.

I saw Dorothy change colour once or twice. When I had done, she told me she did not think I could take Miss Rosamond with me, for that she was my lord's ward, and I had no right over her; and she asked me, would I leave the child that I was so fond of, just for sounds and sights that could do me no harm; and that they had all had to get used to in their turns? I was all

in a hot, trembling passion; and I said it was very well for her
to talk, that knew what these sights and noises betokened, and
that had, perhaps, had something to do with the Spectre-Child
while it was alive. And I taunted her so, that she told me all she
knew, at last; and then I wished I had never been told, for it
only made me more afraid than ever.

She said she had heard the tale from old neighbours, that
were alive when she was first married; when folks used to come
to the hall sometimes, before it had got such a bad name on the
country side: it might not be true, or it might, what she had
been told.

The old lord was Miss Furnivall's father – Miss Grace, as
Dorothy called her, for Miss Maude was the elder, and Miss
Furnivall by rights. The old lord was eaten up with pride. Such
a proud man was never seen or heard of; and his daughters
were like him. No one was good enough to wed them, although
they had choice enough; for they were the great beauties of
their day, as I had seen by their portraits, where they hung in
the state drawing-room. But, as the old saying is, 'Pride will
have a fall;' and these two haughty beauties fell in love with
the same man, and he no better than a foreign musician, whom
their father had down from London to play music with him at
the Manor House. For, above all things, next to his pride, the
old lord loved music. He could play on nearly every instrument
that ever was heard of: and it was a strange thing it did not
soften him; but he was a fierce dour old man, and had broken
his poor wife's heart with his cruelty, they said. He was mad
after music, and would pay any money for it. So he got this
foreigner to come; who made such beautiful music, that they
said the very birds on the trees stopped their singing to listen.
And, by degrees, this foreign gentleman got such a hold over
the old lord, that nothing would serve him but that he must
come every year; and it was he that had the great organ brought
from Holland, and built up in the hall, where it stood now. He
taught the old lord to play on it; but many and many a time,
when Lord Furnivall was thinking of nothing but his fine organ,
and his finer music, the dark foreigner was walking abroad in
the woods with one of the young ladies; now Miss Maude, and
then Miss Grace.

Miss Maude won the day and carried off the prize, such as it was; and he and she were married, all unknown to any one; and before he made his next yearly visit, she had been confined of a little girl at a farm-house on the Moors, while her father and Miss Grace thought she was away at Doncaster Races.[10] But though she was a wife and a mother, she was not a bit softened, but as haughty and as passionate as ever; and perhaps more so, for she was jealous of Miss Grace, to whom her foreign husband paid a deal of court – by way of blinding her – as he told his wife. But Miss Grace triumphed over Miss Maude, and Miss Maude grew fiercer and fiercer, both with her husband and with her sister; and the former – who could easily shake off what was disagreeable, and hide himself in foreign countries – went away a month before his usual time that summer, and half threatened that he would never come back again. Meanwhile, the little girl was left at the farm-house, and her mother used to have her horse saddled and gallop wildly over the hills to see her once every week, at the very least – for where she loved, she loved; and where she hated, she hated. And the old lord went on playing – playing on his organ; and the servants thought the sweet music he made had soothed down his awful temper, of which (Dorothy said) some terrible tales could be told. He grew infirm too, and had to walk with a crutch; and his son – that was the present Lord Furnivall's father – was with the army in America, and the other son at sea;[11] so Miss Maude had it pretty much her own way, and she and Miss Grace grew colder and bitterer to each other every day; till at last they hardly ever spoke, except when the old lord was by. The foreign musician came again the next summer, but it was for the last time; for they led him such a life with their jealousy and their passions, that he grew weary, and went away, and never was heard of again. And Miss Maude, who had always meant to have her marriage acknowledged when her father should be dead, was left now a deserted wife – whom nobody knew to have been married – with a child that she dared not own, although she loved it to distraction; living with a father whom she feared, and a sister whom she hated. When the next summer passed over and the dark foreigner never came, both Miss Maude and Miss Grace grew gloomy and sad; they had a haggard look about them, though they looked handsome as ever. But by-and-by Miss Maude brightened; for her father grew more and more infirm, and more than ever carried away by his music; and she and Miss Grace lived almost entirely apart, having separate rooms, the one on the west side, Miss Maude on the east – those very rooms which were now shut up. So she thought she might have her little girl with her, and no one need ever know except those who dared not speak about it, and were bound to believe that it was, as she said, a cottager's child she had taken a fancy to. All this, Dorothy said, was pretty well known; but what came afterwards no one knew, except Miss Grace, and Mrs Stark, who was even then her maid, and much more of a friend to her than ever her sister had been. But the servants supposed, from words that were dropped, that Miss Maude had triumphed over Miss Grace, and told her that all the time the dark foreigner had been mocking her with pretended love – he was her own husband; the colour left Miss Grace's cheek and lips that very day for ever, and she was heard to say many a time that sooner or later she would have her revenge; and Mrs Stark was for ever spying about the east rooms.

One fearful night, just after the New Year had come in, when the snow was lying thick and deep, and the flakes were still falling – fast enough to blind any one who might be out and abroad – there was a great and violent noise heard, and the old lord's voice above all, cursing and swearing awfully, – and the cries of a little child, – and the proud defiance of a fierce woman, – and the sound of a blow, – and a dead stillness, – and moans and wailings dying away on the hill-side! Then the old lord summoned all his servants, and told them, with terrible oaths, and words more terrible, that his daughter had disgraced herself, and that he had turned her out of doors, – her, and her child, – and that if ever they gave her help, – or food – or shelter, – he prayed that they might never enter Heaven. And, all the while, Miss Grace stood by him, white and still as any stone; and when he had ended she heaved a great sigh, as much as to say her work was done, and her end was accomplished. But the old lord never touched his organ again, and died within the year; and no wonder! for, on the morrow of that wild and fearful night, the shepherds, coming down the Fell side, found Miss Maude sitting, all crazy and smiling, under the holly-trees, nursing a dead child, – with a terrible mark on its right shoulder. 'But that was not what killed it,' said Dorothy; 'it was the frost and the cold; – every wild creature was in its hole, and every beast in its fold, – while the child and its mother were turned out to wander on the Fells! And now you know all! and I wonder if you are less frightened now?'

I was more frightened than ever; but I said I was not. I wished Miss Rosamond and myself well out of that dreadful house for ever; but I would not leave her, and I dared not take her away. But oh! how I watched her, and guarded her! We bolted the doors, and shut the window-shutters fast, an hour or more before dark, rather than leave them open five minutes too late. But my little lady still heard the weird child crying and mourning; and not all we could do or say, could keep her from wanting to go to her, and let her in from the cruel wind and the snow. All this time, I kept away from Miss Furnivall and Mrs Stark, as much as ever I could; for I feared them – I knew no good could be about them, with their grey hard faces, and their dreamy eyes, looking back into the ghastly years that were gone. But, even in my fear, I had a kind of pity – for Miss Furnivall, at least. Those gone down to the pit can hardly have a more hopeless look than that which was ever on her face. At last I even got so sorry for her – who never said a word but what was quite forced from her – that I prayed for her; and I taught Miss Rosamond to pray for one who had done a deadly sin; but often when she came to those words, she would listen, and start up from her knees, and say, 'I hear my little girl plaining and crying very sad – Oh! let her in, or she will die!'

One night – just after New Year's Day had come at last, and the long winter had taken a turn, as I hoped – I heard the west drawing-room bell ring three times, which was the signal for me. I would not leave Miss Rosamond alone, for all she was asleep – for the old lord had been playing wilder than ever – and I feared lest my darling should waken to hear the spectre child; see her I knew she could not. I had fastened the windows too well for that. So, I took her out of her bed and wrapped her up in such outer clothes as were most handy, and carried

her down to the drawing-room, where the old ladies sat at their
tapestry work as usual. They looked up when I came in, and
Mrs Stark asked, quite astounded, 'Why did I bring Miss Rosamond there, out of her warm bed?' I had begun to whisper,
'Because I was afraid of her being tempted out while I was
away, by the wild child in the snow,' when she stopped me
short (with a glance at Miss Furnivall), and said Miss Furnivall
wanted me to undo some work she had done wrong, and which
neither of them could see to unpick. So, I laid my pretty dear
on the sofa, and sat down on a stool by them, and hardened
my heart against them, as I heard the wind rising and howling.

Miss Rosamond slept on sound, for all the wind blew so; and
Miss Furnivall said never a word, nor looked round when the
gusts shook the windows. All at once she started up to her full
height, and put up one hand, as if to bid us listen.

'I hear voices!' said she. 'I hear terrible screams – I hear my
father's voice!'

Just at that moment, my darling wakened with a sudden
start: 'My little girl is crying, oh, how she is crying!' and she
tried to get up and go to her, but she got her feet entangled in
the blanket, and I caught her up; for my flesh had begun to
creep at these noises, which they heard while we could catch
no sound. In a minute or two the noises came, and gathered
fast, and filled our ears; we, too, heard voices and screams, and
no longer heard the winter's wind that raged abroad. Mrs Stark
looked at me, and I at her, but we dared not speak. Suddenly
Miss Furnivall went towards the door, out into the ante-room,
through the west lobby, and opened the door into the great
hall. Mrs Stark followed, and I durst not be left, though my
heart almost stopped beating for fear. I wrapped my darling
tight in my arms, and went out with them. In the hall the
screams were louder than ever; they sounded to come from the
east wing – nearer and nearer – close on the other side of
the locked-up doors – close behind them. Then I noticed that
the great bronze chandelier seemed all alight, though the hall
was dim, and that a fire was blazing in the vast hearth-place,
though it gave no heat; and I shuddered up with terror, and
folded my darling closer to me. But as I did so, the east door
shook, and she, suddenly struggling to get free from me, cried,

'Hester! I must go! My little girl is there; I hear her; she is coming! Hester, I must go!'

I held her tight with all my strength; with a set will, I held her. If I had died, my hands would have grasped her still, I was so resolved in my mind. Miss Furnivall stood listening, and paid no regard to my darling, who had got down to the ground, and whom I, upon my knees now, was holding with both my arms clasped round her neck; she still striving and crying to get free.

All at once, the east door gave way with a thundering crash, as if torn open in a violent passion, and there came into that broad and mysterious light, the figure of a tall old man, with grey hair and gleaming eyes. He drove before him, with many a relentless gesture of abhorrence, a stern and beautiful woman, with a little child clinging to her dress.

'Oh Hester! Hester!' cried Miss Rosamond. 'It's the lady! the lady below the holly-trees; and my little girl is with her. Hester! Hester! let me go to her; they are drawing me to them. I feel them – I feel them. I must go!'

Again she was almost convulsed by her efforts to get away; but I held her tighter and tighter, till I feared I should do her a hurt; but rather that than let her go towards those terrible phantoms. They passed along towards the great hall-door, where the winds howled and ravened for their prey; but before they reached that, the lady turned; and I could see that she defied the old man with a fierce and proud defiance; but then she quailed – and then she threw up her arms wildly and piteously to save her child – her little child – from a blow from his uplifted crutch.

And Miss Rosamond was torn as by a power stronger than mine, and writhed in my arms, and sobbed (for by this time the poor darling was growing faint).

'They want me to go with them on to the Fells – they are drawing me to them. Oh, my little girl! I would come, but cruel, wicked Hester holds me very tight.' But when she saw the uplifted crutch she swooned away, and I thanked God for it. Just at this moment – when the tall old man, his hair streaming as in the blast of a furnace, was going to strike the little shrinking child – Miss Furnivall, the old woman by my side, cried out, 'Oh, father! father! spare the little innocent child!' But just

then I saw – we all saw – another phantom shape itself, and
grow clear out of the blue and misty light that filled the hall;
we had not seen her till now, for it was another lady who stood
by the old man, with a look of relentless hate and triumphant
scorn. That figure was very beautiful to look upon, with a soft
white hat drawn down over the proud brows, and a red and
curling lip. It was dressed in an open robe of blue satin. I had
seen that figure before. It was the likeness of Miss Furnivall in
her youth; and the terrible phantoms moved on, regardless of
old Miss Furnivall's wild entreaty, – and the uplifted crutch fell
on the right shoulder of the little child, and the younger sister
looked on, stony and deadly serene. But at that moment, the
dim lights, and the fire that gave no heat, went out of themselves, and Miss Furnivall lay at our feet stricken down by the
palsy – death-stricken.

Yes! she was carried to her bed that night never to rise again.
She lay with her face to the wall, muttering low but muttering
alway: 'Alas! alas! what is done in youth can never be undone
in age! What is done in youth can never be undone in age!'

FITZ-JAMES O'BRIEN

What Was It?

It is, I confess, with considerable diffidence that I approach the strange narrative which I am about to relate. The events which I purpose detailing are of so extraordinary a character that I am quite prepared to meet with an unusual amount of incredulity and scorn. I accept all such beforehand. I have, I trust, the literary courage to face unbelief. I have, after mature consideration, resolved to narrate, in as simple and straightforward a manner as I can compass, some facts that passed under my observation, in the month of July last, and which, in the annals of the mysteries of physical science, are wholly unparalleled.

I live at No. — Twenty-sixth Street, in New York. The house is in some respects a curious one. It has enjoyed for the last two years the reputation of being haunted. It is a large and stately residence, surrounded by what was once a garden, but which is now only a green enclosure used for bleaching clothes. The dry basin of what has been a fountain, and a few fruit-trees ragged and unpruned, indicate that this spot in past days was a pleasant, shady retreat, filled with fruits and flowers and the sweet murmur of waters.

The house is very spacious. A hall of noble size leads to a large spiral staircase winding through its centre, while the various apartments are of imposing dimensions. It was built some fifteen or twenty years since by Mr A—, the well-known New York merchant, who five years ago threw the commercial world into convulsions by a stupendous bank fraud. Mr A—, as every one knows, escaped to Europe, and died not long after, of a broken heart. Almost immediately after the news of his decease reached this country and was verified, the report spread in Twenty-sixth Street that No. — was haunted. Legal measures

had dispossessed the widow of its former owner, and it was
inhabited merely by a care-taker and his wife, placed there by
the house-agent into whose hands it had passed for purposes
of renting or sale. These people declared that they were troubled
with unnatural noises. Doors were opened without any visible
agency. The remnants of furniture scattered through the various
rooms were, during the night, piled one upon the other by
unknown hands. Invisible feet passed up and down the stairs
in broad daylight, accompanied by the rustle of unseen silk
dresses, and the gliding of viewless hands along the massive
balusters.[1] The care-taker and his wife declared they would live
there no longer. The house-agent laughed, dismissed them, and
put others in their place. The noises and supernatural manifestations continued. The neighbourhood caught up the story, and
the house remained untenanted for three years. Several persons
negotiated for it; but, somehow, always before the bargain was
closed they heard the unpleasant rumours and declined to treat
any further.

It was in this state of things that my landlady, who at that
time kept a boarding-house in Bleecker Street, and who wished
to move further up town, conceived the bold idea of renting
No. — Twenty-sixth Street.[2] Happening to have in her house
rather a plucky and philosophical set of boarders, she laid her
scheme before us, stating candidly everything she had heard
respecting the ghostly qualities of the establishment to which
she wished to remove us. With the exception of two timid
persons, – a sea-captain and a returned Californian who
immediately gave notice that they would leave, – all of Mrs
Moffat's guests declared that they would accompany her in her
chivalric incursion into the abode of spirits.

Our removal was effected in the month of May, and we were
charmed with our new residence. The portion of Twenty-sixth
Street where our house is situated, between Seventh and Eighth
Avenues, is one of the pleasantest localities in New York.[3] The
gardens back of the houses, running down nearly to the
Hudson, form, in the summer time, a perfect avenue of verdure.
The air is pure and invigorating, sweeping, as it does, straight
across the river from the Weehawken heights, and even the
ragged garden which surrounded the house, although dis-

playing on washing days rather too much clothes-line, still gave us a piece of greensward to look at, and a cool retreat in the summer evenings, where we smoked our cigars in the dusk, and watched the fire-flies flashing their dark-lanterns in the long grass.[4]

Of course we had no sooner established ourselves at No. — than we began to expect the ghosts. We absolutely awaited their advent with eagerness. Our dinner conversation was super-natural. One of the boarders, who had purchased Mrs Crowe's 'Night Side of Nature' for his own private delectation, was regarded as a public enemy by the entire household for not having bought twenty copies.[5] The man led a life of supreme wretchedness while he was reading this volume. A system of espionage was established, of which he was the victim. If he incautiously laid the book down for an instant and left the room, it was immediately seized and read aloud in secret places to a select few. I found myself a person of immense importance, it having leaked out that I was tolerably well versed in the history of supernaturalism, and had once written a story the foundation of which was a ghost. If a table or a wainscot panel happened to warp when we were assembled in the large drawing-room, there was an instant silence, and every one was prepared for an immediate clanking of chains and a spectral form.

After a month of psychological excitement, it was with the utmost dissatisfaction that we were forced to acknowledge that nothing in the remotest degree approaching the supernatural had manifested itself. Once the black butler asseverated that his candle had been blown out by some invisible agency while he was undressing himself for the night; but as I had more than once discovered this coloured gentleman in a condition when one candle must have appeared to him like two, I thought it possible that, by going a step further in his potations, he might have reversed this phenomenon, and seen no candle at all where he ought to have beheld one.

Things were in this state when an incident took place so awful and inexplicable in its character that my reason fairly reels at the bare memory of the occurrence. It was the tenth of July. After dinner was over I repaired, with my friend Dr Hammond, to the garden to smoke my evening pipe. Independent of certain

mental sympathies which existed between the Doctor and
myself, we were linked together by a vice. We both smoked
opium.[6] We knew each other's secret, and respected it. We
enjoyed together that wonderful expansion of thought, that
marvellous intensifying of the perceptive faculties, that bound-
less feeling of existence when we seem to have points of contact
with the whole universe, – in short, that unimaginable spiritual
bliss, which I would not surrender for a throne, and which
I hope you, reader, will never – never taste.

Those hours of opium happiness which the Doctor and I
spent together in secret were regulated with a scientific accuracy. We did not blindly smoke the drug of paradise, and leave
our dreams to chance. While smoking, we carefully steered our
conversation through the brightest and calmest channels of
thought. We talked of the East, and endeavoured to recall the
magical panorama of its glowing scenery. We criticized the most
sensuous poets, – those who painted life ruddy with health,
brimming with passion, happy in the possession of youth and
strength and beauty. If we talked of Shakespeare's 'Tempest,'
we lingered over Ariel, and avoided Caliban.[7] Like the Guebers,
we turned our faces to the east, and saw only the sunny side of
the world.[8]

This skilful colouring of our train of thought produced in
our subsequent visions a corresponding tone. The splendours
of Arabian fairy-land dyed our dreams. We paced that narrow
strip of grass with the tread and port of kings.[9] The song of the
rana arborea, while he clung to the bark of the ragged plum-
tree, sounded like the strains of divine musicians.[10] Houses,
walls, and streets melted like rain-clouds, and vistas of unimaginable glory stretched away before us. It was a rapturous
companionship. We enjoyed the vast delight more perfectly
because, even in our most ecstatic moments, we were conscious
of each other's presence. Our pleasures, while individual, were
still twin, vibrating and moving in musical accord.

On the evening in question, the tenth of July, the Doctor and
myself drifted into an unusually metaphysical mood. We lit our
large meerschaums, filled with fine Turkish tobacco, in the core
of which burned a little black nut of opium, that, like the nut
in the fairy tale, held within its narrow limits wonders beyond

the reach of kings; we paced to and fro, conversing.[11] A strange perversity dominated the currents of our thought. They would *not* flow through the sun-lit channels into which we strove to divert them. For some unaccountable reason, they constantly diverged into dark and lonesome beds, where a continual gloom brooded. It was in vain that, after our old fashion, we flung ourselves on the shores of the East, and talked of its gay bazaars, of the splendours of the time of Haroun, of harems and golden palaces.[12] Black afreets continually arose from the depths of our talk, and expanded, like the one the fisherman released from the copper vessel, until they blotted everything bright from our vision.[13] Insensibly, we yielded to the occult force that swayed us, and indulged in gloomy speculation. We had talked some time upon the proneness of the human mind to mysticism, and the almost universal love of the terrible, when Hammond suddenly said to me, 'What do you consider to be the greatest element of terror?'

The question puzzled me. That many things were terrible, I knew. Stumbling over a corpse in the dark; beholding, as I once did, a woman floating down a deep and rapid river, with wildly lifted arms, and awful, upturned face, uttering, as she drifted, shrieks that rent one's heart, while we, the spectators, stood frozen at a window which overhung the river at a height of sixty feet, unable to make the slightest effort to save her, but dumbly watching her last supreme agony and her disappearance. A shattered wreck, with no life visible, encountered floating listlessly on the ocean, is a terrible object, for it suggests a huge terror, the proportions of which are veiled. But it now struck me, for the first time, that there must be one great and ruling embodiment of fear, – a King of Terrors, to which all others must succumb. What might it be? To what train of circumstances would it owe its existence?

'I confess, Hammond,' I replied to my friend, 'I never considered the subject before. That there must be one Something more terrible than any other thing, I feel. I cannot attempt, however, even the most vague definition.'

'I am somewhat like you, Harry,' he answered. 'I feel my capacity to experience a terror greater than anything yet conceived by the human mind; – something combining in fearful

and unnatural amalgamation hitherto supposed incompatible
elements. The calling of the voices in Brockden Brown's novel
of "Wieland" is awful; so is the picture of the Dweller of the
Threshold, in Bulwer's "Zanoni"; but,' he added, shaking his
head gloomily, 'there is something more horrible still than
these.'[14]

'Look here, Hammond,' I rejoined, 'let us drop this kind of
talk, for heaven's sake! We shall suffer for it, depend on it.'

'I don't know what's the matter with me to-night,' he replied,
'but my brain is running upon all sorts of weird and awful
thoughts. I feel as if I could write a story like Hoffman, to-night,
if I were only master of a literary style.'[15]

'Well, if we are going to be Hoffmanesque in our talk, I'm
off to bed. Opium and nightmares should never be brought
together. How sultry it is! Good-night, Hammond.'

'Good-night, Harry. Pleasant dreams to you.'

'To you, gloomy wretch, afreets, ghouls, and enchanters.'[16]

We parted, and each sought his respective chamber. I undressed quickly and got into bed, taking with me, according to
my usual custom, a book, over which I generally read myself
to sleep. I opened the volume as soon as I had laid my head
upon the pillow, and instantly flung it to the other side of the
room. It was Goudon's 'History of Monsters,' – a curious
French work, which I had lately imported from Paris, but
which, in the state of mind I had then reached, was anything
but an agreeable companion.[17] I resolved to go to sleep at once;
so, turning down my gas until nothing but a little blue point of
light glimmered on the top of the tube, I composed myself to rest.

The room was in total darkness. The atom of gas that still
remained alight did not illuminate a distance of three inches
round the burner. I desperately drew my arm across my eyes, as
if to shut out even the darkness, and tried to think of nothing. It
was in vain. The confounded themes touched on by Hammond
in the garden kept obtruding themselves on my brain. I battled
against them. I erected ramparts of would-be blankness of
intellect to keep them out. They still crowded upon me. While
I was lying still as a corpse, hoping that by a perfect physical
inaction I should hasten mental repose, an awful incident
occurred. A Something dropped, as it seemed, from the ceiling,

plumb upon my chest, and the next instant I felt two bony hands encircling my throat, endeavouring to choke me.

I am no coward, and am possessed of considerable physical strength. The suddenness of the attack, instead of stunning me, strung every nerve to its highest tension. My body acted from instinct, before my brain had time to realize the terrors of my position. In an instant I wound two muscular arms around the creature, and squeezed it, with all the strength of despair, against my chest. In a few seconds the bony hands that had fastened on my throat loosened their hold, and I was free to breathe once more. Then commenced a struggle of awful intensity. Immersed in the most profound darkness, totally ignorant of the nature of the Thing by which I was so suddenly attacked, finding my grasp slipping every moment, by reason, it seemed to me, of the entire nakedness of my assailant, bitten with sharp teeth in the shoulder, neck, and chest, having every moment to protect my throat against a pair of sinewy, agile hands, which my utmost efforts could not confine, – these were a combination of circumstances to combat which required all the strength, skill, and courage that I possessed.

At last, after a silent, deadly, exhausting struggle, I got my assailant under by a series of incredible efforts of strength. Once pinned, with my knee on what I made out to be its chest, I knew that I was victor. I rested for a moment to breathe. I heard the creature beneath me panting in the darkness, and felt the violent throbbing of a heart. It was apparently as exhausted as I was; that was one comfort. At this moment I remembered that I usually placed under my pillow, before going to bed, a large yellow silk pocket-handkerchief. I felt for it instantly; it was there. In a few seconds more I had, after a fashion, pinioned the creature's arms.

I now felt tolerably secure. There was nothing more to be done but to turn on the gas, and, having first seen what my midnight assailant was like, arouse the household. I will confess to being actuated by a certain pride in not giving the alarm before; I wished to make the capture alone and unaided.

Never losing my hold for an instant, I slipped from the bed to the floor, dragging my captive with me. I had but a few steps to make to reach the gas-burner; these I made with the greatest caution, holding the creature in a grip like a vice. At last I got within arm's-length of the tiny speck of blue light which told me where the gas-burner lay. Quick as lightning I released my grasp with one hand and let on the full flood of light. Then I turned to look at my captive.

I cannot even attempt to give any definition of my sensations the instant after I turned on the gas. I suppose I must have shrieked with terror, for in less than a minute afterward my room was crowded with the inmates of the house. I shudder now as I think of that awful moment. *I saw nothing!* Yes; I had one arm firmly clasped round a breathing, panting, corporeal shape, my other hand gripped with all its strength a throat as warm, and apparently fleshly, as my own; and yet, with this living substance in my grasp, with its body pressed against my own, and all in the bright glare of a large jet of gas, I absolutely beheld nothing! Not even an outline, – a vapour!

I do not, even at this hour, realize the situation in which I found myself. I cannot recall the astounding incident thoroughly. Imagination in vain tries to compass the awful paradox.

It breathed. I felt its warm breath upon my cheek. It struggled fiercely. It had hands. They clutched me. Its skin was smooth, like my own. There it lay, pressed close up against me, solid as stone, – and yet utterly invisible!

I wonder that I did not faint or go mad on the instant. Some wonderful instinct must have sustained me; for, absolutely, in place of loosening my hold on the terrible Enigma, I seemed to gain an additional strength in my moment of horror, and tightened my grasp with such wonderful force that I felt the creature shivering with agony.

Just then Hammond entered my room at the head of the household. As soon as he beheld my face – which, I suppose, must have been an awful sight to look at – he hastened forward, crying, 'Great heaven, Harry! what has happened?'.

'Hammond! Hammond!' I cried, 'come here. O, this is awful! I have been attacked in bed by something or other, which I have hold of; but I can't see it, – I can't see it!'

Hammond, doubtless struck by the unfeigned horror expressed in my countenance, made one or two steps forward with an anxious yet puzzled expression. A very audible titter burst from the remainder of my visitors. This suppressed laughter made me furious. To laugh at a human being in my position! It was the worst species of cruelty. *Now*, I can understand why the appearance of a man struggling violently, as it would seem, with an airy nothing, and calling for assistance against a vision, should have appeared ludicrous. *Then*, so great was my rage against the mocking crowd that had I the power I would have stricken them dead where they stood.

'Hammond! Hammond!' I cried again, despairingly, 'for God's sake come to me. I can hold the – the thing but a short while longer. It is overpowering me. Help me! Help me!'

'Harry,' whispered Hammond, approaching me, 'you have been smoking too much opium.'

'I swear to you, Hammond, that this is no vision,' I answered, in the same low tone. 'Don't you see how it shakes my whole frame with its struggles? If you don't believe me, convince yourself. Feel it, – touch it.'

Hammond advanced and laid his hand in the spot I indicated. A wild cry of horror burst from him. He *had felt it!*

In a moment he had discovered somewhere in my room a long piece of cord, and was the next instant winding it and knotting it about the body of the unseen being that I clasped in my arms.

'Harry,' he said, in a hoarse, agitated voice, for, though he preserved his presence of mind, he was deeply moved, 'Harry, it's all safe now. You may let go, old fellow, if you're tired. The Thing can't move.'

I was utterly exhausted, and I gladly loosed my hold.

Hammond stood holding the ends of the cord that bound the Invisible, twisted round his hand, while before him, self-supporting as it were, he beheld a rope laced and interlaced, and stretching tightly around a vacant space. I never saw a man look so thoroughly stricken with awe. Nevertheless his face expressed all the courage and determination which I knew him to possess. His lips, although white, were set firmly, and one could perceive at a glance that, although stricken with fear, he was not daunted.

The confusion that ensued among the guests of the house who were witnesses of this extraordinary scene between Hammond

and myself, – who beheld the pantomime of binding this struggling Something, – who beheld me almost sinking from physical
exhaustion when my task of jailer was over, – the confusion
and terror that took possession of the bystanders, when they
saw all this, was beyond description. The weaker ones fled from
the apartment. The few who remained clustered near the door
and could not be induced to approach Hammond and his
Charge. Still incredulity broke out through their terror. They
had not the courage to satisfy themselves, and yet they doubted.
It was in vain that I begged of some of the men to come near
and convince themselves by touch of the existence in that room
of a living being which was invisible. They were incredulous,
but did not dare to undeceive themselves. How could a solid,
living, breathing body be invisible, they asked. My reply was
this. I gave a sign to Hammond, and both of us – conquering
our fearful repugnance to touch the invisible creature – lifted it
from the ground, manacled as it was, and took it to my bed. Its
weight was about that of a boy of fourteen.

'Now, my friends,' I said, as Hammond and myself held the
creature suspended over the bed, 'I can give you self-evident
proof that here is a solid, ponderable body, which, nevertheless,
you cannot see. Be good enough to watch the surface of the bed
attentively.'

I was astonished at my own courage in treating this strange
event so calmly; but I had recovered from my first terror, and
felt a sort of scientific pride in the affair, which dominated every
other feeling.

The eyes of the bystanders were immediately fixed on my
bed. At a given signal Hammond and I let the creature fall.
There was the dull sound of a heavy body alighting on a soft
mass. The timbers of the bed creaked. A deep impression
marked itself distinctly on the pillow, and on the bed itself. The
crowd who witnessed this gave a low cry, and rushed from the
room. Hammond and I were left alone with our Mystery.

We remained silent for some time, listening to the low, irregular breathing of the creature on the bed, and watching the rustle
of the bed-clothes as it impotently struggled to free itself from
confinement. Then Hammond spoke.

'Harry, this is awful.'

'Ay, awful.'

'But not unaccountable.'

'Not unaccountable! What do you mean? Such a thing has never occurred since the birth of the world. I know not what to think, Hammond. God grant that I am not mad, and that this is not an insane fantasy!'

'Let us reason a little, Harry. Here is a solid body which we touch, but which we cannot see. The fact is so unusual that it strikes us with terror. Is there no parallel, though, for such a phenomenon? Take a piece of pure glass. It is tangible and transparent. A certain chemical coarseness is all that prevents its being so entirely transparent as to be totally invisible. It is not *theoretically impossible*, mind you, to make a glass which shall not reflect a single ray of light, – a glass so pure and homogeneous in its atoms that the rays from the sun will pass through it as they do through the air, refracted but not reflected. We do not see the air, and yet we feel it.'

'That's all very well, Hammond, but these are inanimate substances. Glass does not breathe, air does not breathe. *This* thing has a heart that palpitates, – a will that moves it, – lungs that play, and inspire and respire.'

'You forget the phenomena of which we have so often heard of late,' answered the Doctor, gravely. 'At the meetings called "spirit circles," invisible hands have been thrust into the hands of those persons round the table, – warm, fleshly hands that seemed to pulsate with mortal life.'[18]

'What? Do you think, then, that this thing is –'

'I don't know what it is,' was the solemn reply; 'but please the gods I will, with your assistance, thoroughly investigate it.'

We watched together, smoking many pipes, all night long, by the bedside of the unearthly being that tossed and panted until it was apparently wearied out. Then we learned by the low, regular breathing that it slept.

The next morning the house was all astir. The boarders congregated on the landing outside my room, and Hammond and myself were lions. We had to answer a thousand questions as to the state of our extraordinary prisoner, for as yet not one person in the house except ourselves could be induced to set foot in the apartment.

The creature was awake. This was evidenced by the convulsive manner in which the bed-clothes were moved in its efforts to escape. There was something truly terrible in beholding, as it were, those second-hand indications of the terrible writhings and agonized struggles for liberty which themselves were invisible.

Hammond and myself had racked our brains during the long night to discover some means by which we might realize the shape and general appearance of the Enigma. As well as we could make out by passing our hands over the creature's form, its outlines and lineaments were human. There was a mouth; a round, smooth head without hair; a nose, which, however, was little elevated above the cheeks; and its hands and feet felt like those of a boy. At first we thought of placing the being on a smooth surface and tracing its outline with chalk, as shoe-makers trace the outline of the foot. This plan was given up as being of no value. Such an outline would give not the slightest idea of its conformation.

A happy thought struck me. We would take a cast of it in plaster of Paris. This would give us the solid figure, and satisfy all our wishes. But how to do it? The movements of the creature would disturb the setting of the plastic covering, and distort the mould. Another thought. Why not give it chloroform?[19] It had respiratory organs, – that was evident by its breathing. Once reduced to a state of insensibility, we could do with it what we would. Doctor X— was sent for; and after the worthy physician had recovered from the first shock of amazement, he proceeded to administer the chloroform. In three minutes afterward we were enabled to remove the fetters from the creature's body, and a modeller was busily engaged in covering the invisible form with the moist clay. In five minutes more we had a mould, and before evening a rough fac-simile of the Mystery. It was shaped like a man, – distorted, uncouth, and horrible, but still a man. It was small, not over four feet and some inches in height, and its limbs revealed a muscular development that was unparalleled. Its face surpassed in hideousness anything I had ever seen. Gustave Doré, or Callot, or Tony Johannot, never conceived anything so horrible.[20] There is a face in one of the latter's illustrations to *Un Voyage où il vous plaira*, which somewhat approaches the countenance of this creature, but does not equal it.[21] It was the physiognomy of what I should fancy a ghoul might be. It looked as if it was capable of feeding on human flesh.

Having satisfied our curiosity, and bound every one in the house to secrecy, it became a question what was to be done with our Enigma? It was impossible that we should keep such a horror in our house; it was equally impossible that such an awful being should be let loose upon the world. I confess that I would have gladly voted for the creature's destruction. But who would shoulder the responsibility? Who would undertake the execution of this horrible semblance of a human being? Day after day this question was deliberated gravely. The boarders all left the house. Mrs Moffat was in despair, and threatened Hammond and myself with all sorts of legal penalties if we did not remove the Horror. Our answer was, 'We will go if you like, but we decline taking this creature with us. Remove it yourself if you please. It appeared in your house. On you the responsibility rests.' To this there was, of course, no answer. Mrs Moffat could not obtain for love or money a person who would even approach the Mystery.

The most singular part of the affair was that we were entirely ignorant of what the creature habitually fed on. Everything in the way of nutriment that we could think of was placed before it, but was never touched. It was awful to stand by, day after day, and see the clothes toss, and hear the hard breathing, and know that it was starving.

Ten, twelve days, a fortnight passed, and it still lived. The pulsations of the heart, however, were daily growing fainter, and had now nearly ceased. It was evident that the creature was dying for want of sustenance. While this terrible life-struggle was going on, I felt miserable. I could not sleep. Horrible as the creature was, it was pitiful to think of the pangs it was suffering.

At last it died. Hammond and I found it cold and stiff one morning in the bed. The heart had ceased to beat, the lungs to inspire. We hastened to bury it in the garden. It was a strange funeral, the dropping of that viewless corpse into the damp hole. The cast of its form I gave to Doctor X—, who keeps it in his museum in Tenth Street.

As I am on the eve of a long journey from which I may not return, I have drawn up this narrative of an event the most singular that has ever come to my knowledge.

EDWARD BULWER LYTTON

The Haunted and the Haunters: or, The House and the Brain

A friend of mine, who is a man of letters and a philosopher, said to me one day, as if between jest and earnest, – 'Fancy! since we last met, I have discovered a haunted house in the midst of London.'

'Really haunted? – and by what? ghosts?'

'Well, I can't answer that question; all I know is this – six weeks ago I and my wife were in search of a furnished apartment. Passing a quiet street, we saw on the window of one of the houses a bill, "Apartments Furnished." The situation suited us: we entered the house – liked the rooms – engaged them by the week – and left them the third day. No power on earth could have reconciled my wife to have stayed longer; and I don't wonder at it.'

'What did you see?'

'Excuse me – I have no desire to be ridiculed as a superstitious dreamer – nor, on the other hand, could I ask you to accept on my affirmation what you would hold to be incredible without the evidence of your own senses. Let me only say this, it was not so much what we saw or heard (in which you might fairly suppose that we were the dupes of our own excited fancy, or the victims of imposture in others) that drove us away, as it was an undefinable terror which seized both of us whenever we passed by the door of a certain unfurnished room, in which we neither saw nor heard anything. And the strangest marvel of all was, that for once in my life I agreed with my wife, silly woman though she be – and allowed, after the third night, that it was impossible to stay a fourth in that house. Accordingly, on the fourth morning I summoned the woman who kept the house and attended on us, and told her that the rooms did not quite suit us, and we would not stay out our week. She said, dryly, "I know why; you have stayed longer than any other lodger. Few ever stayed a second night; none before you a third. But I take it they have been very kind to you."

' "They? – who?" I asked, affecting a smile.

' "Why, they who haunt the house, whoever they are. I don't mind them; I remember them many years ago, when I lived in this house, not as a servant; but I know they will be the death of me some day. I don't care – I'm old, and must die soon anyhow; and then I shall be with them, and in this house still." The woman spoke with so dreary a calmness, that really it was a sort of awe that prevented my conversing with her further. I paid for my week, and too happy were I and my wife to get off so cheaply.'

'You excite my curiosity,' said I; 'nothing I should like better than to sleep in a haunted house. Pray give me the address of the one which you left so ignominiously.'

My friend gave me the address; and when we parted, I walked straight towards the house thus indicated.

It is situated on the north side of Oxford Street, in a dull but respectable thoroughfare.[1] I found the house shut up – no bill at the window, and no response to my knock. As I was turning away, a beer-boy, collecting pewter pots at the neighbouring areas, said to me, 'Do you want any one at that house, sir?'

'Yes, I heard it was to be let.'

'Let! – why, the woman who kept it is dead – has been dead these three weeks, and no one can be found to stay there, though Mr J— offered ever so much. He offered mother, who chars for him, £1 a week just to open and shut the windows, and she would not.'

'Would not! – and why?'

'The house is haunted; and the old woman who kept it was found dead in her bed, with her eyes wide open. They say the devil strangled her.'

'Pooh! – you speak of Mr J—. Is he the owner of the house?'

'Yes.'

'Where does he live?'

'In G— Street, No.—.'

'What is he? – in any business?'

'No, sir – nothing particular; a single gentleman.'

I gave the pot-boy the gratuity earned by his liberal information, and proceeded to Mr J—, in G— Street, which was
close by the street that boasted the haunted house. I was lucky
enough to find Mr J— at home – an elderly man, with intelligent
countenance and prepossessing manners.

I communicated my name and my business frankly. I said I
heard the house was considered to be haunted – that I had a
strong desire to examine a house with so equivocal a reputation
– that I should be greatly obliged if he would allow me to hire
it, though only for a night. I was willing to pay for that privilege
whatever he might be inclined to ask. 'Sir,' said Mr J—, with
great courtesy, 'the house is at your service, for as short or as
long a time as you please. Rent is out of the question – the
obligation will be on my side should you be able to discover
the cause of the strange phenomena which at present deprive it
of all value. I cannot let it, for I cannot even get a servant to
keep it in order or answer the door. Unluckily the house is
haunted, if I may use that expression, not only by night, but by
day; though at night the disturbances are of a more unpleasant
and sometimes of a more alarming character. The poor old
woman who died in it three weeks ago was a pauper whom I
took out of a workhouse, for in her childhood she had been
known to some of my family, and had once been in such good
circumstances that she had rented that house of my uncle. She
was a woman of superior education and strong mind, and was
the only person I could ever induce to remain in the house.
Indeed, since her death, which was sudden, and the coroner's
inquest, which gave it a notoriety in the neighbourhood, I have
so despaired of finding any person to take charge of the house,
much more a tenant, that I would willingly let it rent-free for a
year to any one who would pay its rates and taxes.'

'How long is it since the house acquired this sinister
character?'

'That I can scarcely tell you, but very many years since. The
old woman I spoke of said it was haunted when she rented it
between thirty and forty years ago. The fact is, that my life has
been spent in the East Indies, and in the civil service of the
Company.[2] I returned to England last year, on inheriting the

fortune of an uncle, among whose possessions was the house in question. I found it shut up and uninhabited. I was told that it was haunted, that no one would inhabit it. I smiled at what seemed to me so idle a story. I spent some money in repairing it – added to its old-fashioned furniture a few modern articles – advertised it, and obtained a lodger for a year. He was a colonel retired on half-pay. He came in with his family, a son and a daughter, and four or five servants: they all left the house the next day; and, although each of them declared that he had seen something different from that which had scared the others, a something still was equally terrible to all. I really could not in conscience sue, nor even blame, the colonel for breach of agreement. Then I put in the old woman I have spoken of, and she was empowered to let the house in apartments. I never had one lodger who stayed more than three days. I do not tell you their stories – to no two lodgers have there been exactly the same phenomena repeated. It is better that you should judge for yourself, than enter the house with an imagination influenced by previous narratives; only be prepared to see and to hear something or other, and take whatever precautions you yourself please.'

'Have you never had a curiosity yourself to pass a night in that house?'

'Yes. I passed not a night but three hours in broad daylight alone in that house. My curiosity is not satisfied, but it is quenched. I have no desire to renew the experiment. You cannot complain, you see, sir, that I am not sufficiently candid; and unless your interest be exceedingly eager and your nerves unusually strong, I honestly add, that I advise you *not* to pass a night in that house.'

'My interest *is* exceedingly keen,' said I, 'and though only a coward will boast of his nerves in situations wholly unfamiliar to him, yet my nerves have been seasoned in such variety of danger that I have the right to rely on them – even in a haunted house.'

Mr J— said very little more; he took the keys of the house out of his bureau, gave them to me, – and, thanking him cordially for his frankness, and his urbane concession to my wish, I carried off my prize.

Impatient for the experiment, as soon as I reached home, I

summoned my confidential servant – a young man of gay spirits, fearless temper, and as free from superstitious prejudice as any one I could think of.

'F—,' said I, 'you remember in Germany how disappointed we were at not finding a ghost in that old castle, which was said to be haunted by a headless apparition? Well, I have heard of a house in London which, I have reason to hope, is decidedly haunted. I mean to sleep there to-night. From what I hear, there is no doubt that something will allow itself to be seen or to be heard – something, perhaps, excessively horrible. Do you think, if I take you with me, I may rely on your presence of mind, whatever may happen?'

'Oh, sir! pray trust me,' answered F—, grinning with delight.

'Very well; then here are the keys of the house – this is the address. Go now, – select for me any bedroom you please; and since the house has not been inhabited for weeks, make up a good fire – air the bed well – see, of course, that there are candles as well as fuel. Take with you my revolver and my dagger – so much for my weapons – arm yourself equally well; and if we are not a match for a dozen ghosts, we shall be but a sorry couple of Englishmen.'

I was engaged for the rest of the day on business so urgent that I had not leisure to think much on the nocturnal adventure to which I had plighted my honour. I dined alone, and very late, and while dining, read, as is my habit. I selected one of the volumes of Macaulay's Essays.[3] I thought to myself that I would take the book with me; there was so much of healthfulness in the style, and practical life in the subjects, that it would serve as an antidote against the influences of superstitious fancy.

Accordingly, about half-past nine, I put the book into my pocket, and strolled leisurely towards the haunted house. I took with me a favourite dog, – an exceedingly sharp, bold, and vigilant bull-terrier, – a dog fond of prowling about strange ghostly corners and passages at night in search of rats – a dog of dogs for a ghost.

It was a summer night, but chilly, the sky somewhat gloomy and overcast. Still there was a moon – faint and sickly, but still a moon – and if the clouds permitted, after midnight it would be brighter.

I reached the house, knocked, and my servant opened with a cheerful smile.

'All right, sir, and very comfortable.'

'Oh!' said I, rather disappointed; 'have you not seen nor heard anything remarkable?'

'Well, sir, I must own I have heard something queer.'

'What? – what?'

'The sound of feet pattering behind me; and once or twice small noises like whispers close at my ear – nothing more.'

'You are not at all frightened?'

'I! not a bit of it, sir;' and the man's bold look reassured me on one point – viz., that, happen what might, he would not desert me.

We were in the hall, the street-door closed, and my attention was now drawn to my dog. He had at first run in eagerly enough, but had sneaked back to the door, and was scratching and whining to get out. After patting him on the head, and encouraging him gently, the dog seemed to reconcile himself to the situation, and followed me and F— through the house, but keeping close at my heels instead of hurrying inquisitively in advance, which was his usual and normal habit in all strange places. We first visited the subterranean apartments, the kitchen and other offices, and especially the cellars, in which last there were two or three bottles of wine still left in a bin, covered with cobwebs, and evidently, by their appearance, undisturbed for many years.[4] It was clear that the ghosts were not winebibbers. For the rest we discovered nothing of interest. There was a gloomy little back-yard, with very high walls. The stones of this yard were very damp; and what with the damp, and what with the dust and smoke-grime on the pavement, our feet left a slight impression where we passed. And now appeared the first strange phenomenon witnessed by myself in this strange abode. I saw, just before me, the print of a foot suddenly form itself, as it were. I stopped, caught hold of my servant, and pointed to it. In advance of that footprint as suddenly dropped another. We both saw it. I advanced quickly to the place; the footprint kept advancing before me, a small footprint – the foot of a child: the impression was too faint thoroughly to distinguish the shape, but it seemed to us both that it was the print of a naked foot. This phenomenon ceased when we arrived at the opposite wall, nor did it repeat itself on returning. We remounted the stairs, and entered the rooms on the ground floor, a dining parlour, a small back-parlour, and a still smaller third room that had been probably appropriated to a footman – all still as death. We then visited the drawing-rooms, which seemed fresh and new. In the front room I seated myself in an arm-chair. F— placed on the table the candlestick with which he had lighted us. I told him to shut the door. As he turned to do so, a chair opposite to me moved from the wall quickly and noiselessly, and dropped itself about a yard from my own chair, immediately fronting it.

'Why, this is better than the turning-tables,' said I, with a half-laugh; and as I laughed, my dog put back his head and howled.[5]

F—, coming back, had not observed the movement of the chair. He employed himself now in stilling the dog. I continued to gaze on the chair, and fancied I saw on it a pale blue misty outline of a human figure, but an outline so indistinct that I could only distrust my own vision. The dog was now quiet. 'Put back that chair opposite to me,' said I to F—; 'put it back to the wall.'

F— obeyed. 'Was that you, sir?' said he, turning abruptly.

'I! – what?'

'Why, something struck me. I felt it sharply on the shoulder – just here.'

'No,' said I. 'But we have jugglers present, and though we may not discover their tricks, we shall catch *them* before they frighten *us*.'

We did not stay long in the drawing-rooms – in fact, they felt so damp and so chilly that I was glad to get to the fire upstairs. We locked the doors of the drawing-rooms – a precaution which, I should observe, we had taken with all the rooms we had searched below. The bedroom my servant had selected for me was the best on the floor – a large one, with two windows fronting the street. The four-posted bed, which took up no inconsiderable space, was opposite to the fire, which burned clear and bright; a door in the wall to the left, between the bed and the window, communicated with the room which my servant appropriated to himself. This last was a small room with a sofa-bed, and had no communication with the landing-place – no other door but that which conducted to the bedroom I was to occupy. On either side of my fire-place was a cupboard, without locks, flush with the wall, and covered with the same dull-brown paper. We examined these cupboards – only hooks to suspend female dresses – nothing else; we sounded the walls – evidently solid – the outer walls of the building. Having finished the survey of these apartments, warmed myself a few moments, and lighted my cigar, I then, still accompanied by F—, went forth to complete my reconnoitre. In the landing-place there was another door; it was closed firmly. 'Sir,' said my servant, in surprise, 'I unlocked this door with all the others when I first came; it cannot have got locked from the inside, for –'

Before he had finished his sentence, the door, which neither of us then was touching, opened quietly of itself. We looked at each other a single instant. The same thought seized both – some human agency might be detected here. I rushed in first, my servant followed. A small blank dreary room without furni-ture – a few empty boxes and hampers in a corner – a small window – the shutters closed – not even a fire-place – no other door but that by which we had entered – no carpet on the floor, and the floor seemed very old, uneven, worm-eaten, mended here and there, as was shown by the whiter patches on the wood; but no living being, and no visible place in which a living being could have hidden. As we stood gazing round, the door by which we had entered closed as quietly as it had before opened: we were imprisoned.

For the first time I felt a creep of undefinable horror. Not so my servant. 'Why, they don't think to trap us, sir; I could break that trumpery door with a kick of my foot.'

'Try first if it will open to your hand,' said I, shaking off the vague apprehension that had seized me, 'while I unclose the shutters and see what is without.'

I unbarred the shutters – the window looked on the little back-yard I have before described; there was no ledge without – nothing to break the sheer descent of the wall. No man getting out of that window would have found any footing till he had fallen on the stones below.

F—, meanwhile, was vainly attempting to open the door. He now turned round to me, and asked my permission to use force. And I should here state, in justice to the servant, that, far from evincing any superstitious terrors, his nerve, composure, and even gaiety amidst circumstances so extraordinary, compelled my admiration, and made me congratulate myself on having secured a companion in every way fitted to the occasion. I willingly gave him the permission he required. But though he was a remarkably strong man, his force was as idle as his milder efforts; the door did not even shake to his stoutest kick. Breathless and panting, he desisted. I then tried the door myself, equally in vain. As I ceased from the effort, again that creep of horror came over me; but this time it was more cold and stubborn. I felt as if some strange and ghastly exhalation were rising up from the chinks of that rugged floor, and filling the atmosphere with a venomous influence hostile to human life. The door now very slowly and quietly opened as if of its own accord. We precipitated ourselves into the landing-place. We both saw a large pale light – as large as the human figure, but shapeless and unsubstantial – move before us, and ascend the stairs that led from the landing into the attics. I followed the light, and my servant followed me. It entered, to the right of the landing, a small garret, of which the door stood open. I entered in the same instant. The light then collapsed into a small globule, exceedingly brilliant and vivid; rested a moment on a bed in the corner, quivered, and vanished. We approached the bed and examined it – a half-tester, such as is commonly found in attics devoted to servants.[6] On the drawers that stood near it we perceived an old faded silk kerchief, with the needle still left in a rent half repaired. The kerchief was covered with dust; probably it had belonged to the old woman who had last died in that house, and this might have been her sleeping-room. I had sufficient curiosity to open the drawers: there were a few odds and ends of female dress, and two letters tied round with a narrow ribbon of faded yellow. I took the liberty to possess myself of the letters. We found nothing else in the room worth noticing – nor did the light reappear; but we distinctly heard, as we turned to go, a pattering footfall on the floor – just before us. We went through the other attics (in all four), the footfall still preceding us. Nothing to be seen – nothing but the footfall heard. I had the letters in my hand: just as I was descending the stairs I distinctly felt my wrist seized, and a faint soft effort made to draw the letters from my clasp. I only held them the more tightly, and the effort ceased.

We regained the bedchamber appropriated to myself, and I then remarked that my dog had not followed us when we had left it. He was thrusting himself close to the fire, and trembling. I was impatient to examine the letters; and while I read them, my servant opened a little box in which he had deposited the weapons I had ordered him to bring; took them out, placed them on a table close at my bed-head, and then occupied himself in soothing the dog, who, however, seemed to heed him very little.

The letters were short – they were dated; the dates exactly thirty-five years ago. They were evidently from a lover to his mistress, or a husband to some young wife. Not only the terms of expression, but a distinct reference to a former voyage, indicated the writer to have been a seafarer. The spelling and handwriting were those of a man imperfectly educated, but still the language itself was forcible. In the expressions of endearment there was a kind of rough wild love; but here and there were dark unintelligible hints at some secret not of love – some secret that seemed of crime. 'We ought to love each other,' was one of the sentences I remember, 'for how every one else would execrate us if all was known.' Again: 'Don't let any one be in the same room with you at night – you talk in your sleep.' And again: 'What's done can't be undone; and I tell you there's nothing against us unless the dead could come to life.' Here there was underlined in a better handwriting (a female's), 'They do!' At the end of the letter latest in date the same female hand had written these words: 'Lost at sea the 4th of June, the same day as—.'

I put down the letters, and began to muse over their contents.

Fearing, however, that the train of thought into which I fell might unsteady my nerves, I fully determined to keep my mind in a fit state to cope with whatever of marvellous the advancing night might bring forth. I roused myself – laid the letters on the table – stirred up the fire which was still bright and cheering –

and opened my volume of Macaulay. I read quietly enough till about half-past eleven. I then threw myself dressed upon the bed, and told my servant he might retire to his own room, but must keep himself awake. I bade him leave open the door between the two rooms. Thus alone, I kept two candles burning on the table by my bed-head. I placed my watch beside the weapons, and calmly resumed my Macaulay. Opposite to me the fire burned clear; and on the hearthrug, seemingly asleep, lay the dog. In about twenty minutes I felt an exceedingly cold air pass by my cheek, like a sudden draught. I fancied the door to my right, communicating with the landing-place, must have got open; but no – it was closed. I then turned my glance to my left, and saw the flame of the candles violently swayed as by a wind. At the same moment the watch beside the revolver softly slid from the table – softly, softly – no visible hand – it was gone. I sprang up, seizing the revolver with the one hand, the dagger with the other: I was not willing that my weapons should share the fate of the watch. Thus armed, I looked round the floor – no sign of the watch. Three slow, loud, distinct knocks were now heard at the bed-head; my servant called out, 'Is that you, sir?'

'No; be on your guard.'

The dog now roused himself and sat on his haunches, his ears moving quickly backwards and forwards. He kept his eyes fixed on me with a look so strange that he concentred all my attention on himself. Slowly he rose up, all his hair bristling, and stood perfectly rigid, and with the same wild stare. I had no time, however, to examine the dog. Presently my servant emerged from his room; and if ever I saw horror in the human face, it was then. I should not have recognized him had we met in the street, so altered was every lineament. He passed by me quickly, saying in a whisper that seemed scarcely to come from his lips, 'Run – run! it is after me!' He gained the door to the landing, pulled it open, and rushed forth. I followed him into the landing involuntarily, calling to him to stop; but, without heeding me, he bounded down the stairs, clinging to the balusters, and taking several steps at a time. I heard, where I stood, the street-door open – heard it again clap to. I was left alone in the haunted house.

It was but for a moment that I remained undecided whether or not to follow my servant; pride and curiosity alike forbade so dastardly a flight. I re-entered my room, closing the door after me, and proceeded cautiously into the interior chamber. I encountered nothing to justify my servant's terror. I again carefully examined the walls, to see if there were any concealed door. I could find no trace of one – not even a seam in the dull-brown paper with which the room was hung. How, then, had the THING, whatever it was, which had so scared him, obtained ingress except through my own chamber?

I returned to my room, shut and locked the door that opened upon the interior one, and stood on the hearth, expectant and prepared. I now perceived that the dog had slunk into an angle of the wall, and was pressing himself close against it, as if literally striving to force his way into it. I approached the animal and spoke to it; the poor brute was evidently beside itself with terror. It showed all its teeth, the slaver dropping from its jaws, and would certainly have bitten me if I had touched it. It did not seem to recognize me. Whoever has seen at the Zoological Gardens a rabbit fascinated by a serpent, cowering in a corner, may form some idea of the anguish which the dog exhibited.[7] Finding all efforts to soothe the animal in vain, and fearing that his bite might be as venomous in that state as in the madness of hydrophobia, I left him alone, placed my weapons on the table beside the fire, seated myself, and recommenced my Macaulay.[8]

Perhaps, in order not to appear seeking credit for a courage, or rather a coolness, which the reader may conceive I exaggerate, I may be pardoned if I pause to indulge in one or two egotistical remarks.

As I hold presence of mind, or what is called courage, to be precisely proportioned to familiarity with the circumstances that lead to it, so I should say that I had been long sufficiently familiar with all experiments that appertain to the Marvellous. I had witnessed many very extraordinary phenomena in various parts of the world – phenomena that would be either totally disbelieved if I stated them, or ascribed to supernatural agencies. Now, my theory is that the Supernatural is the Impossible, and that what is called supernatural is only a something in the laws of nature of which we have been hitherto ignorant. Therefore, if a ghost rise before me, I have not the right to say, 'So, then, the supernatural is possible,' but rather, 'So, then, the apparition of a ghost is, contrary to received opinion, within the laws of nature – *i.e.*, not supernatural.'

Now, in all that I had hitherto witnessed, and indeed in all the wonders which the amateurs of mystery in our age record as facts, a material living agency is always required. On the Continent you will find still magicians who assert that they can raise spirits. Assume for the moment that they assert truly, still the living material form of the magician is present; and he is the material agency by which, from some constitutional peculiarities, certain strange phenomena are represented to your natural senses.

Accept, again, as truthful, the tales of Spirit Manifestation in America – musical or other sounds – writings on paper, produced by no discernible hand – articles of furniture moved without apparent human agency – or the actual sight and touch of hands, to which no bodies seem to belong – still there must be found the MEDIUM or living being, with constitutional peculiarities capable of obtaining these signs.[9] In fine, in all such marvels, supposing even that there is no imposture, there must be a human being like ourselves, by whom, or through whom, the effects presented to human beings are produced. It is so with the now familiar phenomena of mesmerism or electrobiology; the mind of the person operated on is affected through a material living agent.[10] Nor, supposing it true that a mesmerized patient can respond to the will or passes of a mesmerizer a hundred miles distant, is the response less occasioned by a material being; it may be through a material fluid – call it Electric, call it Odic, call it what you will – which has the power of traversing space and passing obstacles, that the material effect is communicated from one to the other.[11] Hence all that I had hitherto witnessed, or expected to witness, in this strange house, I believed to be occasioned through some agency or medium as mortal as myself; and this idea necessarily prevented the awe with which those who regard as supernatural things that are not within the ordinary operations of nature, might have been impressed by the adventures of that memorable night.

As, then, it was my conjecture that all that was presented, or would be presented to my senses, must originate in some human being gifted by constitution with the power so to present them, and having some motive so to do, I felt an interest in my theory which, in its way, was rather philosophical than superstitious. And I can sincerely say that I was in as tranquil a temper for observation as any practical experimentalist could be in awaiting the effects of some rare, though perhaps perilous, chemical combination. Of course, the more I kept my mind detached from fancy, the more the temper fitted for observation would be obtained; and I therefore riveted eye and thought on the strong daylight sense in the page of my Macaulay.

I now became aware that something interposed between the page and the light – the page was overshadowed: I looked up, and I saw what I shall find it very difficult, perhaps impossible, to describe.

It was a Darkness shaping itself forth from the air in very undefined outline. I cannot say it was of a human form, and yet it had more resemblance to a human form, or rather shadow, than to anything else. As it stood, wholly apart and distinct from the air and the light around it, its dimensions seemed gigantic, the summit nearly touching the ceiling. While I gazed, a feeling of intense cold seized me. An iceberg before me could not more have chilled me; nor could the cold of an iceberg have been more purely physical. I feel convinced that it was not the cold caused by fear. As I continued to gaze, I thought – but this I cannot say with precision – that I distinguished two eyes looking down on me from the height. One moment I fancied that I distinguished them clearly, the next they seemed gone; but still two rays of a pale-blue light frequently shot through the darkness, as from the height on which I half believed, half doubted, that I had encountered the eyes.

I strove to speak – my voice utterly failed me; I could only think to myself, 'Is this fear? it is *not* fear!' I strove to rise – in vain; I felt as if weighed down by an irresistible force. Indeed, my impression was that of an immense and overwhelming Power opposed to my volition; – that sense of utter inadequacy to cope with a force beyond man's, which one may feel *physically* in a storm at sea, in a conflagration, or when confronting some terrible wild beast, or rather perhaps, the shark of the ocean, I felt *morally*. Opposed to my will was another will, as far superior to its strength as storm, fire, and shark are superior in material force to the force of man.

And now, as this impression grew on me – now came, at last, horror – horror to a degree that no words can convey. Still I retained pride, if not courage; and in my own mind I said, 'This is horror, but it is not fear; unless I fear, I cannot be harmed; my reason rejects this thing; it is an illusion – I do not fear.' With a violent effort I succeeded at last in stretching out my hand towards the weapon on the table: as I did so, on the arm and shoulder I received a strange shock, and my arm fell to my side powerless. And now, to add to my horror, the light began slowly to wane from the candles – they were not, as it were, extinguished, but their flame seemed very gradually withdrawn: it was the same with the fire – the light was extracted from the fuel; in a few minutes the room was in utter darkness. The dread that came over me, to be thus in the dark with that dark Thing, whose power was so intensely felt, brought a reaction of nerve. In fact, terror had reached that climax, that either my senses must have deserted me, or I must have burst through the spell. I did burst through it. I found voice, though the voice was a shriek. I remember that I broke forth with words like these – 'I do not fear, my soul does not fear;' and at the same time I found the strength to rise. Still in that profound gloom I rushed to one of the windows – tore aside the curtain – flung open the shutters; my first thought was – LIGHT. And when I saw the moon high, clear, and calm, I felt a joy that almost compensated for the previous terror. There was the moon, there was also the light from the gas-lamps in the deserted, slumbrous street. I turned to look back into the room; the moon penetrated its shadow very palely and partially – but still there was light. The dark Thing, whatever it might be, was gone – except that I could yet see a dim shadow, which seemed the shadow of that shade, against the opposite wall.

My eye now rested on the table, and from under the table (which was without cloth or cover – an old mahogany round table) there rose a hand, visible as far as the wrist. It was a hand, seemingly, as much of flesh and blood as my own, but the hand of an aged person – lean, wrinkled, small too – a woman's hand. That hand very softly closed on the two letters that lay on the table: hand and letters both vanished. There then came the same three loud measured knocks I had heard at the bed-head before this extraordinary drama had commenced.

As those sounds slowly ceased, I felt the whole room vibrate sensibly; and at the far end there rose, as from the floor, sparks or globules like bubbles of light, many-coloured – green, yellow, fire-red, azure. Up and down, to and fro, hither, thither, as tiny Will-o'-the-Wisps the sparks moved, slow or swift, each at its own caprice. A chair (as in the drawing-room below) was now advanced from the wall without apparent agency, and placed at the opposite side of the table. Suddenly, as forth from the chair, there grew a shape – a woman's shape. It was distinct as a shape of life – ghastly as a shape of death. The face was that of youth, with a strange mournful beauty; the throat and shoulders were bare, the rest of the form in a loose robe of cloudy white. It began sleeking its long yellow hair, which fell over its shoulders; its eyes were not turned towards me, but to the door; it seemed listening, watching, waiting. The shadow of the shade in the background grew darker; and again I thought I beheld the eyes gleaming out from the summit of the shadow – eyes fixed upon that shape.

As if from the door, though it did not open, there grew out another shape, equally distinct, equally ghastly – a man's shape – a young man's. It was in the dress of the last century, or rather in a likeness of such dress (for both the male shape and the female, though defined, were evidently unsubstantial, impalpable – simulacra – phantasms); and there was something incongruous, grotesque, yet fearful, in the contrast between the elaborate finery, the courtly precision of that old-fashioned garb, with its ruffles and lace and buckles, and the corpse-like aspect and ghost-like stillness of the flitting wearer. Just as the male shape approached the female, the dark Shadow started from the wall, all three for a moment wrapped in darkness. When the pale light returned, the two phantoms were as if in the grasp of the Shadow that towered between them; and there was a blood-stain on the breast of the female; and the phantom male was leaning on its phantom sword, and blood seemed trickling fast from the ruffles, from the lace; and the darkness of the intermediate Shadow swallowed them up – they were gone. And again the bubbles of light shot, and sailed, and undulated, growing thicker and thicker and more wildly confused in their movements.

The closet door to the right of the fire-place now opened, and from the aperture there came the form of an aged woman. In her hand she held letters – the very letters over which I had seen *the* Hand close; and behind her I heard a footstep. She turned round as if to listen, and then she opened the letters and seemed to read; and over her shoulder I saw a livid face, the face as of a man long drowned – bloated, bleached – seaweed tangled in its dripping hair; and at her feet lay a form as of a corpse, and beside the corpse there cowered a child, a miserable squalid child, with famine in its cheeks and fear in its eyes. And as I looked in the old woman's face, the wrinkles and lines vanished, and it became a face of youth – hard-eyed, stony, but still youth; and the Shadow darted forth, and darkened over these phantoms as it had darkened over the last.

Nothing now was left but the Shadow, and on that my eyes were intently fixed, till again eyes grew out of the Shadow – malignant, serpent eyes. And the bubbles of light again rose and fell, and in their disordered, irregular, turbulent maze, mingled with the wan moonlight. And now from these globules themselves, as from the shell of an egg, monstrous things burst out; the air grew filled with them; larvæ so bloodless and so hideous that I can in no way describe them except to remind the reader of the swarming life which the solar microscope brings before his eyes in a drop of water – things transparent, supple, agile, chasing each other, devouring each other – forms like nought ever beheld by the naked eye.[12] As the shapes were without symmetry, so their movements were without order. In their very vagrancies there was no sport; they came round me and round, thicker and faster and swifter, swarming over my head, crawling over my right arm, which was outstretched in involuntary command against all evil beings. Sometimes I felt myself touched, but not by them; invisible hands touched me. Once I felt the clutch as of cold soft fingers at my throat. I was still equally conscious that if I gave way to fear I should be in bodily peril; and I concentrated all my faculties in the single focus of resisting, stubborn will. And I turned my sight from the shadow – above all, from those strange serpent eyes – eyes that had now become distinctly visible. For there, though in nought else around me, I was aware that there was a WILL, and a will of intense, creative, working evil, which might crush down my own.

The pale atmosphere in the room began now to redden as if in the air of some near conflagration. The larvæ grew lurid as things that live in fire. Again the room vibrated; again were heard the three measured knocks; and again all things were swallowed up in the darkness of the dark Shadow, as if out of that darkness all had come, into that darkness all returned.

As the gloom receded, the Shadow was wholly gone. Slowly as it had been withdrawn, the flame grew again into the candles on the table, again into the fuel in the grate. The whole room came once more calmly, healthfully into sight.

The two doors were still closed, the door communicating with the servants' room still locked. In the corner of the wall, into which he had so convulsively niched himself, lay the dog. I called to him – no movement; I approached – the animal was dead; his eyes protruded; his tongue out of his mouth; the froth gathered round his jaws. I took him in my arms; I brought him to the fire; I felt acute grief for the loss of my poor favourite – acute self-reproach; I accused myself of his death; I imagined he had died of fright. But what was my surprise on finding that his neck was actually broken. Had this been done in the dark? – must it not have been by a hand human as mine? – must there not have been a human agency all the while in that room? Good cause to suspect it. I cannot tell. I cannot do more than state the fact fairly; the reader may draw his own inference.

Another surprising circumstance – my watch was restored to the table from which it had been so mysteriously withdrawn; but it had stopped at the very moment it was so withdrawn; nor, despite all the skill of the watchmaker, has it ever gone since – that is, it will go in a strange erratic way for a few hours, and then come to a dead stop – it is worthless.

Nothing more chanced for the rest of the night. Nor, indeed, had I long to wait before the dawn broke. Not till it was broad daylight did I quit the haunted house. Before I did so, I revisited the little blind room in which my servant and myself had been for a time imprisoned. I had a strong impression – for which I could not account – that from that room had originated the mechanism of the phenomena – if I may use the term – which had been experienced in my chamber. And though I entered it now in the clear day, with the sun peering through the filmy window, I still felt, as I stood on its floor, the creep of the horror which I had first there experienced the night before, and which had been so aggravated by what had passed in my own chamber. I could not, indeed, bear to stay more than half a minute within those walls. I descended the stairs, and again I heard the footfall before me; and when I opened the street door, I thought I could distinguish a very low laugh. I gained my own home, expecting to find my runaway servant there. But he had not presented himself; nor did I hear more of him for three days, when I received a letter from him, dated from Liverpool, to this effect: –[13]

'Honoured Sir, – I humbly entreat your pardon, though I can scarcely hope that you will think I deserve it, unless – which Heaven forbid! – you saw what I did. I feel that it will be years before I can recover myself; and as to being fit for service, it is out of the question. I am therefore going to my brother-in-law at Melbourne. The ship sails to-morrow. Perhaps the long voyage may set me up. I do nothing now but start and tremble, and fancy IT is behind me. I humbly beg you, honoured sir, to order my clothes, and whatever wages are due to me, to be sent to my mother's, at Walworth, – John knows her address.'[14]

The letter ended with additional apologies, somewhat incoherent, and explanatory details as to effects that had been under the writer's charge.

This flight may perhaps warrant a suspicion that the man wished to go to Australia, and had been somehow or other fraudulently mixed up with the events of the night. I say nothing in refutation of that conjecture; rather, I suggest it as one that would seem to many persons the most probable solution of

improbable occurrences. My belief in my own theory remained
unshaken. I returned in the evening to the house, to bring away
in a hack cab the things I had left there, with my poor dog's
body. In this task I was not disturbed, nor did any incident
worth note befall me, except that still, on ascending and descending the stairs, I heard the same footfall in advance. On
leaving the house, I went to Mr J—'s. He was at home. I
returned him the keys, told him that my curiosity was sufficiently gratified, and was about to relate quickly what had
passed, when he stopped me and said, though with much politeness, that he had no longer any interest in a mystery which
none had ever solved.

I determined at least to tell him of the two letters I had read,
as well as of the extraordinary manner in which they had
disappeared, and I then inquired if he thought they had been
addressed to the woman who had died in the house, and if there
were anything in her early history which could possibly confirm
the dark suspicions to which the letters gave rise. Mr J— seemed
startled, and, after musing a few moments, answered, 'I am but
little acquainted with the woman's earlier history, except, as I
before told you, that her family were known to mine. But you
revive some vague reminiscences to her prejudice. I will make
inquiries, and inform you of their result. Still, even if we could
admit the popular superstition that a person who had been
either the perpetrator or the victim of dark crimes in life could
revisit, as a restless spirit, the scene in which those crimes had
been committed, I should observe that the house was infested
by strange sights and sounds before the old woman died – you
smile – what would you say?'

'I would say this, that I am convinced, if we could get to
the bottom of these mysteries, we should find a living human
agency.'

'What! you believe it is all an imposture? For what object?'

'Not an imposture in the ordinary sense of the word. If
suddenly I were to sink into a deep sleep, from which you could
not awake me, but in that sleep could answer questions with
an accuracy which I could not pretend to when awake – tell
you what money you had in your pocket – nay, describe your
very thoughts – it is not necessarily an imposture, any more

than it is necessarily supernatural. I should be, unconsciously to myself, under a mesmeric influence, conveyed to me from a distance by a human being who had acquired power over me by previous *rapport*.'[15]

'But if a mesmerizer could so affect another living being, can you suppose that a mesmerizer could also affect inanimate objects: move chairs – open and shut doors?'

'Or impress our senses with the belief in such effects – we never having been *en rapport* with the person acting on us? No. What is commonly called mesmerism could not do this: but there may be a power akin to mesmerism, and superior to it – the power that in the old days was called Magic. That such a power may extend to all inanimate objects of matter, I do not say; but if so, it would not be against nature – it would be only a rare power in nature which might be given to constitutions with certain peculiarities, and cultivated by practice to an extra-ordinary degree. That such a power might extend over the dead – that is, over certain thoughts and memories that the dead may still retain – and compel, not that which ought properly to be called the SOUL, and which is far beyond human reach, but rather a phantom of what has been most earth-stained on earth, to make itself apparent to our senses – is a very ancient though obsolete theory, upon which I will hazard no opinion. But I do not conceive the power would be supernatural. Let me illustrate what I mean from an experiment which Paracelsus describes as not difficult, and which the author of the *Curiosities of Litera-ture* cites as credible: – A flower perishes; you burn it.[16] What-ever were the elements of that flower while it lived are gone, dispersed, you know not whither; you can never discover nor re-collect them. But you can, by chemistry, out of the burnt dust of that flower, raise a spectrum of the flower, just as it seemed in life. It may be the same with the human being. The soul has as much escaped you as the essence or elements of the flower. Still you may make a spectrum of it. And this phantom, though in the popular superstition it is held to be the soul of the departed, must not be confounded with the true soul; it is but the eidolon of the dead form.[17] Hence, like the best-attested stories of ghosts or spirits, the thing that most strikes us is the absence of what we hold to be soul; that is, of superior

emancipated intelligence. These apparitions come for little or
no object – they seldom speak when they do come; if they
speak, they utter no ideas above those of an ordinary person
on earth. American spirit-seers have published volumes of communications in prose and verse, which they assert to be given
in the names of the most illustrious dead – Shakespeare, Bacon
– Heaven knows whom. Those communications, taking the
best, are certainly not a whit of higher order than would be
communications from living persons of fair talent and education; they are wondrously inferior to what Bacon, Shakespeare, and Plato said and wrote when on earth.[18] Nor, what is
more noticeable, do they ever contain an idea that was not on
the earth before. Wonderful, therefore, as such phenomena may
be (granting them to be truthful), I see much that philosophy
may question, nothing that it is incumbent on philosophy to
deny – viz., nothing supernatural. They are but ideas conveyed
somehow or other (we have not yet discovered the means) from
one mortal brain to another. Whether, in so doing, tables walk
of their own accord, or fiend-like shapes appear in a magic
circle, or bodiless hands rise and remove material objects, or a
Thing of Darkness, such as presented itself to me, freeze our
blood – still am I persuaded that these are but agencies conveyed
as by electric wires, to my own brain from the brain of another.
In some constitutions there is a natural chemistry, and those
constitutions may produce chemic wonders – in others a natural
fluid, call it electricity, and these may produce electric wonders.
But the wonders differ from Normal Science in this – they are
alike objectless, purposeless, puerile, frivolous. They lead on to
no grand results; and therefore the world does not heed, and
true sages have not cultivated them. But sure I am, that of all I
saw or heard, a man, human as myself, was the remote originator; and I believe unconsciously to himself as to the exact effects
produced, for this reason: no two persons, you say, have ever
told you that they experienced exactly the same thing. Well,
observe, no two persons ever experience exactly the same
dream. If this were an ordinary imposture, the machinery would
be arranged for results that would but little vary; if it were a
supernatural agency permitted by the Almighty, it would surely
be for some definite end. These phenomena belong to neither

class; my persuasion is, that they originate in some brain now far distant; that that brain had no distinct volition in anything that occurred; that what does occur reflects but its devious, motley, ever-shifting, half-formed thoughts; in short, that it has been but the dreams of such a brain put into action and invested with a semi-substance. That this brain is of immense power, that it can set matter into movement, that it is malignant and destructive, I believe; some material force must have killed my dog; the same force might, for aught I know, have sufficed to kill myself, had I been as subjugated by terror as the dog – had my intellect or my spirit given me no countervailing resistance in my will.'

'It killed your dog! that is fearful! indeed it is strange that no animal can be induced to stay in that house; not even a cat. Rats and mice are never found in it.'

'The instincts of the brute creation detect influences deadly to their existence. Man's reason has a sense less subtle, because it has a resisting power more supreme. But enough; do you comprehend my theory?'

'Yes, though imperfectly – and I accept any crotchet (pardon the word), however odd, rather than embrace at once the notion of ghosts and hobgoblins we imbibed in our nurseries. Still, to my unfortunate house the evil is the same. What on earth can I do with the house?'

'I will tell you what I would do. I am convinced, from my own internal feelings that the small unfurnished room at right angles to the door of the bedroom which I occupied, forms a starting-point or receptacle for the influences which haunt the house; and I strongly advise you to have the walls opened, the floor removed – nay, the whole room pulled down. I observe that it is detached from the body of the house, built over the small back-yard, and could be removed without injury to the rest of the building.'

'And you think if I did that –'

'You would cut off the telegraph wires.[19] Try it. I am so persuaded that I am right, that I will pay half the expense if you will allow me to direct the operations.'

'Nay, I am well able to afford the cost; for the rest, allow me to write to you.'

About ten days afterwards I received a letter from Mr J—, telling me that he had visited the house since I had seen him; that he had found the two letters I had described, replaced in the drawer from which I had taken them; that he had read them with misgivings like my own; that he had instituted a cautious inquiry about the woman to whom I rightly conjectured they had been written. It seemed that thirty-six years ago (a year before the date of the letters) she had married, against the wish of her relations, an American of very suspicious character; in fact, he was generally believed to have been a pirate. She herself was the daughter of very respectable tradespeople, and had served in the capacity of a nursery governess before her marriage. She had a brother, a widower, who was considered wealthy, and who had one child of about six years old. A month after the marriage the body of this brother was found in the Thames, near London Bridge; there seemed some marks of violence about his throat, but they were not deemed sufficient to warrant the inquest in any other verdict than that of 'found drowned.'

The American and his wife took charge of the little boy, the deceased brother having by his will left his sister the guardian of his only child – and in event of the child's death, the sister inherited. The child died about six months afterwards – it was supposed to have been neglected and ill-treated. The neighbours deposed to have heard it shriek at night. The surgeon who had examined it after death, said that it was emaciated as if from want of nourishment, and the body was covered with livid bruises. It seemed that one winter night the child had sought to escape – crept out into the back-yard – tried to scale the wall – fallen back exhausted, and been found at morning on the stones in a dying state. But though there was some evidence of cruelty, there was none of murder; and the aunt and her husband had sought to palliate cruelty by alleging the exceeding stubbornness and perversity of the child, who was declared to be half-witted. Be that as it may, at the orphan's death the aunt inherited her brother's fortune. Before the first wedded year was out, the American quitted England abruptly, and never returned to it. He obtained a cruising vessel, which was lost in the Atlantic two years afterwards. The widow was left in affluence: but reverses of various kinds had befallen her: a bank broke – an investment failed – she went into a small business and became insolvent – then she entered into service, sinking lower and lower, from housekeeper down to maid-of-all-work – never long retaining a place, though nothing decided against her character was ever alleged. She was considered sober, honest, and peculiarly quiet in her ways; still nothing prospered with her. And so she had dropped into the workhouse, from which Mr J— had taken her, to be placed in charge of the very house which she had rented as mistress in the first year of her wedded life.

Mr J— added that he had passed an hour alone in the unfurnished room which I had urged him to destroy, and that his impressions of dread while there were so great, though he had neither heard nor seen anything, that he was eager to have the walls bared and the floors removed as I had suggested. He had engaged persons for the work, and would commence any day I would name.

The day was accordingly fixed. I repaired to the haunted house – we went into the blind dreary room, took up the skirting, and then the floors. Under the rafters, covered with rubbish, was found a trap-door, quite large enough to admit a man. It was closely nailed down, with clamps and rivets of iron. On removing these we descended into a room below, the existence of which had never been suspected. In this room there had been a window and a flue, but they had been bricked over, evidently for many years. By the help of candles we examined this place; it still retained some mouldering furniture – three chairs, an oak settle, a table – all of the fashion of about eighty years ago. There was a chest of drawers against the wall, in which we found, half rotted away, old-fashioned articles of a man's dress, such as might have been worn eighty or a hundred years ago by a gentleman of some rank – costly steel buckles and buttons, like those yet worn in court dresses – a handsome court sword – in a waistcoat which had once been rich with gold lace, but which was now blackened and foul with damp, we found five guineas, a few silver coins, and an ivory ticket, probably for some place of entertainment long since passed away. But our main discovery was in a kind of iron safe fixed to the wall, the lock of which it cost us much trouble to get picked.

In this safe were three shelves, and two small drawers. Ranged on the shelves were several small bottles of crystal, hermetically stopped. They contained colourless volatile essences, of the nature of which I shall only say that they were not poisons – phosphor and ammonia entered into some of them. There were also some very curious glass tubes, and a small pointed rod of iron, with a large lump of rock crystal, and another of amber – also a loadstone of great power.

In one of the drawers we found a miniature portrait set in gold, and retaining the freshness of its colours most remarkably, considering the length of time it had probably been there. The portrait was that of a man who might be somewhat advanced in middle life, perhaps forty-seven or forty-eight.

It was a remarkable face – a most impressive face. If you could fancy some mighty serpent transformed into man, preserving in the human lineaments the old serpent type, you would have a better idea of that countenance than long descriptions can convey: the width and flatness of frontal – the tapering elegance of contour disguising the strength of the deadly jaw – the long, large, terrible eye, glittering and green as the emerald – and withal a certain ruthless calm, as if from the consciousness of an immense power.

Mechanically I turned round the miniature to examine the back of it, and on the back was engraved a pentacle; in the middle of the pentacle a ladder, and the third step of the ladder was formed by the date 1765.[20] Examining still more minutely, I detected a spring; this, on being pressed, opened the back of the miniature as a lid. Withinside the lid were engraved, 'Mariana to thee – Be faithful in life and in death to —.' Here follows a name that I will not mention, but it was not unfamiliar to me. I had heard it spoken of by old men in my childhood as the name borne by a dazzling charlatan who had made a great sensation in London for a year or so, and had fled the country on the charge of a double murder within his own house – that of his mistress and his rival. I said nothing of this to Mr J—, to whom reluctantly I resigned the miniature.

We had found no difficulty in opening the first drawer within the iron safe; we found great difficulty in opening the second: it was not locked, but it resisted all efforts, till we inserted in the chinks the edge of a chisel. When we had thus drawn it forth, we found a very singular apparatus in the nicest order. Upon a small thin book, or rather tablet, was placed a saucer of crystal; this saucer was filled with a clear liquid – on that liquid floated a kind of compass, with a needle shifting rapidly round; but instead of the usual points of a compass were seven strange characters, not very unlike those used by astrologers to denote the planets. A peculiar, but not strong nor displeasing odour, came from this drawer, which was lined with a wood that we afterwards discovered to be hazel. Whatever the cause of this odour, it produced a material effect on the nerves. We all felt it, even the two workmen who were in the room – a creeping, tingling sensation from the tips of the fingers to the roots of the hair. Impatient to examine the tablet I removed the saucer. As I did so the needle of the compass went round and round with exceeding swiftness, and I felt a shock that ran through my whole frame, so that I dropped the saucer on the floor. The liquid was spilt – the saucer was broken – the compass rolled to the end of the room – and at that instant the walls shook to and fro, as if a giant had swayed and rocked them.

The two workmen were so frightened that they ran up the ladder by which we had descended from the trap-door; but seeing that nothing more happened, they were easily induced to return.

Meanwhile I had opened the tablet: it was bound in plain red leather, with a silver clasp; it contained but one sheet of thick vellum, and on that sheet were inscribed, within a double pentacle, words in old monkish Latin, which are literally to be translated thus:[21] – 'On all that it can reach within these walls – sentient or inanimate, living or dead – as moves the needle, so work my will! Accursed be the house, and restless be the dwellers therein.'

We found no more. Mr J— burnt the tablet and its anathema.[22] He razed to the foundations the part of the building containing the secret room with the chamber over it. He had then the courage to inhabit the house himself for a month, and a quieter, better-conditioned house could not be found in all London. Subsequently he let it to advantage, and his tenant has made no complaints.

MARY ELIZABETH BRADDON

The Cold Embrace

He was an artist – such things as happened to him happen sometimes to artists.

He was a German – such things as happened to him happen sometimes to Germans.

He was young, handsome, studious, enthusiastic, metaphysical, reckless, unbelieving, heartless.

And being young, handsome, and eloquent, he was beloved.

He was an orphan, under the guardianship of his dead father's brother, his uncle Wilhelm, in whose house he had been brought up from a little child; and she who loved him was his cousin – his cousin Gertrude, whom he swore he loved in return.

Did he love her? Yes, when he first swore it. It soon wore out, this passionate love; how threadbare and wretched a sentiment it became at last in the selfish heart of the student! But in its first golden dawn, when he was only nineteen, and had just returned from his apprenticeship to a great painter at Antwerp, and they wandered together in the most Romantic outskirts of the city at rosy sunset, by holy moonlight, or bright and joyous morning, how beautiful a dream!

They keep it a secret from Wilhelm, as he has the father's ambition of a wealthy suitor for his only child – a cold and dreary vision beside the lover's dream.

So they are betrothed; and standing side by side when the dying sun and the pale rising moon divide the heavens, he puts the betrothal ring upon her finger, the white and taper finger whose slender shape he knows so well. This ring is a peculiar one, a massive golden serpent, its tail in its mouth, the symbol of eternity; it had been his mother's, and he would know it amongst a thousand. If he were to become blind to-morrow, he could select it from amongst a thousand by the touch alone.

He places it on her finger, and they swear to be true to each other for ever and ever – through trouble and danger – in sorrow and change – in wealth or poverty. Her father must needs be won to consent to their union by and by, for they were now betrothed, and death alone could part them.

But the young student, the scoffer at revelation, yet the enthusiastic adorer of the mystical, asks:

'Can death part us? I would return to you from the grave, Gertrude. My soul would come back to be near my love. And you – you, if you died before me – the cold earth would not hold you from me; if you loved me, you would return, and again these fair arms would be clasped round my neck as they are now.'

But she told him, with a holier light in her deep-blue eyes than had ever shone in his – she told him that the dead who die at peace with God are happy in heaven, and cannot return to the troubled earth; and that it is only the suicide – the lost wretch on whom sorrowful angels shut the door of Paradise – whose unholy spirit haunts the footsteps of the living.

The first year of their betrothal is passed, and she is alone, for he has gone to Italy, on a commission for some rich man, to copy Raphaels, Titians, Guidos, in a gallery at Florence.[1] He has gone to win fame, perhaps; but it is not the less bitter – he is gone!

Of course her father misses his young nephew, who has been as a son to him; and he thinks his daughter's sadness no more than a cousin should feel for a cousin's absence.

In the mean time, the weeks and months pass. The lover writes – often at first, then seldom – at last, not at all.

How many excuses she invents for him! How many times she goes to the distant little post-office, to which he is to address his letters! How many times she hopes, only to be disappointed! How many times she despairs, only to hope again!

But real despair comes at last, and will not be put off any more. The rich suitor appears on the scene, and her father is determined. She is to marry at once. The wedding-day is fixed – the fifteenth of June.

The date seems burnt into her brain.

The date, written in fire, dances for ever before her eyes.

The date, shrieked by the Furies, sounds continually in her ears.

But there is time yet – it is the middle of May – there is time for a letter to reach him at Florence; there is time for him to come to Brunswick, to take her away and marry her, in spite of her father – in spite of the whole world.[2]

But the days and weeks fly by, and he does not write – he does not come. This is indeed despair which usurps her heart, and will not be put away.

It is the fourteenth of June. For the last time she goes to the little post-office; for the last time she asks the old question, and they give her for the last time the dreary answer, 'No; no letter.'

For the last time – for to-morrow is the day appointed for her bridal. Her father will hear no entreaties; her rich suitor will not listen to her prayers. They will not be put off a day – an hour; to-night alone is hers – this night, which she may employ as she will.

She takes another path than that which leads home; she hurries through some by-streets of the city, out on to a lonely bridge, where he and she had stood so often in the sunset, watching the rose-coloured light glow, fade, and die upon the river.

He returns from Florence. He had received her letter. That letter, blotted with tears, entreating, despairing – he had received it, but he loved her no longer. A young Florentine, who had sat to him for a model, had bewitched his fancy – that fancy which with him stood in place of a heart – and Gertrude had been half forgotten. If she had a richer suitor, good; let her marry him; better for her, better far for himself. He had no wish to fetter himself with a wife. Had he not his art always? – his eternal bride, his unchanging mistress.

Thus he thought it wiser to delay his journey to Brunswick, so that he should arrive when the wedding was over – arrive in time to salute the bride.

And the vows – the mystical fancies – the belief in his return, even after death, to the embrace of his beloved? O, gone out of his life; melted away for ever, those foolish dreams of his boyhood.

So on the fifteenth of June he enters Brunswick, by that very bridge on which she stood, the stars looking down on her, the night before. He strolls across the bridge and down by the water's edge, a great rough dog at his heels, and the smoke from his short meerschaum-pipe curling in blue wreaths fantastically in the pure morning air.[3] He has his sketchbook under his arm, and, attracted now and then by some object that catches his artist's eye, stops to draw: a few weeds and pebbles on the river's brink – a crag on the opposite shore – a group of pollard willows in the distance. When he has done, he admires his drawing, shuts his sketch-book, empties the ashes from his pipe, refills from his tobacco-pouch, sings the refrain of a gay drinking-song, calls to his dog, smokes again, and walks on. Suddenly he opens his sketch-book again; this time that which attracts him is a group of figures: but what is it?

It is not a funeral, for there are no mourners.

It is not a funeral, but it is a corpse lying on a rude bier, covered with an old sail, carried between two bearers.

It is not a funeral, for the bearers are fishermen – fishermen in their every-day garb.

About a hundred yards from him they rest their burden on a bank – one stands at the head of the bier, the other throws himself down at the foot of it.

And thus they form a perfect group; he walks back two or three paces, selects his point of sight, and begins to sketch a hurried outline. He has finished it before they move; he hears their voices, though he cannot hear their words, and wonders what they can be talking of. Presently he walks on and joins them.

'You have a corpse there, my friends?' he says.

'Yes; a corpse washed ashore an hour ago.'

'Drowned?'

'Yes, drowned; – a young girl, very handsome.'

'Suicides are always handsome,' says the painter; and then he stands for a little while idly smoking and meditating, looking at the sharp outline of the corpse and the stiff folds of the rough canvas-covering.

Life is such a golden holiday for him – young, ambitious, clever – that it seems as though sorrow and death could have no part in his destiny.

At last he says that, as this poor suicide is so handsome, he should like to make a sketch of her.

He gives the fishermen some money, and they offer to remove the sailcloth that covers her features.

No; he will do it himself. He lifts the rough, coarse, wet canvas from her face. What face?

The face that shone on the dreams of his foolish boyhood; the face which once was the light of his uncle's home. His cousin Gertrude – his betrothed!

He sees, as in one glance, while he draws one breath, the rigid features – the marble arms – the hands crossed on the cold bosom; and, on the third finger of the left hand, the ring which had been his mother's – the golden serpent; the ring which, if he were to become blind, he could select from a thousand others by the touch alone.

But he is a genius and a metaphysician – grief, true grief, is not for such as he. His first thought is flight – flight anywhere out of that accursed city – anywhere far from the brink of that hideous river – anywhere away from memory, away from remorse – anywhere to forget.

He is miles on the road that leads away from Brunswick before he knows that he has walked a step.

It is only when his dog lies down panting at his feet that he feels how exhausted he is himself, and sits down upon a bank to rest. How the landscape spins round and round before his dazzled eyes, while his morning's sketch of the two fishermen and the canvas-covered bier glares redly at him out of the twilight!

At last, after sitting a long time by the roadside, idly playing with his dog, idly smoking, idly lounging, looking as any idle, light-hearted travelling student might look, yet all the while acting over that morning's scene in his burning brain a hundred times a minute; at last he grows a little more composed, and tries presently to think of himself as he is, apart from his cousin's suicide. Apart from that, he was no worse off than he was yesterday. His genius was not gone; the money he had earned at Florence still lined his pocket-book; he was his own master, free to go whither he would.

And while he sits on the roadside, trying to separate himself from the scene of that morning – trying to put away the image of the corpse covered with the damp canvas sail – trying to think of what he should do next, where he should go, to be farthest away from Brunswick and remorse, the old diligence comes rumbling and jingling along.[4] He remembers it; it goes from Brunswick to Aix-la-Chapelle.[5]

He whistles to his dog, shouts to the postillion to stop, and springs into the *coupé*.[6]

During the whole evening, through the long night, though he does not once close his eyes, he never speaks a word; but when morning dawns, and the other passengers awake and begin to talk to each other, he joins in the conversation. He tells them that he is an artist, that he is going to Cologne and to Antwerp to copy the Rubenses, and the great picture by Quentin Matsys, in the museum.[7] He remembered afterwards that he talked and laughed boisterously, and that when he was talking and laughing loudest, a passenger, older and graver than the rest, opened the window near him, and told him to put his head out. He remembered the fresh air blowing in his face, the singing of the birds in his ears, and the flat fields and roadside reeling before his eyes. He remembered this, and then falling in a lifeless heap on the floor of the diligence.

It is a fever that keeps him for six long weeks laid on a bed at a hotel in Aix-la-Chapelle.

He gets well, and, accompanied by his dog, starts on foot for Cologne. By this time he is his former self once more. Again the blue smoke from his short meerschaum curls upwards in the morning air – again he sings some old university drinking-song – again stops here and there, meditating and sketching.

He is happy, and has forgotten his cousin – and so, on to Cologne.

It is by the great cathedral he is standing, with his dog at his side. It is night, the bells have just chimed the hour, and the clocks are striking eleven; the moonlight shines full upon the magnificent pile, over which the artist's eye wanders, absorbed in the beauty of form.

He is not thinking of his drowned cousin, for he has forgotten her and is happy.

Suddenly some one, something from behind him, puts two cold arms round his neck, and clasps its hands on his breast.

And yet there is no one behind him, for on the flags bathed in the broad moonlight there are only two shadows, his own and his dog's. He turns quickly round – there is no one – nothing to be seen in the broad square but himself and his dog; and though he feels, he cannot see the cold arms clasped round his neck.

It is not ghostly, this embrace, for it is palpable to the touch – it cannot be real, for it is invisible.

He tries to throw off the cold caress. He clasps the hands in his own to tear them asunder, and to cast them off his neck. He can feel the long delicate fingers cold and wet beneath his touch, and on the third finger of the left hand he can feel the ring which was his mother's – the golden serpent – the ring which he has always said he would know among a thousand by the touch alone. He knows it now!

His dead cousin's cold arms are round his neck – his dead cousin's wet hands are clasped upon his breast. He asks himself if he is mad. 'Up, Leo!' he shouts. 'Up, up, boy!' and the New-foundland leaps to his shoulders – the dog's paws are on the dead hands, and the animal utters a terrific howl, and springs away from his master.[8]

The student stands in the moonlight, the dead arms round his neck, and the dog at a little distance moaning piteously.

Presently a watchman, alarmed by the howling of the dog, comes into the square to see what is wrong.

In a breath the cold arms are gone.

He takes the watchman home to the hotel with him and gives him money; in his gratitude he could have given that man half his little fortune.

Will it ever come to him again, this embrace of the dead?

He tries never to be alone; he makes a hundred acquaintances, and shares the chamber of another student. He starts up if he is left by himself in the public room at the inn where he is staying, and runs into the street. People notice his strange actions, and begin to think that he is mad.

But, in spite of all, he is alone once more; for one night the public room being empty for a moment, when on some idle pretence he strolls into the street, the street is empty too, and for the second time he feels the cold arms round his neck, and for the second time, when he calls his dog, the animal slinks away from him with a piteous howl.

After this he leaves Cologne, still travelling on foot – of necessity now, for his money is getting low. He joins travelling hawkers, he walks side by side with labourers, he talks to every foot-passenger he falls in with, and tries from morning till night to get company on the road.

At night he sleeps by the fire in the kitchen of the inn at which he stops; but do what he will, he is often alone, and it is now a common thing for him to feel the cold arms around his neck.

Many months have passed since his cousin's death – autumn, winter, early spring. His money is nearly gone, his health is utterly broken, he is the shadow of his former self, and he is getting near Paris. He will reach that city at the time of the Carnival.[9] To this he looks forward. In Paris, in Carnival time, he need never, surely, be alone, never feel that deadly caress; he may even recover his lost gaiety, his lost health, once more resume his profession, once more earn fame and money by his art.

How hard he tries to get over the distance that divides him from Paris, while day by day he grows weaker, and his step slower and more heavy!

But there is an end at last; the long dreary roads are passed. This is Paris, which he enters for the first time – Paris, of which he has dreamed so much – Paris, whose million voices are to exorcise his phantom.

To him to-night Paris seems one vast chaos of lights, music, and confusion – lights which dance before his eyes and will not be still – music that rings in his ears and deafens him – confusion which makes his head whirl round and round.

But, in spite of all, he finds the opera-house, where there is a masked ball. He has enough money left to buy a ticket of admission, and to hire a domino to throw over his shabby dress.[10] It seems only a moment after his entering the gates of

Paris that he is in the very midst of the wild gaiety of the opera-house ball.

No more darkness, no more loneliness, but a mad crowd, shouting and dancing, and a lovely Débardeuse hanging on his arm.[11]

The boisterous gaiety he feels surely is his old light-heartedness come back. He hears the people round him talking of the outrageous conduct of some drunken student, and it is to him they point when they say this – to him, who has not moistened his lips since yesterday at noon, for even now he will not drink; though his lips are parched, and his throat burning, he cannot drink. His voice is thick and hoarse, and his utterance indistinct; but still this must be his old light-heartedness come back that makes him so wildly gay.

The little Débardeuse is wearied out – her arm rests on his shoulder heavier than lead – the other dancers one by one drop off.

The lights in the chandeliers one by one die out.

The decorations look pale and shadowy in that dim light which is neither night nor day.

A faint glimmer from the dying lamps, a pale streak of cold grey light from the new-born day, creeping in through half-opened shutters.

And by this light the bright-eyed Débardeuse fades sadly. He looks her in the face. How the brightness of her eyes dies out! Again he looks her in the face. How white that face has grown! Again – and now it is the shadow of a face alone that looks in his.

Again – and they are gone – the bright eyes, the face, the shadow of the face. He is alone; alone in that vast saloon.

Alone, and, in the terrible silence, he hears the echoes of his own footsteps in that dismal dance which has no music.

No music but the beating of his heart against his breast. For the cold arms are round his neck – they whirl him round, they will not be flung off, or cast away; he can no more escape from their icy grasp than he can escape from death. He looks behind him – there is nothing but himself in the great empty *salle*;[12] but he can feel – cold, deathlike, but O, how palpable! – the long slender fingers, and the ring which was his mother's.

He tries to shout, but he has no power in his burning throat.

The silence of the place is only broken by the echoes of his own
footsteps in the dance from which he cannot extricate himself.
Who says he has no partner? The cold hands are clasped on his
breast, and now he does not shun their caress. No! One more
polka, if he drops down dead.[13]

The lights are all out, and half an hour after, the *gendarmes*
come in with a lantern to see that the house is empty; they are
followed by a great dog that they have found seated howling
on the steps of the theatre.[14] Near the principal entrance they
stumble over –

The body of a student, who has died from want of food,
exhaustion, and the breaking of a blood-vessel.

AMELIA B. EDWARDS
The North Mail

The circumstances I am about to relate to you have truth to
recommend them. They happened to myself, and my recollection of them is as vivid as if they had taken place only yesterday.
Twenty years, however, have gone by since that night. During
those twenty years I have told the story to but one other person.
I tell it now with a reluctance which I find it difficult to overcome. All I entreat, meanwhile, is that you will abstain from
forcing your own conclusions upon me. I want nothing explained away. I desire no arguments. My mind on this subject
is quite made up; and, having the testimony of my own senses
to rely upon, I prefer to abide by it.

Well! It was just twenty years ago, and within a day or two
of the end of the grouse season.[1] I had been out all day with
my gun, and had had no sport to speak of. The wind was due
east; the month, December; the place, a bleak wide moor in the
far north of England. And I had lost my way. It was not a
pleasant place in which to lose one's way, with the first feathery
flakes of a coming snow-storm just fluttering down upon the
heather, and the leaden evening closing in all around. I shaded
my eyes with my hand, and stared anxiously into the gathering
darkness, where the purple moorland melted into a range of
low hills, some ten or twelve miles distant. Not the faintest
smoke-wreath, not the tiniest cultivated patch, or fence, or
sheep-track, met my eyes in any direction. There was nothing
for it but to walk on, and take my chance of finding what
shelter I could, by the way. So I shouldered my gun again, and
pushed wearily forward; for I had been on foot since an hour
after daybreak, and had eaten nothing since breakfast.

Meanwhile, the snow began to come down with ominous

steadiness, and the wind fell. After this, the cold grew more intense, and the night came rapidly up. As for me, my prospects darkened with the darkening sky, and my heart grew heavy as I thought how my young wife was already watching for me through the window of our little inn parlour, and imagined all the suffering in store for her throughout this weary night. We had been married four months, and, having spent our autumn in the Highlands, were now lodging in a remote little village situated just on the verge of the great English moorlands. We were very much in love, and, of course, very happy. This morning, when we parted, she had implored me to return before dusk, and I had promised her that I would. What would I not have given to keep my word!

Even now, weary as I was, I felt that with a supper, an hour's rest, and a guide, I might still get back to her before midnight, if only guide and shelter could be found.

And all this time the snow fell, and the night thickened. I stopped and shouted every now and then, but my shouts seemed only to make the silence deeper. Then a vague sense of uneasiness came upon me, and I began to remember stories of travellers who had walked on and on in the falling snow until, wearied out, they were fain to lie down and sleep their lives away. Would it be possible, I asked myself, to keep on thus through all the long dark night? Would there not come a time when my limbs must fail, and my resolution give way? When I, too, must sleep the sleep of death. Death! I shuddered. How hard to die just now, when life lay all so bright before me! How hard for my darling, whose whole loving heart . . . but that thought was not to be borne! To banish it, I shouted again, louder and longer, and then listened eagerly. Was my shout answered, or did I only fancy that I heard a far-off cry? I hallooed again, and again the echo followed. Then a wavering speck of light came suddenly out of the dark, shifting, disappearing, growing momentarily nearer and brighter. Running towards it at full speed, I found myself, to my great joy, face to face with an old man and a lantern.

'Thank God!' was the exclamation that burst involuntarily from my lips.

Blinking and frowning, he lifted the lantern and peered into my face.

'What for?' growled he, sulkily.

'Well – for you. I began to fear I should be lost in the snow.'

'Eh, then, folks do get cast away hereabouts fra' time to time, an' what's to hinder you from bein' cast away likewise, if the Lord's so minded?'

'If the Lord is so minded that you and I shall be lost together, friend, we must submit,' I replied; 'but I don't mean to be lost without you. How far am I now from Dwolding?'[2]

'A gude twenty mile, more or less.'

'And the nearest village?'

'The nearest village is Wyke, an' that's twelve mile t'other side.'

'Where do you live, then?'

'Out yonder,' said he, with a vague jerk of the lantern.

'You're going home, I presume?'

'Maybe I am.'

'Then I'm going with you.'

The old man shook his head, and rubbed his nose reflectively with the handle of the lantern.

'It ain't o' no use,' growled he. 'He 'ont let you in – not he.'

'We'll see about that,' I replied, briskly. 'Who is He?'

'The master.'

'Who is the master?'

'That's now't to you,' was the unceremonious reply.[3]

'Well, well; you lead the way, and I'll engage that the master shall give me shelter and a supper to-night.'

'Eh, you can try him!' muttered my reluctant guide; and, still shaking his head, he hobbled, gnome-like, away through the falling snow.

A large mass loomed up presently out of the darkness, and a huge dog rushed out barking furiously.

'Is this the house?' I asked.

'Ay, it's the house. Down, Bey!' And he fumbled in his pocket for the key.

I drew up close behind him, prepared to lose no chance of entrance, and saw in the little circle of light shed by the lantern that the door was heavily studded with iron nails, like the door of a prison. In another minute he had turned the key, and I had pushed past him into the house.

Once inside, I looked round with curiosity, and found myself in a great raftered hall, which served, apparently, a variety of uses. One end was piled to the roof with corn, like a barn. The other was stored with flour-sacks, agricultural implements, casks, and all kinds of miscellaneous lumber; while from the beams overhead hung rows of hams, flitches, and bunches of dried herbs for winter use.[4] In the centre of the floor stood some huge object gauntly dressed in a dingy wrapping-cloth, and reaching halfway to the rafters. Lifting a corner of this cloth, I saw, to my surprise, a telescope of very considerable size, mounted on a rude moveable platform with four small wheels. The tube was made of painted wood, bound round with bands of metal rudely fashioned; the speculum, so far as I could estimate its size by the dim light, measured at least fifteen inches in diameter.[5] While I was yet examining the instrument, and asking myself whether it was not the work of some self-taught optician, a bell rang sharply.[6]

'That's for you,' said my guide, with a malicious grin. 'Yonder's his room.'

He pointed to a low black door at the opposite side of the hall. I crossed over, rapped somewhat loudly, and went in, without waiting for an invitation. A huge, white-haired old man rose from a table covered with books and papers, and confronted me sternly.

'Who are you?' said he. 'How came you here? What do you want?'

'James Murray, barrister-at-law. On foot across the moor. Meat, drink, and sleep.'

He bent his bushy brows in a portentous frown.

'Mine is not a house of entertainment,' he said, haughtily. 'Jacob, how dared you admit this stranger?'

'I didn't admit him,' grumbled the old man. 'He followed me over the muir, and shouldered his way in before me. I'm no match for six foot two.'

'And pray, sir, by what right have you forced an entrance into my house?'

'The same by which I should have clung to your boat, if I were drowning. The right of self-preservation.'

'Self-preservation.'

'There's an inch of snow on the ground already,' I replied

briefly; 'and it will be deep enough to cover my body before daybreak.'

He strode to the window, pulled aside a heavy black curtain, and looked out.

'It is true,' he said. 'You can stay, if you choose, till morning. Jacob, serve the supper.'

With this he waved me to a seat, resumed his own, and became at once absorbed in the studies at which I had disturbed him.

I placed my gun in a corner, drew a chair to the hearth, and examined my quarters at leisure. Smaller and less incongruous in its arrangements than the hall, this room contained, nevertheless, much to awaken my curiosity. The floor was carpetless. The whitewashed walls were in parts scrawled over with strange diagrams, and in others covered with shelves crowded with philosophical instruments, the uses of many of which were unknown to me. On one side of the fireplace stood a bookcase filled with dingy folios; on the other, a small organ, fantastically decorated with painted carvings of mediæval saints and devils. Through the half-opened door of a cupboard at the further end of the room, I saw a long array of geological specimens, surgical preparations, crucibles, retorts, and jars of chemicals; while on the mantelshelf beside me, amid a number of small objects, stood a model of the solar system, a small galvanic battery, and a microscope.[7] Every chair had its burden. Every corner was heaped high with books. The very floor was littered over with maps, casts, papers, tracings, and learned lumber of all conceivable kinds.

I stared about me with an amazement increased by every fresh object upon which my eyes chanced to rest. So strange a room I had never seen; yet seemed it stranger still to find such a room in a lone farmhouse, amid these wild and solitary moors! Over and over again, I looked from my host to his surroundings, and from his surroundings back to my host, asking myself who and what he could be? His head was singularly fine; but it was more the head of a poet than a philosopher. Broad in the temples, prominent over the eyes, and clothed with a rough profusion of perfectly white hair, it had all the ideality and much of the ruggedness that characterizes the head of Louis von Beethoven.[8] There were the same deep lines about the mouth, and the same stern furrows in the brow. There was the same concentration of expression. While I was yet observing him, the door opened, and Jacob brought in the supper. His master then closed his book, rose, and with more courtesy of manner than he had yet shown, invited me to the table.

A dish of ham and eggs, a loaf of brown bread, and a bottle of admirable sherry, were placed before me.

'I have but the homeliest farmhouse fare to offer you, sir,' said my entertainer. 'Your appetite, I trust, will make up for the deficiencies of our larder.'

I had already fallen upon the viands, and now protested, with the enthusiasm of a starving sportsman, that I had never eaten anything so delicious.

He bowed stiffly, and sat down to his own supper, which consisted, primitively, of a jug of milk and a basin of porridge. We ate in silence, and, when we had done, Jacob removed the tray. I then drew my chair back to the fireside. My host, somewhat to my surprise, did the same, and turning abruptly towards me said: –

'Sir, I have lived here in strict retirement for three-and-twenty years. During that time, I have not seen as many strange faces, and I have not read a single newspaper. You are the first stranger who has crossed my threshold for more than four years. Will you favour me with a few words of information respecting that outer world from which I have parted company so long?'

'Pray interrogate me,' I replied. 'I am heartily at your service.'

He bent his head in acknowledgement; leaned forward, with his elbows resting on his knees, and his chin supported in the palms of his hands; stared fixedly into the fire, and proceeded to question me.

His inquiries related chiefly to scientific matters, with the later progress of which, as applied to the practical purposes of life, he was almost wholly unacquainted. No student of science myself, I replied as well as my slight information permitted; but the task was far from easy, and I was much relieved when, passing from interrogation to discussion, he began pouring forth his own conclusions upon the facts which I had been attempting to place before him. He talked, and I listened spellbound. He talked till I believe he almost forgot my presence, and only thought aloud. I had never heard anything like it then; I have never heard anything like it since. Familiar with all systems of all philosophies, subtle in analysis, bold in generalization, he poured forth his thoughts in an uninterrupted stream, and, still leaning forward in the same moody attitude with his eyes fixed upon the fire, wandered from topic to topic, from speculation to speculation, like an inspired dreamer. From practical science to mental philosophy; from electricity in the wire to electricity in the nerve; from Watts to Mesmer, from Mesmer to Reichenbach, from Reichenbach to Swedenborg, Spinoza, Condillac, Descartes, Berkeley, Aristotle, Plato, and the Magi and Mystics of the East, were transitions which, however bewildering in their variety and scope, seemed easy and harmonious upon his lips as sequences in music.[9] By-and-by – I forget now by what link of conjecture or illustration – he passed on to that field which lies beyond the boundary line of even conjectural philosophy, and reaches no man knows whither. He spoke of the soul and its aspirations; of the spirit and its powers; of second sight; of prophecy; of those phenomena which, under the names of ghosts, spectres, and supernatural appearances, have been denied by the sceptics and attested by the credulous, of all ages.

'The world,' he said, 'grows hourly more and more sceptical of all that lies beyond its own narrow radius; and our men of science foster the fatal tendency. They condemn as fable all that resists experiment. They reject as false all that cannot be brought to the test of the laboratory or the dissecting-room. Against what superstition have they waged so long and obstinate a war, as against the belief in apparitions? And yet what superstition has maintained its hold upon the minds of men so long and so firmly? Show me any fact in physics, in history, in archæology, which is supported by testimony so wide and so various. Attested by all races of men, in all ages, and in all climates, by the soberest sages of antiquity, by the rudest savages of to-day, by the Christian, the Pagan, the Pantheist, the Materialist, this phenomenon is treated as a nursery tale by the philosophers of our century. Circumstantial evidence weighs with them as a feather in the balance. The comparison of causes with effects, however valuable in physical science, is put aside as worthless and unreliable. The evidence of competent witnesses, however conclusive in a court of justice, counts for nothing. He who pauses before he pronounces, is condemned as a trifler. He who believes, is a dreamer or a fool.'

He spoke with bitterness, and, having said thus, relapsed for some minutes into silence. Presently he raised his head from his hands, and added, with an altered voice and manner –

'I, sir, paused, investigated, believed, and was not ashamed to state my convictions to the world. I, too, was branded as a visionary, held up to ridicule by my contemporaries, and hooted from that field of science in which I had laboured with honour during all the best years of my life. These things happened just three-and-twenty years ago. Since then, I have lived as you see me living now, and the world has forgotten me, as I have forgotten the world. You have my history.'

'It is a very sad one,' I murmured, scarcely knowing what to answer.

'It is a very common one,' he replied. 'I have only suffered for the truth, as many a better and wiser man has suffered before me.'

He rose, as if desirous of ending the conversation, and went over to the window.

'It has ceased snowing,' he observed, as he dropped the curtain, and came back to the fireside.

'Ceased!' I exclaimed, starting eagerly to my feet. 'Oh, if it were only possible – but no! it is hopeless. Even if I could find my way across the moor, I could not walk twenty miles to-night.'

'Walk twenty miles to-night!' repeated my host. 'What are you thinking of?'

'Of my wife,' I replied, impatiently. 'Of my young wife, who does not know that I have lost my way, and who is at this moment breaking her heart with suspense and terror.'

'Where is she?'

'At Dwolding, twenty miles away.'

'At Dwolding,' he echoed, thoughtfully. 'Yes, the distance, it is true, is twenty miles; but – are you so anxious to save the next six or eight hours?'

'So anxious, that I would give ten guineas at this moment for a guide and a horse.'

'Your wish can be gratified at a less costly rate,' said he, smiling. 'The night mail from the north, which changes horses at Dwolding, passes within five miles of this spot, and will be due at a certain cross-road in about an hour and a quarter. If Jacob were to go with you across the moor, and put you into the old coach-road, you could find your way, I suppose, to where it joins the new one?'

'Easily – gladly.'

He smiled again, rang the bell, gave the old servant his directions, and, taking a bottle of whisky and a wine-glass from the cupboard in which he kept his chemicals, said –

'The snow lies deep, and it will be difficult walking to-night on the moor. A glass of usquebaugh before you start.'[10]

I would have declined the spirit, but he pressed it on me, and I drank it. It went down my throat like liquid flame, and almost took my breath away.

'It is strong,' he said; 'but it will help to keep out the cold. And now you have no moments to spare. Good night!'

I thanked him for his hospitality, and would have shaken hands, but that he had turned away before I could finish my sentence. In another minute I had traversed the hall, Jacob had locked the outer door behind me, and we were out on the wide white moor.

Although the wind had fallen, it was still bitterly cold. Not a star glimmered in the black vault overhead. Not a sound, save the rapid crunching of the snow beneath our feet, disturbed the heavy stillness of the night. Jacob, not too well pleased with his mission, shambled on before in sullen silence, his lantern in his hand, and his shadow at his feet. I followed, with my gun over my shoulder, as little inclined for conversation as himself. My thoughts were full of my late host. His voice yet rang in my ears. His eloquence yet held my imagination captive. I remember to this day, with surprise, how my over-excited brain retained whole sentences and parts of sentences, troops of brilliant images, and fragments of splendid reasoning, in the very words in which he had uttered them. Musing thus over what I had heard, and striving to recal a lost link here and there, I strode on at the heels of my guide, absorbed and unobservant.[11] Presently – at the end, as it seemed to me, of only a few minutes – he came to a sudden halt, and said:

'Yon's your road. Keep the stone fence to your right hand, and you can't fail of the way.'

'This, then, is the old coach-road?'

'Ay, 'tis the old coach-road.'

'And how far do I go, before I reach the cross-roads?'

'Nigh upon three miles.'

I pulled out my purse, and he became more communicative.

'The road's a fair road enough,' said he, 'for foot passengers; but 'twas over steep and narrow for the northern traffic. You'll mind where the parapet's broken away, close again the signpost. It's never been mended since the accident.'

'What accident?'

'Eh, the night mail pitched right over into the valley below – a guide sixty feet an' more – just at the worst bit o' road in the whole county.'

'Horrible! Were many lives lost?'

'All. Four were found dead, and t'other two died next morning.'

'How long is it since this happened?'

'Just nine year.'

'Near the sign-post, you say? I will bear it in mind. Good night.'

'Gude night, sir, and thankee.'

Jacob pocketed his half-crown, made a faint pretence of touching his hat, and trudged back by the way he had come.

I watched the light of his lantern till it quite disappeared, and then turned to pursue my way alone. This was no longer a matter of the slightest difficulty, for, despite the dead darkness overhead, the line of stone fence showed distinctly enough against the pale gleam of the snow. How silent it seemed now, with only my own footsteps to listen to; how silent and how solitary! A strange disagreeable sense of loneliness stole over me. I walked faster. I hummed a fragment of a tune. I cast up enormous sums in my head, and accumulated them at compound interest. I did my best, in short, to forget the startling speculations to which I had but just been listening, and, to some extent, I succeeded.

Meanwhile the night air seemed to become colder and colder, and though I walked fast, I found it impossible to keep myself warm. My feet were like ice. I lost sensation in my hands, and grasped my gun mechanically. I even breathed with difficulty, as though, instead of traversing a quiet north country highway, I were scaling the uppermost heights of some gigantic Alp. This last symptom became presently so distressing, that I was forced to stop for a few minutes, and lean against the stone fence. As I did so, I chanced to look back up the road, and there, to my infinite relief, I saw a distant point of light, like the gleam of an approaching lantern. I at first concluded that Jacob had retraced his steps and followed me; but even as the conjecture presented itself, a second light flashed into sight – a light evidently parallel with the first, and approaching at the same rate of motion. It needed no second thought to show me that these must be the carriage-lamps of some private vehicle; though it seemed strange that any private vehicle should take a road professedly disused and dangerous.

There could be no doubt, however, of the fact, for the lamps grew larger and brighter every moment, and I even fancied I could already see the dark outline of the carriage between them. It was coming up very fast, and quite noiselessly; the snow being nearly a foot deep under the wheels.

And now the body of the vehicle became distinctly visible behind the lamps. It looked strangely lofty. A sudden suspicion flashed upon me. Was it possible that I had passed the cross-roads in the dark without observing the sign-post, and could this be the very coach which I had come to meet?

No need to ask myself that question a second time, for here it came round the bend of the road, guard and driver, one outside passenger, and four steaming greys, all wrapped in a soft haze of light, through which the lamps blazed out like a pair of fiery meteors.

I jumped forward, waved my hat, and shouted. The mail came down at full speed, and passed me. For a moment I feared that I had not been seen or heard, but it was only for a moment. The coachman pulled up; the guard, muffled to the eyes in capes and comforters, and apparently sound asleep in the rumble, neither answered my hail nor made the slightest effort to dismount; the outside passenger did not even turn his head. I opened the door for myself, and looked in. There were but three travellers inside, so I stepped in, shut the door, slipped into the vacant corner, and congratulated myself on my good fortune.

The atmosphere of the coach seemed, if possible, colder than that of the outer air, and was pervaded by a singularly damp and disagreeable smell. I looked round at my fellow passengers. They were all three men; and all silent. They did not seem to be asleep, but each leaned back in his corner of the vehicle, as if absorbed in his own reflections. I attempted to open a conversation.

'How intensely cold it is to-night,' I said, addressing my opposite neighbour.

He lifted his head, looked at me, but made no reply.

'The winter,' I added, 'seems to have begun in earnest.'

Although the corner in which he sat was so dim that I could distinguish none of his features very clearly, I saw that his eyes were still turned full upon me. And yet he answered never a word.

At any other time I should have felt, and perhaps expressed, some annoyance; but at that moment I felt too ill to do either. The icy coldness of the night air had struck a chill to my very marrow, and the strange smell inside the coach was affecting me with an intolerable nausea. I shivered from head to foot, and, turning to my left-hand neighbour, asked if he had any objection to an open window.

He neither spoke nor stirred.

I repeated the question somewhat more loudly, but with the same result. Then I lost patience, and let the sash down. As I did so, the leather strap broke in my hand, and I observed that the glass was covered with a thick coat of mildew, the accumulation, apparently, of years. My attention being thus drawn to the condition of the coach, I examined it more narrowly, and saw by the uncertain light of the outer lamps that it was in the last state of dilapidation. Every part of it was not only out of repair, but in a state of actual decay. The sashes splintered at a touch. The leather fittings were crusted over with mould, and literally rotting from the woodwork. The floor was almost breaking away beneath my feet. The whole machine, in short, was foul with damp, and had evidently been dragged from some outhouse in which it had been mouldering away for years, to do another day or two of duty on the road.

I turned to the third passenger, whom I had not yet addressed, and hazarded one more remark.

'This coach,' I said, 'is in a deplorable condition. The regular mail, I suppose, is under repair?'

He moved his head slowly, and looked me in the face, without speaking a word. I shall never forget that look while I live. I turned cold at heart under it. I turn cold at heart even now when I recal it. His eyes glowed with a fiery unnatural lustre. His face was livid as the face of a corpse. His bloodless lips were drawn back as if in the agony of death, and showed the gleaming teeth between.

The words that I was about to utter died upon my lips, and a strange horror came upon me. My sight had by this time become used to the gloom of the coach, and I could see with tolerable distinctness. I turned to my opposite neighbour. He, too, was looking at me, with the same startling pallor in his face, and the same stony glitter in his eyes. I passed my hand across my brow. I turned to the passenger on the seat beside my own, and saw – oh Heaven! how shall I describe what I saw? I saw that he was no living man – that none of them were living men, like myself! A pale phosphorescent light – the light of putrefaction – played upon their awful faces; upon their hair, dank with the dews of the grave; upon their clothes, earth-stained and dropping to pieces; upon their hands, which were as the hands of corpses long buried. Only their eyes, their terrible eyes, were living; and those eyes were all turned menacingly upon me!

A shriek of terror, a wild unintelligible cry for help and mercy, burst from my lips as I flung myself against the door, and strove in vain to open it.

In that single instant, brief and vivid as a landscape beheld in the flash of summer lightning, I saw the moon shining down through a rift of stormy cloud – the ghastly sign-post rearing its warning finger by the wayside – the broken parapet – the plunging horses – the black gulf below. Then the coach reeled like a ship at sea. Then came a mighty crash – a sense of crushing pain – and then, darkness.

It seemed as if years had gone by, when I awoke one morning from a deep sleep, and found my wife watching by my bedside. I will pass over the scene that ensued, and give you, in half a dozen words, the tale she told me with tears of thanksgiving. I had fallen over a precipice, close against the junction of the old coach-road and the new, and had only been saved from certain death by lighting upon a deep snowdrift that had accumulated at the foot of the rock beneath. In this snowdrift I was discovered at daybreak by a couple of shepherds, who carried me to the nearest shelter, and brought a surgeon to my aid. The surgeon found me in a state of raving delirium, with a broken arm and a compound fracture of the skull. The letters in my pocket-book showed my name and address; my wife was summoned to nurse me; and, thanks to youth and a fine constitution, I came out of danger at last. The place of my fall, I need scarcely say, was precisely that at which a frightful accident had happened to the north mail nine years before.

I never told my wife the fearful events which I have just related to you. I told the surgeon who attended me; but he treated the whole adventure as a mere dream born of the fever in my brain. We discussed the question over and over again, until we found that we could discuss it with temper no longer, and then we dropped it. Others may form what conclusions they please – I *know* that twenty years ago I was the fourth inside passenger in that Phantom Coach.

CHARLES DICKENS

No. 1 Branch Line: The Signal-man[1]

'Halloa! Below there!'

When he heard a voice thus calling to him, he was standing at the door of his box, with a flag in his hand, furled round its short pole. One would have thought, considering the nature of the ground, that he could not have doubted from what quarter the voice came; but, instead of looking up to where I stood on the top of the steep cutting nearly over his head, he turned himself about and looked down the Line. There was something remarkable in his manner of doing so, though I could not have said, for my life, what. But, I know it was remarkable enough to attract my notice, even though his figure was foreshortened and shadowed, down in the deep trench, and mine was high above him, so steeped in the glow of an angry sunset that I had shaded my eyes with my hand before I saw him at all.

'Halloa! Below!'

From looking down the Line, he turned himself about again, and, raising his eyes, saw my figure high above him.

'Is there any path by which I can come down and speak to you?'

He looked up at me without replying, and I looked down at him without pressing him too soon with a repetition of my idle question. Just then, there came a vague vibration in the earth and air, quickly changing into a violent pulsation, and an on-coming rush that caused me to start back, as though it had force to draw me down. When such vapour as rose to my height from this rapid train, had passed me and was skimming away over the landscape, I looked down again, and saw him re-furling the flag he had shown while the train went by.

I repeated my inquiry. After a pause, during which he seemed to regard me with fixed attention, he motioned with his rolled-up flag towards a point on my level, some two or three hundred yards distant. I called down to him, 'All right!' and made for that point. There, by dint of looking closely about me, I found a rough zig-zag descending path notched out: which I followed.

The cutting was extremely deep, and unusually precipitate. It was made through a clammy stone that became oozier and wetter as I went down. For these reasons, I found the way long enough to give me time to recal a singular air of reluctance or compulsion with which he had pointed out the path.[2]

When I came down low enough upon the zig-zag descent, to see him again, I saw that he was standing between the rails on the way by which the train had lately passed, in an attitude as if he were waiting for me to appear. He had his left hand at his chin, and that left elbow rested on his right hand crossed over his breast. His attitude was one of such expectation and watchfulness, that I stopped a moment, wondering at it.

I resumed my downward way, and stepping out upon the level of the railroad and drawing nearer to him, saw that he was a dark sallow man, with a dark beard and rather heavy eyebrows. His post was in as solitary and dismal a place as ever I saw. On either side, a dripping-wet wall of jagged stone, excluding all view but a strip of sky; the perspective one way, only a crooked prolongation of this great dungeon; the shorter perspective in the other direction, terminating in a gloomy red light, and the gloomier entrance to a black tunnel, in whose massive architecture there was a barbarous, depressing, and forbidding air. So little sunlight ever found its way to this spot, that it had an earthy deadly smell; and so much cold wind rushed through it, that it struck chill to me, as if I had left the natural world.

Before he stirred, I was near enough to him to have touched him. Not even then removing his eyes from mine, he stepped back one step, and lifted his hand.

This was a lonesome post to occupy (I said), and it had riveted my attention when I looked down from up yonder. A visitor was a rarity, I should suppose; not an unwelcome rarity, I hoped? In me, he merely saw a man who had been shut up within narrow limits all his life, and who, being at last set free, had a newly awakened interest in these great works. To such purpose I spoke to him; but I am far from sure of the terms I used, for, besides that I am not happy in opening any conversation, there was something in the man that daunted me.

He directed a most curious look towards the red light near the tunnel's mouth, and looked all about it, as if something were missing from it, and then looked at me.

That light was part of his charge? Was it not?

He answered in a low voice: 'Don't you know it is?'

The monstrous thought came into my mind as I perused the fixed eyes and the saturnine face, that this was a spirit, not a man. I have speculated since, whether there may have been infection in his mind.

In my turn, I stepped back. But in making the action, I detected in his eyes some latent fear of me. This put the monstrous thought to flight.

'You look at me,' I said, forcing a smile, 'as if you had a dread of me.'

'I was doubtful,' he returned, 'whether I had seen you before.'

'Where?'

He pointed to the red light he had looked at.

'There?' I said.

Intently watchful of me, he replied (but without sound), Yes.

'My good fellow, what should I do there? However, be that as it may, I never was there, you may swear.'

'I think I may,' he rejoined. 'Yes. I am sure I may.'

His manner cleared, like my own. He replied to my remarks with readiness, and in well-chosen words. Had he much to do there? Yes; that was to say, he had enough responsibility to bear; but exactness and watchfulness were what was required of him, and of actual work – manual labour – he had next to none. To change that signal, to trim those lights, and to turn this iron handle now and then, was all he had to do under that head. Regarding those many long and lonely hours of which I seemed to make so much, he could only say that the routine of his life had shaped itself into that form, and he had grown used to it. He had taught himself a language down here – if only to know it by sight, and to have formed his own crude ideas of its pronunciation, could be called learning it. He had also worked at fractions and decimals, and tried a little algebra; but he was, and had been as a boy, a poor hand at figures. Was it necessary for him when on duty, always to remain in that channel of damp air, and could he never rise into the sunshine from between those high stone walls? Why, that depended upon times and circumstances. Under some conditions there would be less upon the Line than under others, and the same held good as to certain hours of the day and night. In bright weather, he did choose occasions for getting a little above these lower shadows; but, being at all times liable to be called by his electric bell, and at such times listening for it with redoubled anxiety, the relief was less than I would suppose.

He took me into his box, where there was a fire, a desk for an official book in which he had to make certain entries, a telegraphic instrument with its dial face and needles, and the little bell of which he had spoken. On my trusting that he would excuse the remark that he had been well educated, and (I hoped I might say without offence) perhaps educated above that station, he observed that instances of slight incongruity in such-wise would rarely be found wanting among large bodies of men; that he had heard it was so in workhouses, in the police force, even in that last desperate resource, the army; and that he knew it was so, more or less, in any great railway staff. He had been, when young (if I could believe it, sitting in that hut; he scarcely could), a student of natural philosophy, and had attended lectures; but he had run wild, misused his opportunities, gone down, and never risen again.[3] He had no complaint to offer about that. He had made his bed, and he lay upon it. It was far too late to make another.

All that I have here condensed, he said in a quiet manner, with his grave dark regards divided between me and the fire. He threw in the word 'Sir' from time to time, and especially when he referred to his youth: as though to request me to understand that he claimed to be nothing but what I found him. He was several times interrupted by the little bell, and had to read off messages, and send replies. Once, he had to stand without the door, and display a flag as a train passed, and make some verbal communication to the driver. In the discharge of his duties I observed him to be remarkably exact and vigilant, breaking off his discourse at a syllable, and remaining silent until what he had to do was done.

In a word, I should have set this man down as one of the safest of men to be employed in that capacity, but for the circumstance that while he was speaking to me he twice broke off with a fallen colour, turned his face towards the little bell when it did NOT ring, opened the door of the hut (which was kept shut to exclude the unhealthy damp), and looked out towards the red light near the mouth of the tunnel. On both of those occasions, he came back to the fire with the inexplicable air upon him which I had remarked, without being able to define, when we were so far asunder.

Said I when I rose to leave him: 'You almost make me think that I have met with a contented man.'

(I am afraid I must acknowledge that I said it to lead him on.)

'I believe I used to be so,' he rejoined, in the low voice in which he had first spoken; 'but I am troubled, sir, I am troubled.'

He would have recalled the words if he could. He had said them, however, and I took them up quickly.

'With what? What is your trouble?'

'It is very difficult to impart, sir. It is very, very, difficult to speak of. If ever you make me another visit, I will try to tell you.'

'But I expressly intend to make you another visit. Say, when shall it be?'

'I go off early in the morning, and I shall be on again at ten to-morrow night, sir.'

'I will come at eleven.'

He thanked me, and went out at the door with me. 'I'll show my white light, sir,' he said, in his peculiar low voice, 'till you have found the way up. When you have found it, don't call out! And when you are at the top, don't call out!'

His manner seemed to make the place strike colder to me, but I said no more than 'Very well.'

'And when you come down to-morrow night, don't call out! Let me ask you a parting question. What made you cry "Halloa! Below there!" to-night?'

'Heaven knows,' said I. 'I cried something to that effect –'

'Not to that effect, sir. Those were the very words. I know them well.'

'Admit those were the very words. I said them, no doubt, because I saw you below.'

'For no other reason?'

'What other reason could I possibly have!'

'You had no feeling that they were conveyed to you in any supernatural way?'

'No.'

He wished me good night, and held up his light. I walked by the side of the down Line of rails (with a very disagreeable sensation of a train coming behind me), until I found the path. It was easier to mount than to descend, and I got back to my inn without any adventure.

Punctual to my appointment, I placed my foot on the first notch of the zig-zag next night, as the distant clocks were striking eleven. He was waiting for me at the bottom, with his white light on. 'I have not called out,' I said, when we came close together; 'may I speak now?' 'By all means, sir.' 'Good night then, and here's my hand.' 'Good night, sir, and here's mine.' With that, we walked side by side to his box, entered it, closed the door, and sat down by the fire.

'I have made up my mind, sir,' he began, bending forward as soon as we were seated, and speaking in a tone but a little above a whisper, 'that you shall not have to ask me twice what troubles me. I took you for some one else yesterday evening. That troubles me.'

'That mistake?'

'No. That some one else.'

'Who is it?'

'I don't know.'

'Like me?'

'I don't know. I never saw the face. The left arm is across the face, and the right arm is waved. Violently waved. This way.'

I followed his action with my eyes, and it was the action of an arm gesticulating with the utmost passion and vehemence: 'For God's sake clear the way!'

'One moonlight night,' said the man, 'I was sitting here, when

I heard a voice cry "Halloa! Below there!" I started up, looked from that door, and saw this Some one else standing by the red light near the tunnel, waving as I just now showed you. The voice seemed hoarse with shouting, and it cried, "Look out! Look out!" And then again "Halloa! Below there! Look out!" I caught up my lamp, turned it on red, and ran towards the figure, calling, "What's wrong? What has happened? Where?" It stood just outside the blackness of the tunnel. I advanced so close upon it that I wondered at its keeping the sleeve across its eyes. I ran right up at it, and had my hand stretched out to pull the sleeve away, when it was gone.'

'Into the tunnel,' said I.

'No. I ran on into the tunnel, five hundred yards. I stopped and held my lamp above my head, and saw the figures of the measured distance, and saw the wet stains stealing down the walls and trickling through the arch. I ran out again, faster than I had run in (for I had a mortal abhorrence of the place upon me), and I looked all round the red light with my own red light, and I went up the iron ladder to the gallery atop of it, and I came down again, and ran back here. I telegraphed both ways: "An alarm has been given. Is anything wrong?" The answer came back, both ways: "All well."'

Resisting the slow touch of a frozen finger tracing out my spine, I showed him how that this figure must be a deception of his sense of sight, and how that figures, originating in disease of the delicate nerves that minister to the functions of the eye, were known to have often troubled patients, some of whom had become conscious of the nature of their affliction, and had even proved it by experiments upon themselves. 'As to an imaginary cry,' said I, 'do but listen for a moment to the wind in this unnatural valley while we speak so low, and to the wild harp it makes of the telegraph wires!'

That was all very well, he returned, after we had sat listening for a while, and he ought to know something of the wind and the wires, he who so often passed long winter nights there, alone and watching. But he would beg to remark that he had not finished.

I asked his pardon, and he slowly added these words, touching my arm:

'Within six hours after the Appearance, the memorable accident on this Line happened, and within ten hours the dead and
wounded were brought along through the tunnel over the spot
where the figure had stood.'

A disagreeable shudder crept over me, but I did my best
against it. It was not to be denied, I rejoined, that this was a
remarkable coincidence, calculated deeply to impress his mind.
But, it was unquestionable that remarkable coincidences did
continually occur, and they must be taken into account in
dealing with such a subject. Though to be sure I must admit, I
added (for I thought I saw that he was going to bring the
objection to bear upon me), men of common sense did not
allow much for coincidences in making the ordinary calculations of life.

He again begged to remark that he had not finished.

I again begged his pardon for being betrayed into inter-
ruptions.

'This,' he said, again laying his hand upon my arm, and
glancing over his shoulder with hollow eyes, 'was just a year
ago. Six or seven months passed, and I had recovered from the
surprise and shock, when one morning, as the day was breaking,
I, standing at that door, looked towards the red light, and saw
the spectre again.' He stopped, with a fixed look at me.

'Did it cry out?'

'No. It was silent.'

'Did it wave its arm?'

'No. It leaned against the shaft of the light, with both hands
before the face. Like this.'

Once more, I followed his action with my eyes. It was an
action of mourning. I have seen such an attitude in stone figures
on tombs.

'Did you go up to it?'

'I came in and sat down, partly to collect my thoughts, partly
because it had turned me faint. When I went to the door again,
daylight was above me, and the ghost was gone.'

'But nothing followed? Nothing came of this?'

He touched me on the arm with his forefinger twice or thrice,
giving a ghastly nod each time:

'That very day, as a train came out of the tunnel, I noticed at a carriage window on my side, what looked like a confusion of hands and heads, and something waved. I saw it, just in time to signal the driver, Stop! He shut off, and put his brake on, but the train drifted past here a hundred and fifty yards or more. I ran after it, and, as I went along, heard terrible screams and cries. A beautiful young lady had died instantaneously in one of the compartments, and was brought in here, and laid down on this floor between us.'

Involuntarily, I pushed my chair back, as I looked from the boards at which he pointed, to himself.

'True, sir. True. Precisely as it happened, so I tell it you.'

I could think of nothing to say, to any purpose, and my mouth was very dry. The wind and the wires took up the story with a long lamenting wail.

He resumed. 'Now, sir, mark this, and judge how my mind is troubled. The spectre came back, a week ago. Ever since, it has been there, now and again, by fits and starts.'

'At the light?'

'At the Danger-light.'

'What does it seem to do?'

He repeated, if possible with increased passion and vehemence, that former gesticulation of 'For God's sake clear the way!'

Then, he went on. 'I have no peace or rest for it. It calls to me, for many minutes together, in an agonized manner, "Below there! Look out! Look out!" It stands waving to me. It rings my little bell —'

I caught at that. 'Did it ring your bell yesterday evening when I was here, and you went to the door?'

'Twice.'

'Why, see,' said I, 'how your imagination misleads you. My eyes were on the bell, and my ears were open to the bell, and if I am a living man, it did NOT ring at those times. No, nor at any other time, except when it was rung in the natural course of physical things by the station communicating with you.'

He shook his head. 'I have never made a mistake as to that, yet, sir. I have never confused the spectre's ring with the man's. The ghost's ring is a strange vibration in the bell that it derives from nothing else, and I have not asserted that the bell stirs to the eye. I don't wonder that you failed to hear it. But *I* heard it.'

'And did the spectre seem to be there, when you looked out?'

'It WAS there.'

'Both times?'

He repeated firmly: 'Both times.'

'Will you come to the door with me, and look for it now?'

He bit his under-lip as though he were somewhat unwilling, but arose. I opened the door, and stood on the step, while he stood in the doorway. There, was the Danger-light. There, was the dismal mouth of the tunnel. There, were the high wet stone walls of the cutting. There, were the stars above them.

'Do you see it?' I asked him, taking particular note of his face. His eyes were prominent and strained; but not very much more so, perhaps, than my own had been when I had directed them earnestly towards the same spot.

'No,' he answered. 'It is not there.'

'Agreed,' said I.

We went in again, shut the door, and resumed our seats. I was thinking how best to improve this advantage, if it might be called one, when he took up the conversation in such a matter of course way, so assuming that there could be no serious question of fact between us, that I felt myself placed in the weakest of positions.

'By this time you will fully understand, sir,' he said, 'that what troubles me so dreadfully, is the question, What does the spectre mean?'

I was not sure, I told him, that I did fully understand.

'What is its warning against?' he said, ruminating, with his eyes on the fire, and only by times turning them on me. 'What is the danger? Where is the danger? There is danger overhanging, somewhere on the Line. Some dreadful calamity will happen. It is not to be doubted this third time, after what has gone before. But surely this is a cruel haunting of *me*. What can *I* do!'

He pulled out his handkerchief, and wiped the drops from his heated forehead.

'If I telegraph Danger, on either side of me, or on both, I can give no reason for it,' he went on, wiping the palms of his hands. 'I should get into trouble, and do no good. They would think I was mad. This is the way it would work: – Message: "Danger! Take care!" Answer: "What Danger? Where?" Message: "Don't know. But for God's sake take care!" They would displace me. What else could they do?'

His pain of mind was most pitiable to see. It was the mental torture of a conscientious man, oppressed beyond endurance by an unintelligible responsibility involving life.

'When it first stood under the Danger-light,' he went on, putting his dark hair back from his head, and drawing his hands outward across and across his temples in an extremity of feverish distress, 'why not tell me where that accident was to happen – if it must happen? Why not tell me how it could be averted – if it could have been averted? When on its second coming it hid its face, why not tell me instead: "She is going to die. Let them keep her at home"? If it came, on those two occasions, only to show me that its warnings were true, and so to prepare me for the third, why not warn me plainly now? And I, Lord help me! A mere poor signalman on this solitary station! Why not go to somebody with credit to be believed, and power to act!'

When I saw him in this state, I saw that for the poor man's sake, as well as for the public safety, what I had to do for the time was, to compose his mind. Therefore, setting aside all question of reality or unreality between us, I represented to him that whoever thoroughly discharged his duty, must do well, and that at least it was his comfort that he understood his duty, though he did not understand these confounding Appearances. In this effort I succeeded far better than in the attempt to reason him out of his conviction. He became calm; the occupations incidental to his post as the night advanced, began to make larger demands on his attention; and I left him at two in the morning. I had offered to stay through the night, but he would not hear of it.

That I more than once looked back at the red light as I ascended the pathway, that I did not like the red light, and that I should have slept but poorly if my bed had been under it, I see no reason to conceal. Nor, did I like the two sequences of the accident and the dead girl. I see no reason to conceal that, either.

But, what ran most in my thoughts was the consideration how ought I to act, having become the recipient of this disclosure? I had proved the man to be intelligent, vigilant, painstaking, and exact; but how long might he remain so, in his state of mind? Though in a subordinate position, still he held a most important trust, and would I (for instance) like to stake my own life on the chances of his continuing to execute it with precision?

Unable to overcome a feeling that there would be something treacherous in my communicating what he had told me, to his superiors in the Company, without first being plain with himself and proposing a middle course to him, I ultimately resolved to offer to accompany him (otherwise keeping his secret for the present) to the wisest medical practitioner we could hear of in those parts, and to take his opinion. A change in his time of duty would come round next night, he had apprised me, and he would be off an hour or two after sunrise, and on again soon after sunset. I had appointed to return accordingly.

Next evening was a lovely evening, and I walked out early to enjoy it. The sun was not yet quite down when I traversed the field-path near the top of the deep cutting. I would extend my walk for an hour, I said to myself, half an hour on and half an hour back, and it would then be time to go to my signalman's box.

Before pursuing my stroll, I stepped to the brink, and mechanically looked down, from the point from which I had first seen him. I cannot describe the thrill that seized upon me, when, close at the mouth of the tunnel, I saw the appearance of a man, with his left sleeve across his eyes, passionately waving his right arm.

The nameless horror that oppressed me, passed in a moment, for in a moment I saw that this appearance of a man was a man indeed, and that there was a little group of other men standing at a short distance, to whom he seemed to be rehearsing the gesture he made. The Danger-light was not yet lighted. Against its shaft, a little low hut, entirely new to me, had been made of some wooden supports and tarpaulin. It looked no bigger than a bed.

With an irresistible sense that something was wrong – with a flashing self-reproachful fear that fatal mischief had come of my leaving the man there, and causing no one to be sent to over-look or correct what he did – I descended the notched path with all the speed I could make.

'What is the matter?' I asked the men.

'Signalman killed this morning, sir.'

'Not the man belonging to that box?'

'Yes, sir.'

'Not the man I know?'

'You will recognize him, sir, if you knew him,' said the man who spoke for the others, solemnly uncovering his own head and raising an end of the tarpaulin, 'for his face is quite composed.'

'O! how did this happen, how did this happen?' I asked, turning from one to another as the hut closed in again.

'He was cut down by an engine, sir. No man in England knew his work better. But somehow he was not clear of the outer rail. It was just at broad day. He had struck the light, and had the lamp in his hand. As the engine came out of the tunnel, his back was towards, her, and she cut him down. That man drove her, and was showing how it happened. Show the gentleman, Tom.'

The man, who wore a rough dark dress, stepped back to his former place at the mouth of the tunnel:

'Coming round the curve in the tunnel, sir,' he said, 'I saw him at the end, like as if I saw him down a perspective-glass.[4] There was no time to check speed, and I knew him to be very careful. As he didn't seem to take heed of the whistle, I shut it off when we were running down upon him, and called to him as loud as I could call.'

'What did you say?'

'I said, Below there! Look out! Look out! For God's sake clear the way!'

I started.

'Ah! it was a dreadful time, sir. I never left off calling to him. I put this arm before my eyes, not to see, and I waved this arm to the last; but it was no use.'

Without prolonging the narrative to dwell on any one of its curious circumstances more than on any other, I may, in closing

it, point out the coincidence that the warning of the Engine-
Driver included, not only the words which the unfortunate
Signalman had repeated to me as haunting him, but also the
words which I myself – not he – had attached, and that only in
my own mind, to the gesticulation he had imitated.

SHERIDAN LE FANU

Green Tea

PROLOGUE

Martin Hesselius, the German Physician

Though carefully educated in medicine and surgery, I have never practised either. The study of each continues, nevertheless, to interest me profoundly. Neither idleness nor caprice caused my secession from the honourable calling which I had just entered. The cause was a very trifling scratch inflicted by a dissecting knife. This trifle cost me the loss of two fingers, amputated promptly, and the more painful loss of my health, for I have never been quite well since, and have seldom been twelve months together in the same place.

In my wanderings I became acquainted with Dr Martin Hesselius, a wanderer like myself, like me a physician, and like me an enthusiast in his profession. Unlike me in this, that his wanderings were voluntary, and he a man, if not of fortune, as we estimate fortune in England, at least in what our forefathers used to term 'easy circumstances.' He was an old man when I first saw him; nearly five-and-thirty years my senior.

In Dr Martin Hesselius, I found my master. His knowledge was immense, his grasp of a case was an intuition. He was the very man to inspire a young enthusiast, like me, with awe and delight. My admiration has stood the test of time and survived the separation of death. I am sure it was well-founded.

For nearly twenty years I acted as his medical secretary. His immense collection of papers he has left in my care, to be arranged, indexed and bound. His treatment of some of these cases is curious. He writes in two distinct characters. He describes what he saw and heard as an intelligent layman might, and when in this style of narrative he had seen the patient either through his own hall-door, to the light of day, or through the gates of darkness to the caverns of the dead, he returns upon the narrative, and in the terms of his art, and with all the force and originality of genius, proceeds to the work of analysis, diagnosis and illustration.

Here and there a case strikes me as of a kind to amuse or horrify a lay reader with an interest quite different from the peculiar one which it may possess for an expert. With slight modifications, chiefly of language, and of course a change of names, I copy the following. The narrator is Dr Martin Hesselius. I find it among the voluminous notes of cases which he made during a tour in England about sixty-four years ago.

It is related in a series of letters to his friend Professor Van Loo of Leyden.[1] The professor was not a physician, but a chemist, and a man who read history and metaphysics and medicine, and had, in his day, written a play.

The narrative is therefore, if somewhat less valuable as a medical record, necessarily written in a manner more likely to interest an unlearned reader.

These letters, from a memorandum attached, appear to have been returned on the death of the professor, in 1819, to Dr Hesselius. They are written, some in English, some in French, but the greater part in German. I am a faithful, though I am conscious, by no means a graceful translator, and although here and there, I omit some passages, and shorten others and disguise names, I have interpolated nothing.

CHAPTER I

Dr Hesselius Relates How He Met the Rev. Mr Jennings

The Rev. Mr Jennings is tall and thin. He is middle-aged, and dresses with a natty, old-fashioned, high-church precision. He is naturally a little stately, but not at all stiff. His features, without being handsome, are well formed, and their expression extremely kind, but also shy.

I met him one evening at Lady Mary Heyduke's. The modesty and benevolence of his countenance are extremely prepossessing.

We were but a small party, and he joined agreeably enough in the conversation. He seems to enjoy listening very much more than contributing to the talk; but what he says is always to the purpose and well said. He is a great favourite of Lady Mary's, who it seems, consults him upon many things, and thinks him the most happy and blessed person on earth. Little knows she about him.

The Rev. Mr Jennings is a bachelor, and has, they say, sixty thousand pounds in the funds.[2] He is a charitable man. He is most anxious to be actively employed in his sacred profession, and yet though always tolerably well elsewhere, when he goes down to his vicarage in Warwickshire, to engage in the actual duties of his sacred calling his health soon fails him, and in a very strange way.[3] So says Lady Mary.

There is no doubt that Mr Jennings' health does break down in, generally a sudden and mysterious way, sometimes in the very act of officiating in his old and pretty church at Kenlis.[4] It may be his heart, it may be his brain. But so it has happened three or four times, or oftener, that after proceeding a certain way in the service, he has on a sudden stopped short, and after a silence, apparently quite unable to resume, he has fallen into solitary, inaudible prayer, his hands and eyes uplifted, and then pale as death, and in the agitation of a strange shame and horror, descended trembling, and got into the vestry-room, leaving his congregation, without explanation, to themselves. This occurred when his curate was absent. When he goes down to Kenlis, now, he always takes care to provide a clergyman to share his duty, and to supply his place on the instant should he become thus suddenly incapacitated.

When Mr Jennings breaks down quite, and beats a retreat from the vicarage, and returns to London, where, in a dark street off Piccadilly, he inhabits a very narrow house, Lady Mary says that he is always perfectly well. I have my own opinion about that. There are degrees of course. We shall see.

Mr Jennings is a perfectly gentleman-like man. People, however, remark something odd. There is an impression a little ambiguous. One thing which certainly contributes to it, people I think don't remember; or, perhaps, distinctly remark. But I did, almost immediately. Mr Jennings has a way of looking sidelong upon the carpet, as if his eye followed the movements of something there. This, of course, is not always. It occurs only now and then. But often enough to give a certain oddity, as I have said to his manner, and in this glance travelling along the floor there is something both shy and anxious.

A medical philosopher, as you are good enough to call me, elaborating theories by the aid of cases sought out by himself, and by him watched and scrutinized with more time at command, and consequently infinitely more minuteness than the ordinary practitioner can afford, falls insensibly into habits of observation, which accompany him everywhere, and are exercised, as some people would say, impertinently, upon every subject that presents itself with the least likelihood of rewarding inquiry.

There was a promise of this kind in the slight, timid, kindly, but reserved gentleman, whom I met for the first time at this agreeable little evening gathering. I observed, of course, more than I here set down; but I reserve all that borders on the technical for a strictly scientific paper.

I may remark, that when I here speak of medical science, I do so, as I hope some day to see it more generally understood, in a much more comprehensive sense than its generally material treatment would warrant. I believe the entire natural world is but the ultimate expression of that spiritual world from which, and in which alone, it has its life. I believe that the essential man is a spirit, that the spirit is an organized substance, but as different in point of material from what we ordinarily understand by matter, as light or electricity is; that the material

body is, in the most literal sense, a vesture, and death consequently no interruption of the living man's existence, but simply
his extrication from the natural body – a process which com-
mences at the moment of what we term death, and the com-
pletion of which, at furthest a few days later, is the resurrection
'in power.'

The person who weighs the consequences of these positions
will probably see their practical bearing upon medical science.
This is, however, by no means the proper place for displaying
the proofs and discussing the consequences of this too generally
unrecognized state of facts.

In pursuance of my habit, I was covertly observing Mr
Jennings, with all my caution – I think he perceived it – and I
saw plainly that he was as cautiously observing me. Lady Mary
happening to address me by my name, as Dr Hesselius, I saw
that he glanced at me more sharply, and then became thoughtful
for a few minutes.

After this, as I conversed with a gentleman at the other end
of the room, I saw him look at me more steadily, and with an
interest which I thought I understood. I then saw him take an
opportunity of chatting with Lady Mary, and was, as one
always is, perfectly aware of being the subject of a distant
inquiry and answer.

This tall clergyman approached me by-and-by: and in a little
time we had got into conversation. When two people, who like
reading, and know books and places, having travelled, wish to
converse, it is very strange if they can't find topics. It was not
accident that brought him near me, and led him into conversation. He knew German, and had read my Essays on Metaphysical Medicine which suggest more than they actually say.

This courteous man, gentle, shy, plainly a man of thought
and reading, who moving and talking among us, was not
altogether of us, and whom I already suspected of leading a life
whose transactions and alarms were carefully concealed, with
an impenetrable reserve from, not only the world, but his best
beloved friends – was cautiously weighing in his own mind the
idea of taking a certain step with regard to me.

I penetrated his thoughts without his being aware of it, and
was careful to say nothing which could betray to his sensitive

vigilance my suspicions respecting his position, or my surmises about his plans respecting myself.

We chatted upon indifferent subjects for a time; but at last he said:

'I was very much interested by some papers of yours, Dr Hesselius, upon what you term Metaphysical Medicine – I read them in German, ten or twelve years ago – have they been translated?'

'No, I'm sure they have not – I should have heard. They would have asked my leave, I think.'

'I asked the publishers here, a few months ago, to get the book for me in the original German; but they tell me it is out of print.'

'So it is, and has been for some years; but it flatters me as an author to find that you have not forgotten my little book, although,' I added, laughing, 'ten or twelve years is a considerable time to have managed without it; but I suppose you have been turning the subject over again in your mind, or something has happened lately to revive your interest in it.'

At this remark, accompanied by a glance of inquiry, a sudden embarrassment disturbed Mr Jennings, analogous to that which makes a young lady blush and look foolish. He dropped his eyes, and folded his hands together uneasily, and looked oddly, and you would have said, guiltily for a moment.

I helped him out of his awkwardness in the best way, by appearing not to observe it, and going straight on, I said: 'Those revivals of interest in a subject happen to me often; one book suggests another, and often sends me back on a wild-goose chase over an interval of twenty years. But if you still care to possess a copy, I shall be only too happy to provide you; I have still got two or three by me – and if you allow me to present one I shall be very much honoured.'

'You are very good indeed,' he said, quite at his ease again, in a moment: 'I almost despaired – I don't know how to thank you.'

'Pray don't say a word; the thing is really so little worth that I am only ashamed of having offered it, and if you thank me any more I shall throw it into the fire in a fit of modesty.'

Mr Jennings laughed. He inquired where I was staying in London, and after a little more conversation on a variety of subjects, he took his departure.

CHAPTER II

The Doctor Questions Lady Mary, and She Answers

'I like your vicar so much, Lady Mary,' said I, so soon as he was gone. 'He has read, travelled, and thought, and having also suffered, he ought to be an accomplished companion.'

'So he is, and, better still, he is a really good man,' said she. 'His advice is invaluable about my schools, and all my little undertakings at Dawlbridge, and he's so painstaking, he takes so much trouble – you have no idea – wherever he thinks he can be of use: he's so good-natured and so sensible.'[5]

'It is pleasant to hear so good an account of his neighbourly virtues. I can only testify to his being an agreeable and gentle companion, and in addition to what you have told me, I think I can tell you two or three things about him,' said I.

'Really!'

'Yes, to begin with, he's unmarried.'

'Yes, that's right, – go on.'

'He has been writing, that is he *was*, but for two or three years perhaps, he has not gone on with his work, and the book was upon some rather abstract subject – perhaps theology.'

'Well, he was writing a book, as you say; I'm not quite sure what it was about, but only that it was nothing that I cared for, very likely you are right, and he certainly did stop – yes.'

'And although he only drank a little coffee here to-night, he likes tea, at least, did like it, extravagantly.'

'Yes, that's *quite* true.'

'He drank green tea, a good deal, didn't he?' I pursued.

'Well, that's very odd! Green tea was a subject on which we used almost to quarrel.'

'But he has quite given that up,' said I.

'So he has.'

'And, now, one more fact. His mother or his father, did you know them?'

'Yes, both; his father is only ten years dead, and their place is near Dawlbridge. We knew them very well,' she answered.

'Well, either his mother or his father – I should rather think his father, saw a ghost,' said I.

'Well, you really are a conjurer, Dr Hesselius.'

'Conjurer or no, haven't I said right?' I answered merrily.

'You certainly have, and it *was* his father: he was a silent, whimsical man, and he used to bore my father about his dreams, and at last he told him a story about a ghost he had seen and talked with, and a very odd story it was. I remember it particularly, because I was so afraid of him. This story was long before he died – when I was quite a child – and his ways were so silent and moping, and he used to drop in, sometimes, in the dusk, when I was alone in the drawing-room, and I used to fancy there were ghosts about him.'

I smiled and nodded.

'And now having established my character as a conjurer I think I must say good-night,' said I.

'But how *did* you find it out?'

'By the planets of course, as the gipsies do,' I answered, and so, gaily, we said good-night.

Next morning I sent the little book he had been inquiring after, and a note to Mr Jennings, and on returning late that evening, I found that he had called, at my lodgings, and left his card. He asked whether I was at home, and asked at what hour he would be most likely to find me.

Does he intend opening his case, and consulting me 'professionally,' as they say? I hope so. I have already conceived a theory about him. It is supported by Lady Mary's answers to my parting questions. I should like much to ascertain from his own lips. But what can I do consistently with good breeding to invite a confession? Nothing. I rather think he meditates one. At all events, my dear Van L., I shan't make myself difficult of access; I mean to return his visit to-morrow. It will be only civil in return for his politeness, to ask to see him. Perhaps something may come of it. Whether much, little, or nothing, my dear Van L., you shall hear.

CHAPTER III

Dr Hesselius Picks Up Something in Latin Books

Well, I have called at Blank-street.

On inquiring at the door, the servant told me that Mr Jennings was engaged very particularly with a gentleman, a clergyman from Kenlis, his parish in the country. Intending to reserve my privilege and to call again, I merely intimated that I should try another time, and had turned to go, when the servant begged my pardon, and asked me, looking at me a little more attentively than well-bred persons of his order usually do, whether I was Dr Hesselius; and, on learning that I was, he said, 'Perhaps then, sir, you would allow me to mention it to Mr Jennings, for I am sure he wishes to see you.'

The servant returned in a moment, with a message from Mr Jennings, asking me to go into his study, which was in effect his back drawing-room, promising to be with me in a very few minutes.

This was really a study – almost a library. The room was lofty, with two tall slender windows, and rich dark curtains. It was much larger than I had expected, and stored with books on every side, from the floor to the ceiling. The upper carpet – for to my tread it felt that there were two or three – was a Turkey carpet. My steps fell noiselessly. The book-cases standing out, placed the windows, particularly narrow ones, in deep recesses. The effect of the room was, although extremely comfortable, and even luxurious, decidedly gloomy, and aided by the silence, almost oppressive. Perhaps, however, I ought to have allowed something for association. My mind had connected peculiar ideas with Mr Jennings. I stepped into this perfectly silent room, of a very silent house, with a peculiar foreboding; and its darkness, and solemn clothing of books, for except where two narrow looking-glasses were set in the wall, they were everywhere, helped this sombre feeling.

While awaiting Mr Jennings' arrival, I amused myself by looking into some of the books with which his shelves were laden. Not among these, but immediately under them, with their backs upward, on the floor, I lighted upon a complete set of Swedenborg's Arcana Cælestia, in the original Latin, a very fine folio set, bound in the natty livery which theology affects, pure vellum, namely, gold letters, and carmine edges.[6] There were paper markers in several of these volumes, I raised and placed them, one after the other, upon the table, and opening where these papers were placed, I read in the solemn Latin phraseology, a series of sentences indicated by a pencilled line at the margin. Of these I copy here a few, translating them into English.

'When man's interior sight is opened, which is that of his spirit, then there appear the things of another life, which cannot possibly be made visible to the bodily sight.'[7] . . .

'By the internal sight it has been granted me to see the things that are in the other life, more clearly than I see those that are in the world. From these considerations, it is evident that external vision exists from interior vision, and this from a vision still more interior, and so on.'[8] . . .

'There are with every man at least two evil spirits.'[9] . . .

'With wicked genii there is also a fluent speech, but harsh and grating. There is also among them a speech which is not fluent, wherein the dissent of the thoughts is perceived as something secretly creeping along within it.'[10] . . .

'The evil spirits associated with man are, indeed, from the hells, but when with man they are not then in hell, but are taken out thence. The place where they then are is in the midst between heaven and hell, and is called the world of spirits – when the evil spirits who are with man, are in that world, they are not in any infernal torment, but in every thought and affection of the man, and so, in all that the man himself enjoys. But when they are remitted into their hell, they return to their former state.'[11] . . .

'If evil spirits could perceive that they were associated with man, and yet that they were spirits separate from him, and if they could flow in into the things of his body, they would attempt by a thousand means to destroy him; for they hate man with a deadly hatred.' . . .

'Knowing, therefore, that I was a man in the body, they were continually striving to destroy me, not as to the body only, but especially as to the soul; for to destroy any man or spirit is the very delight of the life of all who are in hell; but I have been continually protected by the Lord. Hence it appears how dangerous it is for man to be in a living consort with spirits, unless he be in the good of faith.'[12] . . .

'Nothing is more carefully guarded from the knowledge of associate spirits than their being thus conjoint with a man, for if they knew it they would speak to him, with the intention to destroy him.'[13] . . .

'The delight of hell is to do evil to man, and to hasten his eternal ruin.'[14]

A long note, written with a very sharp and fine pencil, in Mr Jennings' neat hand, at the foot of the page, caught my eye. Expecting his criticism upon the text, I read a word or two, and stopped, for it was something quite different, and began with these words, *Deus misereatur mei* – 'May God compassionate me.' Thus warned of its private nature, I averted my eyes, and shut the book, replacing all the volumes as I had found them, except one which interested me, and in which, as men studious and solitary in their habits will do, I grew so absorbed as to take no cognizance of the outer world, nor to remember where I was.

I was reading some pages which refer to 'representatives' and 'correspondents,' in the technical language of Swedenborg, and had arrived at a passage, the substance of which is, that evil spirits, when seen by other eyes than those of their infernal associates, present themselves, by 'correspondence,' in the shape of the beast (*fera*) which represents their particular lust and life, in aspect direful and atrocious.[15] This is a long passage, and particularizes a number of those bestial forms.[16]

CHAPTER IV

Four Eyes were Reading the Passage

I was running the head of my pencil-case along the line as I read it, and something caused me to raise my eyes.

Directly before me was one of the mirrors I have mentioned, in which I saw reflected the tall shape of my friend Mr Jennings leaning over my shoulder, and reading the page at which I was busy, and with a face so dark and wild that I should hardly have known him.

I turned and rose. He stood erect also, and with an effort laughed a little, saying:

'I came in and asked you how you did, but without succeeding in awaking you from your book; so I could not restrain my curiosity, and very impertinently, I'm afraid, peeped over your shoulder. This is not your first time of looking into those pages. You have looked into Swedenborg, no doubt, long ago?'

'Oh dear, yes! I owe Swedenborg a great deal; you will discover traces of him in the little book on Metaphysical Medicine, which you were so good as to remember.'

Although my friend affected a gaiety of manner, there was a slight flush in his face, and I could perceive that he was inwardly much perturbed.

'I'm scarcely yet qualified, I know so little of Swedenborg. I've only had them a fortnight,' he answered, 'and I think they are rather likely to make a solitary man nervous – that is, judging from the very little I have read – I don't say that they have made me so,' he laughed; 'and I'm so very much obliged for the book. I hope you got my note?'

I made all proper acknowledgments and modest disclaimers.

'I never read a book that I go with, so entirely, as that of yours,' he continued. 'I saw at once there is more in it than is quite unfolded. Do you know Dr Harley?' he asked, rather abruptly.

In passing, the editor remarks that the physician here named was one of the most eminent who had ever practised in England.[17]

I did, having had letters to him, and had experienced from him great courtesy and considerable assistance during my visit to England.

'I think that man one of the very greatest fools I ever met in my life,' said Mr Jennings.

This was the first time I had ever heard him say a sharp thing of anybody, and such a term applied to so high a name a little startled me.

'Really! and in what way?' I asked.

'In his profession,' he answered.

I smiled.

'I mean this,' he said: 'he seems to me, one half, blind – I mean one half of all he looks at is dark – preternaturally bright and vivid all the rest; and the worst of it is, it seems *wilful*. I can't get him – I mean he won't – I've had some experience of him as a physician, but I look on him as, in that sense, no better than a paralytic mind, an intellect half dead, I'll tell you – I know I shall some time – all about it,' he said, with a little agitation. 'You stay some months longer in England. If I should be out of town during your stay for a little time, would you allow me to trouble you with a letter?'

'I should be only too happy,' I assured him.

'Very good of you. I am so utterly dissatisfied with Harley.'

'A little leaning to the materialistic school,' I said.

'A *mere* materialist,' he corrected me; 'you can't think how that sort of thing worries one who knows better. You won't tell any one – any of my friends you know – that I am hippish; now, for instance, no one knows – not even Lady Mary – that I have seen Dr Harley, or any other doctor.[18] So pray don't mention it; and, if I should have any threatening of an attack, you'll kindly let me write, or, should I be in town, have a little talk with you.'

I was full of conjecture, and unconsciously I found I had fixed my eyes gravely on him, for he lowered his for a moment, and he said:

'I see you think I might as well tell you now, or else you are forming a conjecture; but you may as well give it up. If you were guessing all the rest of your life, you will never hit on it.'

He shook his head smiling, and over that wintry sunshine a black cloud suddenly came down, and he drew his breath in, through his teeth as men do in pain.

'Sorry, of course, to learn that you apprehend occasion to consult any of us; but, command me when and how you like, and I need not assure you that your confidence is sacred.'

He then talked of quite other things, and in a comparatively cheerful way and after a little time, I took my leave.

CHAPTER V

Doctor Hesselius is Summoned to Richmond

We parted cheerfully, but he was not cheerful, nor was I. There are certain expressions of that powerful organ of spirit – the human face – which, although I have seen them often, and possess a doctor's nerve, yet disturb me profoundly. One look of Mr Jennings haunted me. It had seized my imagination with so dismal a power that I changed my plans for the evening, and went to the opera, feeling that I wanted a change of ideas.

I heard nothing of or from him for two or three days, when a note in his hand reached me. It was cheerful, and full of hope. He said that he had been for some little time so much better – quite well, in fact – that he was going to make a little experiment, and run down for a month or so to his parish, to try whether a little work might not quite set him up. There was in it a fervent religious expression of gratitude for his restoration, as he now almost hoped he might call it.

A day or two later I saw Lady Mary, who repeated what his note had announced, and told me that he was actually in Warwickshire, having resumed his clerical duties at Kenlis; and she added, 'I begin to think that he is really perfectly well, and that there never was anything the matter, more than nerves and fancy; we are all nervous, but I fancy there is nothing like a little hard work for that kind of weakness, and he has made up his mind to try it. I should not be surprised if he did not come back for a year.'

Notwithstanding all this confidence, only two days later I had this note, dated from his house off Piccadilly:

'Dear Sir. – I have returned disappointed. If I should feel at all able to see you, I shall write to ask you kindly to call. At present I am too low, and, in fact, simply unable to say all I wish to say. Pray don't mention my name to my friends. I can see no one. By-and-by, please God, you shall hear from me. I mean to take a run into Shropshire, where some of my people are. God bless you! May we, on my return, meet more happily than I can now write.'

About a week after this I saw Lady Mary at her own house, the last person, she said, left in town, and just on the wing for Brighton, for the London season was quite over.[19] She told me that she had heard from Mr Jennings' niece, Martha, in Shropshire. There was nothing to be gathered from her letter, more than that he was low and nervous. In those words, of which healthy people think so lightly, what a world of suffering is sometimes hidden!

Nearly five weeks passed without any further news of Mr Jennings. At the end of that time I received a note from him. He wrote:

'I have been in the country, and have had change of air, change of scene, change of faces, change of everything and in everything – but *myself*. I have made up my mind, so far as the most irresolute creature on earth can do it, to tell my case fully to you. If your engagements will permit, pray come to me to-day, to-morrow, or the next day; but, pray defer as little as possible. You know not how much I need help. I have a quiet house at Richmond, where I now am. Perhaps you can manage to come to dinner, or to luncheon, or even to tea. You shall have no trouble in finding me out. The servant at Blank street, who takes this note, will have a carriage at your door at any hour you please; and I am always to be found. You will say that I ought not to be alone. I have tried everything. Come and see.'

I called up the servant, and decided on going out the same evening, which accordingly I did.

He would have been much better in a lodging-house, or hotel, I thought, as I drove up through a short double row of sombre elms to a very old-fashioned brick house, darkened by the foliage of these trees, which over-topped, and nearly surrounded it. It was a perverse choice, for nothing could be imagined more triste and silent.[20] The house, I found, belonged to him. He had stayed for a day or two in town, and, finding it for some cause insupportable, had come out here, probably because being furnished and his own, he was relieved of the thought and delay of selection, by coming here.

The sun had already set, and the red reflected light of the western sky illuminated the scene with the peculiar effect with which we are all familiar. The hall seemed very dark, but, getting to the back drawing-room, whose windows command the west, I was again in the same dusky light.

I sat down, looking out upon the richly-wooded landscape that glowed in the grand and melancholy light which was every moment fading. The corners of the room were already dark; all was growing dim, and the gloom was insensibly toning my mind, already prepared for what was sinister. I was waiting alone for his arrival, which soon took place. The door communicating with the front room opened, and the tall figure of Mr Jennings, faintly seen in the ruddy twilight, came, with quiet stealthy steps, into the room.

We shook hands, and, taking a chair to the window, where there was still light enough to enable us to see each other's faces, he sat down beside me, and, placing his hand upon my arm, with scarcely a word of preface began his narrative.

CHAPTER VI

How Mr Jennings Met His Companion

The faint glow of the west, the pomp of the then lonely woods of Richmond, were before us, behind and about us the darkening room, and on the stony face of the sufferer – for the character of his face, though still gentle and sweet, was changed – rested that dim, odd glow which seems to descend and produce, where it touches, lights, sudden though faint, which are lost, almost without gradation, in darkness. The silence, too, was utter; not a distant wheel, or bark, or whistle from without; and within the depressing stillness of an invalid bachelor's house.

I guessed well the nature, though not even vaguely the particulars of the revelations I was about to receive, from that fixed face of suffering that so oddly flushed stood out, like a portrait of Schalken's, before its background of darkness.[21]

'It began,' he said, 'on the 15th of October, three years and eleven weeks ago, and two days – I keep very accurate count, for every day is torment. If I leave anywhere a chasm in my narrative tell me.

'About four years ago I began a work, which had cost me very much thought and reading. It was upon the religious metaphysics of the ancients.'

'I know,' said I; 'the actual religion of educated and thinking paganism, quite apart from symbolic worship? A wide and very interesting field.'

'Yes; but not good for the mind – the Christian mind, I mean. Paganism is all bound together in essential unity, and, with evil sympathy, their religion involves their art, and both their manners, and the subject is a degrading fascination and the nemesis sure.[22] God forgive me!

'I wrote a great deal; I wrote late at night. I was always thinking on the subject, walking about, wherever I was, everywhere. It thoroughly infected me. You are to remember that all the material ideas connected with it were more or less of the beautiful, the subject itself delightfully interesting, and I, then, without a care.'

He sighed heavily.

'I believe that every one who sets about writing in earnest does his work, as a friend of mine phrased it, *on* something – tea, or coffee, or tobacco. I suppose there is a material waste that must be hourly supplied in such occupations, or that we should grow too abstracted, and the mind, as it were, pass out of the body, unless it were reminded often of the connection by actual sensation. At all events, I felt the want, and I supplied it. Tea was my companion – at first the ordinary black tea, made in the usual way, not too strong: but I drank a good deal, and increased its strength as I went on. I never experienced an uncomfortable symptom from it. I began to take a little green tea. I found the effect pleasanter, it cleared and intensified the power of thought so. I had come to take it frequently, but not stronger than one might take it for pleasure. I wrote a great deal out here, it was so quiet, and in this room. I used to sit up very late, and it became a habit with me to sip my tea – green tea – every now and then as my work proceeded. I had a little kettle on my table, that swung over a lamp, and made tea two or three times between eleven o'clock and two or three in the morning, my hours of going to bed. I used to go into town every day. I was not a monk, and, although I spent an hour or two in a library, hunting up authorities and looking out lights upon my theme, I was in no morbid state as far as I can judge. I met my friends pretty much as usual, and enjoyed their society, and, on the whole, existence had never been, I think, so pleasant before.

'I had met with a man who had some odd old books, German editions in mediæval Latin, and I was only too happy to be permitted access to them. This obliging person's books were in the City, a very out-of-the-way part of it. I had rather out-stayed my intended hour, and, on coming out, seeing no cab near, I was tempted to get into the omnibus which used to drive past this house. It was darker than this by the time the 'bus had reached an old house, you may have remarked, with four poplars at each side of the door, and there the last passenger but myself got out. We drove along rather faster. It was twilight now. I leaned back in my corner next the door ruminating pleasantly.

'The interior of the omnibus was nearly dark. I had observed in the corner opposite to me at the other side, and at the end next the horses, two small circular reflections, as it seemed to me of a reddish light. They were about two inches apart, and about the size of those small brass buttons that yachting men used to put upon their jackets. I began to speculate, as listless men will, upon this trifle, as it seemed. From what centre did that faint but deep red light come, and from what – glass beads, buttons, toy decorations – was it reflected? We were lumbering along gently, having nearly a mile still to go. I had not solved the puzzle, and it became in another minute more odd, for these two luminous points, with a sudden jerk, descended nearer the floor, keeping still their relative distance and horizontal position, and then, as suddenly, they rose to the level of the seat on which I was sitting, and I saw them no more.

'My curiosity was now really excited, and, before I had time to think, I saw again these two dull lamps, again together near the floor; again they disappeared, and again in their old corner I saw them.

'So, keeping my eyes upon them, I edged quietly up my own side, towards the end at which I still saw these tiny discs of red.

'There was very little light in the 'bus. It was nearly dark. I leaned forward to aid my endeavour to discover what these little circles really were. They shifted their position a little as I did so. I began now to perceive an outline of something black, and I soon saw with tolerable distinctness the outline of a small black monkey, pushing its face forward in mimicry to meet mine; those were its eyes, and I now dimly saw its teeth grinning at me.

'I drew back, not knowing whether it might not meditate a spring. I fancied that one of the passengers had forgot this ugly pet, and wishing to ascertain something of its temper, though not caring to trust my fingers to it, I poked my umbrella softly towards it. It remained immovable – up to it – *through* it! For through it, and back and forward, it passed, without the slightest resistance.

'I can't, in the least, convey to you the kind of horror that I felt. When I had ascertained that the thing was an illusion, as I then supposed, there came a misgiving about myself and a terror that fascinated me in impotence to remove my gaze from the eyes of the brute for some moments. As I looked, it made a little skip back, quite into the corner, and I, in a panic, found myself at the door, having put my head out, drawing deep breaths of the outer air, and staring at the lights and trees we were passing, too glad to reassure myself of reality.

'I stopped the 'bus and got out. I perceived the man look oddly at me as I paid him. I daresay there was something unusual in my looks and manner, for I had never felt so strangely before.'

CHAPTER VII

The Journey: First Stage

'When the omnibus drove on, and I was alone upon the road, I looked carefully round to ascertain whether the monkey had followed me. To my indescribable relief I saw it nowhere. I can't describe easily what a shock I had received, and my sense of genuine gratitude on finding myself, as I supposed, quite rid of it.

'I had got out a little before we reached this house, two or three hundred steps. A brick wall runs along the footpath, and inside the wall is a hedge of yew or some dark evergreen of that kind, and within that again the row of fine trees which you may have remarked as you came.

'This brick wall is about as high as my shoulder, and happening to raise my eyes I saw the monkey, with that stooping gait, on all fours, walking or creeping, close beside me on top of the wall. I stopped, looking at it with a feeling of loathing and horror. As I stopped so did it. It sat up on the wall with its long hands on its knees looking at me. There was not light enough to see it much more than in outline, nor was it dark enough to bring the peculiar light of its eyes into strong relief. I still saw, however, that red foggy light plainly enough. It did not show its teeth, nor exhibit any sign of irritation, but seemed jaded and sulky, and was observing me steadily.

'I drew back into the middle of the road. It was an unconscious recoil, and there I stood, still looking at it, it did not move.

'With an instinctive determination to try something – anything, I turned about and walked briskly towards town with a skance look, all the time, watching the movements of the beast.[23] It crept swiftly along the wall, at exactly my pace.

'Where the wall ends, near the turn of the road, it came down and with a wiry spring or two brought itself close to my feet, and continued to keep up with me, as I quickened my pace. It was at my left side, so close to my leg that I felt every moment as if I should tread upon it.

'The road was quite deserted and silent, and it was darker every moment. I stopped dismayed and bewildered, turning as I did so, the other way – I mean, towards this house, away from which I had been walking. When I stood still, the monkey drew back to a distance of, I suppose, about five or six yards, and remained stationary, watching me.

'I had been more agitated than I have said. I had read, of course, as every one has, something about "spectral illusions," as you physicians term the phenomena of such cases. I considered my situation, and looked my misfortune in the face.

'These affections, I had read, are sometimes transitory and sometimes obstinate.[24] I had read of cases in which the appearance, at first harmless, had, step by step, degenerated into something direful and insupportable, and ended by wearing its victim out. Still as I stood there, but for my bestial companion, quite alone, I tried to comfort myself by repeating again and again the assurance, "the thing is purely disease, a well-known physical affection, as distinctly as small-pox or neuralgia. Doctors are all agreed on that, philosophy demonstrates it. I must not be a fool. I've been sitting up too late, and I daresay my digestion is quite wrong, and with God's help, I shall be all right, and this is but a symptom of nervous dyspepsia." Did I believe all this? Not one word of it, no more than any other miserable being ever did who is once seized and riveted in this satanic captivity. Against my convictions, I might say my knowledge, I was simply bullying myself into a false courage.

'I now walked homeward. I had only a few hundred yards to go. I had forced myself into a sort of resignation, but I had not got over the sickening shock and the flurry of the first certainty of my misfortune.

'I made up my mind to pass the night at home. The brute moved close beside me, and I fancied there was the sort of anxious drawing toward the house, which one sees in tired horses or dogs, sometimes as they come toward home.

'I was afraid to go into town, I was afraid of any one's seeing and recognizing me. I was conscious of an irrepressible agitation in my manner. Also, I was afraid of any violent change in my habits, such as going to a place of amusement, or walking from home in order to fatigue myself. At the hall door it waited till

I mounted the steps, and when the door was opened entered with me.

'I drank no tea that night. I got cigars and some brandy-and-water. My idea was that I should act upon my material system, and by living for a while in sensation apart from thought, send myself forcibly, as it it were, into a new groove. I came up here to this drawing-room. I sat just here. The monkey then got upon a small table that then stood *there*. It looked dazed and languid. An irrepressible uneasiness as to its movements kept my eyes always upon it. Its eyes were half closed, but I could see them glow. It was looking steadily at me. In all situations, at all hours, it is awake and looking at me. That never changes.

'I shall not continue in detail my narrative of this particular night. I shall describe, rather, the phenomena of the first year, which never varied, essentially. I shall describe the monkey as it appeared in daylight. In the dark, as you shall presently hear, there are peculiarities. It is a small monkey, perfectly black. It had only one peculiarity – a character of malignity – unfathomable malignity. During the first year it looked sullen and sick. But this character of intense malice and vigilance was always underlying that surly languor. During all that time it acted as if on a plan of giving me as little trouble as was consistent with watching me. Its eyes were never off me. I have never lost sight of it, except in my sleep, light or dark, day or night, since it came here, excepting when it withdraws for some weeks at a time, unaccountably.

'In total dark it is visible as in daylight. I do not mean merely its eyes. It is *all* visible distinctly in a halo that resembles a glow of red embers, and which accompanies it in all its movements.

'When it leaves me for a time, it is always at night, in the dark, and in the same way. It grows at first uneasy, and then furious, and then advances towards me, grinning and shaking its paws clenched, and, at the same time, there comes the appearance of fire in the grate. I never have any fire. I can't sleep in the room where there is any, and it draws nearer and nearer to the chimney, quivering, it seems, with rage, and when its fury rises to the highest pitch, it springs into the grate, and up the chimney, and I see it no more.

'When first this happened I thought I was released. I was a

new man. A day passed – a night – and no return, and a blessed week – a week – another week. I was always on my knees, Dr Hesselius, always, thanking God and praying. A whole month passed of liberty, but on a sudden, it was with me again.'

CHAPTER VIII

The Second Stage

'It was with me, and the malice which before was torpid under a sullen exterior, was now active. It was perfectly unchanged in every other respect. This new energy was apparent in its activity and its looks, and soon in other ways.

'For a time, you will understand, the change was shown only in an increased vivacity, and an air of menace, as if it was always brooding over some atrocious plan. Its eyes, as before, were never off me.'

'Is it here now?' I asked.

'No,' he replied, 'it has been absent exactly a fortnight and a day – fifteen days. It has sometimes been away so long as nearly two months, once for three. Its absence always exceeds a fortnight, although it may be but by a single day. Fifteen days having past since I saw it last, it may return now at any moment.'

'Is its return,' I asked, 'accompanied by any peculiar manifestation?'

'Nothing – no,' he said. 'It is simply with me again. On lifting my eyes from a book, or turning my head, I see it, as usual, looking at me, and then it remains, as before, for its appointed time. I have never told so much and so minutely before to any one.'

I perceived that he was agitated, and looking like death, and he repeatedly applied his handkerchief to his forehead; I suggested that he might be tired, and told him that I would call, with pleasure, in the morning, but he said:

'No, if you don't mind hearing it all now. I have got so far, and I should prefer making one effort of it. When I spoke to Dr Harley, I had nothing like so much to tell. You are a philosophic physician. You give spirit its proper rank. If this thing is real –'

He paused, looking at me with agitated inquiry.

'We can discuss it by-and-by, and very fully. I will give you all I think,' I answered, after an interval.

'Well – very well. If it is anything real, I say, it is prevailing, little by little, and drawing me more interiorly into hell. Optic nerves, he talked of. Ah! well – there are other nerves of communication. May God Almighty help me! You shall hear.

'Its power of action, I tell you, had increased. Its malice became, in a way aggressive. About two years ago, some questions that were pending between me and the bishop having been settled, I went down to my parish in Warwickshire, anxious to find occupation in my profession. I was not prepared for what happened, although I have since thought I might have apprehended something like it. The reason of my saying so, is this –'

He was beginning to speak with a great deal more effort and reluctance, and sighed often, and seemed at times nearly overcome. But at this time his manner was not agitated. It was more like that of a sinking patient, who has given himself up.

'Yes, but I will first tell you about Kenlis, my parish.

'It was with me when I left this place for Dawlbridge. It was my silent travelling companion, and it remained with me at the vicarage. When I entered on the discharge of my duties, another change took place. The thing exhibited an atrocious determination to thwart me. It was with me in the church – in the reading-desk – in the pulpit – within the communion rails. At last, it reached this extremity, that while I was reading to the congregation, it would spring upon the open book and squat there, so that I was unable to see the page. This happened more than once.

'I left Dawlbridge for a time. I placed myself in Dr Harley's hands. I did everything he told me. He gave my case a great deal of thought. It interested him, I think. He seemed successful. For nearly three months I was perfectly free from a return. I began to think I was safe. With his full assent I returned to Dawlbridge.

'I travelled in a chaise. I was in good spirits. I was more – I was happy and grateful. I was returning, as I thought delivered from a dreadful hallucination, to the scene of duties which

I longed to enter upon. It was a beautiful sunny evening, every-thing looked serene and cheerful, and I was delighted. I remem-ber looking out of the window to see the spire of my church at Kenlis among the trees, at the point where one has the earliest view of it. It is exactly where the little stream that bounds the parish passes under the road by a culvert, and where it emerges at the road-side, a stone with an old inscription is placed. As we passed this point, I drew my head in and sat down, and in the corner of the chaise was the monkey.

'For a moment I felt faint, and then quite wild with despair and horror. I called to the driver, and got out, and sat down at the road-side, and prayed to God silently for mercy. A despair-ing resignation supervened. My companion was with me as I re-entered the vicarage. The same persecution followed. After a short struggle I submitted, and soon I left the place.

'I told you,' he said, 'that the beast has before this become in certain ways aggressive. I will explain a little. It seemed to be actuated by intense and increasing fury, whenever I said my prayers, or even meditated prayer. It amounted at last to a dreadful interruption. You will ask, how could a silent imma-terial phantom effect that? It was thus, whenever I meditated praying; it was always before me, and nearer and nearer.

'It used to spring on a table, on the back of a chair, on the chimney-piece, and slowly to swing itself from side to side, looking at me all the time. There is in its motion an indefinable power to dissipate thought, and to contract one's attention to that monotony, till the ideas shrink, as it were, to a point, and at last to nothing – and unless I had started up, and shook off the catalepsy I have felt as if my mind were on the point of losing itself. There are other ways,' he sighed heavily; 'thus, for instance, while I pray with my eyes closed, it comes closer and closer, and I see it. I know it is not to be accounted for physi-cally, but I do actually see it, though my lids are closed, and so it rocks my mind, as it were, and overpowers me, and I am obliged to rise from my knees. If you had ever yourself known this, you would be acquainted with desperation.'

CHAPTER IX

The Third Stage

'I see, Dr Hesselius, that you don't lose one word of my statement. I need not ask you to listen specially to what I am now
going to tell you. They talk of the optic nerves, and of spectral
illusions, as if the organ of sight was the only point assailable
by the influences that have fastened upon me – I know better.
For two years in my direful case that limitation prevailed. But
as food is taken in softly at the lips, and then brought under
the teeth, as the tip of the little finger caught in a mill crank
will draw in the hand, and the arm, and the whole body, so the
miserable mortal who has been once caught firmly by the end
of the finest fibre of his nerve, is drawn in and in, by the
enormous machinery of hell, until he is as I am. Yes, Doctor,
as *I* am, for while I talk to you, and implore relief, I feel that
my prayer is for the impossible, and my pleading with the
inexorable.'

I endeavoured to calm his visibly increasing agitation, and
told him that he must not despair.

While we talked the night had overtaken us. The filmy moonlight was wide over the scene which the window commanded,
and I said:

'Perhaps you would prefer having candles. This light, you
know, is odd. I should wish you, as much as possible, under
your usual conditions while I make my diagnosis, shall I call it
– otherwise I don't care.'

'All lights are the same to me,' he said: 'except when I read
or write, I care not if night were perpetual. I am going to tell
you what happened about a year ago. The thing began to speak
to me.'

'Speak! How do you mean – speak as a man does, do you
mean?'

'Yes; speak in words and consecutive sentences, with perfect
coherence and articulation; but there is a peculiarity. It is not
like the tone of a human voice. It is not by my ears it reaches
me – it comes like a singing through my head.

'This faculty, the power of speaking to me, will be my undoing. It won't let me pray, it interrupts me with dreadful blasphemies. I dare not go on, I could not. Oh! Doctor, can the skill, and thought, and prayers of man avail me nothing!'

'You must promise me, my dear sir, not to trouble yourself with unnecessarily exciting thoughts; confine yourself strictly to the narrative of *facts*; and recollect, above all, that even if the thing that infests you be all you seem to suppose, a reality with an actual independent life and will, yet it can have no power to hurt you, unless it be given from above: its access to your senses depends mainly upon your physical condition – this is, under God, your comfort and reliance: we are all alike environed. It is only that in your case, the "*paries*," the veil of the flesh, the screen, is a little out of repair, and sights and sounds are transmitted.²⁵ We must enter on a new course, sir – be encouraged. I'll give to-night to the careful consideration of the whole case.'

'You are very good, sir; you think it worth trying, you don't give me quite up; but, sir, you don't know, it is gaining such an influence over me: it orders me about, it is such a tyrant, and I'm growing so helpless. May God deliver me!'

'It orders you about – of course you mean by speech?'

'Yes, yes; it is always urging me to crimes, to injure others, or myself. You see, Doctor, the situation is urgent, it is indeed. When I was in Shropshire, a few weeks ago' (Mr Jennings was speaking rapidly and trembling now, holding my arm with one hand, and looking in my face), 'I went out one day with a party of friends for a walk: my persecutor, I tell you, was with me at the time. I lagged behind the rest: the country near the Dee, you know, is beautiful.²⁶ Our path happened to lie near a coal mine, and at the verge of the wood is a perpendicular shaft, they say, a hundred and fifty feet deep. My niece had remained behind with me – she knows, of course, nothing of the nature of my sufferings. She knew, however, that I had been ill, and was low, and she remained to prevent my being quite alone. As we loitered slowly on together the brute that accompanied me was urging me to throw myself down the shaft. I tell you now – oh, sir, think of it! – the one consideration that saved me from that hideous death was the fear lest the shock of witnessing the occurrence should be too much for the poor girl. I asked her to go on and take her walk with her friends, saying that I could go no further. She made excuses, and the more I urged her the firmer she became. She looked doubtful and frightened. I suppose there was something in my looks or manner that alarmed her; but she would not go, and that literally saved me. You had no idea, sir, that a living man could be made so abject a slave of Satan,' he said, with a ghastly groan and a shudder.

There was a pause here, and I said, 'You *were* preserved nevertheless. It was the act of God. You are in his hands and in the power of no other being: be therefore confident for the future.'

CHAPTER X
Home

I made him have candles lighted, and saw the room looking cheery and inhabited before I left him. I told him that he must regard his illness strictly as one dependent on physical, though *subtle* physical, causes. I told him that he had evidence of God's care and love in the deliverance which he had just described, and that I had perceived with pain that he seemed to regard its peculiar features as indicating that he had been delivered over to spiritual reprobation. Than such a conclusion nothing could be, I insisted, less warranted; and not only so, but more contrary to facts, as disclosed in his mysterious deliverance from that murderous influence during his Shropshire excursion. First, his niece had been retained by his side without his intending to keep her near him; and, secondly, there had been infused into his mind an irresistible repugnance to execute the dreadful suggestion in her presence.

As I reasoned this point with him, Mr Jennings wept. He seemed comforted. One promise I exacted, which was that should the monkey at any time return, I should be sent for immediately; and, repeating my assurance that I would give neither time nor thought to any other subject until I had thoroughly investigated his case, and that to-morrow he should hear the result, I took my leave.

Before getting into the carriage I told the servant that his master was far from well, and that he should make a point of frequently looking into his room.

My own arrangements I made with a view to being quite secure from interruption.

I merely called at my lodgings, and with a travelling-desk and carpet-bag, set off in a hackney-carriage for an inn about two miles out of town, called The Horns, a very quiet and comfortable house, with good thick walls. And there I resolved, without the possibility of intrusion or distraction, to devote some hours of the night, in my comfortable sitting-room, to Mr Jennings' case, and so much of the morning as it might require.

(There occurs here a careful note of Dr Hesselius' opinion upon the case and of the habits, dietary, and medicines which he prescribed. It is curious – some persons would say mystical. But on the whole I doubt whether it would sufficiently interest a reader of the kind I am likely to meet with, to warrant its being here reprinted. The whole letter was plainly written at the inn where he had hid himself for the occasion. The next letter is dated from his town lodgings.)

I left town for the inn where I slept last night at half-past nine, and did not arrive at my room in town until one o'clock this afternoon. I found a letter in Mr Jennings' hand upon my table. It had not come by post, and, on inquiry, I learned that Mr Jennings' servant had brought it, and on learning that I was not to return until to-day, and that no one could tell him my address, he seemed very uncomfortable, and said that his orders from his master were that he was not to return without an answer.

I opened the letter, and read:

'Dear Dr Hesselius. It is here. You had not been an hour gone when it returned. It is speaking. It knows all that has happened. It knows everything – it knows you, and is frantic and atrocious. It reviles. I send you this. It knows every word I have written –

8 SHERIDAN LE FANU

4

I write. This I promised, and I therefore write, but I fear very confused, very incoherently. I am so interrupted, disturbed.

'Ever yours, sincerely yours,
'ROBERT LYNDER JENNINGS.'

'When did this come?' I asked.

'About eleven last night: the man was here again, and has been here three times to-day. The last time is about an hour since.'

Thus answered, and with the notes I had made upon his case in my pocket, I was in a few minutes driving towards Richmond, to see Mr Jennings.

I by no means, as you perceive, despaired of Mr Jennings' case. He had himself remembered and applied, though quite in a mistaken way, the principle which I lay down in my Metaphysical Medicine, and which governs all such cases. I was about to apply it in earnest. I was profoundly interested, and very anxious to see and examine him while the 'enemy' was actually present.

I drove up to the sombre house, and ran up the steps, and knocked. The door, in a little time, was opened by a tall woman in black silk. She looked ill, and as if she had been crying. She curtseyed, and heard my question, but she did not answer. She turned her face away, extending her hand towards two men who were coming down-stairs; and thus having, as it were, tacitly made me over to them, she passed through a side-door hastily and shut it.

The man who was nearest the hall, I at once accosted, but being now close to him, I was shocked to see that both his hands were covered with blood.

I drew back a little, and the man passing down-stairs merely said in a low tone, 'Here's the servant, sir.'

The servant had stopped on the stairs, confounded and dumb at seeing me. He was rubbing his hands in a handkerchief, and it was steeped in blood.

'Jones, what is it, what has happened?' I asked, while a sickening suspicion overpowered me.

The man asked me to come up to the lobby. I was beside him in a moment, and frowning and pallid, with contracted eyes, he told me the horror which I already half guessed.

His master had made away with himself.

I went upstairs with him to the room – what I saw there I won't tell you. He had cut his throat with his razor. It was a frightful gash. The two men had laid him on the bed and composed his limbs. It had happened, as the immense pool of blood on the floor declared, at some distance between the bed and the window. There was carpet round his bed, and a carpet under his dressing-table, but none on the rest of the floor, for the man said he did not like a carpet on his bedroom. In this sombre, and now terrible room, one of the great elms that darkened the house was slowly moving the shadow of one of its great boughs upon this dreadful floor.

I beckoned to the servant and we went down-stairs together. I turned off the hall into an old-fashioned panelled room, and there standing, I heard all the servant had to tell. It was not a great deal.

'I concluded, sir, from your words, and looks, sir, as you left last night, that you thought my master seriously ill. I thought it might be that you were afraid of a fit, or something. So I attended very close to your directions. He sat up late, till past three o'clock. He was not writing or reading. He was talking a great deal to himself, but that was nothing unusual. At about that hour I assisted him to undress, and left him in his slippers and dressing-gown. I went back softly in about half an hour. He was in his bed, quite undressed, and a pair of candles lighted on the table beside his bed. He was leaning on his elbow and looking out at the other side of the bed when I came in. I asked him if he wanted anything, and he said no.

'I don't know whether it was what you said to me, sir, or something a little unusual about him, but I was uneasy, uncommon uneasy about him last night.

'In another half hour, or it might be a little more, I went up again. I did not hear him talking as before. I opened the door a little. The candles were both out, which was not usual. I had a bedroom candle, and I let the light in, a little bit, looking softly round. I saw him sitting in that chair beside the dressing-table with his clothes on again. He turned round and looked at me. I thought it strange he should get up and dress, and put out the candles to sit in the dark, that way. But I only asked him again if I could do anything for him. He said, no, rather sharp, I thought. I asked if I might light the candles, and he said, "Do as you like, Jones." So I lighted them, and I lingered about the room, and he said, "Tell me truth, Jones, why did you come again – you did not hear any one cursing?" "No, sir," I said, wondering what he could mean.

'"No," said he, after me, "of course, no;" and I said to him, "Wouldn't it be well, sir, you went to bed? It's just five o'clock," and he said nothing but, "Very likely; good-night, Jones." So I went, sir, but in less than an hour I came again. The door was fast, and he heard me, and called as I thought from the bed to know what I wanted, and he desired me not to disturb him again. I lay down and slept for a little. It must have been between six and seven when I went up again. The door was still fast, and he made no answer, so I did not like to disturb him, and thinking he was asleep, I left him till nine. It was his custom to ring when he wished me to come, and I had no particular hour for calling him. I tapped very gently, and getting no answer, I stayed away a good while, supposing he was getting some rest then. It was not till eleven o'clock I grew really uncomfortable about him – for at the latest he was never, that I could remember, later than half-past ten. I got no answer. I knocked and called, and still no answer. So not being able to force the door, I called Thomas from the stables, and together we forced it, and found him in the shocking way you saw.'

Jones had no more to tell. Poor Mr Jennings was very gentle, and very kind. All his people were fond of him. I could see that the servant was very much moved.

So, dejected and agitated, I passed from that terrible house, and its dark canopy of elms, and I hope I shall never see it more. While I write to you I feel like a man who has but half waked from a frightful and monotonous dream. My memory rejects the picture with incredulity and horror. Yet I know it is true. It is the story of the process of a poison, a poison which excites the reciprocal action of spirit and nerve, and paralyses the tissue that separates those cognate functions of the senses, the external and the interior. Thus we find strange bed-fellows, and the mortal and immortal prematurely make acquaintance.

CONCLUSION

A Word for Those Who Suffer

My dear Van L——, you have suffered from an affection similar to that which I have just described. You twice complained of a return of it.

Who, under God, cured you? Your humble servant, Martin Hesselius. Let me rather adopt the more emphasized piety of a certain good old French surgeon of three hundred years ago: 'I treated, and God cured you.'

Come, my friend, you are not to be hippish. Let me tell you a fact.

I have met with, and treated, as my book shows, fifty-seven cases of this kind of vision, which I term indifferently 'sublimated,' 'precocious,' and 'interior.'

There is another class of affections which are truly termed – though commonly confounded with those which I describe – spectral illusions. These latter I look upon as being no less simply curable than a cold in the head or a trifling dyspepsia.

It is those which rank in the first category that test our promptitude of thought. Fifty-seven such cases have I encountered, neither more nor less. And in how many of these have I failed? In no one single instance.

There is no one affliction of mortality more easily and certainly reducible, with a little patience, and a rational confidence in the physician. With these simple conditions, I look upon the cure as absolutely certain.

You are to remember that I had not even commenced to treat Mr Jennings' case. I have not any doubt that I should have cured him perfectly in eighteen months, or possibly it might have extended to two years. Some cases are very rapidly curable, others extremely tedious. Every intelligent physician who will give thought and diligence to the task, will effect a cure.

You know my tract on The Cardinal Functions of the Brain. I there, by the evidence of innumerable facts, prove, as I think, the high probability of a circulation arterial and venous in its mechanism, through the nerves. Of this system, thus considered, the brain is the heart. The fluid, which is propagated hence through one class of nerves, returns in an altered state through another, and the nature of that fluid is spiritual, though not immaterial, any more than, as I before remarked, light or electricity are so.

By various abuses, among which the habitual use of such agents as green tea is one, this fluid may be affected as to its quality, but it is more frequently disturbed as to equilibrium. This fluid being that which we have in common with spirits, a congestion found upon the masses of brain or nerve, connected with the interior sense, forms a surface unduly exposed, on which disembodied spirits may operate: communication is thus more or less effectually established. Between this brain circulation and the heart circulation there is an intimate sympathy. The seat, or rather the instrument of exterior vision, is the eye. The seat of interior vision is the nervous tissue and brain, immediately about and above the eyebrow. You remember how effectually I dissipated your pictures by the simple application of iced eau-de-cologne. Few cases, however, can be treated exactly alike with anything like rapid success. Cold acts powerfully as a repellant of the nervous fluid. Long enough continued it will even produce that permanent insensibility which we call numbness, and a little longer, muscular as well as sensational paralysis.

I have not, I repeat, the slightest doubt that I should have first dimmed and ultimately sealed that inner eye which Mr Jennings had inadvertently opened. The same senses are opened in delirium tremens, and entirely shut up again when the overaction of the cerebral heart, and the prodigious nervous congestions that attend it, are terminated by a decided change in the state of the body.[27] It is by acting steadily upon the body, by a simple process, that this result is produced – and inevitably produced – I have never yet failed.

Poor Mr Jennings made away with himself. But that catastrophe was the result of a totally different malady, which, as it were, projected itself upon that disease which was established. His case was in the distinctive manner a complication, and the complaint under which he really succumbed, was hereditary suicidal mania. Poor Mr Jennings I cannot call a patient of mine, for I had not even begun to treat his case, and he had not yet given me, I am convinced, his full and unreserved confidence. If the patient do not array himself on the side of the disease, his cure is certain.

HARRIET BEECHER STOWE

The Ghost in the Cap'n Brown House

'Now, Sam, tell us certain true, is there any such things as ghosts?'[1]

'Be there ghosts?' said Sam, immediately translating into his vernacular grammar: 'wal, now, that are's jest the question, ye see.'

'Well, grandma thinks there are, and Aunt Lois thinks it's all nonsense. Why, Aunt Lois don't even believe the stories in Cotton Mather's "Magnalia."'[2]

'Wanter know?' said Sam, with a tone of slow, languid meditation.

We were sitting on a bank of the Charles River, fishing.[3] The soft melancholy red of evening was fading off in streaks on the glassy water, and the houses of Oldtown were beginning to loom through the gloom, solemn and ghostly.[4] There are times and tones and moods of nature that make all the vulgar, daily real seem shadowy, vague, and supernatural, as if the outlines of this hard material present were fading into the invisible and unknown. So Oldtown, with its elm-trees, its great square white houses, its meeting-house and tavern and blacksmith's shop and mill, which at high noon seem as real and as commonplace as possible, at this hour of the evening was dreamy and solemn. They rose up blurred, indistinct, dark; here and there winking candles sent long lines of light through the shadows, and little drops of unforeseen rain rippled the sheeny darkness of the water.

'Wal, you see, boys, in them things it's jest as well to mind your granny. There's a consid'able sight o' gumption in grandmas. You look at the folks that's allus tellin' you what they don't believe, – they don't believe this, and they don't believe that, – and what sort o' folks is they? Why, like yer Aunt Lois, sort o' stringy and dry. There ain't no 'sorption got out o' not believin' nothin'.

'Lord a massy! we don't know nothin' 'bout them things.[5] We hain't ben there, and can't say that there ain't no ghosts and sich, can we, now?'

We agreed to that fact, and sat a little closer to Sam in the gathering gloom.

'Tell us about the Cap'n Brown house, Sam.'

'Ye didn't never go over the Cap'n Brown house?'

No, we had not that advantage.

'Wal, yer see, Cap'n Brown he made all his money to sea, in furrin parts, and then come here to Oldtown to settle down.

'Now, there ain't no knowin' 'bout these 'ere old ship-masters, where they's ben, or what they's ben a doin', or how they got their money. Ask me no questions, and I'll tell ye no lies, is 'bout the best philosophy for them. Wal, it didn't do no good to ask Cap'n Brown questions too close, 'cause you didn't git no satisfaction. Nobody rightly knew 'bout who his folks was, or where they come from; and, ef a body asked him, he used to say that the very fust he know'd 'bout himself he was a young man walkin' the streets in London.

'But, yer see, boys, he hed money, and that is about all folks wanter know when a man comes to settle down. And he bought that 'are place, and built that 'are house. He built it all sea-cap'n fashion, so's to feel as much at home as he could. The parlour was like a ship's cabin. The table and chairs was fastened down to the floor, and the closets was made with holes to set the casters and the decanters and bottles in, jest's they be at sea; and there was stanchions to hold on by; and they say that blowy nights the cap'n used to fire up pretty well with his grog, till he hed about all he could carry, and then he'd set and hold on, and hear the wind blow, and kind o' feel out to sea right there to hum. There wasn't no Mis' Cap'n Brown, and there didn't seem likely to be none. And whether there ever hed been one, nobody know'd. He hed an old black Guinea niggerwoman, named Quassia, that did his work.[6] She was shaped pretty much like one o' these 'ere great crookneck-squashes.[7] She wa'n't no gret beauty, I can tell you; and she used to wear a gret red turban and a yaller short gown and red petticoat, and a gret string o' gold beads round her neck, and gret big gold hoops in her ears, made right in the middle o' Africa among the heathen there. For all she was black, she thought a heap o' herself, and was consid'able sort o' predominative over the cap'n. Lordy massy! boys, it's allus so. Get a man and a woman together, – any sort o' woman you're a mind to, don't care who 'tis, – and one way or another she gets the rule over him, and he jest has to train to her fife. Some does it one way, and some does it another; some does it by jawin', and some does it by kissin', and some does it by faculty and contrivance; but one way or another they allers does it. Old Cap'n Brown was a good stout, stocky kind o' John Bull sort o' fellow, and a good judge o' sperits, and allers kep' the best in them 'are cupboards o' his'n; but, fust and last, things in his house went pretty much as old Quassia said.[8]

'Folks got to kind o' respectin' Quassia. She come to meetin' Sunday regular, and sot all fixed up in red and yaller and green, with glass beads and what not, lookin' for all the world like one o' them ugly Indian idols; but she was well-behaved as any Christian. She was a master hand at cookin'. Her bread and biscuits couldn't be beat, and no couldn't her pies, and there wa'n't no such pound-cake as she made nowhere. Wal, this 'ere story I'm a goin' to tell you was told me by Cinthy Pendleton. There ain't a more respectable gal, old or young, than Cinthy nowheres. She lives over to Sherburne now, and I hear tell she's sot up a manty-makin' business; but then she used to do tailorin' in Oldtown.[9] She was a member o' the church, and a good Christian as ever was. Wal, ye see, Quassia she got Cinthy to come up and spend a week to the Cap'n Brown house, a doin' tailorin' and a fixin' over his close: 'twas along toward the fust o' March. Cinthy she sot by the fire in the front parlour with her goose and her press-board and her work: for there wa'n't no company callin', and the snow was drifted four feet deep right across the front door; so there wa'n't much danger o' anybody comin' in.[10] And the cap'n he was a perlite man to wimmen; and Cinthy she liked it jest as well not to have company, 'cause the cap'n he'd make himself entertainin' tellin' on her sea-stories, and all about his adventures among the

THE GHOST IN THE CAP'N BROWN HOUSE

Ammonites, and Perresites, and Jebusites, and all sorts o' heathen people he'd been among.[11]

'Wal, that 'are week there come on the master snow-storm. Of all the snow-storms that hed ben, that 'are was the beater; and I tell you the wind blew as if 'twas the last chance it was ever goin' to have. Wal, it's kind o' scary like to be shet up in a lone house with all natur' a kind o' breakin' out, and goin' on so, and the snow a comin' down so thick ye can't see 'cross the street, and the wind a pipin' and a squeelin' and a rumblin' and a tumblin' fust down this chimney and then down that. I tell you, it sort o' sets a feller thinkin' o' the three great things, – death, judgment, and etarnaty; and I don't care who the folks is, nor how good they be, there's times when they must be feelin' putty consid'able solemn.

'Wal, Cinthy she said she kind o' felt so along, and she hed a sort o' queer feelin' come over her as if there was somebody or somethin' round the house more'n appeared. She said she sort o' felt it in the air; but it seemed to her silly, and she tried to get over it. But two or three times, she said, when it got to be dusk, she felt somebody go by her up the stairs. The front entry wa'n't very light in the daytime and in the storm, come five o'clock, it was so dark that all you could see was jest a gleam o' something, and two or three times when she started to go up stairs she see a soft white suthin' that seemed goin' up before her, and she stopped with her heart a beatin' like a trip-hammer, and she sort o' saw it go up and along the entry to the cap'n's door, and then it seemed to go right through, 'cause the door didn't open.

'Wal, Cinthy says she to old Quassia, says she, "Is there anybody lives in this house but us?"

'"Anybody lives here?" says Quassia; "what you mean?" says she.

'Says Cinthy, "I thought somebody went past me on the stairs last night and to-night."

'Lordy massy! how old Quassia did screech and laugh. "Good Lord!" says she, "how foolish white folks is! Somebody went past you? Was't the capt'in?"

'"No, it wa'n't the cap'n," says she: "it was somethin' soft and white, and moved very still; it was like somethin' in the air," says she.

'Then Quassia she haw-hawed louder. Says she, "It's hy-sterikes, Miss Cinthy; that's all it is."

'Wal, Cinthy she was kind o' 'shamed, but for all that she couldn't help herself. Sometimes evenin's she'd be a settin' with the cap'n, and she'd think she'd hear somebody a movin' in his room overhead; and she knowed it wa'n't Quassia, 'cause Quassia was ironin' in the kitchen. She took pains once or twice to find out that 'are.

'Wal, ye see, the cap'n's room was the gret front upper chamber over the parlour, and then right opposite to it was the gret spare chamber where Cinthy slept. It was jest as grand as could be, with a gret four-post mahogany bedstead and damask curtains brought over from England; but it was cold enough to freeze a white bear solid, – the way spare chambers allers is. Then there was the entry between, run straight through the house: one side was old Quassia's room, and the other was a sort o' store-room, where the old cap'n kep' all sorts o' traps.

'Wal, Cinthy she kep' a hevin' things happen and a seein' things, till she didn't railly know what was in it. Once when she come into the parlour jest at sundown, she was sure she see a white figure a vanishin' out o' the door that went towards the side entry. She said it was so dusk, that all she could see was jest this white figure, and it jest went out still as a cat as she come in.

'Wal, Cinthy didn't like to speak to the cap'n about it. She was a close woman, putty prudent, Cinthy was.

'But one night, 'bout the middle o' the week, this 'ere thing kind o' come to a crisis.

'Cinthy said she'd ben up putty late a sewin' and a finishin' off down in the parlour, and the cap'n he sot up with her, and was consid'able cheerful and entertainin', tellin' her all about things over in the Bermudys, and off to Chiny and Japan, and round the world ginerally. The storm that hed been a blowin' all the week was about as furious as ever; and the cap'n he stirred up a mess o' flip, and hed it for her hot to go to bed on.[12] He was a good-natured critter, and allers had feelin's for lone women; and I s'pose he knew 'twas sort o' desolate for Cinthy.

'Wal, takin' the flip so right the last thing afore goin' to bed, she went right off to sleep as sound as a nut, and slep' on till somewhere about mornin', when she said somethin' waked her broad awake in a minute. Her eyes flew wide open like a spring, and the storm had gone down and the moon come out; and there, standin' right in the moonlight by her bed, was a woman jest as white as a sheet, with black hair hangin' down to her waist, and the brightest, mournfullest black eyes you ever see. She stood there lookin' right at Cinthy; and Cinthy thinks that was what waked her up; 'cause, you know, ef anybody stands and looks steady at folks asleep it's apt to wake 'em.

'Any way, Cinthy said she felt jest as ef she was turnin' to stone. She couldn't move nor speak. She lay a minute, and then she shut her eyes, and begun to say her prayers; and a minute after she opened 'em, and it was gone.

'Cinthy was a sensible gal, and one that allers hed her thoughts about her; and she jest got up and put a shawl round her shoulders, and went first and looked at the doors, and they was both on 'em locked jest as she left 'em when she went to bed. Then she looked under the bed and in the closet, and felt all round the room: where she couldn't see she felt her way, and there wa'n't nothin' there.

'Wal, next mornin' Cinthy got up and went home, and she kep' it to herself a good while. Finally, one day when she was workin' to our house she told Hepsy about it, and Hepsy she told me.'

'Well, Sam,' we said, after a pause, in which we heard only the rustle of leaves and the ticking of branches against each other, 'what do you suppose it was?'

'Wal, there 'tis: you know jest as much about it as I do. Hepsy told Cinthy it might 'a' ben a dream; so it might, but Cinthy she was sure it wa'n't a dream, 'cause she remembers plain hearin' the old clock on the stairs strike four while she had her eyes open lookin' at the woman; and then she only shet 'em a minute, jest to say "Now I lay me," and opened 'em and she was gone.

'Wal, Cinthy told Hepsy, and Hepsy she kep' it putty close. She didn't tell it to nobody except Aunt Sally Dickerson and the Widder Bije Smith and your Grandma Badger and the minister's wife; and they every one o' 'em 'greed it ought to be kep' close, 'cause it would make talk. Wal, come spring, some-how or other it seemed to 'a' got all over Oldtown. I heard on 't to the store and up to the tavern; and Jake Marshall he says to me one day, "What's this 'ere about the cap'n's house?" And the Widder Loker she says to me, "There's ben a ghost seen in the cap'n's house;" and I heard on 't clear over to Needham and Sherburne.[13]

'Some o' the women they drew themselves up putty stiff and proper. Your Aunt Lois was one on 'em.

'"Ghost," says she; "don't tell me! Perhaps it would be best ef 'twas a ghost," says she. She didn't think there ought to be no sich doin's in nobody's house; and your grandma she shet her up, and told her she didn't oughter talk so.'

'Talk how?' said I, interrupting Sam with wonder. 'What did Aunt Lois mean?'

'Why, you see,' said Sam mysteriously, 'there allers is folks in every town that's jest like the Sadducees in old times: they won't believe in angel nor sperit, no way you can fix it; and ef things is seen and done in a house, why, they say, it's 'cause there's somebody there; there's some sort o' deviltry or trick about it.[14]

'So the story got round that there was a woman kep' private in Cap'n Brown's house, and that he brought her from furrin parts; and it growed and growed, till there was all sorts o' ways o' tellin on 't.

'Some said they'd seen her a settin' at an open winder. Some said that moonlight nights they'd seen her a walkin' out in the back garden kind o' in and out 'mong the bean-poles and squash-vines.

'You see, it come on spring and summer; and the winders o' the Cap'n Brown house stood open, and folks was all a watchin' on 'em day and night. Aunt Sally Dickerson told the minister's wife that she'd seen in plain daylight a woman a settin' at the chamber winder atween four and five o'clock in the mornin', – jist a settin' a lookin' out and a doin' nothin', like anybody else. She was very white and pale, and had black eyes.

'Some said that it was a nun the cap'n had brought away from a Roman Catholic convent in Spain, and some said he'd got her out o' the Inquisition.

'Aunt Sally said she thought the minister ought to call and inquire why she didn't come to meetin', and who she was, and all about her: 'cause, you see, she said it might be all right enough ef folks only know'd jest how things was; but ef they didn't, why, folks will talk.'

'Well, did the minister do it?'

'What, Parson Lothrop? Wal, no, he didn't. He made a call on the cap'n in a regular way, and asked arter his health and all his family. But the cap'n he seemed jest as jolly and chipper as a spring robin, and he gin the minister some o' his old Jamaiky;[15] and the minister he come away and said he didn't see nothin'; and no he didn't. Folks never does see nothin' when they aint' lookin' where 'tis. Fact is, Parson Lothrop wa'n't fond o' interferin'; he was a master hand to slick things over. Your grandma she used to mourn about it, 'cause she said he never gin no p'int to the doctrines; but 'twas all of a piece, he kind o' took every thing the smooth way.

'But your grandma she believed in the ghost, and so did Lady Lothrop. I was up to her house t'other day fixin' a door-knob, and says she, "Sam, your wife told me a strange story about the Cap'n Brown house."

'"Yes, ma'am, she did," says I.

'"Well, what do you think of it?" says she.

'"Wall, sometimes I think, and then agin I don't know," says I. "There's Cinthy she's a member o' the church and a good pious gal," says I.

'"Yes, Sam," says Lady Lothrop, says she; "and Sam," says she, "it is jest like something that happened once to my grandmother when she was livin' in the old Province House in Bostin." Says she, "These 'ere things is the mysteries of Providence, and it's jest as well not to have 'em too much talked about."

'"Jest so," says I, – "jest so. That 'are's what every woman I've talked with says; and I guess, fust and last, I've talked with twenty, – good, safe church-members, – and they's every one o' opinion that this 'ere oughtn't to be talked about. Why, over to the deakin's t'other night we went it all over as much as two or three hours, and we concluded that the best way was to keep quite still about it; and that's jest what they say over to Needham and Sherburne. I've been all round a hushin' this 'ere up,

and I hain't found but a few people that hedn't the particulars
one way or another." This 'ere was what I says to Lady Lothrop.
The fact was, I never did see no report spread so, nor make sich
sort o' surchin's o' heart, as this 'ere. It railly did beat all; 'cause,
ef 'twas a ghost, why there was the p'int proved, ye see. Cinthy's
a church-member, and she *see* it, and got right up and sarched
the room: but then agin, ef 'twas a woman, why that are was
kind o' awful; it give cause, ye see, for thinkin' all sorts o'
things. There was Cap'n Brown, to be sure, he wa'n't a church-
member; but yet he was as honest and regular a man as any
goin', as fur as any on us could see. To be sure, nobody know'd
where he come from, but that wa'n't no reason agin' him: this
'ere might a ben a crazy sister, or some poor crittur that he
took out o' the best o' motives; and the Scriptur' says, "Charity
hopeth all things." But then, ye see, folks will talk, – that are's
the pester of all these things, – and they did some on 'em talk
consid'able strong about the cap'n; but somehow or other,
there didn't nobody come to the p'int o' facin' on him down,
and sayin' square out, "Cap'n Brown, have you got a woman
in your house, or hain't you? or is it a ghost, or what is it?"
Folks somehow never does come to that. Ye see, there was the
cap'n so respectable, a settin' up every Sunday there in his pew,
with his ruffles round his hands and his red broadcloth cloak
and his cocked hat. Why, folks' hearts sort o' failed 'em when
it come to sayin' any thing right to him. They thought and kind
o' whispered round that the minister or the deakins oughter do
it: but Lordy massy! ministers, I s'pose, has feelin's like the rest
on us; they don't want to eat all the hard cheeses that nobody
else won't eat. Anyhow, there wasn't nothin' said direct to the
cap'n; and jest for want o' that all the folks in Oldtown kep' a
bilin' and a bilin' like a kettle o' soap, till it seemed all the time
as if they'd bile over.

   'Some o' the wimmen tried to get somethin' out o' Quassy.
Lordy massy! you might as well 'a' tried to get it out an old
tom-turkey, that'll strut and gobble and quitter, and drag his
wings on the ground, and fly at you, but won't say nothin'.
Quassy she screeched her queer sort o' laugh; and she told 'em
that they was a makin' fools o' themselves, and that the cap'n's
matters wa'n't none o' their bus'ness; and that was true enough.

As to goin' into Quassia's room, or into any o' the store-rooms or closets she kep' the keys of, you might as well hev gone into a lion's den. She kep' all her places locked up tight; and there was no gettin' at nothin' in the Cap'n Brown house, else I believe some o' the wimmen would 'a' sent a sarch-warrant.'

'Well,' said I, 'what came of it? Didn't anybody ever find out?'

'Wal,' said Sam, 'it come to an end sort o', and didn't come to an end. It was jest this 'ere way. You see, along in October, jest in the cider-makin' time, Abel Flint he was took down with dysentery and died. You 'member the Flint house: it stood on a little rise o' ground jest lookin' over towards the Brown house. Wal, there was Aunt Sally Dickerson and the Widder Bije Smith, they set up with the corpse. He was laid out in the back chamber, you see, over the milk-room and kitchen; but there was cold victuals and sich in the front chamber, where the watchers sot. Wal, now, Aunt Sally she told me that between three and four o'clock she heard wheels a rumblin', and she went to the winder, and it was clear starlight; and she see a coach come up to the Cap'n Brown house; and she see the cap'n come out bringin' a woman all wrapped in a cloak, and old Quassy came after with her arms full of bundles; and he put her into the kerridge, and shet her in, and it driv off; and she see old Quassy stand lookin' over the fence arter it. She tried to wake up the widder, but 'twas towards mornin', and the widder allers was a hard sleeper; so there wa'n't no witness but her.'

'Well, then, it wasn't a ghost,' said I, 'after all, and it *was* a woman.'

'Wal, there 'tis, you see. Folks don't know that 'are yit, 'cause there it's jest as broad as 'tis long. Now, look at it. There's Cinthy, she's a good, pious gal: she locks her chamber-doors, both on 'em, and goes to bed, and wakes up in the night and there's a woman there. She jest shets her eyes, and the woman's gone. She gits up and looks, and both doors is locked jest as she left 'em. That 'ere woman wa'n't flesh and blood now, no way, – not such flesh and blood as we knows on; but then they say Cinthy might have dreamed it!

'Wal, now, look at it t'other way. There's Aunt Sally Dickerson; she's a good woman and a church-member: wal, she sees a woman in a cloak with all her bundles brought out o' Cap'n Brown's house, and put into a kerridge, and driv off, atween three and four o'clock in the mornin'. Wal, that 'ere shows there must 'a' ben a real live woman kep' there privately, and so what Cinthy saw wasn't a ghost.

'Wal, now, Cinthy says Aunt Sally might 'a' dreamed it, – that she got her head so full o' stories about the Cap'n Brown house, and watched it till she got asleep, and hed this 'ere dream; and, as there didn't nobody else see it, it might 'a' ben, you know. Aunt Sally's clear she didn't dream, and then ag'in Cinthy's clear *she* didn't dream; but which on 'em was awake or which on 'em was asleep, is what ain't settled in Oldtown yet.'

ROBERT LOUIS STEVENSON

Thrawn Janet

The Reverend Murdoch Soulis was long minister of the moorland parish of Balweary, in the vale of Dule.[1] A severe, bleak-
faced old man, dreadful to his hearers, he dwelt in the last years
of his life, without relative or servant or any human company,
in the small and lonely manse under the Hanging Shaw. In spite
of the iron composure of his features, his eye was wild, seared,
and uncertain; and when he dwelt, in private admonitions, on
the future of the impenitent, it seemed as if his eye pierced
through the storms of time to the terrors of eternity. Many
young persons, coming to prepare themselves against the season
of the Holy Communion, were dreadfully affected by his talk.
He had a sermon on 1st Peter, v and 8th, 'The devil as a roaring
lion,' on the Sunday after every seventeenth of August, and he
was accustomed to surpass himself upon that text both by the
appalling nature of the matter and the terror of his bearing in
the pulpit.[2] The children were frightened into fits, and the old
looked more than usually oracular, and were, all that day, full
of those hints that Hamlet deprecated.[3] The manse itself, where
it stood by the water of Dule among some thick trees, with the
Shaw overhanging it on the one side, and on the other many
cold, moorish hilltops rising towards the sky, had begun, at a
very early period of Mr Soulis's ministry, to be avoided in the
dusk hours by all who valued themselves upon their prudence;
and guidmen sitting at the clachan alehouse shook their heads
together at the thought of passing late by that uncanny neighbourhood. There was one spot, to be more particular, which
was regarded with especial awe. The manse stood between the
high road and the water of Dule, with a gable to each; its back
was towards the kirktown of Balweary, nearly half a mile away;

in front of it, a bare garden, hedged with thorn, occupied the land between the river and the road. The house was two stories high, with two large rooms on each. It opened not directly on the garden, but on a causewayed path, or passage, giving on the road on the one hand, and closed on the other by the tall willows and elders that bordered on the stream. And it was this strip of causeway that enjoyed among the young parishioners of Balweary so infamous a reputation. The minister walked there often after dark, sometimes groaning aloud in the instancy of his unspoken prayers; and when he was from home, and the manse door was locked, the more daring schoolboys ventured, with beating hearts, to 'follow my leader' across that legendary spot.

This atmosphere of terror, surrounding, as it did, a man of God of spotless character and orthodoxy, was a common cause of wonder and subject of inquiry among the few strangers who were led by chance or business into that unknown, outlying country. But many even of the people of the parish were ignorant of the strange events which had marked the first year of Mr Soulis's ministrations; and among those who were better informed, some were naturally reticent, and others shy of that particular topic. Now and again, only, one of the older folk would warm into courage over his third tumbler, and recount the cause of the minister's strange looks and solitary life.

Fifty years syne, when Mr Soulis cam first into Ba'weary, he was still a young man – a callant, the folk said – fu' o' book learnin' and grand at the exposition, but, as was natural in sae young a man, wi' nae leevin' experience in religion. The younger sort were greatly taken wi' his gifts and his gab; but auld, concerned, serious men and women were moved even to prayer for the young man, whom they took to be a self-deceiver, and the parish that was like to be sae ill-supplied. It was before the days o' the moderates – weary fa' them; but ill things are like guid – they baith come bit by bit, a pickle at a time; and there were folk even then that said the Lord had left the college professors to their ain devices, an' the lads that went to study wi' them wad hae done mair and better sittin' in a peat-bog, like their forbears of the persecution, wi' a Bible under their oxter and a speerit o' prayer in their heart.[4] There was nae

doubt, onyway, but that Mr Soulis had been ower lang at the
college. He was careful and troubled for mony things besides
the ae thing needful. He had a feck o' books wi' him – mair
than had ever been seen before in a' that presbytery; and a sair
wark the carrier had wi' them, for they were a' like to have
smoored in the Deil's Hag between this and Kilmackerlie. They
were books o' divinity, to be sure, or so they ca'd them; but the
serious were o' opinion there was little service for sae mony,
when the hail o' God's Word would gang in the neuk of a plaid.
Then he wad sit half the day and half the nicht forbye, which
was scant decent – writin', nae less; and first, they were feared
he wad read his sermons; and syne it proved he was writin' a
book himsel', which was surely no fittin' for ane of his years
an' sma' experience.

Onyway it behoved him to get an auld, decent wife to keep
the manse for him an' see to his bit denners; and he was recommended to an auld limmer – Janet M'Clour, they ca'd her – and
sae far left to himsel' as to be ower persuaded. There was mony
advised him to the contrar, for Janet was mair than suspeckit
by the best folk in Ba'weary. Lang or that, she had had a wean
to a dragoon; she hadnae come forrit* for maybe thretty year;
and bairns had seen her mumblin' to hersel' up on Key's Loan in
the gloamin', whilk was an unco time an' place for a God-fearin'
woman. Howsoever, it was the laird himsel' that had first tauld
the minister o' Janet; and in thae days he wad have gane a far
gate to pleesure the laird. When folk tauld him that Janet was
sib to the deil, it was a' superstition by his way of it; an' when
they cast up the Bible to him an' the witch of Endor, he wad
threep it doun their thrapples that thir days were a' gane by,
and the deil was mercifully restrained.[5]

Weel, when it got about the clachan that Janet M'Clour was
to be servant at the manse, the folk were fair mad wi' her an'
him thegither; and some o' the guidwives had nae better to dae
than get round her door cheeks and chairge her wi' a' that was
ken't again her, frae the sodger's bairn to John Tamson's twa
kye. She was nae great speaker; folk usually let her gang her
ain gate, an' she let them gang theirs, wi' neither Fair-guid-een

* To come forrit – to offer oneself as a communicant.

nor Fair-guid-day; but when she buckled to, she had a tongue to deave the miller. Up she got, an' there wasnae an auld story in Ba'weary but she gart somebody lowp for it that day; they couldnae say ae thing but she could say twa to it; till, at the hinder end, the guidwives up and claucht haud of her, and clawcd the coats aff her back, and pu'd her doun the clachan to the water o' Dule, to see if she were a witch or no, soum or droun. The carline skirled till ye could hear her at the Hangin' Shaw, and she focht like ten; there was mony a guidwife bure the mark of her neist day an' mony a lang day after; and just in the hettest o' the collieshangie, wha suld come up (for his sins) but the new minister.

'Women,' said he (and he had a grand voice), 'I charge you in the Lord's name to let her go.'

Janet ran to him – she was fair wud wi' terror – an' clang to him, an' prayed him, for Christ's sake, save her frae the cummers; an' they, for their pairt, tauld him a' that was ken't, and maybe mair.

'Woman,' says he to Janet, 'is this true?'

'As the Lord sees me,' says she, 'as the Lord made me, no a word o't. Forbye the bairn,' says she, 'I've been a decent woman a' my days.'

'Will you,' says Mr Soulis, 'in the name of God, and before me, His unworthy minister, renounce the devil and his works?'

Weel, it wad appear that when he askit that, she gave a girn that fairly frichtit them that saw her, an' they could hear her teeth play dirl thegether in her chafts; but there was naething for it but the ae way or the ither; an' Janet lifted up her hand and renounced the deil before them a'.

'And now,' says Mr Soulis to the guidwives, 'home with ye, one and all, and pray to God for His forgiveness.'

And he gied Janet his arm, though she had little on her but a sark, and took her up the clachan to her ain door like a leddy of the land; an' her scrieghin' and laughin' as was a scandal to be heard.

There were mony grave folk lang ower their prayers that nicht; but when the morn cam' there was sic a fear fell upon a' Ba'weary that the bairns hid theirsels, and even the men folk stood and keekit frae their doors. For there was Janet comin' doun the clachan – her or her likeness, nane could tell – wi' her neck thrawn, and her heid on ae side, like a body that has been hangit, and a girn on her face like an unstreakit corp. By an' by they got used wi' it, and even speered at her to ken what was wrang; but frae that day forth she couldnae speak like a Christian woman, but slavered and played click wi' her teeth like a pair o' shears; and frae that day forth the name o' God cam never on her lips. Whiles she wad try to say it, but it michtnae be. Them that kenned best said least; but they never gied that Thing the name o' Janet M'Clour; for the auld Janet, by their way o't, was in muckle hell that day. But the minister was neither to haud nor to bind; he preached about naething but the folk's cruelty that had gi'en her a stroke of the palsy; he skelpt the bairns that meddled her; and he had her up to the manse that same nicht, and dwalled there a' his lane wi' her under the Hangin' Shaw.

Weel, time gaed by: and the idler sort commenced to think mair lichtly o' that black business. The minister was weel thocht o'; he was aye late at the writing, folk wad see his can'le doon by the Dule water after twal' at e'en; and he seemed pleased wi' himsel' and upsitten as at first, though a' body could see that he was dwining. As for Janet she cam an' she gaed; if she didnae speak muckle afore, it was reason she should speak less then; she meddled naebody; but she was an eldritch thing to see, an' nane wad hae mistrysted wi' her for Ba'weary glebe.[6]

About the end o' July there cam' a spell o' weather, the like o't never was in that country side; it was lown an' het an' heartless; the herds couldnae win up the Black Hill, the bairns were ower weariet to play; an' yet it was gousty too, wi' claps o' het wund that rumm'led in the glens, and bits o' shouers that slockened naething. We aye thocht it but to thun'er on the morn; but the morn cam, an' the morn's morning, and it was aye the same uncanny weather, sair on folks and bestial. Of a' that were the waur, nane suffered like Mr Soulis; he could neither sleep nor eat, he tauld his elders; an' when he wasnae writin' at his weary book, he wad be stravaguin' ower a' the countryside like a man possessed, when a' body else was blythe to keep caller ben the house.

Abune Hangin' Shaw, in the bield o' the Black Hill, there's a bit enclosed grund wi' an iron yett; and it seems, in the auld days, that was the kirkyaird o' Ba'weary, and consecrated by the Papists before the blessed licht shone upon the kingdom. It was a great howff o' Mr Soulis's, onyway; there he would sit an' consider his sermons; and indeed it's a bieldy bit. Weel, as he cam ower the wast end o' the Black Hill, ae day, he saw first twa, an syne fower, an' syne seeven corbie craws fleein' round an' round abune the auld kirkyaird. They flew laigh and heavy, an' squawked to ither as they gaed; and it was clear to Mr Soulis that something had put them frae their ordinar. He wasnae easy fleyed, an' gaed straucht up to the wa's; an' what suld he find there but a man, or the appearance of a man, sittin' in the inside upon a grave. He was of a great stature, an' black as hell, and his e'en were singular to see.* Mr Soulis had heard tell o' black men, mony's the time; but there was something unco about this black man that daunted him. Het as he was, he took a kind o' cauld grue in the marrow o' his banes; but up he spak for a' that; an' says he: 'My friend, are you a stranger in this place?' The black man answered never a word; he got upon his feet, an' begude to hirsle to the wa' on the far side; but he aye lookit at the minister; an' the minister stood an' lookit back; till a' in a meenute the black man was ower the wa' an' rinnin' for the bield o' the trees. Mr Soulis, he hardly kenned why, ran after him; but he was sair forjaskit wi' his walk an' the het, unhalesome weather; and rin as he likit, he got nae mair than a glisk o' the black man amang the birks, till he won doun to the foot o' the hill-side, an' there he saw him ance mair, gaun, hap, step, an' lowp, ower Dule water to the manse.

Mr Soulis wasnae weel pleased that this fearsome gangrel suld mak' sae free wi' Ba'weary manse; an' he ran the harder, an', wet shoon, ower the burn, an' up the walk; but the deil a black man was there to see. He stepped out upon the road, but there was naebody there; he gaed a' ower the gairden, but na, nae black man. At the hinder end, and a bit feared as was but

* It was a common belief in Scotland that the devil appeared as a black man. This appears in several witch trials and I think in Law's *Memorials*, that delightful store-house of the quaint and grisly.[7]

natural, he lifted the hasp and into the manse; and there was Janet M'Clour before his een, wi' her thrawn craig, and nane sae pleased to see him. And he aye minded sinsyne, when first he set his een upon her, he had the same cauld and deidly grue.

'Janet,' says he, 'have you seen a black man?'

'A black man?' quo' she. 'Save us a'! Ye're no wise, minister. There's nae black man in a' Ba'weary.'

But she didnae speak plain, ye maun understand; but yam-yammered, like a powney wi' the bit in its moo.

'Weel,' says he, 'Janet, if there was nae black man, I have spoken with the Accuser of the Brethren.'[8]

And he sat down like ane wi' a fever, an' his teeth chittered in his heid.

'Hoots,' says she, 'think shame to yoursel', minister;' an' gied him a drap brandy that she keept aye by her.

Syne Mr Soulis gaed into his study amang a' his books. It's a lang, laigh, mirk chalmer, perishin' cauld in winter, an' no very dry even in the tap o' the simmer, for the manse stands near the burn. Sae doun he sat, and thocht of a' that had come an' gane since he was in Ba'weary, an' his hame, an' the days when he was a bairn an' ran daffin' on the braes; and that black man aye ran in his heid like the owercome of a sang. Aye the mair he thocht, the mair he thocht o' the black man. He tried the prayer, an' the words wouldnae come to him; an' he tried, they say, to write at his book, but he could nae mak' nae mair o' that. There was whiles he thocht the black man was at his oxter, an' the swat stood upon him cauld as well-water; and there was other whiles, when he cam' to himsel' like a christened bairn and minded naething.

The upshot was that he gaed to the window an' stood glowrin' at Dule water. The trees are unco thick, an' the water lies deep an' black under the manse; an' there was Janet washin' the cla'es wi' her coats kilted. She had her back to the minister, an' he, for his pairt, hardly kenned what he was lookin' at. Syne she turned round, an' shawed her face; Mr Soulis had the same cauld grue as twice that day afore, an' it was borne in upon him what folk said, that Janet was deid lang syne, an' this was a bogle in her clay-cauld flesh. He drew back a pickle and he scanned her narrowly. She was tramp-trampin' in the cla'es,

croonin' to hersel'; and eh! Gude guide us, but it was a fearsome
face. Whiles she sang louder, but there was nae man born o'
woman that could tell the words o' her sang; an' whiles she
lookit side-lang doun, but there was naething there for her to
look at. There gaed a scunner through the flesh upon his banes;
and that was Heeven's advertisement. But Mr Soulis just blamed
himsel', he said, to think sae ill of a puir, auld afflicted wife
that hadnae a freend forbye himsel'; an' he put up a bit prayer
for him and her, an' drank a little caller water – for his heart
rose again the meat – an' – an' gaed up to his naked bed in the
gloaming.

That was a nicht that has never been forgotten in Ba'weary,
the nicht o' the seeventeenth of August, seventeen hun'er' an
twal'. It had been het afore, as I hae said, but that nicht it
was hetter than ever. The sun gaed doun amang unco-lookin'
clouds; it fell as mirk as the pit; no a star, no a breath o' wund;
ye couldnae see your han' afore your face, and even the auld
folk cuist the covers frae their beds and lay pechin' for their
breath. Wi' a' that he had upon his mind, it was gey and unlikely
Mr Soulis wad get muckle sleep. He lay an' he tummled; the
gude, caller bed that he got into brunt his very banes; whiles he
slept, and whiles he waukened; whiles he heard the time o'
nicht, and whiles a tyke yowlin' up the muir, as if somebody
was deid; whiles he thocht he heard bogles claverin' in his lug,
an' whiles he saw spunkies in the room. He behoved, he judged,
to be sick; an' sick he was – little he jaloosed the sickness.

At the hinder end, he got a clearness in his mind, sat up in
his sark on the bed-side, and fell thinkin' ance mair o' the black
man an' Janet. He couldnae weel tell how – maybe it was the
cauld to his feet – but it cam' in upon him wi' a spate that there
was some connection between thir twa, an' that either or baith
o' them were bogles. And just at that moment, in Janet's room,
which was neist to his, there cam' a stramp o' feet as if men
were wars'lin', an' then a loud bang; an' then a wund gaed
reishling round the fower quarters of the house; an' then a' was
aince mair as seelent as the grave.

Mr Soulis was feared for neither man nor deevil. He got his
tinder-box, an' lit a can'le, an' made three steps o't ower to
Janet's door. It was on the hasp, an' he pushed it open, an'

keeked bauldly in. It was a big room, as big as the minister's ain, an' plenished wi' grand, auld, solid gear, for he had naething else. There was a fower-posted bed wi' auld tapestry; and a braw cabinet of aik, that was fu' o' the minister's divinity books, an' put there to be out o' the gate; an' a wheen duds o' Janet's lying here and there about the floor. But nae Janet could Mr Soulis see; nor ony sign of a contention. In he gaed (an' there's few that wad ha'e followed him) an' lookit a' round, an' listened. But there was naethin' to be heard, neither inside the manse nor in a' Ba'weary parish, an' naethin' to be seen but the muckle shadows turnin' round the can'le. An' then a' at aince, the minister's heart played dunt an' stood stock-still; an' a cauld wund blew amang the hairs o' his heid. Whaten a weary sicht was that for the puir man's een! For there was Janet hangin' frae a nail beside the auld aik cabinet: her heid aye lay on her shoother, her een were steeked, the tongue projekit frae her mouth, and her heels were twa feet clear abune the floor.

'God forgive us all!' thocht Mr Soulis; 'poor Janet's dead.'

He cam' a step nearer to the corp; an' then his heart fair whammled in his inside. For by what cantrip it wad ill-beseem a man to judge, she was hingin' frae a single nail an' by a single wursted thread for darnin' hose.

It's an awfu' thing to be your lane at nicht wi' siccan prodigies o' darkness; but Mr Soulis was strong in the Lord. He turned an' gaed his ways oot o' that room, and lockit the door ahint him; and step by step, doon the stairs, as heavy as leed; and set doon the can'le on the table at the stairfoot. He couldnae pray, he couldnae think, he was dreepin' wi' caul' swat, an' naething could he hear but the dunt-dunt-duntin' o' his ain heart. He micht maybe have stood there an hour, or maybe twa, he minded sae little; when a' o' a sudden, he heard a laigh, uncanny steer upstairs; a foot gaed to an' fro in the cha'mer whaur the corp was hingin'; syne the door was opened, though he minded weel that he had lockit it; an' syne there was a step upon the landin', an' it seemed to him as if the corp was lookin' ower the rail and doun upon him whaur he stood.

He took up the can'le again (for he couldnae want the licht), and as saftly as ever he could, gaed straucht out o' the manse an' to the far end o' the causeway. It was aye pit-mirk; the flame o' the can'le, when he set it on the grund, brunt steedy and clear as in a room; naething moved, but the Dule water seepin' and sabbin' doon the glen, an' yon unhaly footstep that cam' ploddin' doun the stairs inside the manse. He kenned the foot over weel, for it was Janet's; and at ilka step that cam' a wee thing nearer, the cauld got deeper in his vitals. He commended his soul to Him that made an' keepit him; 'and O Lord,' said he, 'give me strength this night to war against the powers of evil.'

By this time the foot was comin' through the passage for the door; he could hear a hand skirt alang the wa', as if the fearsome thing was feelin' for its way. The saughs tossed an' maned thegether, a lang sigh cam' ower the hills, the flame o' the can'le was blawn aboot; an' there stood the corp of Thrawn Janet, wi' her grogram goun an' her black mutch, wi' the heid aye upon the shouther, an' the girn still upon the face o't – leevin', ye wad hae said – deid, as Mr Soulis weel kenned – upon the threshold o' the manse.[9]

It's a strange thing that the saul of man should be that thirled into his perishable body; but the minister saw that, an' his heart didnae break.

She didnae stand there lang; she began to move again an' cam' slowly towards Mr Soulis whaur he stood under the saughs. A' the life o' his body, a' the strength o' his speerit, were glowerin' frae his een. It seemed she was gaun to speak, but wanted words, an' made a sign wi' the left hand. There cam' a clap o' wund, like a cat's fuff; oot gaed the can'le, the saughs skrieghed like folk; an' Mr Soulis kenned that, live or die, this was the end o't.

'Witch, beldame, devil!' he cried, 'I charge you, by the power of God, begone – if you be dead, to the grave – if you be damned, to hell.'

An' at that moment the Lord's ain hand out o' the Heevens struck the Horror whaur it stood; the auld, deid, desecrated corp o' the witch-wife, sae lang keepit frae the grave and hirsled round by deils, lowed up like a brunstane spunk and fell in ashes to the grund; the thunder followed, peal on dirling peal, the rairing rain upon the back o' that; and Mr Soulis lowped through the garden hedge, and ran, wi' skelloch upon skelloch, for the clachan.

That same mornin', John Christie saw the Black Man pass the Muckle Cairn as it was chappin' six; before eicht, he gaed by the change-house at Knockdow; an' no lang after, Sandy M'Lellan saw him gaun linkin' doun the braes frae Kilmackerlie.[10] There's little doubt but it was him that dwalled sae lang in Janet's body; but he was awa' at last; and sinsyne the deil has never fashed us in Ba'weary.

But it was a sair dispensation for the minister; lang, lang he lay ravin' in his bed; and frae that hour to this, he was the man ye ken the day.

MARGARET OLIPHANT
The Open Door

I took the house of Brentwood on my return from India in
18—, for the temporary accommodation of my family, until I
could find a permanent home for them.[1] It had many advantages
which made it peculiarly appropriate. It was within reach of
Edinburgh, and my boy Roland, whose education had been
considerably neglected, could go in and out to school, which
was thought to be better for him than either leaving home
altogether or staying there always with a tutor. The first of these
expedients would have seemed preferable to me, the second
commended itself to his mother. The doctor, like a judicious
man, took the midway between. 'Put him on his pony, and let
him ride into the High School every morning; it will do him all
the good in the world,' Dr Simson said; 'and when it is bad
weather there is the train.' His mother accepted this solution of
the difficulty more easily than I could have hoped; and our
pale-faced boy, who had never known anything more invigorating than Simla, began to encounter the brisk breezes of the
North in the subdued severity of the month of May.[2] Before
the time of the vacation in July we had the satisfaction of
seeing him begin to acquire something of the brown and ruddy
complexion of his schoolfellows. The English system did not
commend itself to Scotland in these days. There was no little
Eton at Fettes; nor do I think, if there had been, that a genteel
exotic of that class would have tempted either my wife or me.[3]
The lad was doubly precious to us, being the only one left us
of many; and he was fragile in body, we believed, and deeply
sensitive in mind. To keep him at home, and yet to send him to
school – to combine the advantages of the two systems – seemed
to be everything that could be desired. The two girls also found

at Brentwood everything they wanted. They were near enough
to Edinburgh to have masters and lessons as many as they
required for completing that never-ending education which the
young people seem to require nowadays. Their mother married
me when she was younger than Agatha, and I should like to see
them improve upon their mother! I myself was then no more
than twenty-five – an age at which I see the young fellows now
groping about them, with no notion what they are going to do
with their lives. However, I suppose every generation has a
conceit of itself which elevates it, in its own opinion, above that
which comes after it.

Brentwood stands on that fine and wealthy slope of country,
one of the richest in Scotland, which lies between the Pentland
Hills and the Firth.[4] In clear weather you could see the blue
gleam – like a bent bow, embracing the wealthy fields and
scattered houses – of the great estuary on one side of you; and
on the other the blue heights, not gigantic like those we had
been used to, but just high enough for all the glories of the
atmosphere, the play of clouds, and sweet reflections, which
give to a hilly country an interest and a charm which nothing
else can emulate. Edinburgh, with its two lesser heights – the
Castle and the Calton Hill – its spires and towers piercing
through the smoke, and Arthur's Seat, lying crouched behind,
like a guardian no longer very needful, taking his repose beside
the well-beloved charge, which is now, so to speak, able to take
care of itself without him – lay at our right hand.[5] From the lawn
and drawing-room windows we could see all these varieties
of landscape. The colour was sometimes a little chilly, but
sometimes, also, as animated and full of vicissitude as a drama.
I was never tired of it. Its colour and freshness revived the eyes
which had grown weary of arid plains and blazing skies. It was
always cheery, and fresh, and full of repose.

The village of Brentwood lay almost under the house, on the
other side of the deep little ravine, down which a stream –
which ought to have been a lovely, wild, and frolicsome little
river – flowed between its rocks and trees. The river, like so
many in that district, had, however, in its earlier life been
sacrificed to trade, and was grimy with paper-making.[6] But this
did not affect our pleasure in it so much as I have known it to

affect other streams. Perhaps our water was more rapid – perhaps less clogged with dirt and refuse. Our side of the dell was charmingly *accidenté*, and clothed with fine trees, through which various paths wound down to the river-side and to the village bridge which crossed the stream.[7] The village lay in the hollow, and climbed, with very prosaic houses, the other side. Village architecture does not flourish in Scotland. The blue slates and the grey stone are sworn foes to the picturesque; and though I do not, for my own part, dislike the interior of an old-fashioned pewed and galleried church, with its little family settlements on all sides, the square box outside, with its bit of a spire like a handle to lift it by, is not an improvement to the landscape. Still a cluster of houses on differing elevations – with scraps of garden coming in between, a hedgerow with clothes laid out to dry, the opening of a street with its rural sociability, the women at their doors, the slow waggon lumbering along – gives a centre to the landscape. It was cheerful to look at, and convenient in a hundred ways. Within ourselves we had walks in plenty, the glen being always beautiful in all its phases, whether the woods were green in the spring or ruddy in the autumn. In the park which surrounded the house were the ruins of the former mansion of Brentwood, a much smaller and less important house than the solid Georgian edifice which we inhabited. The ruins were picturesque, however, and gave importance to the place. Even we, who were but temporary tenants, felt a vague pride in them, as if they somehow reflected a certain consequence upon ourselves. The old building had the remains of a tower, an indistinguishable mass of mason-work, overgrown with ivy, and the shells of walls attached to this were half filled up with soil. I had never examined it closely, I am ashamed to say. There was a large room, or what had been a large room, with the lower part of the windows still existing, on the principal floor, and underneath other windows, which were perfect, though half filled up with fallen soil, and waving with a wild growth of brambles and chance growths of all kinds. This was the oldest part of all. At a little distance were some very commonplace and disjointed fragments of building, one of them suggesting a certain pathos by its very commonness and the complete wreck which it showed. This was the end of a low gable, a bit of grey wall, all encrusted with lichens, in which was a common doorway. Probably it had been a servants' entrance, a back-door, or opening into what are called 'the offices' in Scotland.[8] No offices remained to be entered – pantry and kitchen had all been swept out of being; but there stood the doorway open and vacant, free to all the winds, to the rabbits, and every wild creature. It struck my eye, the first time I went to Brentwood, like a melancholy comment upon a life that was over. A door that led to nothing – closed once, perhaps, with anxious care, bolted and guarded, now void of any meaning. It impressed me, I remember, from the first; so perhaps it may be said that my mind was prepared to attach to it an importance which nothing justified.

The summer was a very happy period of repose for us all. The warmth of Indian suns was still in our veins. It seemed to us that we could never have enough of the greenness, the dewiness, the freshness of the northern landscape. Even its mists were pleasant to us, taking all the fever out of us, and pouring in vigour and refreshment. In autumn we followed the fashion of the time, and went away for change which we did not in the least require. It was when the family had settled down for the winter, when the days were short and dark, and the rigorous reign of frost upon us, that the incidents occurred which alone could justify me in intruding upon the world my private affairs. These incidents were, however, of so curious a character, that I hope my inevitable references to my own family and pressing personal interests will meet with a general pardon.

I was absent in London when these events began. In London an old Indian plunges back into the interests with which all his previous life has been associated, and meets old friends at every step. I had been circulating among some half-dozen of these – enjoying the return to my former life in shadow, though I had been so thankful in substance to throw it aside – and had missed some of my home letters, what with going down from Friday to Monday to old Benbow's place in the country, and stopping on the way back to dine and sleep at Sellar's and to take a look into Cross's stables, which occupied another day. It is never safe to miss one's letters. In this transitory life, as the Prayer-book says, how can one ever be certain what is going to happen?' All was well at home. I knew exactly (I thought) what they would have to say to me: 'The weather has been so fine, that Roland has not once gone by train, and he enjoys the ride beyond anything.' 'Dear papa, be sure that you don't forget anything, but bring us so-and-so, and so-and-so' – a list as long as my arm. Dear girls and dearer mother! I would not for the world have forgotten their commissions, or lost their little letters, for all the Benbows and Crosses in the world.

But I was confident in my home-comfort and peacefulness. When I got back to my club, however, three or four letters were lying for me, upon some of which I noticed the 'immediate,' 'urgent,' which old-fashioned people and anxious people still believe will influence the post-office and quicken the speed of the mails. I was about to open one of these, when the club porter brought me two telegrams, one of which, he said, had arrived the night before. I opened, as was to be expected, the last first, and this was what I read: 'Why don't you come or answer? For God's sake, come. He is much worse.' This was a thunderbolt to fall upon a man's head who had one only son, and he the light of his eyes! The other telegram, which I opened with hands trembling so much that I lost time by my haste, was to much the same purport: 'No better; doctor afraid of brain-fever. Calls for you day and night. Let nothing detain you.' The first thing I did was to look up the time-tables to see if there was any way of getting off sooner than by the night-train, though I knew well enough there was not; and then I read the letters, which furnished, alas! too clearly, all the details. They told me that the boy had been pale for some time, with a scared look. His mother had noticed it before I left home, but would not say anything to alarm me. This look had increased day by day; and soon it was observed that Roland came home at a wild gallop through the park, his pony panting and in foam, himself 'as white as a sheet,' but with the perspiration streaming from his forehead. For a long time he had resisted all question-ing, but at length had developed such strange changes of mood, showing a reluctance to go to school, a desire to be fetched in the carriage at night – which was a ridiculous piece of luxury – an unwillingness to go out into the grounds, and nervous start at every sound, that his mother had insisted upon an explanation.

When the boy – our boy Roland, who had never known what fear was – began to talk to her of voices he had heard in the park, and shadows that had appeared to him among the ruins, my wife promptly put him to bed and sent for Dr Simson – which, of course, was the only thing to do.

I hurried off that evening, as may be supposed with an anxious heart. How I got through the hours before the starting of the train, I cannot tell. We must all be thankful for the quickness of the railway when in anxiety; but to have thrown myself into a post-chaise as soon as horses could be put to, would have been a relief. I got to Edinburgh very early in the blackness of the winter morning, and scarcely dared look the man in the face, at whom I gasped 'What news?' My wife had sent the brougham for me, which I concluded, before the man spoke, was a bad sign.[10] His answer was that stereotyped answer which leaves the imagination so wildly free – 'Just the same.' Just the same! What might that mean? The horses seemed to me to creep along the long dark country-road. As we dashed through the park, I thought I heard some one moaning among the trees, and clenched my fist at him (whoever he might be) with fury. Why had the fool of a woman at the gate allowed any one to come in to disturb the quiet of the place? If I had not been in such hot haste to get home, I think I should have stopped the carriage and got out to see what tramp it was that had made an entrance, and chosen my grounds, of all places in the world, – when my boy was ill! – to grumble and groan in. But I had no reason to complain of our slow pace here. The horses flew like lightning along the intervening path, and drew up at the door all panting, as if they had run a race. My wife stood waiting to receive me with a pale face, and a candle in her hand, which made her look paler still as the wind blew the flame about. 'He is sleeping,' she said in a whisper, as if her voice might wake him. And I replied, when I could find my voice, also in a whisper, as though the jingling of the horses' furniture and the sound of their hoofs must not have been more dangerous. I stood on the steps with her a moment, almost afraid to go in, now that I was here; and it seemed to me that I saw without observing, if I may say so, that the horses were unwilling to turn round, though their stables lay that way, or that the men were unwilling. These things occurred to me afterwards, though at the moment I was not capable of anything but to ask questions and to hear of the condition of the boy.

I looked at him from the door of his room, for we were afraid to go near, lest we should disturb that blessed sleep. It looked like actual sleep – not the lethargy into which my wife told me he would sometimes fall. She told me everything in the next room, which communicated with his, rising now and then and going to the door of communication; and in this there was much that was very startling and confusing to the mind. It appeared that ever since the winter began, since it was early dark, and night had fallen before his return from school, he had been hearing voices among the ruins – at first only a groaning, he said, at which his pony was as much alarmed as he was, but by degrees a voice. The tears ran down my wife's cheeks as she described to me how he would start up in the night and cry out, 'Oh, mother, let me in! oh, mother, let me in!' with a pathos which rent her heart. And she sitting there all the time, only longing to do everything his heart could desire! But though she would try to soothe him, crying, 'You are at home, my darling. I am here. Don't you know me? Your mother is here!' he would only stare at her, and after a while spring up again with the same cry. At other times he would be quite reasonable, she said, asking eagerly when I was coming, but declaring that he must go with me as soon as I did so, 'to let them in.' 'The doctor thinks his nervous system must have received a shock,' my wife said. 'Oh, Henry, can it be that we have pushed him on too much with his work – a delicate boy like Roland? – and what is his work in comparison with his health? Even you would think little of honours or prizes if it hurt the boy's health.' Even I! as if I were an inhuman father sacrificing my child to my ambition. But I would not increase her trouble by taking any notice. After a while they persuaded me to lie down, to rest, and to eat – none of which things had been possible since I received their letters. The mere fact of being on the spot, of course, in itself was a great thing; and when I knew that I could be called in a moment, as soon as he was awake and wanted me, I felt capable, even in the dark, chill morning twilight, to snatch an hour or two's sleep. As it happened, I

was so worn out with the strain of anxiety, and he so quieted
and consoled by knowing I had come, that I was not disturbed
till the afternoon, when the twilight had again settled down.
There was just daylight enough to see his face when I went to
him; and what a change in a fortnight! He was paler and more
worn, I thought, than even in those dreadful days in the plains
before we left India. His hair seemed to me to have grown long
and lank; his eyes were like blazing lights projecting out of his
white face. He got hold of my hand in a cold and tremulous
clutch, and waved to everybody to go away. 'Go away – even
mother,' he said, – 'go away.' This went to her heart, for she
did not like that even I should have more of the boy's confidence
than herself; but my wife has never been a woman to think of
herself, and she left us alone. 'Are they all gone?' he said,
eagerly. 'They would not let me speak. The doctor treated me
as if I were a fool. You know I am not a fool, papa.'

'Yes, yes, my boy, I know; but you are ill, and quiet is so necessary. You are not only not a fool, Roland, but you are reasonable and understand. When you are ill you must deny yourself;
you must not do everything that you might do being well.'

He waved his thin hand with a sort of indignation. 'Then,
father, I am not ill,' he cried. 'Oh, I thought when you came
you would not stop me, – you would see the sense of it! What
do you think is the matter with me, all of you? Simson is well
enough, but he is only a doctor. What do you think is the
matter with me? I am no more ill than you are. A doctor, of
course, he thinks you are ill the moment he looks at you – that's
what he's there for – and claps you into bed.'

'Which is the best place for you at present, my dear boy.'

'I made up my mind,' cried the little fellow, 'that I would
stand it till you came home. I said to myself, I won't frighten
mother and the girls. But now, father,' he cried, half jumping
out of bed, 'it's not illness, – it's a secret.'

His eyes shone so wildly, his face was so swept with strong
feeling, that my heart sank within me. It could be nothing but
fever that did it, and fever had been so fatal. I got him into my
arms to put him back into bed. 'Roland,' I said, humouring the
poor child, which I knew was the only way, 'if you are going
to tell me this secret to do any good, you know you must be

quite quiet, and not excite yourself. If you excite yourself,
I must not let you speak.'

'Yes, father,' said the boy. He was quiet directly, like a man,
as if he quite understood. When I had laid him back on his
pillow, he looked up at me with that grateful sweet look with
which children, when they are ill, break one's heart, the water
coming into his eyes in his weakness. 'I was sure as soon as you
were here you would know what to do,' he said.

'To be sure, my boy. Now keep quiet, and tell it all out like a
man.' To think I was telling lies to my own child! for I did it only
to humour him, thinking, poor little fellow, his brain was wrong.

'Yes, father. Father, there is some one in the park, – some
one that has been badly used.'

'Hush, my dear; you remember, there is to be no excitement.
Well, who is this somebody, and who has been ill-using him?
We will soon put a stop to that.'

'Ah,' cried Roland, 'but it is not so easy as you think. I don't
know who it is. It is just a cry. Oh, if you could hear it! It gets
into my head in my sleep. I heard it as clear – as clear; – and
they think that I am dreaming – or raving perhaps,' the boy
said, with a sort of disdainful smile.

This look of his perplexed me; it was less like fever than I
thought. 'Are you quite sure you have not dreamt it, Roland?'
I said.

'Dreamt? – that!' He was springing up again when he suddenly bethought himself, and lay down flat with the same sort
of smile on his face. 'The pony heard it too,' he said. 'She
jumped as if she had been shot. If I had not grasped at the reins,
– for I was frightened, father –'

'No shame to you, my boy,' said I, though I scarcely knew why.

'If I hadn't held to her like a leech, she'd have pitched me
over her head, and never drew breath till we were at the door.
Did the pony dream it?' he said, with a soft disdain, yet indulgence for my foolishness. Then he added slowly: 'It was only a
cry the first time, and all the time before you went away. I
wouldn't tell you, for it was so wretched to be frightened.
I thought it might be a hare or a rabbit snared, and I went in
the morning and looked, but there was nothing. It was after
you went I heard it really first, and this is what he says.' He

raised himself on his elbow close to me, and looked me in the face. '"Oh, mother, let me in! oh, mother, let me in!"' As he said the words a mist came over his face, the mouth quivered, the soft features all melted and changed, and when he had ended these pitiful words, dissolved in a shower of heavy tears.

Was it a hallucination? Was it the fever of the brain? Was it the disordered fancy caused by great bodily weakness? How could I tell? I thought it wisest to accept it as if it were all true.

'This is very touching, Roland,' I said.

'Oh, if you had just heard it, father! I said to myself, if father heard it he would do something; but mamma, you know, she's given over to Simson, and that fellow's a doctor, and never thinks of anything but clapping you into bed.'

'We must not blame Simson for being a doctor, Roland.'

'No, no,' said my boy, with delightful toleration and indulgence; 'oh no; that's the good of him – that's what he's for; I know that. But you – you are different; you are just father: and you'll do something, – directly, papa, directly, this very night.'

'Surely,' I said. 'No doubt it is some little lost child.'

He gave me a sudden, swift look, investigating my face as though to see whether, after all, this was everything my eminence as 'father' came to, – no more than that? Then he got hold of my shoulder, clutching it with his thin hand: 'Look here,' he said, with a quiver in his voice; 'suppose it wasn't – living at all!'

'My dear boy, how then could you have heard it?' I said.

He turned away from me with a pettish exclamation – 'As if you didn't know better than that!'

'Do you want to tell me it is a ghost?' I said.

Roland withdrew his hand; his countenance assumed an aspect of great dignity and gravity; a slight quiver remained about his lips. 'Whatever it was – you always said we were not to call names. It was something – in trouble. Oh, father, in terrible trouble!'

'But, my boy,' I said – I was at my wits' end – 'if it was a child that was lost, or any poor human creature – but, Roland, what do you want me to do?'

'I should know if I was you,' said the child, eagerly. 'That is what I always said to myself – Father will know. 'Oh, papa, papa, to have to face it night after night, in such terrible, terrible

trouble! and never to be able to do it any good. I don't want to
cry; it's like a baby, I know; but what can I do else? – out there
all by itself in the ruin, and nobody to help it. I can't bear it, I
can't bear it!' cried my generous boy. And in his weakness he
burst out, after many attempts to restrain it, into a great childish
fit of sobbing and tears.

I do not know that I ever was in a greater perplexity in my
life; and afterwards, when I thought of it, there was something
comic in it too. It is bad enough to find your child's mind
possessed with the conviction that he has seen – or heard – a
ghost. But that he should require you to go instantly and help
that ghost, was the most bewildering experience that had ever
come my way. I am a sober man myself, and not superstitious
– at least any more than everybody is superstitious. Of course
I do not believe in ghosts; but I don't deny, any more than
other people, that there are stories, which I cannot pretend to
understand. My blood got a sort of chill in my veins at the idea
that Roland should be a ghost-seer; for that generally means a
hysterical temperament and weak health, and all that men most
hate and fear for their children. But that I should take up his
ghost and right its wrongs, and save it from its trouble, was
such a mission as was enough to confuse any man. I did my
best to console my boy without giving any promise of this
astonishing kind; but he was too sharp for me. He would have
none of my caresses. With sobs breaking in at intervals upon
his voice, and the rain-drops hanging on his eyelids, he yet
returned to the charge.

'It will be there now – it will be there all the night. Oh think,
papa, think, if it was me! I can't rest for thinking of it. Don't!'
he cried, putting away my hand – 'don't! You go and help it,
and mother can take care of me.'

'But, Roland, what can I do?'

My boy opened his eyes, which were large with weakness
and fever, and gave me a smile such, I think, as sick children
only know the secret of. 'I was sure you would know as soon
as you came. I always said – Father will know: and mother,' he
cried, with a softening of repose upon his face, his limbs
relaxing, his form sinking with a luxurious ease in his bed –
'mother can come and take care of me.'

I called her, and saw him turn to her with the complete dependence of a child, and then I went away and left them, as perplexed a man as any in Scotland. I must say, however, I had this consolation, that my mind was greatly eased about Roland. He might be under a hallucination, but his head was clear enough, and I did not think him so ill as everybody else did. The girls were astonished even at the ease with which I took it. 'How do you think he is?' they said in a breath, coming round me, laying hold of me. 'Not half so ill as I expected,' I said; 'not very bad at all.' 'Oh, papa, you are a darling!' cried Agatha, kissing me, and crying upon my shoulder; while little Jeanie, who was as pale as Roland, clasped both her arms round mine, and could not speak at all. I knew nothing about it, not half so much as Simson: but they believed in me; they had a feeling that all would go right now. God is very good to you when your children look to you like that. It makes one humble, not proud. I was not worthy of it; and then I recollected that I had to act the part of a father to Roland's ghost, which made me almost laugh, though I might just as well have cried. It was the strangest mission that ever was intrusted to mortal man.

It was then I remembered suddenly the looks of the men when they turned to take the brougham to the stables in the dark that morning: they had not liked it, and the horses had not liked it. I remembered that even in my anxiety about Roland I had heard them tearing along the avenue back to the stables, and had made a memorandum mentally that I must speak of it. It seemed to me that the best thing I could do was to go to the stables now and make a few inquiries. It is impossible to fathom the minds of rustics; there might be some devilry of practical joking, for anything I knew; or they might have some interest in getting up a bad reputation for the Brentwood avenue. It was getting dark by the time I went out, and nobody who knows the country will need to be told how black is the darkness of a November night under high laurel-bushes and yew-trees. I walked into the heart of the shrubberies two or three times, not seeing a step before me, till I came out upon the broader carriage-road, where the trees opened a little, and there was a faint grey glimmer of sky visible, under which the great limes

and elms stood darkling like ghosts; but it grew black again as
I approached the corner where the ruins lay. Both eyes and ears
were on the alert, as may be supposed; but I could see nothing
in the absolute gloom, and, so far as I can recollect, I heard
nothing. Nevertheless there came a strong impression upon me
that somebody was there. It is a sensation which most people
have felt. I have seen when it has been strong enough to awake
me out of sleep, the sense of some one looking at me. I suppose
my imagination had been affected by Roland's story; and the
mystery of the darkness is always full of suggestions. I stamped
my feet violently on the gravel to rouse myself, and called out
sharply, 'Who's there?' Nobody answered, nor did I expect any
one to answer, but the impression had been made. I was so
foolish that I did not like to look back, but went sideways,
keeping an eye on the gloom behind. It was with great relief
that I spied the light in the stables, making a sort of oasis in the
darkness. I walked very quickly into the midst of that lighted
and cheerful place, and thought the clank of the groom's pail
one of the pleasantest sounds I had ever heard. The coachman
was the head of this little colony, and it was to his house I went
to pursue my investigations. He was a native of the district, and
had taken care of the place in the absence of the family for
years; it was impossible but that he must know everything that
was going on, and all the traditions of the place. The men, I
could see, eyed me anxiously when I thus appeared at such an
hour among them, and followed me with their eyes to Jarvis's
house, where he lived alone with his old wife, their children
being all married and out in the world. Mrs Jarvis met me with
anxious questions. How was the poor young gentleman? but
the others knew, I could see by their faces, that not even this
was the foremost thing in my mind.

'Noises? – ou ay, there'll be noises – the wind in the trees, and
the water soughing down the glen. As for tramps, Cornel, no,
there's little o' that kind o' cattle about here; and Merran
at the gate's a careful body.' Jarvis moved about with some
embarrassment from one leg to another as he spoke. He kept
in the shade, and did not look at me more than he could help.
Evidently his mind was perturbed, and he had reasons for

keeping his own counsel. His wife sat by, giving him a quick look now and then, but saying nothing. The kitchen was very snug, and warm, and bright – as different as could be from the chill and mystery of the night outside.

'I think you are trifling with me, Jarvis,' I said.

'Triflin', Cornel? no me. What would I trifle for? If the deevil himsel was in the auld hoose, I have no interest in't one way or another –'

'Sandy, hold your peace!' cried his wife, imperatively.

'And what am I to hold my peace for, wi' the Cornel standing there asking a' thae questions? I'm saying, if the deevil himself –'

'And I'm telling ye hold your peace!' cried the woman, in great excitement. 'Dark November weather and lang nichts, and us that ken a' we ken. How daur ye name – a name that shouldna be spoken?' She threw down her stocking and got up, also in great agitation. 'I tell't ye you never could keep it. It's no a thing that will hide; and the haill toun kens as weel as you or me. Tell the Cornel straight out – or see, I'll do it. I dinna hold wi' your secrets: and a secret that the haill toun kens!' She snapped her fingers with an air of large disdain. As for Jarvis, ruddy and big as he was, he shrank to nothing before this decided woman. He repeated to her two or three times her own adjuration, 'Hold your peace!' then, suddenly changing his tone, cried out, 'Tell him then, confound ye! I'll wash my hands o't. If a' the ghosts in Scotland were in the auld hoose, is that ony concern o' mine?'

After this I elicited without much difficulty the whole story. In the opinion of the Jarvises, and of everybody about, the certainty that the place was haunted was beyond all doubt. As Sandy and his wife warmed to the tale, one tripping up another in their eagerness to tell everything, it gradually developed as distinct a superstition as I ever heard, and not without poetry and pathos. How long it was since the voice had been heard first, nobody could tell with certainty. Jarvis's opinion was that his father, who had been coachman at Brentwood before him, had never heard anything about it, and that the whole thing had arisen within the last ten years, since the complete dismantling of the old house: which was a wonderfully modern date for a tale so well authenticated. According to these witnesses, and to several whom I questioned afterwards, and who were all in perfect agreement, it was only in the months of November and December that 'the visitation' occurred. During these months, the darkest of the year, scarcely a night passed without the recurrence of these inexplicable cries. Nothing, it was said, had ever been seen – at least nothing that could be identified. Some people, bolder or more imaginative than the others, had seen the darkness moving, Mrs Jarvis said, with unconscious poetry. It began when night fell, and continued, at intervals, till day broke. Very often it was only an inarticulate cry and moan-ing, but sometimes the words which had taken possession of my poor boy's fancy had been distinctly audible – 'Oh, mother, let me in!' The Jarvises were not aware that there had ever been any investigation into it. The estate of Brentwood had lapsed into the hands of a distant branch of the family, who had lived but little there; and of the many people who had taken it, as I had done, few had remained through two Decembers. And nobody had taken the trouble to make a very close examination into the facts. 'No, no,' Jarvis said, shaking his head, 'no, no, Cornel. Wha wad set themsels up for a laughin'-stock to a' the country-side, making a wark about a ghost? Naebody believes in ghosts. It bid to be the wind in the trees, the last gentleman said, or some effec' o' the water wrastlin' among the rocks. He said it was a' quite easy explained: but he gave up the hoose. And when you cam, Cornel, we were awfu' anxious you should never hear. What for should I have spoiled the bargain and hairmed the property for no-thing?'

'Do you call my child's life nothing?' I said in the trouble of the moment, unable to restrain myself. 'And instead of telling this all to me, you have told it to him – to a delicate boy, a child unable to sift evidence, or judge for himself, a tender-hearted young creature –'

I was walking about the room with an anger all the hotter that I felt it to be most likely quite unjust. My heart was full of bitterness against the stolid retainers of a family who were content to risk other people's children and comfort rather than let a house lie empty. If I had been warned I might have taken precautions, or left the place, or sent Roland away, a hundred

things which now I could not do; and here I was with my boy
in a brain-fever, and his life, the most precious life on earth,
hanging in the balance, dependent on whether or not I could
get to the reason of a commonplace ghost-story! I paced about
in high wrath, not seeing what I was to do; for, to take Roland
away, even if he were able to travel, would not settle his agitated
mind; and I feared even that a scientific explanation of refracted
sound, or reverberation, or any other of the easy certainties
with which we elder men are silenced, would have very little
effect upon the boy.[11]

'Cornel,' said Jarvis, solemnly, 'and *she'll* bear me witness –
the young gentleman never heard a word from me – no, nor
from either groom or gardener; I'll gie ye my word for that. In
the first place, he's no a lad that invites ye to talk. There are
some that are, and some that arena. Some will draw ye on, till
ye've tellt them a' the clatter of the toun, and a' ye ken, and
whiles mair. But Maister Roland, his mind's fu' of his books.
He's aye civil and kind, and a fine lad; but no that sort. And ye
see it's for a' our interest, Cornel, that you should stay at
Brentwood. I took it upon me mysel to pass the word – "No
a syllable to Maister Roland, nor to the young leddies –
no a syllable." The women-servants, that have little reason to
be out at night, ken little or nothing about it. And some think
it grand to have a ghost so long as they're no in the way of
coming across it. If you had been tellt the story to begin with,
maybe ye would have thought so yourself.'

This was true enough, though it did not throw any light
upon my perplexity. If we had heard of it to start with, it is
possible that all the family would have considered the possession of a ghost a distinct advantage. It is the fashion of the
times. We never think what a risk it is to play with young
imaginations, but cry out, in the fashionable jargon, 'A ghost!
– nothing else was wanted to make it perfect.' I should not have
been above this myself. I should have smiled, of course, at the
idea of the ghost at all, but then to feel that it was mine would
have pleased my vanity. Oh yes, I claim no exemption. The
girls would have been delighted. I could fancy their eagerness,
their interest, and excitement. No; if we had been told, it would
have done no good – we should have made the bargain all the

more eagerly, the fools that we are. 'And there has been no
attempt to investigate it,' I said, 'to see what it really is?'

'Eh, Cornel,' said the coachman's wife, 'wha would investigate, as ye call it, a thing that nobody believes in? Ye would be
the laughin'-stock of a' the country-side, as my man says.'

'But you believe in it,' I said, turning upon her hastily. The
woman was taken by surprise. She made a step backward out
of my way.

'Lord, Cornel, how ye frichten a body! Me! – there's awfu'
strange things in this world. An unlearned person doesna ken
what to think. But the minister and the gentry they just laugh
in your face. Inquire into the thing that is not! Na, na, we just
let it be.'

'Come with me, Jarvis,' I said, hastily, 'and we'll make an
attempt at least. Say nothing to the men or to anybody. I'll
come back after dinner, and we'll make a serious attempt to
see what it is, if it is anything. If I hear it – which I doubt – you
may be sure I shall never rest till I make it out. Be ready for me
about ten o'clock.'

'Me, Cornel!' Jarvis said, in a faint voice. I had not been
looking at him in my own preoccupation, but when I did so, I
found that the greatest change had come over the fat and ruddy
coachman. 'Me, Cornel!' he repeated, wiping the perspiration
from his brow. His ruddy face hung in flabby folds, his knees
knocked together, his voice seemed half extinguished in his
throat. Then he began to rub his hands and smile upon me in
a deprecating, imbecile way. 'There's nothing I wouldna do to
pleasure ye, Cornel,' taking a step further back. 'I'm sure, *she*
kens I've aye said I never had to do with a mair fair, weel-spoken
gentleman –' Here Jarvis came to a pause, again looking at me,
rubbing his hands.

'Well?' I said.

'But eh, sir!' he went on, with the same imbecile yet insinuat-
ing smile, 'if ye'll reflect that I am no used to my feet. With a
horse atween my legs, or the reins in my hand, I'm maybe nae
worse than other men; but on fit, Cornel – It's no the – bogles;
– but I've been cavalry, ye see,' with a little hoarse laugh, 'a'
my life. To face a thing ye didna understan' – on your feet,
Cornel.'

'Well, sir, if *I* do it,' said I tartly, 'why shouldn't you?'

'Eh, Cornel, there's an awfu' difference. In the first place, ye tramp about the haill country-side, and think naething of it; but a walk tires me mair than a hunard miles' drive: and then ye're a gentleman, and do your ain pleasure; and you're no so auld as me; and it's for your ain bairn, ye see, Cornel; and then –'

'He believes in it, Cornel, and you dinna believe in it,' the woman said.

'Will you come with me?' I said, turning to her.

She jumped back, upsetting her chair in her bewilderment. 'Me!' with a scream, and then fell into a sort of hysterical laugh. 'I wouldna say but what I would go; but what would the folk say to hear of Cornel Mortimer with an auld silly woman at his heels?'

The suggestion made me laugh too, though I had little inclination for it. 'I'm sorry you have so little spirit, Jarvis,' I said. 'I must find some one else, I suppose.'

Jarvis, touched by this, began to remonstrate, but I cut him short. My butler was a soldier who had been with me in India, and was not supposed to fear anything – man or devil, – certainly not the former; and I felt that I was losing time. The Jarvises were too thankful to get rid of me. They attended me to the door with the most anxious courtesies. Outside, the two grooms stood close by, a little confused by my sudden exit. I don't know if perhaps they had been listening – at least standing as near as possible, to catch any scrap of the conversation. I waved my hand to them as I went past, in answer to their salutations, and it was very apparent to me that they also were glad to see me go.

And it will be thought very strange, but it would be weak not to add, that I myself, though bent on the investigation I have spoken of, pledged to Roland to carry it out, and feeling that my boy's health, perhaps his life, depended on the result of my inquiry, – I felt the most unaccountable reluctance to pass these ruins on my way home. My curiosity was intense; and yet it was all my mind could do to pull my body along. I daresay the scientific people would describe it the other way, and attribute my cowardice to the state of my stomach. I went

on; but if I had followed my impulse, I should have turned and
bolted. Everything in me seemed to cry out against it; my heart
thumped, my pulses all began, like sledge-hammers, beating
against my ears and every sensitive part. It was very dark, as I
have said; the old house, with its shapeless tower, loomed a
heavy mass through the darkness, which was only not entirely
so solid as itself. On the other hand, the great dark cedars of
which we were so proud seemed to fill up the night. My foot
strayed out of the path in my confusion and the gloom together,
and I brought myself up with a cry as I felt myself knock against
something solid. What was it? The contact with hard stone and
lime, and prickly bramble-bushes restored me a little to myself.
'Oh, it's only the old gable,' I said aloud, with a little laugh to
reassure myself. The rough feeling of the stones reconciled me.
As I groped about thus, I shook off my visionary folly. What
so easily explained as that I should have strayed from the path
in the darkness? This brought me back to common existence,
as if I had been shaken by a wise hand out of all the silliness of
superstition. How silly it was, after all! What did it matter
which path I took? I laughed again, this time with better heart
– when suddenly, in a moment, the blood was chilled in my
veins, a shiver stole along my spine, my faculties seemed to
forsake me. Close by me at my side, at my feet, there was a
sigh. No, not a groan, not a moaning, not anything so tangible
– a perfectly soft, faint, inarticulate sigh. I sprang back, and my
heart stopped beating. Mistaken! no, mistake was impossible.
I heard it as clearly as I hear myself speak; a long, soft, weary
sigh, as if drawn to the utmost, and emptying out a load of
sadness that filled the breast. To hear this in the solitude, in the
dark, in the night (though it was still early), had an effect which
I cannot describe. I feel it now – something cold creeping over
me, up into my hair, and down to my feet, which refused to
move. I cried out, with a trembling voice, 'Who is there?' as
I had done before – but there was no reply.

I got home I don't quite know how; but in my mind there
was no longer any indifference as to the thing, whatever it was,
that haunted these ruins. My scepticism disappeared like a mist.
I was as firmly determined that there was something as Roland
was. I did not for a moment pretend to myself that it was

possible I could be deceived; there were movements and noises which I understood all about, cracklings of small branches in the frost, and little rolls of gravel on the path, such as have a very eerie sound sometimes, and perplex you with wonder as to who has done it, *when there is no real mystery*; but I assure you all these little movements of nature don't affect you one bit *when there is something*. I understood *them*. I did not understand the sigh. That was not simple nature; there was meaning in it – feeling, the soul of a creature invisible. This is the thing that human nature trembles at – a creature invisible, yet with sensations, feelings, a power somehow of expressing itself. I had not the same sense of unwillingness to turn my back upon the scene of the mystery which I had experienced in going to the stables; but I almost ran home, impelled by eagerness to get everything done that had to be done, in order to apply myself to finding it out. Bagley was in the hall as usual when I went in. He was always there in the afternoon, always with the appearance of perfect occupation, yet, so far as I know, never doing anything. The door was open, so that I hurried in without any pause, breathless; but the sight of his calm regard, as he came to help me off with my overcoat, subdued me in a moment. Anything out of the way, anything incomprehensible, faded to nothing in the presence of Bagley. You saw and wondered how *he* was made: the parting of his hair, the tie of his white neckcloth, the fit of his trousers, all perfect as works of art; but you could see how they were done, which makes all the difference. I flung myself upon him, so to speak, without waiting to note the extreme unlikeness of the man to anything of the kind I meant. 'Bagley,' I said, 'I want you to come out with me to-night to watch for – '

'Poachers, Colonel,' he said, a gleam of pleasure running all over him.

'No, Bagley; a great deal worse,' I cried.

'Yes, Colonel; at what hour, sir?' the man said; but then I had not told him what it was.

It was ten o'clock when we set out. All was perfectly quiet indoors. My wife was with Roland, who had been quite calm, she said, and who (though, no doubt, the fever must run its course) had been better ever since I came. I told Bagley to put on a thick greatcoat over his evening coat, and did the same myself – with strong boots; for the soil was like a sponge, or worse. Talking to him, I almost forgot what we were going to do. It was darker even than it had been before, and Bagley kept very close to me as we went along. I had a small lantern in my hand, which gave us a partial guidance. We had come to the corner where the path turns. On one side was the bowling-green, which the girls had taken possession of for their croquet-ground – a wonderful enclosure surrounded by high hedges of holly, three hundred years old and more; on the other, the ruins. Both were black as night; but before we got so far, there was a little opening in which we could just discern the trees and the lighter line of the road. I thought it best to pause there and take breath. 'Bagley,' I said, 'there is something about these ruins I don't understand. It is there I am going. Keep your eyes open and your wits about you. Be ready to pounce upon any stranger you see – anything, man or woman. Don't hurt, but seize – anything you see.' 'Colonel,' said Bagley, with a little tremor in his breath, 'they do say there's things there – as is neither man nor woman.' There was no time for words. 'Are you game to follow me, my man? that's the question,' I said. Bagley fell in without a word, and saluted. I knew then I had nothing to fear.

We went, so far as I could guess, exactly as I had come, when I heard that sigh. The darkness, however, was so complete that all marks, as of trees or paths, disappeared. One moment we felt our feet on the gravel, another sinking noiselessly into the slippery grass, that was all. I had shut up my lantern, not wishing to scare any one, whoever it might be. Bagley followed, it seemed to me, exactly in my footsteps as I made my way, as I supposed, towards the mass of the ruined house. We seemed to take a long time groping along seeking this; the squash of the wet soil under our feet was the only thing that marked our progress. After a while I stood still to see, or rather feel, where we were. The darkness was very still, but no stiller than is usual in a winter's night. The sounds I have mentioned – the crackling of twigs, the roll of a pebble, the sound of some rustle in the dead leaves, or creeping creature on the grass – were audible when you listened, all mysterious enough when your mind is disengaged, but to me cheering now as signs of the livingness of nature, even in the death of the frost. As we stood still there came up from the trees in the glen the prolonged hoot of an owl. Bagley started with alarm, being in a state of general nervousness, and not knowing what he was afraid of. But to me the sound was encouraging and pleasant, being so comprehensible. 'An owl,' I said, under my breath. 'Y-es, Colonel,' said Bagley, his teeth chattering. We stood still about five minutes, while it broke into the still brooding of the air, the sound widening out in circles, dying upon the darkness. This sound, which is not a cheerful one, made me almost gay. It was natural, and relieved the tension of the mind. I moved on with new courage, my nervous excitement calming down.

When all at once, quite suddenly, close to us, at our feet, there broke out a cry. I made a spring backwards in the first moment of surprise and horror, and in doing so came sharply against the same rough masonry and brambles that had struck me before. This new sound came upwards from the ground – a low, moaning, wailing voice, full of suffering and pain. The contrast between it and the hoot of the owl was indescribable; the one with a wholesome wildness and naturalness that hurt nobody – the other, a sound that made one's blood curdle, full of human misery. With a great deal of fumbling – for in spite of everything I could do to keep up my courage my hands shook – I managed to remove the slide of my lantern. The light leaped out like something living, and made the place visible in a moment. We were what would have been inside the ruined building had anything remained but the gable-wall which I have described. It was close to us, the vacant doorway in it going out straight into the blackness outside. The light showed the bit of wall, the ivy glistening upon it in clouds of dark green, the bramble-branches waving, and below, the open door – a door that led to nothing. It was from this the voice came which died out just as the light flashed upon this strange scene. There was a moment's silence, and then it broke forth again. The sound was so near, so penetrating, so pitiful, that, in the nervous start I gave, the light fell out of my hand. As I groped for it in the dark my hand was clutched by Bagley, who I think must have dropped upon his knees; but I was too much perturbed myself

to think much of this. He clutched at me in the confusion of
his terror, forgetting all his usual decorum. 'For God's sake,
what is it, sir?' he gasped. If I yielded, there was evidently an
end of both of us. 'I can't tell,' I said, 'any more than you; that's
what we've got to find out: up, man, up!' I pulled him to his
feet. 'Will you go round and examine the other side, or will you
stay here with the lantern?' Bagley gasped at me with a face of
horror. 'Can't we stay together, Colonel?' he said – his knees
were trembling under him. I pushed him against the corner of
the wall, and put the light into his hands. 'Stand fast till I come
back; shake yourself together, man; let nothing pass you,' I
said. The voice was within two or three feet of us, of that there
could be no doubt.

I went myself to the other side of the wall, keeping close to
it. The light shook in Bagley's hand, but, tremulous though it
was, shone out through the vacant door, one oblong block of
light marking all the crumbling corners and hanging masses of
foliage. Was that something dark huddled in a heap by the side
of it? I pushed forward across the light in the doorway, and fell
upon it with my hands; but it was only a juniper-bush growing
close against the wall. Meanwhile, the sight of my figure crossing the doorway had brought Bagley's nervous excitement to a
height: he flew at me, gripping my shoulder. 'I've got him,
Colonel! I've got him!' he cried, with a voice of sudden exultation. He thought it was a man, and was at once relieved. But
at that moment the voice burst forth again between us, at our
feet – more close to us than any separate being could be. He
dropped off from me, and fell against the wall, his jaw dropping
as if he were dying. I suppose, at the same moment, he saw that
it was me whom he had clutched. I, for my part, had scarcely
more command of myself. I snatched the light out of his hand,
and flashed it all about me wildly. Nothing, – the juniper-bush
which I thought I had never seen before, the heavy growth of
the glistening ivy, the brambles waving. It was close to my ears
now, crying, crying, pleading as if for life. Either I heard the
same words Roland had heard, or else, in my excitement, his
imagination got possession of mine. The voice went on, growing
into distinct articulation, but wavering about, now from one
point, now from another, as if the owner of it were moving

slowly back and forward. 'Mother! mother!' and then an outburst of wailing. As my mind steadied, getting accustomed (as
one's mind gets accustomed to anything), it seemed to me as if
some uneasy, miserable creature was pacing up and down
before a closed door. Sometimes – but that must have been
excitement – I thought I heard a sound like knocking, and then
another burst, 'Oh, mother! mother!' All this close, close to the
space where I was standing with my lantern – now before me,
now behind me: a creature restless, unhappy, moaning, crying,
before the vacant doorway, which no one could either shut or
open more.

'Do you hear it, Bagley? do you hear what it is saying?' I
cried, stepping in through the doorway. He was lying against
the wall – his eyes glazed, half dead with terror. He made a
motion of his lips as if to answer me, but no sounds came;
then lifted his hand with a curious imperative movement as if
ordering me to be silent and listen. And how long I did so I
cannot tell. It began to have an interest, an exciting hold upon
me, which I could not describe. It seemed to call up visibly a
scene any one could understand – a something shut out, restlessly wandering to and fro; sometimes the voice dropped, as if
throwing itself down – sometimes wandered off a few paces,
growing sharp and clear. 'Oh, mother, let me in! oh, mother,
mother, let me in! oh, let me in!' every word was clear to me.
No wonder the boy had gone wild with pity. I tried to steady
my mind upon Roland, upon his conviction that I could do
something, but my head swam with the excitement, even when
I partially overcame the terror. At last the words died away,
and there was a sound of sobs and moaning. I cried out, 'In the
name of God who are you?' with a kind of feeling in my mind
that to use the name of God was profane, seeing that I did not
believe in ghosts or anything supernatural; but I did it all the
same, and waited, my heart giving a leap of terror lest there
should be a reply. Why this should have been I cannot tell, but I
had a feeling that if there was an answer it would be more than
I could bear. But there was no answer; the moaning went on, and
then, as if it had been real, the voice rose a little higher again, the
words recommenced, 'Oh, mother, let me in! oh, mother, let me
in!' with an expression that was heart-breaking to hear.

As if it had been real! What do I mean by that? I suppose I
got less alarmed as the thing went on. I began to recover the
use of my senses – I seemed to explain it all to myself by saying
that this had once happened, that it was a recollection of a
real scene. Why there should have seemed something quite
satisfactory and composing in this explanation I cannot tell,
but so it was. I began to listen almost as if it had been a play,
forgetting Bagley, who, I almost think, had fainted, leaning
against the wall. I was startled out of this strange spectatorship
that had fallen upon me by the sudden rush of something which
made my heart jump once more, a large black figure in the
doorway waving its arms. 'Come in! come in! come in!' it shouted
out hoarsely at the top of a deep bass voice, and then poor Bagley
fell down senseless across the threshold. He was less sophisticated than I, – he had not been able to bear it any longer. I took
him for something supernatural, as he took me, and it was some
time before I awoke to the necessities of the moment. I remembered only after, that from the time I began to give my attention
to the man, I heard the other voice no more. It was some time
before I brought him to. It must have been a strange scene; the
lantern making a luminous spot in the darkness, the man's
white face lying on the black earth, I over him, doing what I
could for him. Probably I should have been thought to be
murdering him had any one seen us. When at last I succeeded
in pouring a little brandy down his throat, he sat up and looked
about him wildly. 'What's up?' he said; then recognizing me,
tried to struggle to his feet with a faint 'Beg your pardon,
Colonel.' I got him home as best I could, making him lean upon
my arm. The great fellow was as weak as a child. Fortunately
he did not for some time remember what had happened. From
the time Bagley fell the voice had stopped, and all was still.

'You've got an epidemic in your house, Colonel,' Simson said
to me next morning. 'What's the meaning of it all? Here's your
butler raving about a voice. This will never do, you know; and
so far as I can make out, you are in it too.'

'Yes, I am in it, doctor. I thought I had better speak to you.
Of course you are treating Roland all right – but the boy is not
raving, he is as sane as you or me. It's all true.'

'As sane as – I – or you. I never thought the boy insane. He's got cerebral excitement, fever. I don't know what you've got. There's something very queer about the look of your eyes.'

'Come,' said I, 'you can't put us all to bed, you know. You had better listen and hear the symptoms in full.'

The doctor shrugged his shoulders, but he listened to me patiently. He did not believe a word of the story, that was clear; but he heard it all from beginning to end. 'My dear fellow,' he said, 'the boy told me just the same. It's an epidemic. When one person falls a victim to this sort of thing, it's as safe as can be – there's always two or three.'

'Then how do you account for it?' I said.

'Oh, account for it! – that's a different matter; there's no accounting for the freaks our brains are subject to. If it's delusion; if it's some trick of the echoes or the winds – some phonetic disturbance or other –'[12]

'Come with me to-night, and judge for yourself,' I said.

Upon this he laughed aloud, then said, 'That's not such a bad idea; but it would ruin me for ever if it were known that John Simson was ghost-hunting.'

'There it is,' said I; 'you dart down on us who are unlearned with your phonetic disturbances, but you daren't examine what the thing really is for fear of being laughed at. That's science!'

'It's not science – it's common-sense,' said the doctor. 'The thing has delusion on the front of it. It is encouraging an unwholesome tendency even to examine. What good could come of it? Even if I am convinced, I shouldn't believe.'

'I should have said so yesterday; and I don't want you to be convinced or to believe,' said I. 'If you prove it to be a delusion, I shall be very much obliged to you for one. Come; somebody must go with me.'

'You are cool,' said the doctor. 'You've disabled this poor fellow of yours, and made him – on that point – a lunatic for life; and now you want to disable me. But for once, I'll do it. To save appearance, if you'll give me a bed, I'll come over after my last rounds.'

It was agreed that I should meet him at the gate, and that we should visit the scene of last night's occurrences before we came to the house, so that nobody might be the wiser. It was scarcely

possible to hope that the cause of Bagley's sudden illness should
not somehow steal into the knowledge of the servants at least,
and it was better that all should be done as quietly as possible.
The day seemed to me a very long one. I had to spend a certain
part of it with Roland, which was a terrible ordeal for me – for
what could I say to the boy? The improvement continued,
but he was still in a very precarious state, and the trembling
vehemence with which he turned to me when his mother left
the room filled me with alarm. 'Father?' he said, quietly. 'Yes,
my boy; I am giving my best attention to it – all is being done
that I can do. I have not come to any conclusion – yet. I am
neglecting nothing you said,' I cried. What I could not do was
to give his active mind any encouragement to dwell upon the
mystery. It was a hard predicament, for some satisfaction had
to be given him. He looked at me very wistfully, with the great
blue eyes which shone so large and brilliant out of his white
and worn face. 'You must trust me,' I said. 'Yes, father. Father
understands,' he said to himself, as if to soothe some inward
doubt. I left him as soon as I could. He was about the most
precious thing I had on earth, and his health my first thought;
but yet somehow, in the excitement of this other subject, I put
that aside, and preferred not to dwell upon Roland, which was
the most curious part of it all.

That night at eleven I met Simson at the gate. He had come
by train, and I let him in gently myself. I had been so much
absorbed in the coming experiment that I passed the ruins in
going to meet him, almost without thought, if you can understand that. I had my lantern; and he showed me a coil of taper
which he had ready for use. 'There is nothing like light,' he
said, in his scoffing tone. It was a very still night, scarcely a
sound, but not so dark. We could keep the path without difficulty as we went along. As we approached the spot we could
hear a low moaning, broken occasionally by a bitter cry. 'Perhaps that is your voice,' said the doctor; 'I thought it must be
something of the kind. That's a poor brute caught in some of
these infernal traps of yours; you'll find it among the bushes
somewhere.' I said nothing. I felt no particular fear, but a
triumphant satisfaction in what was to follow. I led him to the
spot where Bagley and I had stood on the previous night. All

was silent as a winter night could be – so silent that we heard far off the sound of the horses in the stables, the shutting of a window at the house. Simson lighted his taper and went peering about, poking into all the corners. We looked like two conspirators lying in wait for some unfortunate traveller; but not a sound broke the quiet. The moaning had stopped before we came up; a star or two shone over us in the sky, looking down as if surprised at our strange proceedings. Dr Simson did nothing but utter subdued laughs under his breath. 'I thought as much,' he said. 'It is just the same with tables and all other kinds of ghostly apparatus; a sceptic's presence stops everything. When I am present nothing ever comes off. How long do you think it will be necessary to stay here? Oh, I don't complain; only, when *you* are satisfied, *I* am – quite.'

I will not deny that I was disappointed beyond measure by this result. It made me look like a credulous fool. It gave the doctor such a pull over me as nothing else could. I should point all his morals for years to come, and his materialism, his scepticism, would be increased beyond endurance. 'It seems, indeed,' I said, 'that there is to be no –' 'Manifestation,' he said, laughing; 'that is what all the mediums say.[13] No manifestations, in consequence of the presence of an unbeliever.' His laugh sounded very uncomfortable to me in the silence; and it was now near midnight. But that laugh seemed the signal; before it died away the moaning we had heard before was resumed. It started from some distance off, and came towards us, nearer and nearer, like some one walking along and moaning to himself. There could be no idea now that it was a hare caught in a trap. The approach was slow, like that of a weak person with little halts and pauses. We heard it coming along the grass straight towards the vacant doorway. Simson had been a little startled by the first sound. He said hastily, 'That child has no business to be out so late.' But he felt, as well as I, that this was no child's voice. As it came nearer, he grew silent, and, going to the doorway with his taper, stood looking out towards the sound. The taper being unprotected blew about in the night air, though there was scarcely any wind. I threw the light of my lantern steady and white across the same space. It was in a blaze of light in the midst of the blackness. A little icy thrill had

gone over me at the first sound, but as it came close, I confess
that my only feeling was satisfaction. The scoffer could scoff
no more. The light touched his own face, and showed a very
perplexed countenance. If he was afraid, he concealed it with
great success, but he was perplexed. And then all that had
happened on the previous night was enacted once more. It fell
strangely upon me with a sense of repetition. Every cry, every
sob seemed the same as before. I listened almost without any
emotion at all in my own person, thinking of its effect upon
Simson. He maintained a very bold front on the whole. All that
coming and going of the voice was, if our ears could be trusted,
exactly in front of the vacant, blank doorway, blazing full of
light, which caught and shone in the glistening leaves of the
great hollies at a little distance. Not a rabbit could have crossed
the turf without being seen; – but there was nothing. After a
time, Simson, with a certain caution and bodily reluctance, as
it seemed to me, went out with his roll of taper into this space.
His figure showed against the holly in full outline. Just at this
moment the voice sank, as was its custom, and seemed to fling
itself down at the door. Simson recoiled violently, as if some
one had come up against him, then turned, and held his taper
low as if examining something. 'Do you see anybody?' I cried
in a whisper, feeling the chill of nervous panic steal over me at
this action. 'It's nothing but a – confounded juniper-bush,' he
said. This I knew very well to be nonsense, for the juniper-bush
was on the other side. He went about after this round and
round, poking his taper everywhere, then returned to me on
the inner side of the wall. He scoffed no longer; his face was
contracted and pale. 'How long does this go on?' he whispered
to me, like a man who does not wish to interrupt some one
who is speaking. I had become too much perturbed myself to
remark whether the successions and changes of the voice were
the same as last night. It suddenly went out in the air almost as
he was speaking, with a soft reiterated sob dying away. If there
had been anything to be seen, I should have said that the person
was at that moment crouching on the ground close to the door.

We walked home very silent afterwards. It was only when we
were in sight of the house that I said, 'What do you think of
it?' 'I can't tell what to think of it,' he said, quickly. He took –

though he was a very temperate man – not the claret I was going to offer him, but some brandy from the tray, and swallowed it almost undiluted. 'Mind you, I don't believe a word of it,' he said, when he had lighted his candle; 'but I can't tell what to think,' he turned round to add, when he was half-way up-stairs.

All of this, however, did me no good with the solution of my problem. I was to help this weeping, sobbing thing, which was already to me as distinct a personality as anything I knew – or what should I say to Roland? It was on my heart that my boy would die if I could not find some way of helping this creature. You may be surprised that I should speak of it in this way. I did not know if it was man or woman; but I no more doubted that it was a soul in pain than I doubted my own being; and it was my business to soothe this pain – to deliver it, if that was possible. Was ever such a task given to an anxious father trembling for his only boy? I felt in my heart, fantastic as it may appear, that I must fulfil this somehow, or part with my child; and you may conceive that rather than do that I was ready to die. But even my dying would not have advanced me – unless by bringing me into the same world with that seeker at the door.

Next morning Simson was out before breakfast, and came in with evident signs of the damp grass on his boots, and a look of worry and weariness, which did not say much for the night he had passed. He improved a little after breakfast, and visited his two patients, for Bagley was still an invalid. I went out with him on his way to the train, to hear what he had to say about the boy. 'He is going on very well,' he said; 'there are no complications as yet. But mind you, that's not a boy to be trifled with, Mortimer. Not a word to him about last night.' I had to tell him then of my last interview with Roland, and of the impossible demand he had made upon me – by which, though he tried to laugh, he was much discomposed, as I could see. 'We must just perjure ourselves all round,' he said, 'and swear you exorcised it;' but the man was too kind-hearted to be satisfied with that. 'It's frightfully serious for you, Mortimer. I can't laugh as I should like to. I wish I saw a way out of it, for your sake. By the way,' he added shortly, 'didn't you notice that juniper-bush on the left-hand side?' 'There was one on the right hand of the door. I noticed you made that mistake last night.' 'Mistake!' he cried, with a curious low laugh, pulling up the collar of his coat as though he felt the cold, – 'there's no juniper there this morning, left or right. Just go and see.' As he stepped into the train a few minutes after, he looked back upon me and beckoned me for a parting word. 'I'm coming back to-night,' he said.

I don't think I had any feeling about this as I turned away from that common bustle of the railway which made my private preoccupations feel so strangely out of date. There had been a distinct satisfaction in my mind before that his scepticism had been so entirely defeated. But the more serious part of the matter pressed upon me now. I went straight from the railway to the manse, which stood on a little plateau on the side of the river opposite to the woods of Brentwood. The minister was one of a class which is not so common in Scotland as it used to be. He was a man of good family, well educated in the Scotch way, strong in philosophy, not so strong in Greek, strongest of all in experience, – a man who had 'come across,' in the course of his life, most people of note that had ever been in Scotland – and who was said to be very sound in doctrine, without infringing the toleration with which old men, who are good men, are generally endowed. He was old-fashioned; perhaps he did not think so much about the troublous problems of theology as many of the young men, nor ask himself any hard questions about the Confession of Faith – but he understood human nature, which is perhaps better. He received me with a cordial welcome. 'Come away, Colonel Mortimer,' he said; 'I'm all the more glad to see you, that I feel it's a good sign for the boy. He's doing well? – God be praised – and the Lord bless him and keep him. He has many a poor body's prayers – and that can do nobody harm.'

'He will need them all, Dr Moncrieff,' I said, 'and your counsel too.' And I told him the story – more than I had told Simson. The old clergyman listened to me with many suppressed exclamations, and at the end the water stood in his eyes.

'That's just beautiful,' he said. 'I do not mind to have heard anything like it; it's as fine as Burns when he wished deliverance

to one – that is prayed for in no kirk.[14] Ay, ay! so he would
have you console the poor lost spirit? God bless the boy! There's
something more than common in that, Colonel Mortimer. And
also the faith of him in his father! – I would like to put that
into a sermon.' Then the old gentleman gave me an alarmed
look, and said, 'No, no; I was not meaning a sermon; but I
must write it down for the "Children's Record." '[15] I saw the
thought that passed through his mind. Either he thought, or he
feared I would think, of a funeral sermon. You may believe this
did not make me more cheerful.

I can scarcely say that Dr Moncrieff gave me any advice.
How could any one advise on such a subject? But he said, 'I
think I'll come too. I'm an old man; I'm less liable to be frighted
than those that are further off the world unseen. It behoves me
to think of my own journey there. I've no cut-and-dry beliefs
on the subject. I'll come too: and maybe at the moment the
Lord will put into our heads what to do.'

This gave me a little comfort – more than Simson had given
me. To be clear about the cause of it was not my grand desire.
It was another thing that was in my mind – my boy. As for the
poor soul at the open door, I had no more doubt, as I have
said, of its existence than I had of my own. It was no ghost to
me. I knew the creature, and it was in trouble. That was my
feeling about it, as it was Roland's. To hear it first was a great
shock to my nerves, but not now; a man will get accustomed
to anything. But to do something for it was the great problem;
how was I to be serviceable to a being that was invisible, that
was mortal no longer? 'Maybe at the moment the Lord will put
it into our heads.' This is very old-fashioned phraseology, and
a week before, most likely, I should have smiled (though always
with kindness) at Dr Moncrieff's credulity; but there was a
great comfort, whether rational or otherwise I cannot say, in
the mere sound of the words.

The road to the station and the village lay through the glen
– not by the ruins; but though the sunshine and the fresh air,
and the beauty of the trees, and the sound of the water were all
very soothing to the spirits, my mind was so full of my own
subject that I could not refrain from turning to the right hand
as I got to the top of the glen, and going straight to the place

which I may call the scene of all my thoughts. It was lying full in the sunshine, like all the rest of the world. The ruined gable looked due east, and in the present aspect of the sun the light streamed down through the doorway as our lantern had done, throwing a flood of light upon the damp grass beyond. There was a strange suggestion in the open door – so futile, a kind of emblem of vanity – all free around, so that you could go where you pleased, and yet that semblance of an enclosure – that way of entrance, unnecessary, leading to nothing. And why any creature should pray and weep to get in – to nothing: or be kept out – by nothing! You could not dwell upon it, or it made your brain go round. I remembered, however, what Simson said about the juniper, with a little smile on my own mind as to the inaccuracy of recollection, which even a scientific man will be guilty of. I could see now the light of my lantern gleaming upon the wet glistening surface of the spiky leaves at the right hand – and he ready to go to the stake for it that it was the left! I went round to make sure. And then I saw what he had said. Right or left there was no juniper at all. I was confounded by this, though it was entirely a matter of detail: nothing at all: a bush of brambles waving, the grass growing up to the very walls. But after all, though it gave me a shock for a moment, what did that matter? There were marks as if a number of footsteps had been up and down in front of the door; but these might have been our steps; and all was bright, and peaceful, and still. I poked about the other ruin – the larger ruins of the old house – for some time, as I had done before. There were marks upon the grass here and there, I could not call them footsteps, all about; but that told for nothing one way or another. I had examined the ruined rooms closely the first day. They were half filled up with soil and *débris*, withered brackens and bramble – no refuge for any one there. It vexed me that Jarvis should see me coming from that spot when he came up to me for his orders. I don't know whether my nocturnal expeditions had got wind among the servants. But there was a significant look in his face. Something in it I felt was like my own sensation when Simson in the midst of his scepticism was struck dumb. Jarvis felt satisfied that his veracity had been put beyond question. I never spoke to a servant of mine in such a peremptory tone before. I sent him away 'with a flea in his lug,' as the man described it afterwards. Interference of any kind was intolerable to me at such a moment.

But what was strangest of all was, that I could not face Roland. I did not go up to his room as I would have naturally done at once. This the girls could not understand. They saw there was some mystery in it. 'Mother has gone to lie down,' Agatha said; 'he has had such a good night.' 'But he wants you so, papa!' cried little Jeanie, always with her two arms embracing mine in a pretty way she had. I was obliged to go at last – but what could I say? I could only kiss him, and tell him to keep still – that I was doing all I could. There is something mystical about the patience of a child. 'It will come all right, won't it, father?' he said. 'God grant it may! I hope so, Roland.' 'Oh yes, it will come all right.' Perhaps he understood that in the midst of my anxiety I could not stay with him as I should have done otherwise. But the girls were more surprised than it is possible to describe. They looked at me with wondering eyes. 'If I were ill, papa, and you only stayed with me a moment, I should break my heart,' said Agatha. But the boy had a sympathetic feeling. He knew that of my own will I would not have done it. I shut myself up in the library, where I could not rest, but kept pacing up and down like a caged beast. What could I do? and if I could do nothing, what would become of my boy? These were the questions that, without ceasing, pursued each other through my mind.

Simson came out to dinner, and when the house was all still, and most of the servants in bed, we went out and met Dr Moncrieff, as we had appointed, at the head of the glen. Simson, for his part, was disposed to scoff at the Doctor. 'If there are to be any spells, you know, I'll cut the whole concern,' he said. I did not make him any reply. I had not invited him; he could go or come as he pleased. He was very talkative, far more so than suited my humour, as we went on. 'One thing is certain, you know, there must be some human agency,' he said. 'It is all bosh about apparitions. I never have investigated the laws of sound to any great extent, and there's a great deal in ventriloquism that we don't know much about.'[16] 'If it's the same to you,' I said, 'I wish you'd keep all that to yourself, Simson. It

doesn't suit my state of mind.' 'Oh, I hope I know how to
respect idiosyncrasy,' he said. The very tone of his voice irritated
me beyond measure. These scientific fellows, I wonder people
put up with them as they do, when you have no mind for their
cold-blooded confidence. Dr Moncrieff met us about eleven
o'clock, the same time as on the previous night. He was a large
man, with a venerable countenance and white hair – old, but
in full vigour, and thinking less of a cold night walk than many
a younger man. He had his lantern as I had. We were fully
provided with means of lighting the place, and we were all of
us resolute men. We had a rapid consultation as we went up,
and the result was that we divided to different posts. Dr Moncrieff remained inside the wall – if you can call that inside where
there was no wall but one. Simson placed himself on the side
next the ruins, so as to intercept any communication with the
old house, which was what his mind was fixed upon. I was
posted on the other side. To say that nothing could come near
without being seen was self-evident. It had been so also on the
previous night. Now, with our three lights in the midst of the
darkness, the whole place seemed illuminated. Dr Moncrieff's
lantern, which was a large one, without any means of shutting
up – an old-fashioned lantern with a pierced and ornamental
top – shone steadily, the rays shooting out of it upward into
the gloom. He placed it on the grass, where the middle of the
room, if this had been a room, would have been. The usual
effect of the light streaming out of the doorway was prevented
by the illumination which Simson and I on either side supplied.
With these differences, everything seemed as on the previous
night.

And what occurred was exactly the same, with the same air
of repetition, point for point, as I had formerly remarked. I
declare that it seemed to me as if I were pushed against, put
aside, by the owner of the voice as he paced up and down in
his trouble, – though these are perfectly futile words, seeing
that the stream of light from my lantern, and that from Simson's
taper, lay broad and clear, without a shadow, without the
smallest break, across the entire breadth of the grass. I had
ceased even to be alarmed, for my part. My heart was rent with
pity and trouble – pity for the poor suffering human creature

that moaned and pleaded so, and trouble for myself and my boy. God! if I could not find any help – and what help could I find? – Roland would die.

We were all perfectly still till the first outburst was exhausted, as I knew (by experience) it would be. Dr Moncrieff, to whom it was new, was quite motionless on the other side of the wall, as we were in our places. My heart had remained almost at its usual beating during the voice. I was used to it; it did not rouse all my pulses as it did at first. But just as it threw itself sobbing at the door (I cannot use other words), there suddenly came something which sent the blood coursing through my veins and my heart into my mouth. It was a voice inside the wall – the minister's well-known voice. I would have been prepared for it in any kind of adjuration, but I was not prepared for what I heard. It came out with a sort of stammering, as if too much moved for utterance. 'Willie, Willie! Oh, God preserve us! is it you?'

These simple words had an effect upon me that the voice of the invisible creature had ceased to have. I thought the old man, whom I had brought into this danger, had gone mad with terror. I made a dash round to the other side of the wall, half crazed myself with the thought. He was standing where I had left him, his shadow thrown vague and large upon the grass by the lantern which stood at his feet. I lifted my own light to see his face as I rushed forward. He was very pale, his eyes wet and glistening, his mouth quivering with parted lips. He neither saw nor heard me. We that had gone through this experience before, had crouched towards each other to get a little strength to bear it. But he was not even aware that I was there. His whole being seemed absorbed in anxiety and tenderness. He held out his hands, which trembled, but it seemed to me with eagerness, not fear. He went on speaking all the time. 'Willie, if it is you – and it's you, if it is not a delusion of Satan, – Willie, lad! why come ye here frighting them that know you not? Why came ye not to me?'

He seemed to wait for an answer. When his voice ceased, his countenance, every line moving, continued to speak. Simson gave me another terrible shock, stealing into the open doorway with his light, as much awe-stricken, as wildly curious, as I. But the minister resumed, without seeing Simson, speaking to some one else. His voice took a tone of expostulation –

'Is this right to come here? Your mother's gone with your
name on her lips. Do you think she would ever close her door
on her own lad? Do ye think the Lord will close the door, ye
faint-hearted creature? No! – I forbid ye! I forbid ye!' cried the
old man. The sobbing voice had begun to resume its cries. He
made a step forward, calling out the last words in a voice of
command. 'I forbid ye! Cry out no more to man. Go home, ye
wandering spirit! go home! Do you hear me? – me that christened ye, that have struggled with ye, that have wrestled for ye
with the Lord!' Here the loud tones of his voice sank into
tenderness. 'And her too, poor woman! poor woman! her you
are calling upon. She's no here. You'll find her with the Lord.
Go there and seek her, not here. Do you hear me, lad? go after
her there. He'll let you in, though it's late. Man, take heart! if
you will lie and sob and greet, let it be at heaven's gate, and no
your poor mother's ruined door.'

He stopped to get his breath: and the voice had stopped, not
as it had done before, when its time was exhausted and all its
repetitions said, but with a sobbing catch in the breath as if
overruled. Then the minister spoke again, 'Are you hearing me,
Will? Oh, laddie, you've liked the beggarly elements all your
days. Be done with them now. Go home to the Father – the
Father! Are you hearing me?' Here the old man sank down
upon his knees, his face raised upwards, his hands held up with
a tremble in them, all white in the light in the midst of the
darkness. I resisted as long as I could, though I cannot tell why,
– then I, too, dropped upon my knees. Simson all the time stood
in the doorway, with an expression in his face such as words
could not tell, his under lip dropped, his eyes wild, staring. It
seemed to be to him, that image of blank ignorance and wonder,
that we were praying. All the time the voice, with a low arrested
sobbing, lay just where he was standing, as I thought.

'Lord,' the minister said – 'Lord, take him into Thy everlast-
ing habitations. The mother he cries to is with Thee. Who can
open to him but Thee? Lord, when is it too late for Thee, or
what is too hard for Thee? Lord, let that woman there draw
him inower! Let her draw him inower!'

I sprang forward to catch something in my arms that flung
itself wildly within the door. The illusion was so strong, that I

never paused till I felt my forehead graze against the wall and my hands clutch the ground – for there was nobody there to save from falling, as in my foolishness I thought. Simson held out his hand to me to help me up. He was trembling and cold, his lower lip hanging, his speech almost inarticulate. 'It's gone,' he said, stammering, – 'it's gone!' We leant upon each other for a moment, trembling so much both of us that the whole scene trembled as if it were going to dissolve and disappear; and yet as long as I live I will never forget it – the shining of the strange lights, the blackness all round, the kneeling figure with all the whiteness of the light concentrated on its white venerable head and uplifted hands. A strange solemn stillness seemed to close all round us. By intervals a single syllable, 'Lord! Lord!' came from the old minister's lips. He saw none of us, nor thought of us. I never knew how long we stood, like sentinels guarding him at his prayers, holding our lights in a confused dazed way, not knowing what we did. But at last he rose from his knees, and standing up at his full height, raised his arms, as the Scotch manner is at the end of a religious service, and solemnly gave the apostolical benediction – to what? to the silent earth, the dark woods, the wide breathing atmosphere – for we were but spectators gasping an Amen![17]

It seemed to me that it must be the middle of the night, as we all walked back. It was in reality very late. Dr Moncrieff put his arm into mine. He walked slowly, with an air of exhaustion. It was as if we were coming from a deathbed. Something hushed and solemnized the very air. There was that sense of relief in it which there always is at the end of a death-struggle. And nature, persistent, never daunted, came back in all of us, as we returned into the ways of life. We said nothing to each other, indeed, for a time; but when we got clear of the trees and reached the opening near the house, where we could see the sky, Dr Moncrieff himself was the first to speak. 'I must be going,' he said; 'it's very late, I'm afraid. I will go down the glen, as I came.'

'But not alone. I am going with you, Doctor.'

'Well, I will not oppose it. I am an old man, and agitation wearies more than work. Yes; I'll be thankful of your arm. To-night, Colonel, you've done me more good turns than one.'

I pressed his hand on my arm, not feeling able to speak. But Simson, who turned with us, and who had gone along all this time with his taper flaring, in entire unconsciousness, came to himself, apparently at the sound of our voices, and put out that wild little torch with a quick movement, as if of shame. 'Let me carry your lantern,' he said; 'it is heavy.' He recovered with a spring, and in a moment, from the awe-stricken spectator he had been, became himself, sceptical and cynical. 'I should like to ask you a question,' he said. 'Do you believe in Purgatory, Doctor? It's not in the tenets of the Church, so far as I know.'

'Sir,' said Dr Moncrieff, 'an old man like me is sometimes not very sure what he believes. There is just one thing I am certain of – and that is the loving-kindness of God.'

'But I thought that was in this life. I am no theologian –'

'Sir,' said the old man again, with a tremor in him which I could feel going over all his frame, 'if I saw a friend of mine within the gates of hell, I would not despair but his Father would take him by the hand still – if he cried like *yon*.'

'I allow it is very strange – very strange. I cannot see through it. That there must be human agency, I feel sure. Doctor, what made you decide upon the person and the name?'

The minister put out his hand with the impatience which a man might show if he were asked how he recognized his brother. 'Tuts!' he said, in familiar speech – then more solemnly, 'how should I not recognize a person that I know better – far better – than I know you?'

'Then you saw the man?'

Dr Moncrieff made no reply. He moved his hand again with a little impatient movement, and walked on, leaning heavily on my arm. And we went on for a long time without another word, threading the dark paths, which were steep and slippery with the damp of the winter. The air was very still – not more than enough to make a faint sighing in the branches, which mingled with the sound of the water to which we were descending. When we spoke again, it was about indifferent matters – about the height of the river, and the recent rains. We parted with the minister at his own door, where his old housekeeper appeared in great perturbation, waiting for him. 'Eh me, minister! the young gentleman will be worse?' she cried.

'Far from that – better. God bless him!' Dr Moncrieff said.

I think if Simson had begun again to me with his questions, I should have pitched him over the rocks as we returned up the glen; but he was silent, by a good inspiration. And the sky was clearer than it had been for many nights, shining high over the trees, with here and there a star faintly gleaming through the wilderness of dark and bare branches. The air, as I have said, was very soft in them, with a subdued and peaceful cadence. It was real, like every natural sound, and came to us like a hush of peace and relief. I thought there was a sound in it as of the breath of a sleeper, and it seemed clear to me that Roland must be sleeping, satisfied and calm. We went up to his room when we went in. There we found the complete hush of rest. My wife looked up out of a doze, and gave me a smile; 'I think he is a great deal better: but you are very late,' she said in a whisper, shading the light with her hand that the doctor might see his patient. The boy had got back something like his own colour. He woke as we stood all round his bed. His eyes had the happy half-awakened look of childhood, glad to shut again, yet pleased with the interruption and glimmer of the light. I stooped over him and kissed his forehead, which was moist and cool. 'All is well, Roland,' I said. He looked up at me with a glance of pleasure, and took my hand and laid his cheek upon it, and so went to sleep.

For some nights after, I watched among the ruins, spending all the dark hours up to midnight patrolling about the bit of wall which was associated with so many emotions; but I heard nothing, and saw nothing beyond the quiet course of nature: nor, so far as I am aware, has anything been heard again. Dr Moncrieff gave me the history of the youth, whom he never hesitated to name. I did not ask, as Simson did, how he recognized him. He had been a prodigal – weak, foolish, easily imposed upon, and 'led away,' as people say.[18] All that we had heard had passed actually in life, the Doctor said. The young man had come home thus a day or two after his mother died – who was no more than the housekeeper in the old house – and distracted with the news, had thrown himself down at the door and called upon her to let him in. The old man could scarcely speak of it for tears. To me it seemed as if – heaven help us, how little do we know about anything! – a scene like that might impress itself somehow upon the hidden heart of nature. I do not pretend to know how, but the repetition had struck me at the time as, in its terrible strangeness and incomprehensibility, almost mechanical – as if the unseen actor could not exceed or vary, but was bound to re-enact the whole. One thing that struck me, however, greatly, was the likeness between the old minister and my boy in the manner of regarding these strange phenomena. Dr Moncrieff was not terrified, as I had been myself, and all the rest of us. It was no 'ghost,' as I fear we all vulgarly considered it, to him – but a poor creature whom he knew under these conditions, just as he had known him in the flesh, having no doubt of his identity. And to Roland it was the same. This spirit in pain – if it was a spirit – this voice out of the unseen – was a poor fellow-creature in misery, to be suc-coured and helped out of his trouble, to my boy. He spoke to me quite frankly about it when he got better. 'I knew father would find out some way,' he said. And this was when he was strong and well, and all idea that he would turn hysterical or become a seer of visions had happily passed away.

I must add one curious fact which does not seem to me to have any relation to the above, but which Simson made great use of, as the human agency which he was determined to find some-how. We had examined the ruins very closely at the time of these occurrences; but afterwards, when all was over, as we went casually about them one Sunday afternoon in the idleness of that unemployed day, Simson with his stick penetrated an old window which had been entirely blocked up with fallen soil. He jumped down into it in great excitement, and called me to follow. There we found a little hole – for it was more a hole than a room – entirely hidden under the ivy and ruins, in which there was a quantity of straw laid in a corner, as if some one had made a bed there, and some remains of crusts about the floor. Some one had lodged there, and not very long before, he made out; and that this unknown being was the author of all the mysterious sounds we heard he is convinced. 'I told you it was human agency,' he said, triumphantly. He forgets, I suppose, how he and I stood with our lights seeing nothing, while the space between us was audibly traversed by something that could speak, and sob, and suffer. There is no argument with men of this kind. He is ready to get up a laugh against me on this slender ground. 'I was puzzled myself – I could not make it out – but I always felt convinced human agency was at the bottom of it. And here it is – and a clever fellow he must have been,' the Doctor says.

Bagley left my service as soon as he got well. He assured me it was no want of respect; but he could not stand 'them kind of things,' and the man was so shaken and ghastly that I was glad to give him a present and let him go. For my own part, I made a point of staying out the time, two years, for which I had taken Brentwood; but I did not renew my tenancy. By that time we had settled, and found for ourselves a pleasant home of our own.

I must add that when the doctor defies me, I can always bring back gravity to his countenance, and a pause in his railing, when I remind him of the juniper-bush. To me that was a matter of little importance. I could believe I was mistaken. I did not care about it one way or other; but on his mind the effect was different. The miserable voice, the spirit in pain, he could think of as the result of ventriloquism, or reverberation, or – anything you please: an elaborate prolonged hoax executed somehow by the tramp that had found a lodging in the old tower. But the juniper-bush staggered him. Things have effects so different on the minds of different men.

RUDYARD KIPLING

At the End of the Passage

The sky is lead and our faces are red,
    And the gates of Hell are opened and riven,
    And the winds of Hell are loosened and driven,
And the dust flies up in the face of Heaven,
    And the clouds come down in a fiery sheet,
Heavy to raise and hard to be borne.
And the soul of man is turned from his meat,
    Turned from the trifles for which he has striven
    Sick in his body, and heavy hearted,
    And his soul flies up like the dust in the sheet
    Breaks from his flesh and is gone and departed,
As the blasts they blow on the cholera-horn.

Himalayan[1]

Four men, each entitled to 'life, liberty, and the pursuit of happiness,' sat at a table playing whist.[2] The thermometer marked – for them – one hundred and one degrees of heat. The room was darkened till it was only just possible to distinguish the pips of the cards and the very white faces of the players. A tattered, rotten punkah of whitewashed calico was puddling the hot air and whining dolefully at each stroke.[3] Outside lay gloom of a November day in London. There was neither sky, sun, nor horizon, – nothing but a brown purple haze of heat. It was as though the earth were dying of apoplexy.[4]

From time to time clouds of tawny dust rose from the ground without wind or warning, flung themselves tablecloth-wise among the tops of the parched trees, and came down again. Then a whirling dust-devil would scutter across the plain for a couple of miles, break, and fall outward, though there was nothing to check its flight save a long low line of piled railway-sleepers white with the dust, a cluster of huts made of mud, condemned rails, and canvas, and the one squat four-roomed bungalow that belonged to the assistant engineer in charge of a section of the Gaudhari State line then under construction.[5]

The four, stripped to the thinnest of sleeping-suits, played whist crossly, with wranglings as to leads and returns. It was not the best kind of whist, but they had taken some trouble to arrive at it. Mottram of the Indian Survey had ridden thirty and railed one hundred miles from his lonely post in the desert since the night before; Lowndes of the Civil Service, on special duty in the political department, had come as far to escape for an instant the miserable intrigues of an impoverished native State whose king alternately fawned and blustered for more money from the pitiful revenues contributed by hard-wrung peasants and despairing camel-breeders; Spurstow, the doctor of the line, had left a cholera-stricken camp of coolies to look after itself for forty-eight hours while he associated with white men once more.[6] Hummil, the assistant engineer, was the host. He stood fast and received his friends thus every Sunday if they could come in. When one of them failed to appear, he would send a telegram to his last address, in order that he might know whether the defaulter were dead or alive. There are very many places in the East where it is not good or kind to let your acquaintances drop out of sight even for one short week.

The players were not conscious of any special regard for each other. They squabbled whenever they met; but they ardently desired to meet, as men without water desire to drink. They were lonely folk who understood the dread meaning of loneliness. They were all under thirty years of age, – which is too soon for any man to possess that knowledge.

'Pilsener?' said Spurstow, after the second rubber, mopping his forehead.[7]

'Beer's out, I'm sorry to say, and there's hardly enough soda-water for to-night,' said Hummil.

'What filthy bad management!' Spurstow snarled.

'Can't help it. I've written and wired; but the trains don't come through regularly yet. Last week the ice ran out, – as Lowndes knows.'

'Glad I didn't come. I could ha' sent you some if I had known, though. Phew! it's too hot to go on playing bumblepuppy.'[8]

This with a savage scowl at Lowndes, who only laughed. He
was a hardened offender.

Mottram rose from the table and looked out of a chink in
the shutters.

'What a sweet day!' said he.

The company yawned all together and betook themselves to
an aimless investigation of all Hummil's possessions, – guns,
tattered novels, saddlery, spurs, and the like. They had fingered
them a score of times before, but there was really nothing else
to do.

'Got anything fresh?' said Lowndes.

'Last week's *Gazette of India*, and a cutting from a home
paper.⁹ My father sent it out. It's rather amusing.'

'One of those vestrymen that call 'emselves MP's again, is
it?' said Spurstow, who read his newspapers when he could get
them.

'Yes. Listen to this. It's to your address, Lowndes. The man
was making a speech to his constituents, and he piled it on.
Here's a sample, "And I assert unhesitatingly that the Civil
Service in India is the preserve – the pet preserve – of the
aristocracy of England. What does the democracy – what do
the masses – get from that country, which we have step by step
fraudulently annexed? I answer, nothing whatever. It is farmed
with a single eye to their own interests by the scions of the
aristocracy. They take good care to maintain their lavish scale
of incomes, to avoid or stifle any inquiries into the nature and
conduct of their administration, while they themselves force the
unhappy peasant to pay with the sweat of his brow for all the
luxuries in which they are lapped."' Hummil waved the cutting
above his head. ''Ear! 'ear!' said his audience.

Then Lowndes, meditatively, 'I'd give – I'd give three months'
pay to have that gentleman spend one month with me and see
how the free and independent native prince works things. Old
Timbersides' – this was his flippant title for an honoured and
decorated feudatory prince – 'has been wearing my life out this
week past for money. By Jove, his latest performance was to
send me one of his women as a bribe!'

'Good for you! Did you accept it?' said Mottram.

'No. I rather wish I had, now. She was a pretty little person, and she yarned away to me about the horrible destitution among the king's women-folk. The darlings haven't had any new clothes for nearly a month, and the old man wants to buy a new drag from Calcutta, – solid silver railings and silver lamps, and trifles of that kind.[10] I've tried to make him understand that he has played the deuce with the revenues for the last twenty years and must go slow. He can't see it.'

'But he has the ancestral treasure-vaults to draw on. There must be three millions at least in jewels and coin under his palace,' said Hummil.

'Catch a native king disturbing the family treasure! The priests forbid it except as the last resort. Old Timbersides has added something like a quarter of a million to the deposit in his reign.'

'Where the mischief does it all come from?' said Mottram.

'The country. The state of the people is enough to make you sick. I've known the tax-men wait by a milch-camel till the foal was born and then hurry off the mother for arrears. And what can I do? I can't get the court clerks to give me any accounts; I can't raise anything more than a fat smile from the commander-in-chief when I find out the troops are three months in arrears; and old Timbersides begins to weep when I speak to him. He has taken to the King's Peg heavily, – liqueur brandy for whisky, and Heidsieck for soda-water.'[11]

'That's what the Rao of Jubela took to.[12] Even a native can't last long at that,' said Spurstow. 'He'll go out.'

'And a good thing, too. Then I suppose we'll have a council of regency, and a tutor for the young prince, and hand him back his kingdom with ten years' accumulations.'

'Whereupon that young prince, having been taught all the vices of the English, will play ducks and drakes with the money and undo ten years' work in eighteen months. I've seen that business before,' said Spurstow. 'I should tackle the king with a light hand, if I were you, Lowndes. They'll hate you quite enough under any circumstances.'

'That's all very well. The man who looks on can talk about the light hand; but you can't clean a pig-stye with a pen dipped in rose-water. I know my risks; but nothing has happened yet. My servant's an old Pathan, and he cooks for me.[13] They are

hardly likely to bribe him, and I don't accept food from my
true friends, as they call themselves. Oh, but it's weary work! I'd
sooner be with you, Spurstow. There's shooting near your camp.'

'Would you? I don't think it. About fifteen deaths a day don't
incite a man to shoot anything but himself. And the worst of it
is that the poor devils look at you as though you ought to save
them. Lord knows, I've tried everything. My last attempt was
empirical, but it pulled an old man through. He was brought
to me apparently past hope, and I gave him gin and Worcester
sauce with cayenne. It cured him; but I don't recommend it.'

'How do the cases run generally?' said Hummil.

'Very simply indeed. Chlorodyne, opium pill, chlorodyne,
collapse, nitre, bricks to the feet, and then – the burning-ghat.[14]
The last seems to be the only thing that stops the trouble. It's
black cholera, you know. Poor devils! But, I will say, little
Bunsee Lal, my apothecary, works like a demon. I've recommended him for promotion if he comes through it all alive.'

'And what are your chances, old man?' said Mottram.

'Don't know; don't care much; but I've sent the letter in.
What are you doing with yourself generally?'

'Sitting under a table in the tent and spitting on the sextant
to keep it cool,' said the man of the survey. 'Washing my eyes
to avoid ophthalmia, which I shall certainly get, and trying to
make a sub-surveyor understand that an error of five degrees
in an angle isn't quite so small as it looks. I'm altogether alone,
y' know, and shall be till the end of the hot weather.'

'Hummil's the lucky man,' said Lowndes, flinging himself
into a long chair. 'He has an actual roof – torn as to the
ceiling-cloth, but still a roof – over his head. He sees one train
daily. He can get beer and soda-water and ice 'em when God is
good. He has books, pictures,' – they were torn from the
Graphic, – 'and the society of the excellent sub-contractor
Jevins, besides the pleasure of receiving us weekly.'[15]

Hummil smiled grimly. 'Yes, I'm the lucky man, I suppose.
Jevins is luckier.'

'How? Not –'

'Yes. Went out. Last Monday.'

'By his own hand?' said Spurstow quickly, hinting the suspicion that was in everybody's mind. There was no cholera near

Hummil's section. Even fever gives a man at least a week's grace, and sudden death generally implied self-slaughter.

'I judge no man this weather,' said Hummil. 'He had a touch of the sun, I fancy; for last week, after you fellows had left, he came into the verandah and told me that he was going home to see his wife, in Market Street, Liverpool, that evening.

'I got the apothecary in to look at him, and we tried to make him lie down. After an hour or two he rubbed his eyes and said he believed he had had a fit, – hoped he hadn't said anything rude. Jevins had a great idea of bettering himself socially. He was very like Chucks in his language.'[16]

'Well?'

'Then he went to his own bungalow and began cleaning a rifle. He told the servant that he was going to shoot buck in the morning. Naturally he fumbled with the trigger, and shot himself through the head – accidentally. The apothecary sent in a report to my chief, and Jevins is buried somewhere out there. I'd have wired to you, Spurstow, if you could have done anything.'

'You're a queer chap,' said Mottram. 'If you'd killed the man yourself you couldn't have been more quiet about the business.'

'Good Lord! what does it matter?' said Hummil calmly. 'I've got to do a lot of his overseeing work in addition to my own. I'm the only person that suffers. Jevins is out of it, – by pure accident, of course, but out of it. The apothecary was going to write a long screed on suicide. Trust a babu to drivel when he gets the chance.'[17]

'Why didn't you let it go in as suicide?' said Lowndes.

'No direct proof. A man hasn't many privileges in this country, but he might at least be allowed to mishandle his own rifle. Besides, some day I may need a man to smother up an accident to myself. Live and let live. Die and let die.'

'You take a pill,' said Spurstow, who had been watching Hummil's white face narrowly. 'Take a pill, and don't be an ass. That sort of talk is skittles. Anyhow, suicide is shirking your work. If I were Job ten times over, I should be so interested in what was going to happen next that I'd stay on and watch.'[18]

'Ah! I've lost that curiosity,' said Hummil.

'Liver out of order?' said Lowndes feelingly.

'No. Can't sleep. That's worse.'

'By Jove, it is!' said Mottram. 'I'm that way every now and then, and the fit has to wear itself out. What do you take for it?'

'Nothing. What's the use? I haven't had ten minutes' sleep since Friday morning.'

'Poor chap! Spurstow, you ought to attend to this,' said Mottram. 'Now you mention it, your eyes are rather gummy and swollen.'

Spurstow, still watching Hummil, laughed lightly. 'I'll patch him up, later on. Is it too hot, do you think, to go for a ride?'

'Where to?' said Lowndes wearily. 'We shall have to go away at eight, and there'll be riding enough for us then. I hate a horse, when I have to use him as a necessity. Oh, heavens! what is there to do?'

'Begin whist again, at chick points ["a chick" is supposed to be eight shillings] and a gold mohur on the rub,' said Spurstow promptly.[19]

'Poker. A month's pay all round for the pool, – no limit, – and fifty-rupee raises. Somebody would be broken before we got up,' said Lowndes.

'Can't say that it would give me any pleasure to break any man in this company,' said Mottram. 'There isn't enough excitement in it, and it's foolish.' He crossed over to the worn and battered little camp-piano, – wreckage of a married household that had once held the bungalow, – and opened the case.

'It's used up long ago,' said Hummil. 'The servants have picked it to pieces.'

The piano was indeed hopelessly out of order, but Mottram managed to bring the rebellious notes into a sort of agreement, and there rose from the ragged keyboard something that might once have been the ghost of a popular music-hall song. The men in the long chairs turned with evident interest as Mottram banged the more lustily.

'That's good!' said Lowndes. 'By Jove! the last time I heard that song was in '79, or thereabouts, just before I came out.'

'Ah!' said Spurstow with pride, 'I was home in '80.' And he mentioned a song of the streets popular at that date.

Mottram executed it roughly. Lowndes criticized and volunteered emendations. Mottram dashed into another ditty, not of the music-hall character, and made as if to rise.

'Sit down,' said Hummil. 'I didn't know that you had any music in your composition. Go on playing until you can't think of anything more. I'll have that piano tuned up before you come again. Play something festive.'

Very simple indeed were the tunes to which Mottram's art and the limitations of the piano could give effect, but the men listened with pleasure, and in the pauses talked all together of what they had seen or heard when they were last at home. A dense dust-storm sprung up outside, and swept roaring over the house, enveloping it in the choking darkness of midnight, but Mottram continued unheeding, and the crazy tinkle reached the ears of the listeners above the flapping of the tattered ceiling-cloth.

In the silence after the storm he glided from the more directly personal songs of Scotland, half humming them as he played, into the Evening Hymn.

'Sunday,' said he, nodding his head.

'Go on. Don't apologize for it,' said Spurstow.

Hummil laughed long and riotously. 'Play it, by all means. You're full of surprises to-day. I didn't know you had such a gift of finished sarcasm. How does that thing go?'

Mottram took up the tune.

'Too slow by half. You miss the note of gratitude,' said Hummil. 'It ought to go to the "Grasshopper's Polka," – this way.' And he chanted, *prestissimo*, –[20]

> 'Glory to thee, my God, this night,
> For all the blessings of the light.

That shows we really feel our blessings. How does it go on? –

> 'If in the night I sleepless lie,
> My soul with sacred thoughts supply;
> May no ill dreams disturb my rest, –

Quicker, Mottram! –

> 'Or powers of darkness me molest!'[21]

'Bah! what an old hypocrite you are!'

'Don't be an ass,' said Lowndes. 'You are at full liberty to make fun of anything else you like, but leave that hymn alone. It's associated in my mind with the most sacred recollections – '

'Summer evenings in the country, – stained-glass window, – light going out, and you and she jamming your heads together over one hymn-book,' said Mottram.

'Yes, and a fat old cockchafer hitting you in the eye when you walked home.[22] Smell of hay, and a moon as big as a bandbox sitting on the top of a haycock; bats, – roses, – milk and midges,' said Lowndes.

'Also mothers. I can just recollect my mother singing me to sleep with that when I was a little chap,' said Spurstow.

The darkness had fallen on the room. They could hear Hummil squirming in his chair.

'Consequently,' said he testily, 'you sing it when you are seven fathom deep in Hell! It's an insult to the intelligence of the Deity to pretend we're anything but tortured rebels.'

'Take *two* pills,' said Spurstow; 'that's tortured liver.'

'The usually placid Hummil is in a vile bad temper. I'm sorry for his coolies to-morrow,' said Lowndes, as the servants brought in the lights and prepared the table for dinner.

As they were settling into their places about the miserable goat-chops, and the smoked tapioca pudding, Spurstow took occasion to whisper to Mottram, 'Well done, David!'[23]

'Look after Saul, then,' was the reply.

'What are you two whispering about?' said Hummil suspiciously.

'Only saying that you are a damned poor host. This fowl can't be cut,' returned Spurstow with a sweet smile. 'Call this a dinner?'

'I can't help it. You don't expect a banquet, do you?'

Throughout that meal Hummil contrived laboriously to insult directly and pointedly all his guests in succession, and at each insult Spurstow kicked the aggrieved persons under the table; but he dared not exchange a glance of intelligence with either of them. Hummil's face was white and pinched, while his eyes were unnaturally large. No man dreamed for a moment of resenting his savage personalities, but as soon as the meal was over they made haste to get away.

'Don't go. You're just getting amusing, you fellows. I hope I haven't said anything that annoyed you. You're such touchy devils.' Then, changing the note into one of almost abject entreaty, Hummil added, 'I say, you surely aren't going?'

'In the language of the blessed Jorrocks, where I dines I sleeps,' said Spurstow.[24] 'I want to have a look at your coolies to-morrow, if you don't mind. You can give me a place to lie down in, I suppose?'

The others pleaded the urgency of their several duties next day, and, saddling up, departed together, Hummil begging them to come next Sunday. As they jogged off, Lowndes unbosomed himself to Mottram –

'. . . And I never felt so like kicking a man at his own table in my life. He said I cheated at whist, and reminded me I was in debt! 'Told you you were as good as a liar to your face! You aren't half indignant enough over it.'

'Not I,' said Mottram. 'Poor devil! Did you ever know old Hummy behave like that before or within a hundred miles of it?'

'That's no excuse. Spurstow was hacking my shin all the time, so I kept a hand on myself. Else I should have –'

'No, you wouldn't. You'd have done as Hummy did about Jevins; judge no man this weather. By Jove! the buckle of my bridle is hot in my hand! Trot out a bit, and 'ware rat-holes.'

Ten minutes' trotting jerked out of Lowndes one very sage remark when he pulled up, sweating from every pore –

' 'Good thing Spurstow's with him to-night.'

'Ye-es. Good man, Spurstow. Our roads turn here. See you again next Sunday, if the sun doesn't bowl me over.'

'S'pose so, unless old Timbersides' finance minister manages to dress some of my food. Good-night, and – God bless you!'

'What's wrong now?'

'Oh, nothing.' Lowndes gathered up his whip, and, as he flicked Mottram's mare on the flank, added, 'You're not a bad little chap, – that's all.' And the mare bolted half a mile across the sand, on the word.

In the assistant engineer's bungalow Spurstow and Hummil smoked the pipe of silence together, each narrowly watching the other. The capacity of a bachelor's establishment is as elastic as its arrangements are simple. A servant cleared away the dining-room table, brought in a couple of rude native bedsteads made of tape strung on a light wood frame, flung a square of cool Calcutta matting over each, set them side by side, pinned two towels to the punkah so that their fringes should just sweep clear of the sleepers' nose and mouth, and announced that the couches were ready.

The men flung themselves down, ordering the punkah-coolies by all the powers of Hell to pull. Every door and window was shut, for the outside air was that of an oven. The atmosphere within was only 104°, as the thermometer bore witness, and heavy with the foul smell of badly-trimmed kerosene lamps; and this stench, combined with that of native tobacco, baked brick, and dried earth, sends the heart of many a strong man down to his boots, for it is the smell of the Great Indian Empire when she turns herself for six months into a house of torment. Spurstow packed his pillows craftily so that he reclined rather than lay, his head at a safe elevation above his feet. It is not good to sleep on a low pillow in the hot weather if you happen to be of thick-necked build, for you may pass with lively snores and gugglings from natural sleep into the deep slumber of heat-apoplexy.[25]

'Pack your pillows,' said the doctor sharply, as he saw Hummil preparing to lie down at full length.

The night-light was trimmed; the shadow of the punkah wavered across the room, and the '*flick*' of the punkah-towel and the soft whine of the rope through the wall-hole followed it. Then the punkah flagged, almost ceased. The sweat poured from Spurstow's brow. Should he go out and harangue the coolie? It started forward again with a savage jerk, and a pin came out of the towels. When this was replaced, a tomtom in the coolie-lines began to beat with the steady throb of a swollen artery inside some brain-fevered skull. Spurstow turned on his side and swore gently. There was no movement on Hummil's part. The man had composed himself as rigidly as a corpse, his hands clinched at his sides. The respiration was too hurried for any suspicion of sleep. Spurstow looked at the set face. The jaws were clinched, and there was a pucker round the quivering eyelids.

'He's holding himself as tightly as ever he can,' thought
Spurstow. 'What in the world is the matter with him? –
Hummil!'

'Yes,' in a thick constrained voice.

'Can't you get to sleep?'

'No.'

'Head hot? 'Throat feeling bulgy? or how?'

'Neither, thanks. I don't sleep much, you know.'

''Feel pretty bad?'

'Pretty bad, thanks. There is a tomtom outside, isn't there? I
thought it was my head at first . . . Oh Spurstow, for pity's sake
give me something that will put me asleep, – sound asleep, – if
it's only for six hours!' He sprang up, trembling from head to
foot. 'I haven't been able to sleep naturally for days, and I can't
stand it! – I can't stand it!'

'Poor old chap!'

'That's no use. Give me something to make me sleep. I tell
you I'm nearly mad. I don't know what I say half my time. For
three weeks I've had to think and spell out every word that has
come through my lips before I dared say it. Isn't that enough
to drive a man mad? I can't see things correctly now, and I've
lost my sense of touch. My skin aches – my skin aches! Make
me sleep. Oh Spurstow, for the love of God make me sleep
sound. It isn't enough merely to let me dream. Let me sleep!'

'All right, old man, all right. Go slow; you aren't half as bad
as you think.'

The flood-gates of reserve once broken, Hummil was clinging
to him like a frightened child. 'You're pinching my arm to pieces.'

'I'll break your neck if you don't do something for me. No, I
didn't mean that. Don't be angry, old fellow.' He wiped the
sweat off himself as he fought to regain composure. 'I'm a bit
restless and off my oats, and perhaps you could recommend
some sort of sleeping mixture, – bromide of potassium.'

'Bromide of skittles! Why didn't you tell me this before? Let
go of my arm, and I'll see if there's anything in my cigarette-case
to suit your complaint.' Spurstow hunted among his day-
clothes, turned up the lamp, opened a little silver cigarette-case,
and advanced on the expectant Hummil with the daintiest of
fairy squirts.

'The last appeal of civilization,' said he, 'and a thing I hate to use. Hold out your arm. Well, your sleeplessness hasn't ruined your muscle; and what a thick hide it is! Might as well inject a buffalo subcutaneously. Now in a few minutes the morphia will begin working. Lie down and wait.'

A smile of unalloyed and idiotic delight began to creep over Hummil's face. 'I think,' he whispered, – 'I think I'm going off now. Gad! it's positively heavenly! Spurstow, you must give me that case to keep; you –' The voice ceased as the head fell back.

'Not for a good deal,' said Spurstow to the unconscious form. 'And now, my friend, sleeplessness of your kind being very apt to relax the moral fibre in little matters of life and death, I'll just take the liberty of spiking your guns.'²⁶

He paddled into Hummil's saddle-room in his bare feet and uncased a twelve-bore rifle, an express, and a revolver.²⁷ Of the first he unscrewed the nipples and hid them in the bottom of a saddlery-case; of the second he abstracted the lever, kicking it behind a big wardrobe.²⁸ The third he merely opened, and knocked the doll-head bolt of the grip up with the heel of a riding-boot.²⁹

'That's settled,' he said, as he shook the sweat off his hands. 'These little precautions will at least give you time to turn. You have too much sympathy with gun-room accidents.'

And as he rose from his knees, the thick muffled voice of Hummil cried in the doorway, 'You fool!'

Such tones they use who speak in the lucid intervals of delirium to their friends a little before they die.

Spurstow started, dropping the pistol. Hummil stood in the doorway, rocking with helpless laughter.

'That was awf'ly good of you, I'm sure,' he said, very slowly, feeling for his words. 'I don't intend to go out by my own hand at present. I say, Spurstow, that stuff won't work. What shall I do? What shall I do?' And panic terror stood in his eyes.

'Lie down and give it a chance. Lie down at once.'

'I daren't. It will only take me half-way again, and I shan't be able to get away this time. Do you know it was all I could do to come out just now? Generally I am as quick as lightning; but you had clogged my feet. I was nearly caught.'

'Oh yes, I understand. Go and lie down.'

'No, it isn't delirium; but it was an awfully mean trick to play on me. Do you know I might have died?'

As a sponge rubs a slate clean, so some power unknown to Spurstow had wiped out of Hummil's face all that stamped it for the face of a man, and he stood at the doorway in the expression of his lost innocence. He had slept back into terrified childhood.

'Is he going to die on the spot?' thought Spurstow. Then, aloud, 'All right, my son. Come back to bed, and tell me all about it. You couldn't sleep; but what was all the rest of the nonsense?'

'A place, – a place down there,' said Hummil, with simple sincerity. The drug was acting on him by waves, and he was flung from the fear of a strong man to the fright of a child as his nerves gathered sense or were dulled.

'Good God! I've been afraid of it for months past, Spurstow. It has made every night hell to me; and yet I'm not conscious of having done anything wrong.'

'Be still, and I'll give you another dose. We'll stop your nightmares, you unutterable idiot!'

'Yes, but you must give me so much that I can't get away. You must make me quite sleepy, – not just a little sleepy. It's so hard to run then.'

'I know it; I know it. I've felt it myself. The symptoms are exactly as you describe.'

'Oh, don't laugh at me, confound you! Before this awful sleeplessness came to me I've tried to rest on my elbow and put a spur in the bed to sting me when I fell back. Look!'

'By Jove! the man has been rowelled like a horse![30] Ridden by the nightmare with a vengeance! And we all thought him sensible enough. Heaven send us understanding! You like to talk, don't you?'

'Yes, sometimes. Not when I'm frightened. *Then* I want to run. Don't you?'

'Always. Before I give you your second dose try to tell me exactly what your trouble is.'

Hummil spoke in broken whispers for nearly ten minutes, whilst Spurstow looked into the pupils of his eyes and passed his hand before them once or twice.

At the end of the narrative the silver cigarette-case was

produced, and the last words that Hummil said as he fell back for the second time were, 'Put me quite to sleep; for if I'm caught I die, – I die!'

'Yes, yes; we all do that sooner or later, – thank Heaven who has set a term to our miseries,' said Spurstow, settling the cushions under the head. 'It occurs to me that unless I drink something I shall go out before my time. I've stopped sweating, and – I wear a seventeen-inch collar.' He brewed himself scalding hot tea, which is an excellent remedy against heat-apoplexy if you take three or four cups of it in time.[30] Then he watched the sleeper.

'A blind face that cries and can't wipe its eyes, a blind face that chases him down corridors![31] H'm! Decidedly, Hummil ought to go on leave as soon as possible; and, sane or otherwise, he undoubtedly did rowel himself most cruelly. Well, Heaven send us understanding!'

At mid-day Hummil rose, with an evil taste in his mouth, but an unclouded eye and a joyful heart.

'I was pretty bad last night, wasn't I?' said he.

'I have seen healthier men. You must have had a touch of the sun. Look here: if I write you a swingeing medical certificate, will you apply for leave on the spot?'

'No.'

'Why not? You want it.'

'Yes, but I can hold on till the weather's a little cooler.'

'Why should you, if you can get relieved on the spot?'

'Burkett is the only man who could be sent; and he's a born fool.'

'Oh, never mind about the line. You aren't so important as all that. Wire for leave, if necessary.'

Hummil looked very uncomfortable.

'I can hold on till the Rains,' he said evasively.[32]

'You can't. Wire to headquarters for Burkett.'

'I won't. If you want to know why, particularly, Burkett is married, and his wife's just had a kid, and she's up at Simla, in the cool, and Burkett has a very nice billet that takes him into Simla from Saturday to Monday.[33] That little woman isn't at all well. If Burkett was transferred she'd try to follow him. If she left the baby behind she'd fret herself to death. If she came,

– and Burkett's one of those selfish little beasts who are always talking about a wife's place being with her husband, – she'd die. It's murder to bring a woman here just now. Burkett hasn't the physique of a rat. If he came here he'd go out; and I know she hasn't any money, and I'm pretty sure she'd go out too. I'm salted in a sort of way, and I'm not married. Wait till the Rains, and then Burkett can get thin down here. It'll do him heaps of good.'

'Do you mean to say that you intend to face – what you have faced, till the Rains break?'

'Oh, it won't be so bad, now you've shown me a way out of it. I can always wire to you. Besides, now I've once got into the way of sleeping, it'll be all right. Anyhow, I shan't put in for leave. That's the long and the short of it.'

'My great Scott! I thought all that sort of thing was dead and done with.'[34]

'Bosh! You'd do the same yourself. I feel a new man, thanks to that cigarette-case. You're going over to camp now, aren't you?'

'Yes; but I'll try to look you up every other day, if I can.'

'I'm not bad enough for that. I don't want you to bother. Give the coolies gin and ketchup.'

'Then you feel all right?'

'Fit to fight for my life, but not to stand out in the sun talking to you. Go along, old man, and bless you!'

Hummil turned on his heel to face the echoing desolation of his bungalow, and the first thing he saw standing in the verandah was the figure of himself. He had met a similar apparition once before, when he was suffering from overwork and the strain of the hot weather.

'This is bad, – already,' he said, rubbing his eyes. 'If the thing slides away from me all in one piece, like a ghost, I shall know it is only my eyes and stomach that are out of order. If it walks – my head is going.'

He approached the figure, which naturally kept at an unvarying distance from him, as is the use of all spectres that are born of overwork. It slid through the house and dissolved into swimming specks within the eyeball as soon as it reached the burning light of the garden. Hummil went about his business

till even. When he came in to dinner he found himself sitting at
the table. The vision rose and walked out hastily. Except that
it cast no shadow it was in all respects real.

No living man knows what that week held for Hummil. An
increase of the epidemic kept Spurstow in camp among the
coolies, and all he could do was to telegraph to Mottram,
bidding him go to the bungalow and sleep there. But Mottram
was forty miles away from the nearest telegraph, and knew
nothing of anything save the needs of the survey till he met, early
on Sunday morning, Lowndes and Spurstow heading towards
Hummil's for the weekly gathering.

'Hope the poor chap's in a better temper,' said the former,
swinging himself off his horse at the door. 'I suppose he isn't
up yet.'

'I'll just have a look at him,' said the doctor. 'If he's asleep
there's no need to wake him.'

And an instant later, by the tone of Spurstow's voice calling
upon them to enter, the men knew what had happened. There
was no need to wake him.

The punkah was still being pulled over the bed, but Hummil
had departed this life at least three hours.

The body lay on its back, hands clinched by the side, as
Spurstow had seen it lying seven nights previously. In the staring
eyes was written terror beyond the expression of any pen.

Mottram, who had entered behind Lowndes, bent over the
dead and touched the forehead lightly with his lips. 'Oh, you
lucky, lucky devil!' he whispered.

But Lowndes had seen the eyes, and withdrew shuddering to
the other side of the room.

'Poor chap! poor old chap! And the last time I met him I was
angry. Spurstow, we should have watched him. Has he –?'

Deftly Spurstow continued his investigations, ending by a
search round the room.

'No, he hasn't,' he snapped. 'There's no trace of anything.
Call the servants.'

They came, eight or ten of them, whispering and peering over
each other's shoulders.

'When did your Sahib go to bed?' said Spurstow.[35]

'At eleven or ten, we think,' said Hummil's personal servant.

'He was well then? But how should you know?'

'He was not ill, as far as our comprehension extended. But he had slept very little for three nights. This I know, because I saw him walking much, and specially in the heart of the night.'

As Spurstow was arranging the sheet, a big straight-necked hunting-spur tumbled on the ground. The doctor groaned. The personal servant peeped at the body.

'What do you think, Chuma?' said Spurstow, catching the look on the dark face.

'Heaven-born, in my poor opinion, this that was my master has descended into the Dark Places, and there has been caught because he was not able to escape with sufficient speed. We have the spur for evidence that he fought with Fear. Thus have I seen men of my race do with thorns when a spell was laid upon them to overtake them in their sleeping hours and they dared not sleep.'

'Chuma, you're a mud-head. Go out and prepare seals to be set on the Sahib's property.'

'God has made the Heaven-born. God has made me. Who are we, to inquire into the dispensations of God? I will bid the other servants hold aloof while you are reckoning the tale of the Sahib's property. They are all thieves, and would steal.'

'As far as I can make out, he died from – oh, anything; stoppage of the heart's action, heat-apoplexy, or some other visitation,' said Spurstow to his companions. 'We must make an inventory of his effects, and so on.'

'He was scared to death,' insisted Lowndes. 'Look at those eyes! For pity's sake don't let him be buried with them open!'

'Whatever it was, he's clear of all the trouble now,' said Mottram softly.

Spurstow was peering into the open eyes.

'Come here,' said he. 'Can you see anything there?'

'I can't face it!' whimpered Lowndes. 'Cover up the face! Is there any fear on earth that can turn a man into that likeness? It's ghastly. Oh, Spurstow, cover it up!'

'No fear – on earth,' said Spurstow. Mottram leaned over his shoulder and looked intently.

'I see nothing except some grey blurs in the pupil. There can be nothing there, you know.'

'Even so. Well, let's think. It'll take half a day to knock up any sort of coffin; and he must have died at midnight. Lowndes, old man, go out and tell the coolies to break ground next to Jevins's grave. Mottram, go round the house with Chuma and see that the seals are put on things. Send a couple of men to me here, and I'll arrange.'

The strong-armed servants when they returned to their own kind told a strange story of the doctor Sahib vainly trying to call their master back to life by magic arts, – to wit, the holding of a little green box that clicked to each of the dead man's eyes, and of a bewildered muttering on the part of the doctor Sahib, who took the little green box away with him.

The resonant hammering of a coffin-lid is no pleasant thing to hear, but those who have experience maintain that much more terrible is the soft swish of the bed-linen, the reeving and unreeving of the bed-tapes, when he who has fallen by the roadside is apparelled for burial, sinking gradually as the tapes are tied over, till the swaddled shape touches the floor and there is no protest against the indignity of hasty disposal.

At the last moment Lowndes was seized with scruples of conscience. 'Ought you to read the service, – from beginning to end?' said he to Spurstow.

'I intend to. You're my senior as a civilian. You can take it if you like.'

'I didn't mean that for a moment. I only thought if we could get a chaplain from somewhere, – I'm willing to ride anywhere, – and give poor Hummil a better chance. That's all.'

'Bosh!' said Spurstow, as he framed his lips to the tremendous words that stand at the head of the burial service.

After breakfast they smoked a pipe in silence to the memory of the dead. Then Spurstow said absently –

' 'Tisn't in medical science.'

'What?'

'Things in a dead man's eye.'

'For goodness' sake leave that horror alone!' said Lowndes. 'I've seen a native die of pure fright when a tiger chivied him. I know what killed Hummil.'

'The deuce you do! I'm going to try to see.' And the doctor

retreated into the bath-room with a Kodak camera.[36] After a few minutes there was the sound of something being hammered to pieces, and he emerged, very white indeed.

'Have you got a picture?' said Mottram. 'What does the thing look like?'

'It was impossible, of course. You needn't look, Mottram. I've torn up the films. There was nothing there. It was impossible.'

'That,' said Lowndes, very distinctly, watching the shaking hand striving to relight the pipe, 'is a damned lie.'

Mottram laughed uneasily. 'Spurstow's right,' he said. 'We're all in such a state now that we'd believe anything. For pity's sake let's try to be rational.'

There was no further speech for a long time. The hot wind whistled without, and the dry trees sobbed. Presently the daily train, winking brass, burnished steel, and spouting steam, pulled up panting in the intense glare. 'We'd better go on on that,' said Spurstow. 'Go back to work. I've written my certificate. We can't do any more good here, and work'll keep our wits together. Come on.'

No one moved. It is not pleasant to face railway journeys at mid-day in June. Spurstow gathered up his hat and whip, and, turning in the doorway, said –

> 'There may be Heaven, – there must be Hell.
> Meantime, there is our life here. We-ell?'[37]

Neither Mottram nor Lowndes had any answer to the question.

LAFCADIO HEARN

Nightmare-Touch

I

What *is* the fear of ghosts among those who believe in ghosts?

All fear is the result of experience, – experience of the individual or of the race, – experience either of the present life or of lives forgotten. Even the fear of the unknown can have no other origin. And the fear of ghosts must be a product of past pain.

Probably the fear of ghosts, as well as the belief in them, had its beginning in dreams. It is a peculiar fear. No other fear is so intense; yet none is so vague. Feelings thus voluminous and dim are super-individual mostly, – feelings inherited, – feelings made within us by the experience of the dead.

What experience?

Nowhere do I remember reading a plain statement of the reason why ghosts are feared. Ask any ten intelligent persons of your acquaintance, who remember having once been afraid of ghosts, to tell you exactly why they were afraid, – to define the fancy behind the fear; – and I doubt whether even one will be able to answer the question. The literature of folk-lore – oral and written – throws no clear light upon the subject. We find, indeed, various legends of men torn asunder by phantoms; but such gross imaginings could not explain the peculiar quality of ghostly fear. It is not a fear of bodily violence. It is not even a reasoning fear, – not a fear that can readily explain itself, – which would not be the case if it were founded upon definite ideas of physical danger. Furthermore, although primitive ghosts may have been imagined as capable of tearing and devouring, the common idea of a ghost is certainly that of a being intangible and imponderable. *

Now I venture to state boldly that the common fear of ghosts is *the fear of being touched by ghosts*, – or, in other words, that the imagined Supernatural is dreaded mainly because of its imagined power to touch. Only to *touch*, remember! – not to wound or to kill.

But this dread of the touch would itself be the result of experience, – chiefly, I think, of prenatal experience stored up in the individual by inheritance, like the child's fear of darkness. And who can ever have had the sensation of being touched by ghosts? The answer is simple: – *Everybody who has been seized by phantoms in a dream*.

Elements of primeval fears – fears older than humanity – doubtless enter into the child-terror of darkness. But the more definite fear of ghosts may very possibly be composed with inherited results of dream-pain, – ancestral experience of nightmare. And the intuitive terror of supernatural touch can thus be evolutionally explained.

Let me now try to illustrate my theory by relating some typical experiences.

II

When about five years old I was condemned to sleep by myself in a certain isolated room, thereafter always called the Child's Room. (At that time I was scarcely ever mentioned by name, but only referred to as 'the Child.') The room was narrow, but very high, and, in spite of one tall window, very gloomy. It contained a fire-place wherein no fire was ever kindled; and the Child suspected that the chimney was haunted.

A law was made that no light should be left in the Child's

---

* I may remark here that in many old Japanese legends and ballads, ghosts are represented as having power to *pull off* people's heads. But so far as the origin of the fear of ghosts is concerned, such stories explain nothing, – since the experiences that evolved the fear must have been real, not imaginary, experiences.

Room at night, – simply because the Child was afraid of the
dark. His fear of the dark was judged to be a mental disorder
requiring severe treatment. But the treatment aggravated the
disorder. Previously I had been accustomed to sleep in a well-
lighted room, with a nurse to take care of me. I thought that I
should die of fright when sentenced to lie alone in the dark,
and – what seemed to me then abominably cruel – actually
locked into my room, the most dismal room of the house. Night
after night when I had been warmly tucked into bed, the lamp
was removed; the key clicked in the lock; the protecting light
and the footsteps of my guardian receded together. Then an
agony of fear would come upon me. Something in the black air
would seem to gather and grow – (I thought that I could even
hear it grow) – till I had to scream. Screaming regularly brought
punishment; but it also brought back the light, which more
than consoled for the punishment. This fact being at last found
out, orders were given to pay no further heed to the screams of
the Child.

Why was I thus insanely afraid? Partly because the dark had
always been peopled for me with shapes of terror. So far back
as memory extended, I had suffered from ugly dreams; and
when aroused from them I could always *see* the forms dreamed
of, lurking in the shadows of the room. They would soon fade
out; but for several moments they would appear like tangible
realities. And they were always the same figures . . . Sometimes,
without any preface of dreams, I used to see them at twilight-
time, – following me about from room to room, or reaching
long dim hands after me, from story to story, up through the
interspaces of the deep stairways.

I had complained of these haunters only to be told that I
must never speak of them, and that they did not exist. I had
complained to everybody in the house; and everybody in the
house had told me the very same thing. But there was the
evidence of my eyes! The denial of that evidence I could explain
only in two ways: – Either the shapes were afraid of big people,
and showed themselves to me alone, because I was little and
weak; or else the entire household had agreed, for some ghastly
reason, to say what was not true. This latter theory seemed to

me the more probable one, because I had several times perceived the shapes when I was not unattended; – and the consequent appearance of secrecy frightened me scarcely less than the visions did. Why was I forbidden to talk about what I saw, and even heard, – on creaking stairways, – behind wavering curtains?

'Nothing will hurt you,' – this was the merciless answer to all my pleadings not to be left alone at night. But the haunters *did* hurt me. Only – they would wait until after I had fallen asleep, and so into their power, – for they possessed occult means of preventing me from rising or moving or crying out.

Needless to comment upon the policy of locking me up alone with these fears in a black room. Unutterably was I tormented in that room – for years! Therefore I felt relatively happy when sent away at last to a children's boarding-school, where the haunters very seldom ventured to show themselves.

They were not like any people that I had ever known. They were shadowy dark-robed figures, capable of atrocious self-distortion, – capable, for instance, of growing up to the ceiling, and then across it, and then lengthening themselves, head-downwards, along the opposite wall. Only their faces were distinct; and I tried not to look at their faces. I tried also in my dreams – or thought that I tried – to awaken myself from the sight of them by pulling at my eyelids with my fingers; but the eyelids would remain closed, as if sealed ... Many years afterwards, the frightful plates in Orfila's *Traité des Exhumés*, beheld for the first time, recalled to me with a sickening start the dream-terrors of childhood.[1] But to understand the Child's experience, you must imagine Orfila's drawings intensely alive, and continually elongating or distorting, as in some monstrous anamorphosis.[2]

Nevertheless the mere sight of those nightmare-faces was not the worst of the experiences in the Child's Room. The dreams always began with a suspicion, or sensation of something heavy in the air, – slowly quenching will, – slowly numbing my power to move. At such times I usually found myself alone in a large unlighted apartment; and, almost simultaneously with the first sensation of fear, the atmosphere of the room would become suffused, half-way to the ceiling, with a sombre-yellowish glow, making objects dimly visible, – though the ceiling itself remained pitch-black. This was not a true appearance of light: rather it seemed as if the black air were changing colour from beneath ... Certain terrible aspects of sunset, on the eve of storm, offer like effects of sinister colour ... Forthwith I would try to escape, – (feeling at every step a sensation *as of wading*), – and would sometimes succeed in struggling half-way across the room; – but there I would always find myself brought to a standstill, – paralysed by some innominable opposition. Happy voices I could hear in the next room; – I could see light through the transom over the door that I had vainly endeavoured to reach; – I knew that one loud cry would save me.[3] But not even by the most frantic effort could I raise my voice above a whisper ... And all this signified only that the Nameless was coming, – was nearing, – was mounting the stairs. I could hear the step, – booming like the sound of a muffled drum, – and I wondered why nobody else heard it. A long, long time the haunter would take to come, – malevolently pausing after each ghastly footfall. Then, without a creak, the bolted door would open, – slowly, slowly, – and the thing would enter, gibbering soundlessly, – and put out hands, – and clutch me, – and toss me to the black ceiling, – and catch me descending to toss me up again, and again, and again ... In those moments the feeling was not fear: fear itself had been torpified by the first seizure. It was a sensation that has no name in the language of the living. For every touch brought a shock of something infinitely worse than pain, – something that thrilled into the innermost secret being of me, – a sort of abominable electricity, discovering unimagined capacities of suffering in totally unfamiliar regions of sentiency ... This was commonly the work of a single tormentor; but I can also remember having been caught by a group, and tossed from one to another, – seemingly for a time of many minutes.

III

Whence the fancy of those shapes? I do not know. Possibly from some impression of fear in earliest infancy; possibly from some experience of fear in other lives than mine. That mystery is forever insoluble. But the mystery of the shock of the touch admits of a definite hypothesis.

First, allow me to observe that the experience of the sensation itself cannot be dismissed as 'mere imagination.' Imagination means cerebral activity: its pains and its pleasures are alike inseparable from nervous operation, and their physical importance is sufficiently proved by their physiological effects. Dream-fear may kill as well as other fear; and no emotion thus powerful can be reasonably deemed undeserving of study.

One remarkable fact in the problem to be considered is that the sensation of seizure in dreams differs totally from all sensations familiar to ordinary waking life. Why this differentiation? How interpret the extraordinary massiveness and depth of the thrill?

I have already suggested that the dreamer's fear is most probably not a reflection of relative experience, but represents the incalculable total of ancestral experience of dream-fear. If the sum of the experience of active life be transmitted by inheritance, so must likewise be transmitted the summed experience of the life of sleep. And in normal heredity either class of transmissions would probably remain distinct.

Now, granting this hypothesis, the sensation of dream-seizure would have had its beginnings in the earliest phases of dream-consciousness, – long prior to the apparition of man. The first creatures capable of thought and fear must often have dreamed of being caught by their natural enemies. There could not have been much imagining of pain in these primal dreams. But higher nervous development in later forms of being would have been accompanied with larger susceptibility to dream-pain. Still later, with the growth of reasoning-power, ideas of the supernatural would have changed and intensified the character of dream-fear. Furthermore, through all the course of evolution, heredity would have been accumulating the

experience of such feeling. Under those forms of imaginative
pain evolved through reaction of religious beliefs, there would
persist some dim survival of savage primitive fears, and again,
under this, a dimmer but incomparably deeper substratum of
ancient animal-terrors. In the dreams of the modern child all
these latencies might quicken, – one below another, – unfath-
omably, – with the coming and the growing of nightmare.

It may be doubted whether the phantasms of any particular
nightmare have a history older than the brain in which they
move. But the shock of the touch would seem to indicate *some
point of dream-contact with the total race-experience of shadowy seizure.* It may be that profundities of Self, – abysses never
reached by any ray from the life of sun, – are strangely stirred in
slumber, and that out of their blackness immediately responds a
shuddering of memory, measureless even by millions of years.

W. W. JACOBS
The Monkey's Paw

I

Without, the night was cold and wet, but in the small parlour of Laburnam Villa the blinds were drawn and the fire burned brightly. Father and son were at chess, the former, who possessed ideas about the game involving radical changes, putting his king into such sharp and unnecessary perils that it even provoked comment from the white-haired old lady knitting placidly by the fire.

'Hark at the wind,' said Mr White, who, having seen a fatal mistake after it was too late, was amiably desirous of preventing his son from seeing it.

'I'm listening,' said the latter, grimly surveying the board as he stretched out his hand. 'Check.'

'I should hardly think that he'd come to-night,' said his father, with his hand poised over the board.

'Mate,' replied the son.

'That's the worst of living so far out,' bawled Mr White, with sudden and unlooked-for violence; 'of all the beastly, slushy, out-of-the-way places to live in, this is the worst. Pathway's a bog, and the road's a torrent. I don't know what people are thinking about. I suppose because only two houses in the road are let, they think it doesn't matter.'

'Never mind, dear,' said his wife, soothingly; 'perhaps you'll win the next one.'

Mr White looked up sharply, just in time to intercept a knowing glance between mother and son. The words died away on his lips, and he hid a guilty grin in his thin grey beard.

'There he is,' said Herbert White, as the gate banged to loudly and heavy footsteps came toward the door.

The old man rose with hospitable haste, and opening the door, was heard condoling with the new arrival. The new arrival also condoled with himself, so that Mrs White said, 'Tut, tut!' and coughed gently as her husband entered the room, followed by a tall, burly man, beady of eye and rubicund of visage.

'Sergeant-Major Morris,' he said, introducing him.

The sergeant-major shook hands, and taking the proffered seat by the fire, watched contentedly while his host got out whiskey and tumblers and stood a small copper kettle on the fire.

At the third glass his eyes got brighter, and he began to talk, the little family circle regarding with eager interest this visitor from distant parts, as he squared his broad shoulders in the chair and spoke of wild scenes and doughty deeds; of wars and plagues and strange peoples.

'Twenty-one years of it,' said Mr White, nodding at his wife and son. 'When he went away he was a slip of a youth in the warehouse. Now look at him.'

'He don't look to have taken much harm,' said Mrs White, politely.

'I'd like to go to India myself,' said the old man, 'just to look round a bit, you know.'

'Better where you are,' said the sergeant-major, shaking his head. He put down the empty glass, and sighing softly, shook it again.

'I should like to see those old temples and fakirs and jugglers,' said the old man.[1] 'What was that you started telling me the other day about a monkey's paw or something, Morris?'

'Nothing,' said the soldier, hastily. 'Leastways nothing worth hearing.'

'Monkey's paw?' said Mrs White, curiously.

'Well, it's just a bit of what you might call magic, perhaps,' said the sergeant-major, off-handedly.

His three listeners leaned forward eagerly. The visitor absent-mindedly put his empty glass to his lips and then set it down again. His host filled it for him.

'To look at,' said the sergeant-major, fumbling in his pocket, 'it's just an ordinary little paw, dried to a mummy.'

He took something out of his pocket and proffered it. Mrs White drew back with a grimace, but her son, taking it, examined it curiously.

'And what is there special about it?' inquired Mr White as he took it from his son, and having examined it, placed it upon the table.

'It had a spell put on it by an old fakir,' said the sergeant-major, 'a very holy man. He wanted to show that fate ruled people's lives, and that those who interfered with it did so to their sorrow. He put a spell on it so that three separate men could each have three wishes from it.'

His manner was so impressive that his hearers were conscious that their light laughter jarred somewhat.

'Well, why don't you have three, sir?' said Herbert White, cleverly.

The soldier regarded him in the way that middle age is wont to regard presumptuous youth. 'I have,' he said, quietly, and his blotchy face whitened.

'And did you really have the three wishes granted?' asked Mrs White.

'I did,' said the sergeant-major, and his glass tapped against his strong teeth.

'And has anybody else wished?' persisted the old lady.

'The first man had his three wishes. Yes,' was the reply; 'I don't know what the first two were, but the third was for death. That's how I got the paw.'

His tones were so grave that a hush fell upon the group.

'If you've had your three wishes, it's no good to you now, then, Morris,' said the old man at last. 'What do you keep it for?'

The soldier shook his head. 'Fancy, I suppose,' he said, slowly. 'I did have some idea of selling it, but I don't think I will. It has caused enough mischief already. Besides, people won't buy. They think it's a fairy tale; some of them, and those who do think anything of it want to try it first and pay me afterward.'

'If you could have another three wishes,' said the old man, eyeing him keenly, 'would you have them?'

'I don't know,' said the other. 'I don't know.'

He took the paw, and dangling it between his forefinger and thumb, suddenly threw it upon the fire. White, with a slight cry, stooped down and snatched it off.

'Better let it burn,' said the soldier, solemnly.

'If you don't want it, Morris,' said the other, 'give it to me.'

'I won't,' said his friend, doggedly. 'I threw it on the fire. If you keep it, don't blame me for what happens. Pitch it on the fire again like a sensible man.'

The other shook his head and examined his new possession closely. 'How do you do it?' he inquired.

'Hold it up in your right hand and wish aloud,' said the sergeant-major, 'but I warn you of the consequences.'

'Sounds like the *Arabian Nights*,' said Mrs White, as she rose and began to set the supper.[2] 'Don't you think you might wish for four pairs of hands for me?'

Her husband drew the talisman from his pocket, and then all three burst into laughter as the sergeant-major, with a look of alarm on his face, caught him by the arm.

'If you must wish,' he said, gruffly, 'wish for something sensible.'

Mr White dropped it back in his pocket, and placing chairs, motioned his friend to the table. In the business of supper the talisman was partly forgotten, and afterward the three sat listening in an enthralled fashion to a second instalment of the soldier's adventures in India.

'If the tale about the monkey's paw is not more truthful than those he has been telling us,' said Herbert, as the door closed behind their guest, just in time for him to catch the last train, 'we sha'nt make much out of it.'

'Did you give him anything for it, father?' inquired Mrs White, regarding her husband closely.

'A trifle,' said he, colouring slightly. 'He didn't want it, but I made him take it. And he pressed me again to throw it away.'

'Likely,' said Herbert, with pretended horror. 'Why, we're going to be rich, and famous and happy. Wish to be an emperor, father, to begin with; then you can't be henpecked.'

He darted round the table, pursued by the maligned Mrs White armed with an antimacassar.

Mr White took the paw from his pocket and eyed it dubiously. 'I don't know what to wish for, and that's a fact,' he said, slowly. 'It seems to me I've got all I want.'

'If you only cleared the house, you'd be quite happy, wouldn't you?' said Herbert, with his hand on his shoulder. 'Well, wish for two hundred pounds, then; that'll just do it.'

His father, smiling shamefacedly at his own credulity, held up the talisman, as his son, with a solemn face, somewhat marred by a wink at his mother, sat down at the piano and struck a few impressive chords.

'I wish for two hundred pounds,' said the old man distinctly.

A fine crash from the piano greeted the words, interrupted by a shuddering cry from the old man. His wife and son ran toward him.

'It moved,' he cried, with a glance of disgust at the object as it lay on the floor. 'As I wished, it twisted in my hand like a snake.'

'Well, I don't see the money,' said his son as he picked it up and placed it on the table, 'and I bet I never shall.'

'It must have been your fancy, father,' said his wife, regarding him anxiously.

He shook his head. 'Never mind, though; there's no harm done, but it gave me a shock all the same.'

They sat down by the fire again while the two men finished their pipes. Outside, the wind was higher than ever, and the old man started nervously at the sound of a door banging upstairs. A silence unusual and depressing settled upon all three, which lasted until the old couple rose to retire for the night.

'I expect you'll find the cash tied up in a big bag in the middle of your bed,' said Herbert, as he bade them good-night, 'and something horrible squatting up on top of the wardrobe watching you as you pocket your ill-gotten gains.'

He sat alone in the darkness, gazing at the dying fire, and seeing faces in it. The last face was so horrible and so simian that he gazed at it in amazement. It got so vivid that, with a little uneasy laugh, he felt on the table for a glass containing a little water to throw over it. His hand grasped the monkey's paw, and with a little shiver he wiped his hand on his coat and went up to bed.

II

In the brightness of the wintry sun next morning as it streamed over the breakfast table he laughed at his fears. There was an air of prosaic wholesomeness about the room which it had lacked on the previous night, and the dirty, shrivelled little paw was pitched on the sideboard with a carelessness which betokened no great belief in its virtues.

'I suppose all old soldiers are the same,' said Mrs White. 'The idea of our listening to such nonsense! How could wishes be granted in these days? And if they could, how could two hundred pounds hurt you, father?'

'Might drop on his head from the sky,' said the frivolous Herbert.

'Morris said the things happened so naturally,' said his father, 'that you might if you so wished attribute it to coincidence.'

'Well, don't break into the money before I come back,' said Herbert as he rose from the table. 'I'm afraid it'll turn you into a mean, avaricious man, and we shall have to disown you.'

His mother laughed, and following him to the door, watched him down the road; and returning to the breakfast table, was very happy at the expense of her husband's credulity. All of which did not prevent her from scurrying to the door at the postman's knock, nor prevent her from referring somewhat shortly to retired sergeant-majors of bibulous habits when she found that the post brought a tailor's bill.[3]

'Herbert will have some more of his funny remarks, I expect, when he comes home,' she said, as they sat at dinner.

'I dare say,' said Mr White, pouring himself out some beer; 'but for all that, the thing moved in my hand; that I'll swear to.'

'You thought it did,' said the old lady soothingly.

'I say it did,' replied the other. 'There was no thought about it; I had just – What's the matter?'

His wife made no reply. She was watching the mysterious movements of a man outside, who, peering in an undecided fashion at the house, appeared to be trying to make up his mind to enter. In mental connection with the two hundred pounds, she noticed that the stranger was well dressed, and wore a silk hat of glossy newness. Three times he paused at the gate, and then walked on again. The fourth time he stood with his hand upon it, and then with sudden resolution flung it open and walked up the path. Mrs White at the same moment placed her hands behind her, and hurriedly unfastening the strings of her apron, put that useful article of apparel beneath the cushion of her chair.

She brought the stranger, who seemed ill at ease, into the room. He gazed at her furtively, and listened in a preoccupied fashion as the old lady apologized for the appearance of the room, and her husband's coat, a garment which he usually reserved for the garden. She then waited as patiently as her sex would permit, for him to broach his business, but he was at first strangely silent.

'I – was asked to call,' he said at last, and stooped and picked a piece of cotton from his trousers. 'I come from "Maw and Meggins."'

The old lady started. 'Is anything the matter?' she asked, breathlessly. 'Has anything happened to Herbert? What is it? What is it?'

Her husband interposed. 'There, there, mother,' he said, hastily. 'Sit down, and don't jump to conclusions. You've not brought bad news, I'm sure, sir;' and he eyed the other wistfully.

'I'm sorry –' began the visitor.

'Is he hurt?' demanded the mother, wildly.

The visitor bowed in assent. 'Badly hurt,' he said, quietly, 'but he is not in any pain.'

'Oh, thank God!' said the old woman, clasping her hands. 'Thank God for that! Thank –'

She broke off suddenly as the sinister meaning of the assurance dawned upon her and she saw the awful confirmation of her fears in the other's perverted face. She caught her breath, and turning to her slower-witted husband, laid her trembling old hand upon his. There was a long silence.

'He was caught in the machinery,' said the visitor at length in a low voice.

'Caught in the machinery,' repeated Mr White, in a dazed fashion, 'yes.'

He sat staring blankly out at the window, and taking his wife's hand between his own, pressed it as he had been wont to do in their old courting-days nearly forty years before.

'He was the only one left to us,' he said, turning gently to the visitor. 'It is hard.'

The other coughed, and rising, walked slowly to the window. 'The firm wished me to convey their sincere sympathy with you in your great loss,' he said, without looking round. 'I beg that you will understand I am only their servant and merely obeying orders.'

There was no reply; the old woman's face was white, her eyes staring, and her breath inaudible; on the husband's face was a look such as his friend the sergeant might have carried into his first action.

'I was to say that Maw and Meggins disclaim all responsibility,' continued the other. 'They admit no liability at all, but in consideration of your son's services, they wish to present you with a certain sum as compensation.'

Mr White dropped his wife's hand, and rising to his feet, gazed with a look of horror at his visitor. His dry lips shaped the words, 'How much?'

'Two hundred pounds,' was the answer.

Unconscious of his wife's shriek, the old man smiled faintly, put out his hands like a sightless man, and dropped, a senseless heap, to the floor.

III

In the huge new cemetery, some two miles distant, the old people buried their dead, and came back to a house steeped in shadow and silence. It was all over so quickly that at first they could hardly realize it, and remained in a state of expectation as though of something else to happen – something else which was to lighten this load, too heavy for old hearts to bear.

But the days passed, and expectation gave place to resignation – the hopeless resignation of the old, sometimes miscalled, apathy. Sometimes they hardly exchanged a word, for now they had nothing to talk about, and their days were long to weariness.

It was about a week after that the old man, waking suddenly in the night, stretched out his hand and found himself alone. The room was in darkness, and the sound of subdued weeping came from the window. He raised himself in bed and listened.

'Come back,' he said, tenderly. 'You will be cold.'

'It is colder for my son,' said the old woman, and wept afresh.

The sound of her sobs died away on his ears. The bed was warm, and his eyes heavy with sleep. He dozed fitfully, and then slept until a sudden wild cry from his wife awoke him with a start.

'*The paw!*' she cried wildly. 'The monkey's paw!'

He started up in alarm. 'Where? Where is it? What's the matter?'

She came stumbling across the room toward him. 'I want it,' she said, quietly. 'You've not destroyed it?'

'It's in the parlour, on the bracket,' he replied, marvelling. 'Why?'

She cried and laughed together, and bending over, kissed his cheek.

'I only just thought of it,' she said, hysterically. 'Why didn't I think of it before? Why didn't *you* think of it?'

'Think of what?' he questioned.

'The other two wishes,' she replied, rapidly. 'We've only had one.'

'Was not that enough?' he demanded, fiercely.

'No,' she cried, triumphantly; 'we'll have one more. Go down and get it quickly, and wish our boy alive again.'

The man sat up in bed and flung the bedclothes from his quaking limbs. 'Good God, you are mad!' he cried, aghast.

'Get it,' she panted; 'get it quickly, and wish – Oh, my boy, my boy!'

Her husband struck a match and lit the candle. 'Get back to bed,' he said, unsteadily. 'You don't know what you are saying.'

'We had the first wish granted,' said the old woman, feverishly; 'why not the second?'

'A coincidence,' stammered the old man.

'Go and get it and wish,' cried his wife, quivering with
excitement.

The old man turned and regarded her, and his voice shook.
'He has been dead ten days, and besides he – I would not tell
you else, but – I could only recognize him by his clothing. If he
was too terrible for you to scc then, how now?'

'Bring him back,' cried the old woman, and dragged him
toward the door. 'Do you think I fear the child I have nursed?'

He went down in the darkness, and felt his way to the parlour,
and then to the mantelpiece. The talisman was in its place, and
a horrible fear that the unspoken wish might bring his mutilated
son before him ere he could escape from the room seized upon
him, and he caught his breath as he found that he had lost the
direction of the door. His brow cold with sweat, he felt his way
round the table, and groped along the wall until he found himself
in the small passage with the unwholesome thing in his hand.

Even his wife's face seemed changed as he entered the room.
It was white and expectant, and to his fears seemed to have an
unnatural look upon it. He was afraid of her.

'*Wish!*' she cried, in a strong voice.

'It is foolish and wicked,' he faltered.

'*Wish!*' repeated his wife.

He raised his hand. 'I wish my son alive again.'

The talisman fell to the floor, and he regarded it fearfully.
Then he sank trembling into a chair as the old woman, with
burning eyes, walked to the window and raised the blind.

He sat until he was chilled with the cold, glancing occasionally at the figure of the old woman peering through the window.
The candle-end, which had burned below the rim of the china
candlestick, was throwing pulsating shadows on the ceiling and
walls, until, with a flicker larger than the rest, it expired. The
old man, with an unspeakable sense of relief at the failure of
the talisman, crept back to his bed, and a minute or two afterward the old woman came silently and apathetically beside him.

Neither spoke, but lay silently listening to the ticking of the
clock. A stair creaked, and a squeaky mouse scurried noisily
through the wall. The darkness was oppressive, and after lying
for some time screwing up his courage, he took the box of
matches, and striking one, went downstairs for a candle.

At the foot of the stairs the match went out, and he paused to strike another; and at the same moment a knock, so quiet and stealthy as to be scarcely audible, sounded on the front door.

The matches fell from his hand and spilled in the passage. He stood motionless, his breath suspended until the knock was repeated. Then he turned and fled swiftly back to his room, and closed the door behind him. A third knock sounded through the house.

'*What's that?*' cried the old woman, starting up.

'A rat,' said the old man in shaking tones – 'a rat. It passed me on the stairs.'

His wife sat up in bed listening. A loud knock resounded through the house.

'It's Herbert!' she screamed. 'It's Herbert!'

She ran to the door, but her husband was before her, and catching her by the arm, held her tightly.

'What are you going to do?' he whispered hoarsely.

'It's my boy; it's Herbert!' she cried, struggling mechanically. 'I forgot it was two miles away. What are you holding me for? Let go. I must open the door.'

'For God's sake don't let it in,' cried the old man, trembling.

'You're afraid of your own son,' she cried, struggling. 'Let me go. I'm coming, Herbert; I'm coming.'

There was another knock, and another. The old woman with a sudden wrench broke free and ran from the room. Her husband followed to the landing, and called after her appealingly as she hurried downstairs. He heard the chain rattle back and the bottom bolt drawn slowly and stiffly from the socket. Then the old woman's voice, strained and panting.

'The bolt,' she cried, loudly. 'Come down. I can't reach it.'

But her husband was on his hands and knees groping wildly on the floor in search of the paw. If he could only find it before the thing outside got in. A perfect fusillade of knocks reverberated through the house, and he heard the scraping of a chair as his wife put it down in the passage against the door. He heard the creaking of the bolt as it came slowly back, and at the same moment he found the monkey's paw, and frantically breathed his third and last wish.

The knocking ceased suddenly, although the echoes of it were still in the house. He heard the chair drawn back, and the door opened. A cold wind rushed up the staircase, and a long loud wail of disappointment and misery from his wife gave him courage to run down to her side, and then to the gate beyond. The street lamp flickering opposite shone on a quiet and deserted road.

MARY WILKINS FREEMAN

The Wind in the Rose-Bush

Ford Village has no railroad station, being on the other side of the river from Porter's Falls, and accessible only by the ford which gives it its name, and a ferry line.[1]

The ferry-boat was waiting when Rebecca Flint got off the train with her bag and lunch basket. When she and her small trunk were safely embarked she sat stiff and straight and calm in the ferry-boat as it shot swiftly and smoothly across stream. There was a horse attached to a light country wagon on board, and he pawed the deck uneasily. His owner stood near, with a wary eye upon him, although he was chewing, with as dully reflective an expression as a cow. Beside Rebecca sat a woman of about her own age, who kept looking at her with furtive curiosity; her husband, short and stout and saturnine, stood near her. Rebecca paid no attention to either of them. She was tall and spare and pale, the type of a spinster, yet with rudimentary lines and expressions of matronhood. She all unconsciously held her shawl, rolled up in a canvas bag, on her left hip, as if it had been a child. She wore a settled frown of dissent at life, but it was the frown of a mother who regarded life as a froward child, rather than as an overwhelming fate.[2]

The other woman continued staring at her; she was mildly stupid, except for an over-developed curiosity which made her at times sharp beyond belief. Her eyes glittered, red spots came on her flaccid cheeks; she kept opening her mouth to speak, making little abortive motions. Finally she could endure it no longer; she nudged Rebecca boldly.

'A pleasant day,' said she.

Rebecca looked at her and nodded coldly.

'Yes, very,' she assented.

'Have you come far?'

'I have come from Michigan.'

'Oh!' said the woman, with awe. 'It's a long way,' she remarked presently.

'Yes, it is,' replied Rebecca, conclusively.

Still the other woman was not daunted; there was something which she determined to know, possibly roused thereto by a vague sense of incongruity in the other's appearance. 'It's a long ways to come and leave a family,' she remarked with painful slyness.

'I ain't got any family to leave,' returned Rebecca shortly.

'Then you ain't –'

'No, I ain't.'

'Oh!' said the woman.

Rebecca looked straight ahead at the race of the river.

It was a long ferry. Finally Rebecca herself waxed unexpectedly loquacious. She turned to the other woman and inquired if she knew John Dent's widow who lived in Ford Village. 'Her husband died about three years ago,' said she, by way of detail.

The woman started violently. She turned pale, then she flushed; she cast a strange glance at her husband, who was regarding both women with a sort of stolid keenness.

'Yes, I guess I do,' faltered the woman finally.

'Well, his first wife was my sister,' said Rebecca with the air of one imparting important intelligence.

'Was she?' responded the other woman feebly. She glanced at her husband with an expression of doubt and terror, and he shook his head forbiddingly.

'I'm going to see her, and take my niece Agnes home with me,' said Rebecca.

Then the woman gave such a violent start that she noticed it.

'What is the matter?' she asked.

'Nothin', I guess,' replied the woman, with eyes on her husband, who was slowly shaking his head, like a Chinese toy.

'Is my niece sick?' asked Rebecca with quick suspicion.

'No, she ain't sick,' replied the woman with alacrity, then she caught her breath with a gasp.

'When did you see her?'

'Let me see; I ain't seen her for some little time,' replied the woman. Then she caught her breath again.

'She ought to have grown up real pretty, if she takes after my sister. She was a real pretty woman,' Rebecca said wistfully.

'Yes, I guess she did grow up pretty,' replied the woman in a trembling voice.

'What kind of a woman is the second wife?'

The woman glanced at her husband's warning face. She continued to gaze at him while she replied in a choking voice to Rebecca:

'I – guess she's a nice woman,' she replied. 'I – don't know, I – guess so. I – don't see much of her.'

'I felt kind of hurt that John married again so quick,' said Rebecca; 'but I suppose he wanted his house kept, and Agnes wanted care. I wasn't so situated that I could take her when her mother died. I had my own mother to care for, and I was school-teaching. Now mother has gone, and my uncle died six months ago and left me quite a little property, and I've given up my school, and I've come for Agnes. I guess she'll be glad to go with me, though I suppose her stepmother is a good woman, and has always done for her.'

The man's warning shake at his wife was fairly portentous.

'I guess so,' said she.

'John always wrote that she was a beautiful woman,' said Rebecca.

Then the ferry-boat grated on the shore.

John Dent's widow had sent a horse and wagon to meet her sister-in-law. When the woman and her husband went down the road, on which Rebecca in the wagon with her trunk soon passed them, she said reproachfully:

'Seems as if I'd ought to have told her, Thomas.'

'Let her find it out herself,' replied the man. 'Don't you go to burnin' your fingers in other folks' puddin', Maria.'

'Do you s'pose she'll see anything?' asked the woman with a spasmodic shudder and a terrified roll of her eyes.

'See!' returned her husband with stolid scorn. 'Better be sure there's anything to see.'

'Oh, Thomas, they say –'

'Lord, ain't you found out that what they say is mostly lies?'

'But if it should be true, and she's a nervous woman, she might be scared enough to lose her wits,' said his wife, staring uneasily after Rebecca's erect figure in the wagon disappearing over the crest of the hilly road.

'Wits that so easy upset ain't worth much,' declared the man. 'You keep out of it, Maria.'

Rebecca in the meantime rode on in the wagon, beside a flaxen-headed boy, who looked, to her understanding, not very bright. She asked him a question, and he paid no attention. She repeated it, and he responded with a bewildered and incoherent grunt. Then she let him alone, after making sure that he knew how to drive straight.

They had travelled about half a mile, passed the village square, and gone a short distance beyond, when the boy drew up with a sudden Whoa! before a very prosperous-looking house. It had been one of the aboriginal cottages of the vicinity, small and white, with a roof extending on one side over a piazza, and a tiny 'L' jutting out in the rear, on the right hand. Now the cottage was transformed by dormer windows, a bay window on the piazzaless side, a carved railing down the front steps, and a modern hard-wood door.[3]

'Is this John Dent's house?' asked Rebecca.

The boy was as sparing of speech as a philosopher. His only response was in flinging the reins over the horse's back, stretching out one foot to the shaft, and leaping out of the wagon, then going around to the rear for the trunk. Rebecca got out and went toward the house. Its white paint had a new gloss; its blinds were an immaculate apple green; the lawn was trimmed as smooth as velvet, and it was dotted with scrupulous groups of hydrangeas and cannas.[4]

'I always understood that John Dent was well-to-do,' Rebecca reflected comfortably. 'I guess Agnes will have considerable. I've got enough, but it will come in handy for her schooling. She can have advantages.'

The boy dragged the trunk up the fine gravel-walk, but before he reached the steps leading up to the piazza, for the house stood on a terrace, the front door opened and a fair, frizzled head of a very large and handsome woman appeared. She held up her black silk skirt, disclosing voluminous ruffles of starched embroidery, and waited for Rebecca. She smiled placidly, her pink, double-chinned face widened and dimpled, but her blue eyes were wary and calculating. She extended her hand as Rebecca climbed the steps.

'This is Miss Flint, I suppose,' said she.

'Yes, ma'am,' replied Rebecca, noticing with bewilderment a curious expression compounded of fear and defiance on the other's face.

'Your letter only arrived this morning,' said Mrs Dent, in a steady voice. Her great face was a uniform pink, and her china-blue eyes were at once aggressive and veiled with secrecy.

'Yes, I hardly thought you'd get my letter,' replied Rebecca. 'I felt as if I could not wait to hear from you before I came. I supposed you would be so situated that you could have me a little while without putting you out too much, from what John used to write me about his circumstances, and when I had that money so unexpected I felt as if I must come for Agnes. I suppose you will be willing to give her up. You know she's my own blood, and of course she's no relation to you, though you must have got attached to her. I know from her picture what a sweet girl she must be, and John always said she looked like her own mother, and Grace was a beautiful woman, if she was my sister.'

Rebecca stopped and stared at the other woman in amazement and alarm. The great handsome blonde creature stood speechless, livid, gasping, with her hand to her heart, her lips parted in a horrible caricature of a smile.

'Are you sick!' cried Rebecca, drawing near. 'Don't you want me to get you some water!'

Then Mrs Dent recovered herself with a great effort. 'It is nothing,' she said. 'I am subject to – spells. I am over it now. Won't you come in, Miss Flint?'

As she spoke, the beautiful deep-rose colour suffused her face, her blue eyes met her visitor's with the opaqueness of turquoise – with a revelation of blue, but a concealment of all behind.

Rebecca followed her hostess in, and the boy, who had waited quiescently, climbed the steps with the trunk. But before they entered the door a strange thing happened. On the upper terrace, close to the piazza-post, grew a great rose-bush, and on it, late in the season though it was, one small red, perfect rose.

Rebecca looked at it, and the other woman extended her hand with a quick gesture. 'Don't you pick that rose!' she brusquely cried.

Rebecca drew herself up with stiff dignity.

'I ain't in the habit of picking other folks' roses without leave,' said she.

As Rebecca spoke she started violently, and lost sight of her resentment, for something singular happened. Suddenly the rose-bush was agitated violently as if by a gust of wind, yet it was a remarkably still day. Not a leaf of the hydrangea standing on the terrace close to the rose trembled.

'What on earth –' began Rebecca, then she stopped with a gasp at the sight of the other woman's face. Although a face, it gave somehow the impression of a desperately clutched hand of secrecy.

'Come in!' said she in a harsh voice, which seemed to come forth from her chest with no intervention of the organs of speech. 'Come into the house. I'm getting cold out here.'

'What makes that rose-bush blow so when there isn't any wind?' asked Rebecca, trembling with vague horror, yet resolute.

'I don't see as it is blowing,' returned the woman calmly. And as she spoke, indeed, the bush was quiet.

'It was blowing,' declared Rebecca.

'It isn't now,' said Mrs Dent. 'I can't try to account for everything that blows out-of-doors. I have too much to do.'

She spoke scornfully and confidently, with defiant, unflinching eyes, first on the bush, then on Rebecca, and led the way into the house.

'It looked queer,' persisted Rebecca, but she followed, and also the boy with the trunk.

Rebecca entered an interior, prosperous, even elegant, according to her simple ideas. There were Brussels carpets, lace curtains, and plenty of brilliant upholstery and polished wood.[5]

'You're real nicely situated,' remarked Rebecca, after she had become a little accustomed to her new surroundings and the two women were seated at the tea-table.

Mrs Dent stared with a hard complacency from behind her silver-plated service. 'Yes, I be,' said she.

'You got all the things new?' said Rebecca hesitatingly, with a jealous memory of her dead sister's bridal furnishings.

'Yes,' said Mrs Dent; 'I was never one to want dead folks' things, and I had money enough of my own, so I wasn't beholden to John. I had the old duds put up at auction.[6] They didn't bring much.'

'I suppose you saved some for Agnes. She'll want some of her poor mother's things when she is grown up,' said Rebecca with some indignation.

The defiant stare of Mrs Dent's blue eyes waxed more intense. 'There's a few things up garret,' said she.

'She'll be likely to value them,' remarked Rebecca. As she spoke she glanced at the window. 'Isn't it most time for her to be coming home?' she asked.

'Most time,' answered Mrs Dent carelessly; 'but when she gets over to Addie Slocum's she never knows when to come home.'

'Is Addie Slocum her intimate friend?'

'Intimate as any.'

'Maybe we can have her come out to see Agnes when she's living with me,' said Rebecca wistfully. 'I suppose she'll be likely to be homesick at first.'

'Most likely,' answered Mrs Dent.

'Does she call you mother?' Rebecca asked.

'No, she calls me Aunt Emeline,' replied the other woman shortly. 'When did you say you were going home?'

'In about a week, I thought, if she can be ready to go so soon,' answered Rebecca with a surprised look.

She reflected that she would not remain a day longer than she could help after such an inhospitable look and question.

'Oh, as far as that goes,' said Mrs Dent, 'it wouldn't make any difference about her being ready. You could go home whenever you felt that you must, and she could come afterward.'

'Alone?'

'Why not? She's a big girl now, and you don't have to change cars.'

'My niece will go home when I do, and not travel alone; and if I can't wait here for her, in the house that used to be her mother's and my sister's home, I'll go and board somewhere,' returned Rebecca with warmth.

'Oh, you can stay here as long as you want to. You're welcome,' said Mrs Dent.

Then Rebecca started. 'There she is!' she declared in a trembling, exultant voice. Nobody knew how she longed to see the girl.

'She isn't as late as I thought she'd be,' said Mrs Dent, and again that curious, subtle change passed over her face, and again it settled into that stony impassiveness.

Rebecca stared at the door, waiting for it to open. 'Where is she?' she asked presently.

'I guess she's stopped to take off her hat in the entry,' suggested Mrs Dent.

Rebecca waited. 'Why don't she come? It can't take her all this time to take off her hat.'

For answer Mrs Dent rose with a stiff jerk and threw open the door.

'Agnes!' she called. 'Agnes!' Then she turned and eyed Rebecca. 'She ain't there.'

'I saw her pass the window,' said Rebecca in bewilderment.

'You must have been mistaken.'

'I know I did,' persisted Rebecca.

'You couldn't have.'

'I did. I saw first a shadow go over the ceiling, then I saw her in the glass there' – she pointed to a mirror over the sideboard opposite – 'and then the shadow passed the window.'

'How did she look in the glass?'

'Little and light-haired, with the light hair kind of tossing over her forehead.'

'You couldn't have seen her.'

'Was that like Agnes?'

'Like enough; but of course you didn't see her. You've been thinking so much about her that you thought you did.'

'You thought *you* did.'

'I thought I saw a shadow pass the window, but I must have been mistaken. She didn't come in, or we would have seen her before now. I knew it was too early for her to get home from Addie Slocum's, anyhow.'

When Rebecca went to bed Agnes had not returned. Rebecca had resolved that she would not retire until the girl came, but she was very tired, and she reasoned with herself that she was foolish. Besides, Mrs Dent suggested that Agnes might go to the church social with Addie Slocum. When Rebecca suggested that she be sent for and told that her aunt had come, Mrs Dent laughed meaningly.

'I guess you'll find out that a young girl ain't so ready to leave a sociable, where there's boys, to see her aunt,' said she.

'She's too young,' said Rebecca incredulously and indignantly.

'She's sixteen,' replied Mrs Dent; 'and she's always been great for the boys.'

'She's going to school four years after I get her before she thinks of boys,' declared Rebecca.

'We'll see,' laughed the other woman.

After Rebecca went to bed, she lay awake a long time listening for the sound of girlish laughter and a boy's voice under her window; then she fell asleep.

The next morning she was down early. Mrs Dent, who kept no servants, was busily preparing breakfast.

'Don't Agnes help you about breakfast?' asked Rebecca.

'No, I let her lay,' replied Mrs Dent shortly.

'What time did she get home last night?'

'She didn't get home.'

'What?'

'She didn't get home. She stayed with Addie. She often does.'

'Without sending you word?'

'Oh, she knew I wouldn't worry.'

'When will she be home?'

'Oh, I guess she'll be along pretty soon.'

Rebecca was uneasy, but she tried to conceal it, for she knew of no good reason for uneasiness. What was there to occasion alarm in the fact of one young girl staying overnight with another? She could not eat much breakfast. Afterward she went out on the little piazza, although her hostess strove furtively to stop her.

'Why don't you go out back of the house? It's real pretty – a view over the river,' she said.

'I guess I'll go out here,' replied Rebecca. She had a purpose: to watch for the absent girl.

252 MARY WILKINS FREEMAN

Presently Rebecca came hustling into the house through the sitting-room, into the kitchen where Mrs Dent was cooking.

'That rose-bush!' she gasped.

Mrs Dent turned and faced her.

'What of it?'

'It's a-blowing.'

'What of it?'

'There isn't a mite of wind this morning.'

Mrs Dent turned with an inimitable toss of her fair head. 'If you think I can spend my time puzzling over such nonsense as –' she began, but Rebecca interrupted her with a cry and a rush to the door.

'There she is now!' she cried.

She flung the door wide open, and curiously enough a breeze came in and her own grey hair tossed, and a paper blew off the table to the floor with a loud rustle, but there was nobody in sight.

'There's nobody here,' Rebecca said.

She looked blankly at the other woman, who brought her rolling-pin down on a slab of pie-crust with a thud.

'I didn't hear anybody,' she said calmly.

'*I saw somebody pass that window!*'

'You were mistaken again.'

'I *know* I saw somebody.'

'You couldn't have. Please shut that door.'

Rebecca shut the door. She sat down beside the window and looked out on the autumnal yard, with its little curve of footpath to the kitchen door.

'What smells so strong of roses in this room?' she said presently. She sniffed hard.

'I don't smell anything but these nutmegs.'

'It is not nutmeg.'

'I don't smell anything else.'

'Where do you suppose Agnes is?'

'Oh, perhaps she has gone over the ferry to Porter's Falls with Addie. She often does. Addie's got an aunt over there, and Addie's got a cousin, a real pretty boy.'

'You suppose she's gone over there?'

'Mebbe. I shouldn't wonder.'

'When should she be home?'

'Oh, not before afternoon.'

Rebecca waited with all the patience she could muster. She kept reassuring herself, telling herself that it was all natural, that the other woman could not help it, but she made up her mind that if Agnes did not return that afternoon she should be sent for.

When it was four o'clock she started up with resolution. She had been furtively watching the onyx clock on the sitting-room mantel; she had timed herself. She had said that if Agnes was not home by that time she should demand that she be sent for. She rose and stood before Mrs Dent, who looked up coolly from her embroidery.

'I've waited just as long as I'm going to,' she said. 'I've come 'way from Michigan to see my own sister's daughter and take her home with me. I've been here ever since yesterday – twenty-four hours – and I haven't seen her. Now I'm going to. I want her sent for.'

Mrs Dent folded her embroidery and rose.

'Well, I don't blame you,' she said. 'It is high time she came home. I'll go right over and get her myself.'

Rebecca heaved a sigh of relief. She hardly knew what she had suspected or feared, but she knew that her position had been one of antagonism if not accusation, and she was sensible of relief.

'I wish you would,' she said gratefully, and went back to her chair, while Mrs Dent got her shawl and her little white head-tie. 'I wouldn't trouble you, but I do feel as if I couldn't wait any longer to see her,' she remarked apologetically.

'Oh, it ain't any trouble at all,' said Mrs Dent as she went out. 'I don't blame you; you have waited long enough.'

Rebecca sat at the window watching breathlessly until Mrs Dent came stepping through the yard alone. She ran to the door and saw, hardly noticing it this time, that the rose-bush was again violently agitated, yet with no wind evident elsewhere.

'Where is she?' she cried.

Mrs Dent laughed with stiff lips as she came up the steps over the terrace. 'Girls will be girls,' said she. 'She's gone with Addie to Lincoln.[7] Addie's got an uncle who's conductor on the train, and lives there, and he got 'em passes, and they're goin' to stay to Addie's Aunt Margaret's a few days. Mrs Slocum said Agnes didn't have time to come over and ask me before the train went, but she took it on herself to say it would be all right, and –'

'Why hadn't she been over to tell you?' Rebecca was angry, though not suspicious. She even saw no reason for her anger.

'Oh, she was putting up grapes. She was coming over just as soon as she got the black off her hands. She heard I had company, and her hands were a sight. She was holding them over sulphur matches.'

'You say she's going to stay a few days?' repeated Rebecca dazedly.

'Yes; till Thursday, Mrs Slocum said.'

'How far is Lincoln from here?'

'About fifty miles. It'll be a real treat to her. Mrs Slocum's sister is a real nice woman.'

'It is goin' to make it pretty late about my goin' home.'

'If you don't feel as if you could wait, I'll get her ready and send her on just as soon as I can,' Mrs Dent said sweetly.

'I'm going to wait,' said Rebecca grimly.

The two women sat down again, and Mrs Dent took up her embroidery.

'Is there any sewing I can do for her?' Rebecca asked finally in a desperate way. 'If I can get her sewing along some –'

Mrs Dent arose with alacrity and fetched a mass of white from the closet. 'Here,' she said, 'if you want to sew the lace on this nightgown. I was going to put her to it, but she'll be glad enough to get rid of it. She ought to have this and one more before she goes. I don't like to send her away without some good underclothing.'

Rebecca snatched at the little white garment and sewed feverishly.

That night she wakened from a deep sleep a little after midnight and lay a minute trying to collect her faculties and explain to herself what she was listening to. At last she discovered that it was the then popular strains of 'The Maiden's Prayer' floating up through the floor from the piano in the sitting-room below.[8]

She jumped up, threw a shawl over her nightgown, and hurried downstairs trembling. There was nobody in the sitting-room; the piano was silent. She ran to Mrs Dent's bedroom and called hysterically:

'Emeline! Emeline!'

'What is it?' asked Mrs Dent's voice from the bed. The voice was stern, but had a note of consciousness in it.

'Who – who was that playing "The Maiden's Prayer" in the sitting-room, on the piano?'

'I didn't hear anybody.'

'There was some one.'

'I didn't hear anything.'

'I tell you there was some one. But – *there ain't anybody there.*'

'I didn't hear anything.'

'I did – somebody playing "The Maiden's Prayer" on the piano. Has Agnes got home? I *want to know.*'

'Of course Agnes hasn't got home,' answered Mrs Dent with rising inflection. 'Be you gone crazy over that girl? The last boat from Porter's Falls was in before we went to bed. Of course she ain't come.'

'I heard –'

'You were dreaming.'

'I wasn't; I was broad awake.'

Rebecca went back to her chamber and kept her lamp burning all night.

The next morning her eyes upon Mrs Dent were wary and blazing with suppressed excitement. She kept opening her mouth as if to speak, then frowning, and setting her lips hard. After breakfast she went upstairs, and came down presently with her coat and bonnet.

'Now, Emeline,' she said, 'I want to know where the Slocums live.'

Mrs Dent gave a strange, long, half-lidded glance at her. She was finishing her coffee.

'Why?' she asked.

'I'm going over there and find out if they have heard anything from her daughter and Agnes since they went away. I don't like what I heard last night.'

'You must have been dreaming.'

'I don't make any odds whether I was or not. Does she play "The Maiden's Prayer" on the piano? I want to know.'

'What if she does? She plays it a little, I believe. I don't know. She don't half play it, anyhow; she ain't got an ear.'

'That wasn't half played last night. I don't like such things happening. I ain't superstitious, but I don't like it. I'm going. Where do the Slocum's live?'

'You go down the road over the bridge past the old grist mill, then you turn to the left; it's the only house for half a mile. You can't miss it. It has a barn with a ship in full sail on the cupola.'

'Well, I'm going. I don't feel easy.'

About two hours later Rebecca returned. There were red spots on her cheeks. She looked wild. 'I've been there,' she said, 'and there isn't a soul at home. Something *has* happened.'

'What has happened?'

'I don't know. Something. I had a warning last night. There wasn't a soul there. They've been sent for to Lincoln.'

'Did you see anybody to ask?' asked Mrs Dent with thinly concealed anxiety.

'I asked the woman that lives on the turn of the road. She's stone deaf. I suppose you know. She listened while I screamed at her to know where the Slocums were, and then she said, "Mrs Smith don't live here." I didn't see anybody on the road, and that's the only house. What do you suppose it means?'

'I don't suppose it means much of anything,' replied Mrs Dent coolly. 'Mr Slocum is conductor on the railroad, and he'd be away anyway, and Mrs Slocum often goes early when he does, to spend the day with her sister in Porter's Falls. She'd be more likely to go away than Addie.'

'And you don't think anything has happened?' Rebecca asked with diminishing distrust before the reasonableness of it.

'Land, no!'

Rebecca went upstairs to lay aside her coat and bonnet. But she came hurrying back with them still on.

'Who's been in my room?' she gasped. Her face was pale as ashes.

Mrs Dent also paled as she regarded her.

'What do you mean?' she asked slowly.

'I found when I went upstairs that – little nightgown of – Agnes's on – the bed, laid out. It was – *laid out*. The sleeves were folded across the bosom, and there was that little red rose between them. Emeline, what is it? Emeline, what's the matter? Oh!'

Mrs Dent was struggling for breath in great, choking gasps. She clung to the back of a chair. Rebecca, trembling herself so she could scarcely keep on her feet, got her some water.

As soon as she recovered herself Mrs Dent regarded her with eyes full of the strangest mixture of fear and horror and hostility.

'What do you mean talking so?' she said in a hard voice.

'It *is there*.'

'Nonsense. You threw it down and it fell that way.'

'It was folded in my bureau drawer.'

'It couldn't have been.'

'Who picked that red rose?'

'Look on the bush,' Mrs Dent replied shortly.

Rebecca looked at her; her mouth gaped. She hurried out of the room. When she came back her eyes seemed to protrude. (She had in the meantime hastened upstairs, and come down with tottering steps, clinging to the banisters.)

'Now I want to know what all this means?' she demanded.

'What what means?'

'The rose is on the bush, and it's gone from the bed in my room! Is this house haunted, or what?'

'I don't know anything about a house being haunted. I don't believe in such things. Be you crazy?' Mrs Dent spoke with gathering force. The colour flashed back to her cheeks.

'No,' said Rebecca shortly. 'I ain't crazy yet, but I shall be if this keeps on much longer. I'm going to find out where that girl is before night.'

Mrs Dent eyed her.

'What be you going to do?'

'I'm going to Lincoln.'

A faint triumphant smile overspread Mrs Dent's large face.

'You can't,' said she; 'there ain't any train.'

'No train?'

'No; there ain't any afternoon train from the Falls to Lincoln.'

'Then I'm going over to the Slocums' again to-night.'

However, Rebecca did not go; such a rain came up as deterred even her resolution, and she had only her best dresses with her. Then in the evening came the letter from the Michigan village which she had left nearly a week ago. It was from her cousin, a single woman, who had come to keep her house while she was away. It was a pleasant unexciting letter enough, all the first of it, and related mostly how she missed Rebecca; how she hoped she was having pleasant weather and kept her health; and how her friend, Mrs Greenaway, had come to stay with her since she had felt lonesome the first night in the house; how she hoped Rebecca would have no objections to this, although nothing had been said about it, since she had not realized that she might be nervous alone. The cousin was painfully conscientious, hence the letter. Rebecca smiled in spite of her disturbed mind as she read it, then her eye caught the postscript. That was in a different hand, purporting to be written by the friend, Mrs Hannah Greenaway, informing her that the cousin had fallen down the cellar stairs and broken her hip, and was in a dangerous condition, and begging Rebecca to return at once, as she herself was rheumatic and unable to nurse her properly, and no one else could be obtained.

Rebecca looked at Mrs Dent, who had come to her room with the letter quite late; it was half-past nine, and she had gone upstairs for the night.

'Where did this come from?' she asked.

'Mr Amblecrom brought it,' she replied.

'Who's he?'

'The postmaster. He often brings the letters that come on the late mail. He knows I ain't anybody to send. He brought yours about your coming. He said he and his wife came over on the ferry-boat with you.'

'I remember him,' Rebecca replied shortly. 'There's bad news in this letter.'

Mrs Dent's face took on an expression of serious inquiry.

'Yes, my Cousin Harriet has fallen down the cellar stairs – they were always dangerous – and she's broken her hip, and I've got to take the first train home to-morrow.'

'You don't say so. I'm dreadfully sorry.'

'No, you ain't sorry!' said Rebecca, with a look as if she leaped. 'You're glad. I don't know why, but you're glad. You've wanted to get rid of me for some reason ever since I came. I don't know why. You're a strange woman. Now you've got your way, and I hope you're satisfied.'

'How you talk.'

Mrs Dent spoke in a faintly injured voice, but there was a light in her eyes.

'I talk the way it is. Well, I'm going to-morrow morning, and I want you, just as soon as Agnes Dent comes home, to send her out to me. Don't you wait for anything. You pack what clothes she's got, and don't wait even to mend them, and you buy her ticket. I'll leave the money, and you send her along. She don't have to change cars. You start her off, when she gets home, on the next train!'

'Very well,' replied the other woman. She had an expression of covert amusement.

'Mind you do it.'

'Very well, Rebecca.'

Rebecca started on her journey the next morning. When she arrived, two days later, she found her cousin in perfect health. She found, moreover, that the friend had not written the postscript in the cousin's letter. Rebecca would have returned to Ford Village the next morning, but the fatigue and nervous strain had been too much for her. She was not able to move from her bed. She had a species of low fever induced by anxiety and fatigue. But she could write, and she did, to the Slocums, and she received no answer. She also wrote to Mrs Dent; she even sent numerous telegrams, with no response. Finally she wrote to the postmaster, and an answer arrived by the first possible mail. The letter was short, curt, and to the purpose. Mr Amblecrom, the postmaster, was a man of few words, and especially wary as to his expressions in a letter.

'Dear madam,' he wrote, 'your favour rec'ed. No Slocums in Ford's Village. All dead. Addie ten years ago, her mother two years later, her father five. House vacant. Mrs John Dent said to have neglected stepdaughter. Girl was sick. Medicine not

given. Talk of taking action. Not enough evidence. House said
to be haunted. Strange sights and sounds. Your niece, Agnes
Dent, died a year ago, about this time.

'Yours truly,

'THOMAS AMBLECROM.'

M. R. JAMES

'Oh, Whistle, and I'll Come to You, My Lad'[1]

'I suppose you will be getting away pretty soon, now Full term is over, Professor,' said a person not in the story to the Professor of Ontography, soon after they had sat down next to each other at a feast in the hospitable hall of St James's College.[2]

The Professor was young, neat, and precise in speech.

'Yes,' he said; 'my friends have been making me take up golf this term, and I mean to go to the East Coast – in point of fact to Burnstow – (I dare say you know it) for a week or ten days, to improve my game.[3] I hope to get off to-morrow.'

'Oh, Parkins,' said his neighbour on the other side, 'if you are going to Burnstow, I wish you would look at the site of the Templars' preceptory, and let me know if you think it would be any good to have a dig there in the summer.'[4]

It was, as you might suppose, a person of antiquarian pursuits who said this, but, since he merely appears in this prologue, there is no need to give his entitlements.

'Certainly,' said Parkins, the Professor: 'if you will describe to me whereabouts the site is, I will do my best to give you an idea of the lie of the land when I get back; or I could write to you about it, if you would tell me where you are likely to be.'

'Don't trouble to do that, thanks. It's only that I'm thinking of taking my family in that direction in the Long, and it occurred to me that, as very few of the English preceptories have ever been properly planned, I might have an opportunity of doing something useful on off-days.'[5]

The Professor rather sniffed at the idea that planning out a preceptory could be described as useful. His neighbour continued:

'The site – I doubt if there is anything showing above ground

– must be down quite close to the beach now. The sea has encroached tremendously, as you know, all along that bit of coast. I should think, from the map, that it must be about three-quarters of a mile from the Globe Inn, at the north end of the town. Where are you going to stay?'

'Well, *at* the Globe Inn, as a matter of fact,' said Parkins; 'I have engaged a room there. I couldn't get in anywhere else; most of the lodging-houses are shut up in winter, it seems; and, as it is, they tell me that the only room of any size I can have is really a double-bedded one, and that they haven't a corner in which to store the other bed, and so on.'6 But I must have a fairly large room, for I am taking some books down, and mean to do a bit of work; and though I don't quite fancy having an empty bed – not to speak of two – in what I may call for the time being my study, I suppose I can manage to rough it for the short time I shall be there.'

'Do you call having an extra bed in your room roughing it, Parkins?' said a bluff person opposite. 'Look here, I shall come down and occupy it for a bit; it'll be company for you.'

The Professor quivered, but managed to laugh in a courteous manner.

'By all means, Rogers; there's nothing I should like better. But I'm afraid you would find it rather dull; you don't play golf, do you?'

'No, thank Heaven!' said rude Mr Rogers.

'Well, you see, when I'm not writing I shall most likely be out on the links, and that, as I say, would be rather dull for you, I'm afraid.'

'Oh, I don't know! There's certain to be somebody I know in the place; but, of course, if you don't want me, speak the word, Parkins; I shan't be offended. Truth, as you always tell us, is never offensive.'

Parkins was, indeed, scrupulously polite and strictly truthful. It is to be feared that Mr Rogers sometimes practised upon his knowledge of these characteristics. In Parkins's breast there was a conflict now raging, which for a moment or two did not allow him to answer. That interval being over, he said:

'Well, if you want the exact truth, Rogers, I was considering whether the room I speak of would really be large enough to accommodate us both comfortably; and also whether (mind, I shouldn't have said this if you hadn't pressed me) you would not constitute something in the nature of a hindrance to my work.'

Rogers laughed loudly.

'Well done, Parkins!' he said. 'It's all right. I promise not to interrupt your work; don't you disturb yourself about that. No, I won't come if you don't want me; but I thought I should do so nicely to keep the ghosts off.' Here he might have been seen to wink and to nudge his next neighbour. Parkins might also have been seen to become pink. 'I beg pardon, Parkins,' Rogers continued; 'I oughtn't to have said that. I forgot you didn't like levity on these topics.'

'Well,' Parkins said, 'as you have mentioned the matter, I freely own that I do *not* like careless talk about what you call ghosts. A man in my position,' he went on, raising his voice a little, 'cannot, I find, be too careful about appearing to sanction the current beliefs on such subjects. As you know, Rogers, or as you ought to know; for I think I have never concealed my views –'

'No, you certainly have not, old man,' put in Rogers *sotto voce*.

'– I hold that any semblance, any appearance of concession to the view that such things might exist is to me a renunciation of all that I hold most sacred. But I'm afraid I have not succeeded in securing your attention.'

'Your *undivided* attention, was what Dr Blimber actually *said*,'* Rogers interrupted, with every appearance of an earnest desire for accuracy. 'But I beg your pardon, Parkins: I'm stopping you.'

'No, not at all,' said Parkins. 'I don't remember Blimber; perhaps he was before my time. But I needn't go on. I'm sure you know what I mean.'

'Yes, yes,' said Rogers, rather hastily – 'just so. We'll go into it fully at Burnstow, or somewhere.'

In repeating the above dialogue I have tried to give the impression which it made on me, that Parkins was something of an old woman – rather henlike, perhaps, in his little ways;

* Mr Rogers was wrong, *vide* 'Dombey and Son,' chapter xii.[7]

totally destitute, alas! of the sense of humour, but at the same time dauntless and sincere in his convictions, and a man deserving of the greatest respect. Whether or not the reader has gathered so much, that was the character which Parkins had.

On the following day Parkins did, as he had hoped, succeed in getting away from his college, and in arriving at Burnstow. He was made welcome at the Globe Inn, was safely installed in the large double-bedded room of which we have heard, and was able before retiring to rest to arrange his materials for work in apple-pie order upon a commodious table which occupied the outer end of the room, and was surrounded on three sides by windows looking out seaward;[8] that is to say, the central window looked straight out to sea, and those on the left and right commanded prospects along the shore to the north and south respectively. On the south you saw the village of Burnstow. On the north no houses were to be seen, but only the beach and the low cliff backing it. Immediately in front was a strip – not considerable – of rough grass, dotted with old anchors, capstans, and so forth; then a broad path; then the beach. Whatever may have been the original distance between the Globe Inn and the sea, not more than sixty yards now separated them.

The rest of the population of the inn was, of course, a golfing one, and included few elements that call for a special description. The most conspicuous figure was, perhaps, that of an *ancien militaire*, secretary of a London club, and possessed of a voice of incredible strength, and of views of a pronouncedly Protestant type.[9] These were apt to find utterance after his attendance upon the ministrations of the Vicar, an estimable man with inclinations towards a picturesque ritual, which he gallantly kept down as far as he could out of deference to East Anglian tradition.[10]

Professor Parkins, one of whose principal characteristics was pluck, spent the greater part of the day following his arrival at Burnstow in what he had called improving his game, in company with this Colonel Wilson: and during the afternoon – whether the process of improvement were to blame or not, I am not sure – the Colonel's demeanour assumed a colouring so lurid that even Parkins jibbed at the thought of walking home with him from the links. He determined, after a short and furtive look at that bristling moustache and those incarnadined features, that it would be wiser to allow the influences of tea and tobacco to do what they could with the Colonel before the dinner-hour should render a meeting inevitable.[11]

'I might walk home to-night along the beach,' he reflected – 'yes, and take a look – there will be light enough for that – at the ruins of which Disney was talking.[12] I don't exactly know where they are, by the way; but I expect I can hardly help stumbling on them.'

This he accomplished, I may say, in the most literal sense, for in picking his way from the links to the shingle beach his foot caught, partly in a gorse-root and partly in a biggish stone, and over he went. When he got up and surveyed his surroundings, he found himself in a patch of somewhat broken ground covered with small depressions and mounds. These latter, when he came to examine them, proved to be simply masses of flints embedded in mortar and grown over with turf. He must, he quite rightly concluded, be on the site of the preceptory he had promised to look at. It seemed not unlikely to reward the spade of the explorer; enough of the foundations was probably left at no great depth to throw a good deal of light on the general plan. He remembered vaguely that the Templars, to whom this site had belonged, were in the habit of building round churches, and he thought a particular series of the humps or mounds near him did appear to be arranged in something of a circular form.[13] Few people can resist the temptation to try a little amateur research in a department quite outside their own, if only for the satisfaction of showing how successful they would have been had they only taken it up seriously. Our Professor, however, if he felt something of this mean desire, was also truly anxious to oblige Mr Disney. So he paced with care the circular area he had noticed, and wrote down its rough dimensions in his pocket-book. Then he proceeded to examine an oblong eminence which lay east of the centre of the circle, and seemed to his thinking likely to be the base of a platform or altar. At one end of it, the northern, a patch of the turf was gone – removed by some boy or other creature *ferae naturae*.[14] It might, he thought, be as well to probe the soil here for evidences of masonry, and he took out his knife and began scraping away the earth. And now followed another little discovery: a portion of soil fell inward as he scraped, and disclosed a small cavity. He lighted one match after another to help him to see of what nature the hole was, but the wind was too strong for them all. By tapping and scratching the sides with his knife, however, he was able to make out that it must be an artificial hole in masonry. It was rectangular, and the sides, top, and bottom, if not actually plastered, were smooth and regular. Of course it was empty. No! As he withdrew the knife he heard a metallic clink, and when he introduced his hand it met with a cylindrical object lying on the floor of the hole. Naturally enough, he picked it up, and when he brought it into the light, now fast fading, he could see that it, too, was of man's making – a metal tube about four inches long, and evidently of some considerable age.

By the time Parkins had made sure that there was nothing else in this odd receptacle, it was too late and too dark for him to think of undertaking any further search. What he had done had proved so unexpectedly interesting that he determined to sacrifice a little more of the daylight on the morrow to archæology. The object which he now had safe in his pocket was bound to be of some slight value at least, he felt sure.

Bleak and solemn was the view on which he took a last look before starting homeward. A faint yellow light in the west showed the links, on which a few figures moving towards the club-house were still visible, the squat martello tower, the light of Aldsey village, the pale ribbon of sands intersected at intervals by black wooden groynings, the dim and murmuring sea.[15] The wind was bitter from the north, but was at his back when he set out for the Globe. He quickly rattled and clashed through the shingle and gained the sand, upon which, but for the groynings which had to be got over every few yards, the going was both good and quiet. One last look behind, to measure the distance he had made since leaving the ruined Templars' church, showed him a prospect of company on his walk, in the shape of a rather indistinct personage in the distance, who seemed to be making great efforts to catch up with him, but made little, if any, progress. I mean that there was an appearance of running about his movements, but that the distance between him and Parkins did not seem materially to lessen. So, at least, Parkins thought, and decided that he almost certainly did not know him, and that it would be absurd to wait until he came up. For all that, company, he began to think, would really be very welcome on that lonely shore, if only you could choose your companion. In his unenlightened days he had read of meetings in such places which even now would hardly bear thinking of. He went on thinking of them, however, until he reached home, and particularly of one which catches most people's fancy at some time of their childhood. 'Now I saw in my dream that Christian had gone but a very little way when he saw a foul fiend coming over the field to meet him.'[16] 'What should I do now,' he thought, 'if I looked back and caught sight of a black figure sharply defined against the yellow sky, and saw that it had horns and wings? I wonder whether I should stand or run for it. Luckily, the gentleman behind is not of that kind, and he seems to be about as far off now as when I saw him first. Well, at this rate he won't get his dinner as soon as I shall; and, dear me! it's within a quarter of an hour of the time now. I must run!'

Parkins had, in fact, very little time for dressing. When he met the Colonel at dinner, Peace – or as much of her as that gentleman could manage – reigned once more in the military bosom; nor was she put to flight in the hours of bridge that followed dinner, for Parkins was a more than respectable player. When, therefore, he retired towards twelve o'clock, he felt that he had spent his evening in quite a satisfactory way, and that, even for so long as a fortnight or three weeks, life at the Globe would be supportable under similar conditions – 'especially,' thought he, 'if I go on improving my game.'

As he went along the passages he met the boots of the Globe, who stopped and said:[17]

'Beg your pardon, sir, but as I was a-brushing your coat just now there was somethink fell out of the pocket. I put it on your chest of drawers, sir, in your room, sir – a piece of a pipe or somethink of that, sir. Thank you, sir. You'll find it on your chest of drawers, sir – yes, sir. Good-night, sir.'

The speech served to remind Parkins of his little discovery of that afternoon. It was with some considerable curiosity that he turned it over by the light of his candles. It was of bronze, he now saw, and was shaped very much after the manner of the modern dog-whistle; in fact it was – yes, certainly it was – actually no more nor less than a whistle. He put it to his lips, but it was quite full of a fine, caked-up sand or earth, which would not yield to knocking, but must be loosened with a knife. Tidy as ever in his habits, Parkins cleared out the earth on to a piece of paper, and took the latter to the window to empty it out. The night was clear and bright, as he saw when he had opened the casement, and he stopped for an instant to look at the sea and note a belated wanderer stationed on the shore in front of the inn. Then he shut the window, a little surprised at the late hours people kept at Burnstow, and took his whistle to the light again. Why, surely there were marks on it, and not merely marks, but letters! A very little rubbing rendered the deeply-cut inscription quite legible, but the Professor had to confess, after some earnest thought, that the meaning of it was as obscure to him as the writing on the wall to Belshazzar.[18] There were legends both on the front and on the back of the whistle. The one read thus:

$$\text{FUR} \quad \begin{matrix} \text{FLA} \\ \text{FLE} \end{matrix} \quad \text{BIS}$$

The other:

$$\maltese \text{QUIS EST ISTE QUI UENIT} \maltese_\cdot{}^{19}$$

'I ought to be able to make it out,' he thought; 'but I suppose I am a little rusty in my Latin. When I come to think of it, I don't believe I even know the word for a whistle. The long one does seem simple enough. It ought to mean, "Who is this who is coming?" Well, the best way to find out is evidently to whistle for him.'

He blew tentatively and stopped suddenly, startled and yet pleased at the note he had elicited. It had a quality of infinite

distance in it, and, soft as it was, he somehow felt it must be
audible for miles round. It was a sound, too, that seemed to
have the power (which many scents possess) of forming pictures
in the brain. He saw quite clearly for a moment a vision of a
wide, dark expanse at night, with a fresh wind blowing, and in
the midst a lonely figure – how employed, he could not tell.
Perhaps he would have seen more had not the picture been
broken by the sudden surge of a gust of wind against his casement, so sudden that it made him look up, just in time to see
the white glint of a sea-bird's wing somewhere outside the
dark panes.

The sound of the whistle had so fascinated him that he could
not help trying it once more, this time more boldly. The note
was little, if at all, louder than before, and repetition broke the
illusion – no picture followed, as he had half hoped it might.
'But what is this? Goodness! what force the wind can get up in
a few minutes! What a tremendous gust! There! I knew that
window-fastening was no use! Ah! I thought so – both candles
out. It is enough to tear the room to pieces.'

The first thing was to get the window shut. While you might
count twenty Parkins was struggling with the small casement,
and felt almost as if he were pushing back a sturdy burglar, so
strong was the pressure. It slackened all at once, and the
window banged to and latched itself. Now to relight the
candles and see what damage, if any, had been done. No,
nothing seemed amiss; no glass even was broken in the casement. But the noise had evidently roused at least one member
of the household: the Colonel was to be heard stumping in his
stockinged feet on the floor above, and growling.

Quickly as it had risen, the wind did not fall at once. On it
went, moaning and rushing past the house, at times rising to a
cry so desolate that, as Parkins disinterestedly said, it might
have made fanciful people feel quite uncomfortable; even the
unimaginative, he thought after a quarter of an hour, might be
happier without it.

Whether it was the wind, or the excitement of golf, or of the
researches in the preceptory that kept Parkins awake, he was
not sure. Awake he remained, in any case, long enough to fancy
(as I am afraid I often do myself under such conditions) that he

was the victim of all manner of fatal disorders: he would lie
counting the beats of his heart, convinced that it was going to
stop work every moment, and would entertain grave suspicions
of his lungs, brain, liver, etc. – suspicions which he was sure
would be dispelled by the return of daylight, but which until
then refused to be put aside. He found a little vicarious comfort
in the idea that some one else was in the same boat. A near
neighbour (in the darkness it was not easy to tell his direction)
was tossing and rustling in his bed, too.

The next stage was that Parkins shut his eyes and determined
to give sleep every chance. Here again over-excitement asserted
itself in another form – that of making pictures. *Experto crede*,
pictures do come to the closed eyes of one trying to sleep, and
often his pictures are so little to his taste that he must open his
eyes and disperse the images.[20]

Parkins's experience on this occasion was a very distressing
one. He found that the picture which presented itself to him
was continuous. When he opened his eyes, of course, it went;
but when he shut them once more it framed itself afresh, and
acted itself out again, neither quicker nor slower than before.
What he saw was this:

A long stretch of shore – shingle edged by sand, and intersected at short intervals with black groynes running down to
the water – a scene, in fact, so like that of his afternoon's
walk that, in the absence of any landmark, it could not be
distinguished therefrom. The light was obscure, conveying an
impression of gathering storm, late winter evening, and slight
cold rain. On this bleak stage at first no actor was visible. Then,
in the distance, a bobbing black object appeared; a moment
more, and it was a man running, jumping, clambering over the
groynes, and every few seconds looking eagerly back. The
nearer he came the more obvious it was that he was not only
anxious, but even terribly frightened, though his face was not
to be distinguished. He was, moreover, almost at the end of his
strength. On he came; each successive obstacle seemed to cause
him more difficulty than the last. 'Will he get over this next
one?' thought Parkins; 'it seems a little higher than the others.'
Yes; half climbing, half throwing himself, he did get over, and
fell all in a heap on the other side (the side nearest to the

spectator). There, as if really unable to get up again, he remained crouching under the groyne, looking up in an attitude of painful anxiety.

So far no cause whatever for the fear of the runner had been shown; but now there began to be seen, far up the shore, a little flicker of something light-coloured moving to and fro with great swiftness and irregularity. Rapidly growing larger, it, too, declared itself as a figure in pale, fluttering draperies, ill-defined. There was something about its motion which made Parkins very unwilling to see it at close quarters. It would stop, raise arms, bow itself toward the sand, then run stooping across the beach to the water-edge and back again; and then, rising upright, once more continue its course forward at a speed that was startling and terrifying. The moment came when the pursuer was hovering about from left to right only a few yards beyond the groyne where the runner lay in hiding. After two or three ineffectual castings hither and thither it came to a stop, stood upright, with arms raised high, and then darted straight forward towards the groyne.

It was at this point that Parkins always failed in his resolution to keep his eyes shut. With many misgivings as to incipient failure of eyesight, overworked brain, excessive smoking, and so on, he finally resigned himself to light his candle, get out a book, and pass the night waking, rather than be tormented by this persistent panorama, which he saw clearly enough could only be a morbid reflection of his walk and his thoughts on that very day.

The scraping of match on box and the glare of light must have startled some creatures of the night – rats or what not – which he heard scurry across the floor from the side of his bed with much rustling. Dear, dear! the match is out! Fool that it is! But the second one burnt better, and a candle and book were duly procured, over which Parkins pored till sleep of a wholesome kind came upon him, and that in no long space. For about the first time in his orderly and prudent life he forgot to blow out the candle, and when he was called next morning at eight there was still a flicker in the socket and a sad mess of guttered grease on the top of the little table.

After breakfast he was in his room, putting the finishing touches to his golfing costume – fortune had again allotted the

Colonel to him for a partner – when one of the maids came in.

'Oh, if you please,' she said, 'would you like any extra blankets on your bed, sir?'

'Ah! thank you,' said Parkins. 'Yes, I think I should like one. It seems likely to turn rather colder.'

In a very short time the maid was back with the blanket.

'Which bed should I put it on, sir?' she asked.

'What? Why, that one – the one I slept in last night,' he said, pointing to it.

'Oh yes! I beg your pardon, sir, but you seemed to have tried both of 'em; leastways, we had to make 'em both up this morning.'

'Really? How very absurd!' said Parkins. 'I certainly never touched the other, except to lay some things on it. Did it actually seem to have been slept in?'

'Oh yes, sir!' said the maid. 'Why, all the things was crumpled and throwed about all ways, if you'll excuse me, sir – quite as if any one 'adn't passed but a very poor night, sir.'

'Dear me,' said Parkins. 'Well, I may have disordered it more than I thought when I unpacked my things. I'm very sorry to have given you the extra trouble, I'm sure. I expect a friend of mine soon, by the way – a gentleman from Cambridge – to come and occupy it for a night or two. That will be all right, I suppose, won't it?'

'Oh yes, to be sure, sir. Thank you, sir. It's no trouble, I'm sure,' said the maid, and departed to giggle with her colleagues.

Parkins set forth, with a stern determination to improve his game.

I am glad to be able to report that he succeeded so far in this enterprise that the Colonel, who had been rather repining at the prospect of a second day's play in his company, became quite chatty as the morning advanced; and his voice boomed out over the flats, as certain also of our own minor poets have said, 'like some great bourdon in a minster tower.'[21]

'Extraordinary wind, that, we had last night,' he said. 'In my old home we should have said some one had been whistling for it.'

'Should you, indeed!' said Parkins. 'Is there a superstition of that kind still current in your part of the country?'

'I don't know about superstition,' said the Colonel. 'They believe in it all over Denmark and Norway, as well as on the Yorkshire coast; and my experience is, mind you, that there's generally something at the bottom of what these country-folk hold to, and have held to for generations. But it's your drive' (or whatever it might have been: the golfing reader will have to imagine appropriate digressions at the proper intervals).

When conversation was resumed, Parkins said, with a slight hesitancy:

'Apropos of what you were saying just now, Colonel, I think I ought to tell you that my own views on such subjects are very strong. I am, in fact, a convinced disbeliever in what is called the "supernatural."'

'What!' said the Colonel, 'do you mean to tell me you don't believe in second-sight, or ghosts, or anything of that kind?'

'In nothing whatever of that kind,' returned Parkins firmly.

'Well,' said the Colonel, 'but it appears to me at that rate, sir, that you must be little better than a Sadducee.'[22]

Parkins was on the point of answering that, in his opinion, the Sadducees were the most sensible persons he had ever read of in the Old Testament; but, feeling some doubt as to whether much mention of them was to be found in that work, he preferred to laugh the accusation off.[23]

'Perhaps I am,' he said; 'but – Here, give me my cleek, boy![24] – Excuse me one moment, Colonel.' A short interval. 'Now, as to whistling for the wind, let me give you my theory about it. The laws which govern winds are really not at all perfectly known – to fisher-folk and such, of course, not known at all. A man or woman of eccentric habits, perhaps, or a stranger, is seen repeatedly on the beach at some unusual hour, and is heard whistling. Soon afterwards a violent wind rises; a man who could read the sky perfectly or who possessed a barometer could have foretold that it would. The simple people of a fishing-village have no barometers, and only a few rough rules for prophesying weather. What more natural than that the eccentric personage I postulated should be regarded as having raised the wind, or that he or she should clutch eagerly at the reputation of being able to do so? Now, take last night's wind: as it happens, I myself was whistling. I blew a whistle twice,

and the wind seemed to come absolutely in answer to my call.
If any one had seen me –'

The audience had been a little restive under this harangue,
and Parkins had, I fear, fallen somewhat into the tone of a
lecturer; but at the last sentence the Colonel stopped.

'Whistling, were you?' he said. 'And what sort of whistle did
you use? Play this stroke first.' Interval.

'About that whistle you were asking, Colonel. It's rather a
curious one. I have it in my – No; I see I've left it in my room.
As a matter of fact, I found it yesterday.'

And then Parkins narrated the manner of his discovery of the
whistle, upon hearing which the Colonel grunted, and opined
that, in Parkins's place, he should himself be careful about using
a thing that had belonged to a set of Papists, of whom, speaking
generally, it might be affirmed that you never knew what they
might not have been up to. From this topic he diverged to the
enormities of the Vicar, who had given notice on the previous
Sunday that Friday would be the Feast of St Thomas the
Apostle, and that there would be service at eleven o'clock in
the church.[25] This and other similar proceedings constituted
in the Colonel's view a strong presumption that the Vicar was
a concealed Papist, if not a Jesuit; and Parkins, who could not
very readily follow the Colonel in this region, did not disagree
with him. In fact, they got on so well together in the morning
that there was no talk on either side of their separating after
lunch.

Both continued to play well during the afternoon, or, at least,
well enough to make them forget everything else until the light
began to fail them. Not until then did Parkins remember that
he had meant to do some more investigating at the preceptory;
but it was of no great importance, he reflected. One day was as
good as another; he might as well go home with the Colonel.

As they turned the corner of the house, the Colonel was
almost knocked down by a boy who rushed into him at the very
top of his speed, and then, instead of running away, remained
hanging on to him and panting. The first words of the warrior
were naturally those of reproof and objurgation, but he very
quickly discerned that the boy was almost speechless with
fright. Inquiries were useless at first. When the boy got his

breath he began to howl, and still clung to the Colonel's legs. He was at last detached, but continued to howl.

'What in the world *is* the matter with you? What have you been up to? What have you seen?' said the two men.

'Ow, I seen it wive at me out of the winder,' wailed the boy, 'and I don't like it.'[26]

'What window?' said the irritated Colonel. 'Come, pull yourself together, my boy.'

'The front winder it was, at the 'otel,' said the boy.

At this point Parkins was in favour of sending the boy home, but the Colonel refused; he wanted to get to the bottom of it, he said; it was most dangerous to give a boy such a fright as this one had had, and if it turned out that people had been playing jokes, they should suffer for it in some way. And by a series of questions he made out this story: The boy had been playing about on the grass in front of the Globe with some others; then they had gone home to their teas, and he was just going, when he happened to look up at the front winder and see it a-wiving at him. *It* seemed to be a figure of some sort, in white as far as he knew – couldn't see its face; but it wived at him, and it warn't a right thing – not to say not a right person. Was there a light in the room? No, he didn't think to look if there was a light. Which was the window? Was it the top one or the second one? The seckind one it was – the big winder what got two little uns at the sides.

'Very well, my boy,' said the Colonel, after a few more questions. 'You run away home now. I expect it was some person trying to give you a start. Another time, like a brave English boy, you just throw a stone – well, no, not that exactly, but you go and speak to the waiter, or to Mr Simpson, the landlord, and – yes – and say that I advised you to do so.'

The boy's face expressed some of the doubt he felt as to the likelihood of Mr Simpson's lending a favourable ear to his complaint, but the Colonel did not appear to perceive this, and went on:

'And here's a sixpence – no, I see it's a shilling – and you be off home, and don't think any more about it.'[27]

The youth hurried off with agitated thanks, and the Colonel and Parkins went round to the front of the Globe and reconnoitred. There was only one window answering to the description they had been hearing.

'Well, that's curious,' said Parkins; 'it's evidently my window the lad was talking about. Will you come up for a moment, Colonel Wilson? We ought to be able to see if any one has been taking liberties in my room.'

They were soon in the passage, and Parkins made as if to open the door. Then he stopped and felt in his pockets.

'This is more serious than I thought,' was his next remark. 'I remember now that before I started this morning I locked the door. It is locked now, and, what is more, here is the key.' And he held it up. 'Now,' he went on, 'if the servants are in the habit of going into one's room during the day when one is away, I can only say that – well, that I don't approve of it at all.' Conscious of a somewhat weak climax, he busied himself in opening the door (which was indeed locked) and in lighting candles. 'No,' he said, 'nothing seems disturbed.'

'Except your bed,' put in the Colonel.

'Excuse me, that isn't my bed,' said Parkins. 'I don't use that one. But it does look as if some one had been playing tricks with it.'

It certainly did: the clothes were bundled up and twisted together in a most tortuous confusion. Parkins pondered.

'That must be it,' he said at last: 'I disordered the clothes last night in unpacking, and they haven't made it since. Perhaps they came in to make it, and that boy saw them through the window; and then they were called away and locked the door after them. Yes, I think that must be it.'

'Well, ring and ask,' said the Colonel, and this appealed to Parkins as practical.

The maid appeared, and, to make a long story short, deposed that she had made the bed in the morning when the gentleman was in the room, and hadn't been there since. No, she hadn't no other key. Mr Simpson he kep' the keys; he'd be able to tell the gentleman if any one had been up.

This was a puzzle. Investigation showed that nothing of value had been taken, and Parkins remembered the disposition of the small objects on tables and so forth well enough to be pretty sure that no pranks had been played with them. Mr and Mrs

Simpson furthermore agreed that neither of them had given the duplicate key of the room to any person whatever during the day. Nor could Parkins, fair-minded man as he was, detect anything in the demeanour of master, mistress, or maid that indicated guilt. He was much more inclined to think that the boy had been imposing on the Colonel.

The latter was unwontedly silent and pensive at dinner and throughout the evening. When he bade good-night to Parkins, he murmured in a gruff undertone:

'You know where I am if you want me during the night.'

'Why, yes, thank you, Colonel Wilson, I think I do; but there isn't much prospect of my disturbing you, I hope. By the way,' he added, 'did I show you that old whistle I spoke of? I think not. Well, here it is.'

The Colonel turned it over gingerly in the light of the candle.

'Can you make anything of the inscription?' asked Parkins, as he took it back.

'No, not in this light. What do you mean to do with it?'

'Oh, well, when I get back to Cambridge I shall submit it to some of the archæologists there, and see what they think of it; and very likely, if they consider it worth having, I may present it to one of the museums.'

''M!' said the Colonel. 'Well, you may be right. All I know is that, if it were mine, I should chuck it straight into the sea. It's no use talking, I'm well aware, but I expect that with you it's a case of live and learn. I hope so, I'm sure, and I wish you a good-night.'

He turned away, leaving Parkins in act to speak at the bottom of the stair, and soon each was in his own bedroom.

By some unfortunate accident, there were neither blinds nor curtains to the windows of the Professor's room. The previous night he had thought little of this, but to-night there seemed every prospect of a bright moon rising to shine directly on his bed, and probably wake him later on. When he noticed this he was a good deal annoyed, but, with an ingenuity which I can only envy, he succeeded in rigging up, with the help of a railway-rug, some safety-pins, and a stick and umbrella, a screen which, if it only held together, would completely keep the moonlight off his bed.[28] And shortly afterwards he was comfortably in that bed. When he had read a somewhat solid work long enough to produce a decided wish for sleep, he cast a drowsy glance round the room, blew out the candle, and fell back upon the pillow.

He must have slept soundly for an hour or more, when a sudden clatter shook him up in a most unwelcome manner. In a moment he realized what had happened: his carefully-constructed screen had given way, and a very bright frosty moon was shining directly on his face. This was highly annoying. Could he possibly get up and reconstruct the screen? or could he manage to sleep if he did not?

For some minutes he lay and pondered over the possibilities; then he turned over sharply, and with all his eyes open lay breathlessly listening. There had been a movement, he was sure, in the empty bed on the opposite side of the room. To-morrow he would have it moved, for there must be rats or something playing about in it. It was quiet now. No! the commotion began again. There was a rustling and shaking: surely more than any rat could cause.

I can figure to myself something of the Professor's bewilderment and horror, for I have in a dream thirty years back seen the same thing happen; but the reader will hardly, perhaps, imagine how dreadful it was to him to see a figure suddenly sit up in what he had known was an empty bed. He was out of his own bed in one bound, and made a dash towards the window, where lay his only weapon, the stick with which he had propped his screen. This was, as it turned out, the worst thing he could have done, because the personage in the empty bed, with a sudden smooth motion, slipped from the bed and took up a position, with outspread arms, between the two beds, and in front of the door. Parkins watched it in a horrid perplexity. Somehow, the idea of getting past it and escaping through the door was intolerable to him; he could not have borne – he didn't know why – to touch it; and as for its touching him, he would sooner dash himself through the window than have that happen. It stood for the moment in a band of dark shadow, and he had not seen what its face was like. Now it began to move, in a stooping posture, and all at once the spectator realized, with some horror and some relief, that it must be blind, for it seemed to feel about it with its muffled arms in a groping and random fashion. Turning half away from him, it became suddenly conscious of the bed he had just left, and darted towards it, and bent and felt over the pillows in a way which made Parkins shudder as he had never in his life thought it possible. In a very few moments it seemed to know that the bed was empty, and then, moving forward into the area of light and facing the window, it showed for the first time what manner of thing it was.

Parkins, who very much dislikes being questioned about it, did once describe something of it in my hearing, and I gathered that what he chiefly remembers about it is a horrible, an intensely horrible, face of *crumpled linen*. What expression he read upon it he could not or would not tell, but that the fear of it went nigh to maddening him is certain.

But he was not at leisure to watch it for long. With formidable quickness it moved into the middle of the room, and, as it groped and waved, one corner of its draperies swept across Parkins's face. He could not, though he knew how perilous a sound was – he could not keep back a cry of disgust, and this gave the searcher an instant clue. It leapt towards him upon the instant, and the next moment he was halfway through the window backwards, uttering cry upon cry at the utmost pitch of his voice, and the linen face was thrust close into his own. At this, almost the last possible second, deliverance came, as you will have guessed: the Colonel burst the door open, and was just in time to see the dreadful group at the window. When he reached the figures only one was left. Parkins sank forward into the room in a faint, and before him on the floor lay a tumbled heap of bed-clothes.

Colonel Wilson asked no questions, but busied himself keeping every one else out of the room and in getting Parkins back to his bed; and himself, wrapped in a rug, occupied the other bed, for the rest of the night. Early on the next day Rogers arrived, more welcome than he would have been a day before, and the three of them held a very long consultation in the Professor's room. At the end of it the Colonel left the hotel door carrying a small object between his finger and thumb, which he cast as far into the sea as a very brawny arm could send it. Later on the smoke of a burning ascended from the back premises of the Globe.

Exactly what explanation was patched up for the staff and visitors at the hotel I must confess I do not recollect. The Professor was somehow cleared of the ready suspicion of delirium tremens, and the hotel of the reputation of a troubled house.[29]

There is not much question as to what would have happened to Parkins if the Colonel had not intervened when he did. He would either have fallen out of the window or else lost his wits. But it is not so evident what more the creature that came in answer to the whistle could have done than frighten. There seemed to be absolutely nothing material about it save the bed-clothes of which it had made itself a body. The Colonel, who remembered a not very dissimilar occurrence in India, was of opinion that if Parkins had closed with it it could really have done very little, and that its one power was that of frightening. The whole thing, he said, served to confirm his opinion of the Church of Rome.

There is really nothing more to tell, but, as you may imagine, the Professor's views on certain points are less clear cut than they used to be. His nerves, too, have suffered: he cannot even now see a surplice hanging on a door quite unmoved, and the spectacle of a scarecrow in a field late on a winter afternoon has cost him more than one sleepless night.[30]

AMBROSE BIERCE
The Moonlit Road

I
Statement of Joel Hetman, Jr

I am the most unfortunate of men. Rich, respected, fairly well educated and of sound health – with many other advantages usually valued by those having them and coveted by those who have them not – I sometimes think that I should be less unhappy if they had been denied me, for then the contrast between my outer and my inner life would not be continually demanding a painful attention. In the stress of privation and the need of effort I might sometimes forget the sombre secret ever baffling the conjecture that it compels.

I am the only child of Joel and Julia Hetman. The one was a well-to-do country gentleman, the other a beautiful and accomplished woman to whom he was passionately attached with what I now know to have been a jealous and exacting devotion. The family home was a few miles from Nashville, Tennessee, a large, irregularly built dwelling of no particular order of architecture, a little way off the road, in a park of trees and shrubbery.

At the time of which I write I was nineteen years old, a student at Yale.[1] One day I received a telegram from my father of such urgency that in compliance with its unexplained demand I left at once for home. At the railway station in Nashville a distant relative awaited me to apprise me of the reason for my recall: my mother had been barbarously murdered – why and by whom none could conjecture, but the circumstances were these:

My father had gone to Nashville, intending to return the next afternoon. Something prevented his accomplishing the business in hand, so he returned on the same night, arriving just before the dawn. In his testimony before the coroner he explained that having no latchkey and not caring to disturb the sleeping servants, he had, with no clearly defined intention, gone round to the rear of the house. As he turned an angle of the building, he heard a sound as of a door gently closed, and saw in the darkness, indistinctly, the figure of a man, which instantly disappeared among the trees of the lawn. A hasty pursuit and brief search of the grounds in the belief that the trespasser was some one secretly visiting a servant proving fruitless, he entered at the unlocked door and mounted the stairs to my mother's chamber. Its door was open, and stepping into black darkness he fell headlong over some heavy object on the floor. I may spare myself the details; it was my poor mother, dead of strangulation by human hands!

Nothing had been taken from the house, the servants had heard no sound, and excepting those terrible finger-marks upon the dead woman's throat – dear God! that I might forget them! – no trace of the assassin was ever found.

I gave up my studies and remained with my father, who, naturally, was greatly changed. Always of a sedate, taciturn disposition, he now fell into so deep a dejection that nothing could hold his attention, yet anything – a footfall, the sudden closing of a door – aroused in him a fitful interest; one might have called it an apprehension. At any small surprise of the senses he would start visibly and sometimes turn pale, then relapse into a melancholy apathy deeper than before. I suppose he was what is called a 'nervous wreck.' As to me, I was younger then than now – there is much in that. Youth is Gilead, in which is balm for every wound.[2] Ah, that I might again dwell in that enchanted land! Unacquainted with grief, I knew not how to appraise my bereavement; I could not rightly estimate the strength of the stroke.

One night, a few months after the dreadful event, my father and I walked home from the city. The full moon was about three hours above the eastern horizon; the entire countryside had the solemn stillness of a summer night; our footfalls and the ceaseless song of the katydids were the only sound aloof.[3] Black shadows of bordering trees lay athwart the road, which, in the short reaches between, gleamed a ghostly white. As we approached the gate to our dwelling, whose front was in shadow, and in which no light shone, my father suddenly stopped and clutched my arm, saying, hardly above his breath:

'God! God! what is that?'

'I hear nothing,' I replied.

'But see – see!' he said, pointing along the road, directly ahead.

I said: 'Nothing is there. Come, father, let us go in – you are ill.'

He had released my arm and was standing rigid and motionless in the centre of the illuminated roadway, staring like one bereft of sense. His face in the moonlight showed a pallor and fixity inexpressibly distressing. I pulled gently at his sleeve, but he had forgotten my existence. Presently he began to retire backward, step by step, never for an instant removing his eyes from what he saw, or thought he saw. I turned half round to follow, but stood irresolute. I do not recall any feeling of fear, unless a sudden chill was its physical manifestation. It seemed as if an icy wind had touched my face and enfolded my body from head to foot; I could feel the stir of it in my hair.

At that moment my attention was drawn to a light that suddenly streamed from an upper window of the house: one of the servants, awakened by what mysterious premonition of evil who can say, and in obedience to an impulse that she was never able to name, had lit a lamp. When I turned to look for my father he was gone, and in all the years that have passed no whisper of his fate has come across the borderland of conjecture from the realm of the unknown.

II

Statement of Caspar Grattan[4]

To-day I am said to live; to-morrow, here in this room, will lie a senseless shape of clay that all too long was I. If any one lift the cloth from the face of that unpleasant thing it will be in gratification of a mere morbid curiosity. Some, doubtless, will go further and inquire, 'Who was he?' In this writing I supply the only answer that I am able to make – Caspar Grattan. Surely, that should be enough. The name has served my small need for more than twenty years of a life of unknown length. True, I gave it to myself, but lacking another I had the right. In this world one must have a name; it prevents confusion, even when it does not establish identity. Some, though, are known by numbers, which also seem inadequate distinctions.

One day, for illustration, I was passing along a street of a city, far from here, when I met two men in uniform, one of whom, half pausing and looking curiously into my face, said to his companion, 'That man looks like 767.' Something in the number seemed familiar and horrible. Moved by an uncontrollable impulse, I sprang into a side street and ran until I fell exhausted in a country lane.

I have never forgotten that number, and always it comes to memory attended by gibbering obscenity, peals of joyless laughter, the clang of iron doors. So I say a name, even if self-bestowed, is better than a number. In the register of the potter's field I shall soon have both.[5] What wealth!

Of him who shall find this paper I must beg a little consideration. It is not the history of my life; the knowledge to write that is denied me. This is only a record of broken and apparently unrelated memories, some of them as distinct and sequent as brilliant beads upon a thread, others remote and strange, having the character of crimson dreams with interspaces blank and black – witch-fires glowing still and red in a great desolation.

Standing upon the shore of eternity, I turn for a last look landward over the course by which I came. There are twenty years of footprints fairly distinct, the impressions of bleeding feet. They lead through poverty and pain, devious and unsure, as of one staggering beneath a burden –

Remote, unfriended, melancholy, slow.[6]

Ah, the poet's prophecy of Me – how admirable, how dreadfully admirable!

Backward beyond the beginning of this *via dolorosa* – this epic of suffering with episodes of sin – I see nothing clearly; it comes out of a cloud.[7] I know that it spans only twenty years, yet I am an old man.

One does not remember one's birth – one has to be told. But with me it was different; life came to me full-handed and dowered me with all my faculties and powers. Of a previous existence I know no more than others, for all have stammering intimations that may be memories and may be dreams. I know only that my first consciousness was of maturity in body and mind – a consciousness accepted without surprise or conjecture. I merely found myself walking in a forest, half-clad, footsore, unutterably weary and hungry. Seeing a farmhouse, I approached and asked for food, which was given me by one who inquired my name. I did not know, yet knew that all had names. Greatly embarrassed, I retreated, and night coming on, lay down in the forest and slept.

The next day I entered a large town which I shall not name. Nor shall I recount further incidents of the life that is now to end – a life of wandering, always and everywhere haunted by an overmastering sense of crime in punishment of wrong and of terror in punishment of crime. Let me see if I can reduce it to narrative.

I seem once to have lived near a great city, a prosperous planter, married to a woman whom I loved and distrusted. We had, it sometimes seems, one child, a youth of brilliant parts and promise. He is at all times a vague figure, never clearly drawn, frequently altogether out of the picture.

One luckless evening it occurred to me to test my wife's fidelity in a vulgar, commonplace way familiar to every one who has acquaintance with the literature of fact and fiction. I went to the city, telling my wife that I should be absent until the following afternoon. But I returned before daybreak and went to the rear of the house, purposing to enter by a door with which I had secretly so tampered that it would seem to lock, yet not actually fasten. As I approached it, I heard it gently open and close, and saw a man steal away into the darkness. With murder in my heart, I sprang after him, but he had vanished without even the bad luck of identification. Sometimes now I cannot even persuade myself that it was a human being.

Crazed with jealousy and rage, blind and bestial with all the elemental passions of insulted manhood, I entered the house and sprang up the stairs to the door of my wife's chamber. It was closed, but having tampered with its lock also, I easily entered and despite the black darkness soon stood by the side of her bed. My groping hands told me that although disarranged it was unoccupied.

'She is below,' I thought, 'and terrified by my entrance has evaded me in the darkness of the hall.'

With the purpose of seeking her I turned to leave the room, but took a wrong direction – the right one! My foot struck her, cowering in a corner of the room. Instantly my hands were at her throat, stifling a shriek, my knees were upon her struggling body; and there in the darkness, without a word of accusation or reproach, I strangled her till she died!

There ends the dream. I have related it in the past tense, but the present would be the fitter form, for again and again the sombre tragedy reenacts itself in my consciousness – over and over I lay the plan, I suffer the confirmation, I redress the wrong. Then all is blank; and afterward the rains beat against the grimy window-panes, or the snows fall upon my scant attire, the wheels rattle in the squalid streets where my life lies in poverty and mean employment. If there is ever sunshine I do not recall it; if there are birds they do not sing.

There is another dream, another vision of the night. I stand among the shadows in a moonlit road. I am aware of another presence, but whose I cannot rightly determine. In the shadow of a great dwelling I catch the gleam of white garments; then the figure of a woman confronts me in the road – my murdered wife! There is death in the face; there are marks upon the throat. The eyes are fixed on mine with an infinite gravity which is not reproach, nor hate, nor menace, nor anything less terrible than recognition. Before this awful apparition I retreat in terror – a terror that is upon me as I write. I can no longer rightly shape the words. See! they –

Now I am calm, but truly there is no more to tell: the incident ends where it began – in darkness and in doubt.

Yes, I am again in control of myself: 'the captain of my soul.'[8] But that is not respite; it is another stage and phase of expiation.

My penance, constant in degree, is mutable in kind: one of its variants is tranquillity. After all, it is only a life-sentence. 'To Hell for life' – that is a foolish penalty: the culprit chooses the duration of his punishment. To-day my term expires.

To each and all, the peace that was not mine.

III

Statement of the Late Julia Hetman, Through the Medium Bayrolles[9]

I had retired early and fallen almost immediately into a peaceful sleep, from which I awoke with that indefinable sense of peril which is, I think, a common experience in that other, earlier life. Of its unmeaning character, too, I was entirely persuaded, yet that did not banish it. My husband, Joel Hetman, was away from home; the servants slept in another part of the house. But these were familiar conditions; they had never before distressed me. Nevertheless, the strange terror grew so insupportable that conquering my reluctance to move I sat up and lit the lamp at my bedside. Contrary to my expectation this gave me no relief; the light seemed rather an added danger, for I reflected that it would shine out under the door, disclosing my presence to whatever evil thing might lurk outside. You that are still in the flesh, subject to horrors of the imagination, think what a monstrous fear that must be which seeks in darkness security from malevolent existences of the night. That is to spring to close quarters with an unseen enemy – the strategy of despair!

Extinguishing the lamp I pulled the bedclothing about my head and lay trembling and silent, unable to shriek, forgetful to pray. In this pitiable state I must have lain for what you call hours – with us there are no hours, there is no time.

At last it came – a soft, irregular sound of footfalls on the stairs! They were slow, hesitant, uncertain, as of something that did not see its way; to my disordered reason all the more terrifying for that, as the approach of some blind and mindless malevolence to which is no appeal. I even thought that I must have left the hall lamp burning and the groping of this creature proved it a monster of the night. This was foolish and inconsistent with my previous dread of the light, but what would you have? Fear has no brains; it is an idiot. The dismal witness that it bears and the cowardly counsel that it whispers are unrelated. We know this well, we who have passed into the Realm of Terror, who skulk in eternal dusk among the scenes of our former lives, invisible even to ourselves and one another, yet hiding forlorn in lonely places; yearning for speech with our loved ones, yet dumb, and as fearful of them as they of us. Sometimes the disability is removed, the law suspended: by the deathless power of love or hate we break the spell – we are seen by those whom we would warn, console, or punish. What form we seem to them to bear we know not; we know only that we terrify even those whom we most wish to comfort, and from whom we most crave tenderness and sympathy.

Forgive, I pray you, this inconsequent digression by what was once a woman. You who consult us in this imperfect way – you do not understand. You ask foolish questions about things unknown and things forbidden. Much that we know and could impart in our speech is meaningless in yours. We must communicate with you through a stammering intelligence in that small fraction of our language that you yourselves can speak. You think that we are of another world. No, we have knowledge of no world but yours, though for us it holds no sunlight, no warmth, no music, no laughter, no song of birds, nor any companionship. O God! what a thing it is to be a ghost, cowering and shivering in an altered world, a prey to apprehension and despair!

No, I did not die of fright: the Thing turned and went away. I heard it go down the stairs, hurriedly, I thought, as if itself in sudden fear. Then I rose to call for help. Hardly had my shaking hand found the door-knob when – merciful heaven! – I heard it returning. Its footfalls as it remounted the stairs were rapid, heavy and loud; they shook the house. I fled to an angle of the wall and crouched upon the floor. I tried to pray. I tried to call the name of my dear husband. Then I heard the door thrown open. There was an interval of unconsciousness, and when I revived I felt a strangling clutch upon my throat – felt my arms feebly beating against something that bore me backward – felt my tongue thrusting itself from between my teeth! And then I passed into this life.

No, I have no knowledge of what it was. The sum of what we knew at death is the measure of what we know afterward of all that went before. Of this existence we know many things, but no new light falls upon any page of that; in memory is written all of it that we can read. Here are no heights of truth overlooking the confused landscape of that dubitable domain. We still dwell in the Valley of the Shadow, lurk in its desolate places, peering from brambles and thickets at its mad, malign inhabitants.[10] How should we have new knowledge of that fading past?

What I am about to relate happened on a night. We know when it is night, for then you retire to your houses and we can venture from our places of concealment to move unafraid about our old homes, to look in at the windows, even to enter and gaze upon your faces as you sleep. I had lingered long near the dwelling where I had been so cruelly changed to what I am, as we do while any that we love or hate remain. Vainly I had sought some method of manifestation, some way to make my continued existence and my great love and poignant pity understood by my husband and son. Always if they slept they would wake, or if in my desperation I dared approach them when they were awake, would turn toward me the terrible eyes of the living, frightening me by the glances that I sought from the purpose that I held.

On this night I had searched for them without success, fearing to find them; they were nowhere in the house, nor about the moonlit lawn. For, although the sun is lost to us forever, the moon, full-orbed or slender, remains to us. Sometimes it shines by night, sometimes by day, but always it rises and sets, as in that other life.

I left the lawn and moved in the white light and silence along the road, aimless and sorrowing. Suddenly I heard the voice of my poor husband in exclamations of astonishment, with that of my son in reassurance and dissuasion; and there by the shadow of a group of trees they stood – near, so near! Their faces were toward me, the eyes of the elder man fixed upon

mine. He saw me – at last, at last, he saw me! In the consciousness of that, my terror fled as a cruel dream. The death-spell
was broken: Love had conquered Law! Mad with exultation I
shouted – I *must* have shouted, 'He sees, he sees: he will understand!' Then, controlling myself, I moved forward, smiling and
consciously beautiful, to offer myself to his arms, to comfort
him with endearments, and, with my son's hand in mine, to
speak words that should restore the broken bonds between the
living and the dead.

Alas! alas! his face went white with fear, his eyes were as
those of a hunted animal. He backed away from me, as I
advanced, and at last turned and fled into the wood – whither,
it is not given to me to know.

To my poor boy, left doubly desolate, I have never been able
to impart a sense of my presence. Soon he, too, must pass to
this Life Invisible and be lost to me forever.

HENRY JAMES
The Jolly Corner

I

'Every one asks me what I "think" of everything,' said Spencer
Brydon; 'and I make answer as I can – begging or dodging the
question, putting them off with any nonsense. It wouldn't
matter to any of them really,' he went on, 'for, even were it
possible to meet in that stand-and-deliver way so silly a demand
on so big a subject, my "thoughts" would still be almost
altogether about something that concerns only myself.' He was
talking to Miss Staverton, with whom for a couple of months
now he had availed himself of every possible occasion to talk;
this disposition and this resource, this comfort and support, as
the situation in fact presented itself, having promptly enough
taken the first place in the considerable array of rather unattenu-
ated surprises attending his so strangely belated return to
America. Everything was somehow a surprise; and that might
be natural when one had so long and so consistently neglected
everything, taken pains to give surprises so much margin for
play. He had given them more than thirty years – thirty-three,
to be exact; and they now seemed to him to have organized
their performance quite on the scale of that licence. He had
been twenty-three on leaving New York – he was fifty-six to-
day: unless indeed he were to reckon as he had sometimes, since
his repatriation, found himself feeling; in which case he would
have lived longer than is often allotted to man. It would have
taken a century, he repeatedly said to himself, and said also to
Alice Staverton, it would have taken a longer absence and a
more averted mind than those even of which he had been guilty,
to pile up the differences, the newnesses, the queernesses, above

all the bignesses, for the better or the worse, that at present assaulted his vision wherever he looked.

The great fact all the while however had been the incalculability; since he *had* supposed himself, from decade to decade, to be allowing, and in the most liberal and intelligent manner, for brilliancy of change. He actually saw that he had allowed for nothing; he missed what he would have been sure of finding, he found what he would never have imagined. Proportions and values were upside-down; the ugly things he had expected, the ugly things of his far-away youth, when he had too promptly waked up to a sense of the ugly – these uncanny phenomena placed him rather, as it happened, under the charm; whereas the 'swagger' things, the modern, the monstrous, the famous things, those he had more particularly, like thousands of ingenuous enquirers every year, come over to see, were exactly his sources of dismay. They were as so many set traps for displeasure, above all for reaction, of which his restless tread was constantly pressing the spring. It was interesting, doubtless, the whole show, but it would have been too disconcerting hadn't a certain finer truth saved the situation. He had distinctly not, in this steadier light, come over *all* for the monstrosities; he had come, not only in the last analysis but quite on the face of the act, under an impulse with which they had nothing to do. He had come – putting the thing pompously – to look at his 'property,' which he had thus for a third of a century not been within four thousand miles of; or, expressing it less sordidly, he had yielded to the humour of seeing again his house on the jolly corner, as he usually, and quite fondly, described it – the one in which he had first seen the light, in which various members of his family had lived and had died, in which the holidays of his overschooled boyhood had been passed and the few social flowers of his chilled adolescence gathered, and which, alienated then for so long a period, had, through the successive deaths of his two brothers and the termination of old arrangements, come wholly into his hands. He was the owner of another, not quite so 'good' – the jolly corner having been, from far back, superlatively extended and consecrated; and the value of the pair represented his main capital, with an income consisting, in these later years, of their respective rents which (thanks precisely to their original excellent type) had never been depressingly low. He could live in 'Europe,' as he had been in the habit of living, on the product of these flourishing New York leases, and all the better since, that of the second structure, the mere number in its long row, having within a twelvemonth fallen in, renovation at a high advance had proved beautifully possible.

These were items of property indeed, but he had found himself since his arrival distinguishing more than ever between them. The house within the street, two bristling blocks westward, was already in course of reconstruction as a tall mass of flats; he had acceded, some time before, to overtures for this conversion – in which, now that it was going forward, it had been not the least of his astonishments to find himself able, on the spot, and though without a previous ounce of such experience, to participate with a certain intelligence, almost with a certain authority. He had lived his life with his back so turned to such concerns and his face addressed to those of so different an order that he scarce knew what to make of this lively stir, in a compartment of his mind never yet penetrated, of a capacity for business and a sense for construction. These virtues, so common all round him now, had been dormant in his own organism – where it might be said of them perhaps that they had slept the sleep of the just. At present, in the splendid autumn weather – the autumn at least was a pure boon in the terrible place – he loafed about his 'work' undeterred, secretly agitated; not in the least 'minding' that the whole proposition, as they said, was vulgar and sordid, and ready to climb ladders, to walk the plank, to handle materials and look wise about them, to ask questions, in fine, and challenge explanations and really 'go into' figures.

It amused, it verily quite charmed him; and, by the same stroke, it amused, and even more, Alice Staverton, though perhaps charming her perceptibly less. She wasn't however going to be better-off for it, as *he* was – and so astonishingly much: nothing was now likely, he knew, ever to make her better-off than she found herself, in the afternoon of life, as the delicately frugal possessor and tenant of the small house in Irving Place to which she had subtly managed to cling through her almost

unbroken New York career.[1] If he knew the way to it now
better than to any other address among the dreadful multiplied
numberings which seemed to him to reduce the whole place
to some vast ledger-page, overgrown, fantastic, of ruled and
criss-crossed lines and figures – if he had formed, for his consolation, that habit, it was really not a little because of the charm
of his having encountered and recognized, in the vast wilderness
of the wholesale, breaking through the mere gross generalization of wealth and force and success, a small still scene where
items and shades, all delicate things, kept the sharpness of the
notes of a high voice perfectly trained, and where economy
hung about like the scent of a garden. His old friend lived with
one maid and herself dusted her relics and trimmed her lamps
and polished her silver; she stood off, in the awful modern
crush, when she could, but she sallied forth and did battle
when the challenge was really to 'spirit,' the spirit she after
all confessed to, proudly and a little shyly, as to that of the
better time, that of *their* common, their quite far-away and
antediluvian social period and order. She made use of the street-
cars when need be, the terrible things that people scrambled
for as the panic-stricken at sea scramble for the boats; she
affronted, inscrutably, under stress, all the public concussions
and ordeals; and yet, with that slim mystifying grace of her
appearance, which defied you to say if she were a fair young
woman who looked older through trouble, or a fine smooth
older one who looked young through successful indifference;
with her precious reference, above all, to memories and histories
into which he could enter, she was as exquisite for him as some
pale pressed flower (a rarity to begin with), and, failing other
sweetnesses, she was a sufficient reward of his effort. They had
communities of knowledge, 'their' knowledge (this discrimi-
nating possessive was always on her lips) of presences of the
other age, presences all overlaid, in his case, by the experience
of a man and the freedom of a wanderer, overlaid by pleasure,
by infidelity, by passages of life that were strange and dim to
her, just by 'Europe' in short, but still unobscured, still exposed
and cherished, under that pious visitation of the spirit from
which she had never been diverted.

She had come with him one day to see how his 'apartment-house' was rising; he had helped her over gaps and explained to her plans, and while they were there had happened to have, before her, a brief but lively discussion with the man in charge, the representative of the building-firm that had undertaken his work. He had found himself quite 'standing-up' to this personage over a failure on the latter's part to observe some detail of one of their noted conditions, and had so lucidly argued his case that, besides ever so prettily flushing, at the time, for sympathy in his triumph, she had afterwards said to him (though to a slightly greater effect of irony) that he had clearly for too many years neglected a real gift. If he had but stayed at home he would have anticipated the inventor of the sky-scraper.[2] If he had but stayed at home he would have discovered his genius in time really to start some new variety of awful architectural hare and run it till it burrowed in a gold-mine. He was to remember these words, while the weeks elapsed, for the small silver ring they had sounded over the queerest and deepest of his own lately most disguised and most muffled vibrations.

It had begun to be present to him after the first fortnight, it had broken out with the oddest abruptness, this particular wanton wonderment: it met him there – and this was the image under which he himself judged the matter, or at least, not a little, thrilled and flushed with it – very much as he might have been met by some strange figure, some unexpected occupant, at a turn of one of the dim passages of an empty house. The quaint analogy quite hauntingly remained with him, when he didn't indeed rather improve it by a still intenser form: that of his opening a door behind which he would have made sure of finding nothing, a door into a room shuttered and void, and yet so coming, with a great suppressed start, on some quite erect confronting presence, something planted in the middle of the place and facing him through the dusk. After that visit to the house in construction he walked with his companion to see the other and always so much the better one, which in the eastward direction formed one of the corners, the 'jolly' one precisely, of the street now so generally dishonoured and dis-figured in its westward reaches, and of the comparatively con-servative Avenue. The Avenue still had pretensions, as Miss

Staverton said, to decency; the old people had mostly gone, the old names were unknown, and here and there an old association seemed to stray, all vaguely, like some very aged person, out too late, whom you might meet and feel the impulse to watch or follow, in kindness, for safe restoration to shelter.

They went in together, our friends; he admitted himself with his key, as he kept no one there, he explained, preferring, for his reasons, to leave the place empty, under a simple arrangement with a good woman living in the neighbourhood and who came for a daily hour to open windows and dust and sweep. Spencer Brydon had his reasons and was growingly aware of them; they seemed to him better each time he was there, though he didn't name them all to his companion, any more than he told her as yet how often, how quite absurdly often, he himself came. He only let her see for the present, while they walked through the great blank rooms, that absolute vacancy reigned and that, from top to bottom, there was nothing but Mrs Muldoon's broomstick, in a corner, to tempt the burglar.[3] Mrs Muldoon was then on the premises, and she loquaciously attended the visitors, preceding them from room to room and pushing back shutters and throwing up sashes – all to show them, as she remarked, how little there was to see. There was little indeed to see in the great gaunt shell where the main dispositions and the general apportionment of space, the style of an age of ampler allowances, had nevertheless for its master their honest pleading message, affecting him as some good old servant's, some lifelong retainer's appeal for a character, or even for a retiring-pension; yet it was also a remark of Mrs Muldoon's that, glad as she was to oblige him by her noonday round, there was a request she greatly hoped he would never make of her. If he should wish her for any reason to come in after dark she would just tell him, if he 'plased,' that he must ask it of somebody else.

The fact that there was nothing to see didn't militate for the worthy woman against what one *might* see, and she put it frankly to Miss Staverton that no lady could be expected to like, could she? 'craping up to thim top storeys in the ayvil hours.' The gas and the electric light were off the house, and she fairly evoked a gruesome vision of her march through the

great grey rooms – so many of them as there were too! – with
her glimmering taper. Miss Staverton met her honest glare with
a smile and the profession that she herself certainly would recoil
from such an adventure. Spencer Brydon meanwhile held his
peace – for the moment; the question of the 'evil' hours in his
old home had already become too grave for him. He had begun
some time since to 'crape,' and he knew just why a packet of
candles addressed to that pursuit had been stowed by his own
hand, three weeks before, at the back of a drawer of the fine
old sideboard that occupied, as a 'fixture,' the deep recess in
the dining-room. Just now he laughed at his companions –
quickly however changing the subject; for the reason that, in
the first place, his laugh struck him even at that moment as
starting the odd echo, the conscious human resonance (he scarce
knew how to qualify it) that sounds made while he was there
alone sent back to his ear or his fancy; and that, in the second,
he imagined Alice Staverton for the instant on the point of
asking him, with a divination, if he ever so prowled. There were
divinations he was unprepared for, and he had at all events
averted enquiry by the time Mrs Muldoon had left them, passing on to other parts.

There was happily enough to say, on so consecrated a spot,
that could be said freely and fairly; so that a whole train of
declarations was precipitated by his friend's having herself
broken out, after a yearning look round: 'But I hope you don't
mean they want you to pull *this* to pieces!' His answer came,
promptly, with his re-awakened wrath: it was of course exactly
what they wanted, and what they were 'at' him for, daily, with
the iteration of people who couldn't for their life understand a
man's liability to decent feelings. He had found the place, just
as it stood and beyond what he could express, an interest and
a joy. There were values other than the beastly rent-values, and
in short, in short –! But it was thus Miss Staverton took him
up. 'In short you're to make so good a thing of your sky-scraper
that, living in luxury on *those* ill-gotten gains, you can afford
for a while to be sentimental here!' Her smile had for him, with
the words, the particular mild irony with which he found half
her talk suffused; an irony without bitterness and that came,
exactly, from her having so much imagination – not, like the

cheap sarcasms with which one heard most people, about the
world of 'society,' bid for the reputation of cleverness, from
nobody's really having any. It was agreeable to him at this very
moment to be sure that when he had answered, after a brief
demur, 'Well yes: so, precisely, you may put it!' her imagination
would still do him justice. He explained that even if never a
dollar were to come to him from the other house he would
nevertheless cherish this one; and he dwelt, further, while they
lingered and wandered, on the fact of the stupefaction he was
already exciting, the positive mystification he felt himself create.

He spoke of the value of all he read into it, into the mere
sight of the walls, mere shapes of the rooms, mere sound of
the floors, mere feel, in his hand, of the old silver-plated knobs
of the several mahogany doors, which suggested the pressure
of the palms of the dead; the seventy years of the past in
fine that these things represented, the annals of nearly three
generations, counting his grandfather's, the one that had ended
there, and the impalpable ashes of his long-extinct youth, afloat
in the very air like microscopic motes. She listened to everything; she was a woman who answered intimately but who
utterly didn't chatter. She scattered abroad therefore no cloud
of words; she could assent, she could agree, above all she could
encourage, without doing that. Only at the last she went a little
further than he had done himself. 'And then how do you know?
You may still, after all, want to live here.' It rather indeed pulled
him up, for it wasn't what he had been thinking, at least in her
sense of the words. 'You mean I may decide to stay on for the
sake of it?'

'Well, *with* such a home –!' But, quite beautifully, she had
too much tact to dot so monstrous an *i*, and it was precisely an
illustration of the way she didn't rattle. How could any one
– of any wit – insist on any one else's 'wanting' to live in
New York?

'Oh,' he said, 'I *might* have lived here (since I had my opportunity early in life); I might have put in here all these years.
Then everything would have been different enough – and, I
dare say, "funny" enough. But that's another matter. And then
the beauty of it – I mean of my perversity, of my refusal to
agree to a "deal" – is just in the total absence of a reason. Don't

you see that if I had a reason about the matter at all it would *have* to be the other way, and would then be inevitably a reason of dollars? There are no reasons here *but* of dollars. Let us therefore have none whatever – not the ghost of one.'

They were back in the hall then for departure, but from where they stood the vista was large, through an open door, into the great square main saloon, with its almost antique felicity of brave spaces between windows. Her eyes came back from that reach and met his own a moment. 'Are you very sure the "ghost" of one doesn't, much rather, serve – ?'

He had a positive sense of turning pale. But it was as near as they were then to come. For he made answer, he believed, between a glare and a grin: 'Oh ghosts – of course the place must swarm with them! I should be ashamed of it if it didn't. Poor Mrs Muldoon's right, and it's why I haven't asked her to do more than look in.'

Miss Staverton's gaze again lost itself, and things she didn't utter, it was clear, came and went in her mind. She might even for the minute, off there in the fine room, have imagined some element dimly gathering. Simplified like the death-mask of a handsome face, it perhaps produced for her just then an effect akin to the stir of an expression in the 'set' commemorative plaster. Yet whatever her impression may have been she produced instead a vague platitude. 'Well, if it were only furnished and lived in – !'

She appeared to imply that in case of its being still furnished he might have been a little less opposed to the idea of a return. But she passed straight into the vestibule, as if to leave her words behind her, and the next moment he had opened the house-door and was standing with her on the steps. He closed the door and, while he re-pocketed his key, looking up and down, they took in the comparatively harsh actuality of the Avenue, which reminded him of the assault of the outer light of the Desert on the traveller emerging from an Egyptian tomb. But he risked before they stepped into the street his gathered answer to her speech. 'For me it *is* lived in. For me it *is* furnished.' At which it was easy for her to sigh 'Ah yes – !' all vaguely and discreetly; since his parents and his favourite sister, to say nothing of other kin, in numbers, had run their course and met their end there. That represented, within the walls, ineffaceable life.

It was a few days after this that, during an hour passed with her again, he had expressed his impatience of the too flattering curiosity – among the people he met – about his appreciation of New York. He had arrived at none at all that was socially producible, and as for that matter of his 'thinking' (thinking the better or the worse of anything there) he was wholly taken up with one subject of thought. It was mere vain egoism, and it was moreover, if she liked, a morbid obsession. He found all things come back to the question of what he personally might have been, how he might have led his life and 'turned out,' if he had not so, at the outset, given it up. And confessing for the first time to the intensity within him of this absurd speculation – which but proved also, no doubt, the habit of too selfishly thinking – he affirmed the impotence there of any other source of interest, any other native appeal. 'What would it have made of me, what would it have made of me? I keep for ever wondering, all idiotically; as if I could possibly know! I see what it has made of dozens of others, those I meet, and it positively aches within me, to the point of exasperation, that it would have made something of me as well. Only I can't make out *what*, and the worry of it, the small rage of curiosity never to be satisfied, brings back what I remember to have felt, once or twice, after judging best, for reasons, to burn some important letter unopened. I've been sorry, I've hated it – I've never known what was in the letter. You may of course say it's a trifle –!'

'I don't say it's a trifle,' Miss Staverton gravely interrupted.

She was seated by her fire, and before her, on his feet and restless, he turned to and fro between this intensity of his idea and a fitful and unseeing inspection, through his single eye-glass, of the dear little old objects on her chimney-piece. Her interruption made him for an instant look at her harder. 'I shouldn't care if you did!' he laughed, however; 'and it's only a figure, at any rate, for the way I now feel. *Not* to have followed my perverse young course – and almost in the teeth of my father's curse, as I may say; not to have kept it up, so, "over there," from that day to this, without a doubt or a pang; not, above all, to have liked it, to have loved it, so much, loved it, no doubt, with such an abysmal conceit of my own preference: some variation from *that*, I say, must have produced some different effect for my life and for my "form." I should have stuck here – if it had been possible; and I was too young, at twenty-three, to judge, *pour deux sous*, whether it *were* possible.[4] If I had waited I might have seen it was, and then I might have been, by staying here, something nearer to one of these types who have been hammered so hard and made so keen by their conditions. It isn't that I admire them so much – the question of any charm in them, or of any charm, beyond that of the rank money-passion, exerted by their conditions *for* them, has nothing to do with the matter: it's only a question of what fantastic, yet perfectly possible, development of my own nature I mayn't have missed. It comes over me that I had then a strange *alter ego* deep down somewhere within me, as the full-blown flower is in the small tight bud, and that I just took the course, I just transferred him to the climate, that blighted him for once and for ever.'

'And you wonder about the flower,' Miss Staverton said. 'So do I, if you want to know; and so I've been wondering these several weeks. I believe in the flower,' she continued, 'I feel it would have been quite splendid, quite huge and monstrous.'

'Monstrous above all!' her visitor echoed; 'and I imagine, by the same stroke, quite hideous and offensive.'

'You don't believe that,' she returned; 'if you did you wouldn't wonder. You'd know, and that would be enough for you. What you feel – and what I feel *for* you – is that you'd have had power.'

'You'd have liked me that way?' he asked.

She barely hung fire. 'How should I not have liked you?'

'I see. You'd have liked me, have preferred me, a billionaire!'

'How should I not have liked you?' she simply again asked.

He stood before her still – her question kept him motionless. He took it in, so much there was of it; and indeed his not otherwise meeting it testified to that. 'I know at least what I am,' he simply went on; 'the other side of the medal's clear enough. I've not been edifying – I believe I'm thought in a hundred quarters to have been barely decent. I've followed strange paths and worshipped strange gods; it must have come to you again and again – in fact you've admitted to me as much – that I was leading, at any time these thirty years, a selfish frivolous scandalous life.[5] And you see what it has made of me.'

She just waited, smiling at him. 'You see what it has made of *me*.'

'Oh you're a person whom nothing can have altered. You were born to be what you are, anywhere, anyway: you've the perfection nothing else could have blighted. And don't you see how, without my exile, I shouldn't have been waiting till now – ?' But he pulled up for the strange pang.

'The great thing to see,' she presently said, 'seems to me to be that it has spoiled nothing. It hasn't spoiled your being here at last. It hasn't spoiled this. It hasn't spoiled your speaking – ' She also however faltered.

He wondered at everything her controlled emotion might mean. 'Do you believe then – too dreadfully! – that I *am* as good as I might ever have been?'

'Oh no! Far from it!' With which she got up from her chair and was nearer to him. 'But I don't care,' she smiled.

'You mean I'm good enough?'

She considered a little. 'Will you believe it if I say so? I mean will you let that settle your question for you?' And then as if making out in his face that he drew back from this, that he had some idea which, however absurd, he couldn't yet bargain away: 'Oh you don't care either – but very differently: you don't care for anything but yourself.'

Spencer Brydon recognized it – it was in fact what he had absolutely professed. Yet he importantly qualified. '*He* isn't myself. He's the just so totally other person. But I do want to see him,' he added. 'And I can. And I shall.'

Their eyes met for a minute while he guessed from something in hers that she divined his strange sense. But neither of them otherwise expressed it, and her apparent understanding, with no protesting shock, no easy derision, touched him more deeply than anything yet, constituting for his stifled perversity, on the spot, an element that was like breatheable air. What she said however was unexpected. 'Well, *I've* seen him.'

'You – ?'

'I've seen him in a dream.'

'Oh a "dream" – !' It let him down.

'But twice over,' she continued. 'I saw him as I see you now.'

'You've dreamed the same dream – ?'

'Twice over,' she repeated. 'The very same.'

This did somehow a little speak to him, as it also gratified him. 'You dream about me at that rate?'

'Ah about *him*!' she smiled.

His eyes again sounded her. 'Then you know all about him.' And as she said nothing more: 'What's the wretch like?'

She hesitated, and it was as if he were pressing her so hard that, resisting for reasons of her own, she had to turn away. 'I'll tell you some other time!'

II

It was after this that there was most of a virtue for him, most of a cultivated charm, most of a preposterous secret thrill, in the particular form of surrender to his obsession and of address to what he more and more believed to be his privilege. It was what in these weeks he was living for – since he really felt life to begin but after Mrs Muldoon had retired from the scene and, visiting the ample house from attic to cellar, making sure he was alone, he knew himself in safe possession and, as he tacitly expressed it, let himself go. He sometimes came twice in the twenty-four hours; the moments he liked best were those of gathering dusk, of the short autumn twilight; this was the time of which, again and again, be found himself hoping most. Then he could, as seemed to him, most intimately wander and wait, linger and listen, feel his fine attention, never in his life before so fine, on the pulse of the great vague place: he preferred the lampless hour and only wished he might have prolonged each day the deep crepuscular spell. Later – rarely much before midnight, but then for a considerable vigil – he watched with his glimmering light; moving slowly, holding it high, playing it far, rejoicing above all, as much as he might, in open vistas, reaches of communication between rooms and by passages; the long straight chance or show, as he would have called it, for the revelation he pretended to invite. It was a practice he found he could perfectly 'work' without exciting remark; no one was in the least the wiser for it; even Alice Staverton, who was moreover a well of discretion, didn't quite fully imagine.

He let himself in and let himself out with the assurance of calm proprietorship; and accident so far favoured him that, if a fat Avenue 'officer' had happened on occasion to see him entering at eleven-thirty, he had never yet, to the best of his belief, been noticed as emerging at two. He walked there on the crisp November nights, arrived regularly at the evening's end; it was as easy to do this after dining out as to take his way to a club or to his hotel. When he left his club, if he hadn't been dining out, it was ostensibly to go to his hotel; and when he left his hotel, if he had spent a part of the evening there, it was ostensibly to go to his club. Everything was easy in fine; everything conspired and promoted: there was truly even in the strain of his experience something that glossed over, something that salved and simplified, all the rest of consciousness. He circulated, talked, renewed, loosely and pleasantly, old relations – met indeed, so far as he could, new expectations and seemed to make out on the whole that in spite of the career, of such different contacts, which he had spoken of to Miss Staverton as ministering so little, for those who might have watched it, to edification, he was positively rather liked than not. He was a dim secondary social success – and all with people who had truly not an idea of him. It was all mere surface sound, this murmur of their welcome, this popping of their corks – just as his gestures of response were the extravagant shadows, emphatic in proportion as they meant little, of some game of *ombres chinoises*.[6] He projected himself all day, in thought, straight over the bristling line of hard unconscious heads and into the other, the real, the waiting life; the life that, as soon as he had heard behind him the click of his great house-door, began for him, on the jolly corner, as beguilingly as the slow opening bars of some rich music follows the tap of the conductor's wand.

He always caught the first effect of the steel point of his stick on the old marble of the hall pavement, large black-and-white squares that he remembered as the admiration of his childhood

and that had then made in him, as he now saw, for the growth
of an early conception of style. This effect was the dim reverber-
ating tinkle as of some far-off bell hung who should say where?
– in the depths of the house, of the past, of that mystical other
world that might have flourished for him had he not, for weal
or woe, abandoned it. On this impression he did ever the same
thing; he put his stick noiselessly away in a corner – feeling the
place once more in the likeness of some great glass bowl, all
precious concave crystal, set delicately humming by the play of
a moist finger round its edge. The concave crystal held, as
it were, this mystical other world, and the indescribably fine
murmur of its rim was the sigh there, the scarce audible pathetic
wail to his strained ear, of all the old baffled forsworn possibilities. What he did therefore by this appeal of his hushed presence
was to wake them into such measure of ghostly life as they
might still enjoy. They were shy, all but unappeasably shy, but
they weren't really sinister; at least they weren't as he had
hitherto felt them – before they had taken the Form he so
yearned to make them take, the Form he at moments saw
himself in the light of fairly hunting on tiptoe, the points of his
evening-shoes, from room to room and from storey to storey.

That was the essence of his vision – which was all rank folly,
if one would, while he was out of the house and otherwise
occupied, but which took on the last verisimilitude as soon as
he was placed and posted. He knew what he meant and what
he wanted; it was as clear as the figure on a cheque presented
in demand for cash. His *alter ego* 'walked' – that was the note
of his image of him, while his image of his motive for his own
odd pastime was the desire to waylay him and meet him. He
roamed, slowly, warily, but all restlessly, he himself did – Mrs
Muldoon had been right, absolutely, with her figure of their
'craping'; and the presence he watched for would roam restlessly too. But it would be as cautious and as shifty; the conviction of its probable, in fact its already quite sensible, quite
audible evasion of pursuit grew for him from night to night,
laying on him finally a rigour to which nothing in his life had
been comparable. It had been the theory of many superficially-
judging persons, he knew, that he was wasting that life in a
surrender to sensations, but he had tasted of no pleasure so fine

as his actual tension, had been introduced to no sport that demanded at once the patience and the nerve of this stalking of a creature more subtle, yet at bay perhaps more formidable, than any beast of the forest. The terms, the comparisons, the very practices of the chase positively came again into play; there were even moments when passages of his occasional experience as a sportsman, stirred memories, from his younger time, of moor and mountain and desert, revived for him – and to the increase of his keenness – by the tremendous force of analogy. He found himself at moments – once he had placed his single light on some mantel-shelf or in some recess – stepping back into shelter or shade, effacing himself behind a door or in an embrasure, as he had sought of old the vantage of rock and tree; he found himself holding his breath and living in the joy of the instant, the supreme suspense created by big game alone.

He wasn't afraid (though putting himself the question as he believed gentlemen on Bengal tiger-shoots or in close quarters with the great bear of the Rockies had been known to confess to having put it); and this indeed – since here at least he might be frank! – because of the impression, so intimate and so strange, that he himself produced as yet a dread, produced certainly a strain, beyond the liveliest he was likely to feel. They fell for him into categories, they fairly became familiar, the signs, for his own perception, of the alarm his presence and his vigilance created; though leaving him always to remark, portentously, on his probably having formed a relation, his probably enjoying a consciousness, unique in the experience of man. People enough, first and last, had been in terror of apparitions, but who had ever before so turned the tables and become himself, in the apparitional world, an incalculable terror? He might have found this sublime had he quite dared to think of it; but he didn't too much insist, truly, on that side of his privilege. With habit and repetition he gained to an extraordinary degree the power to penetrate the dusk of dis-tances and the darkness of corners, to resolve back into their innocence the treacheries of uncertain light, the evil-looking forms taken in the gloom by mere shadows, by accidents of the air, by shifting effects of perspective; putting down his dim luminary he could still wander on without it, pass into other rooms and, only knowing it was there behind him in case of need, see his way about, visually project for his purpose a comparative clearness. It made him feel, this acquired faculty, like some monstrous stealthy cat; he wondered if he would have glared at these moments with large shining yellow eyes, and what it mightn't verily be, for the poor hard-pressed *alter ego*, to be confronted with such a type.

He liked however the open shutters; he opened everywhere those Mrs Muldoon had closed, closing them as carefully afterwards, so that she shouldn't notice: he liked – oh this he did like, and above all in the upper rooms! – the sense of the hard silver of the autumn stars through the window-panes, and scarcely less the flare of the street-lamps below, the white electric lustre which it would have taken curtains to keep out. This was human actual social; this was of the world he had lived in, and he was more at his ease certainly for the countenance, coldly general and impersonal, that all the while and in spite of his detachment it seemed to give him. He had support of course mostly in the rooms at the wide front and the prolonged side; it failed him considerably in the central shades and the parts at the back. But if he sometimes, on his rounds, was glad of his optical reach, so none the less often the rear of the house affected him as the very jungle of his prey. The place was there more subdivided; a large 'extension' in particular, where small rooms for servants had been multiplied, abounded in nooks and corners, in closets and passages, in the ramifications especially of an ample back staircase over which he leaned, many a time, to look far down – not deterred from his gravity even while aware that he might, for a spectator, have figured some solemn simpleton playing at hide-and-seek. Outside in fact he might himself make that ironic *rapprochement*; but within the walls, and in spite of the clear windows, his consistency was proof against the cynical light of New York.[7]

It had belonged to that idea of the exasperated consciousness of his victim to become a real test for him; since he had quite put it to himself from the first that, oh distinctly! he could 'cultivate' his whole perception. He had felt it as above all open to cultivation – which indeed was but another name for his manner of spending his time. He was bringing it on, bringing it to perfection, by practice; in consequence of which it had grown so fine that he was now aware of impressions, attestations of his general postulate, that couldn't have broken upon him at once. This was the case more specifically with a phenomenon at last quite frequent for him in the upper rooms, the recognition – absolutely unmistakeable, and by a turn dating from a particular hour, his resumption of his campaign after a diplomatic drop, a calculated absence of three nights – of his being definitely followed, tracked at a distance carefully taken and to the express end that he should the less confidently, less arrogantly, appear to himself merely to pursue. It worried, it finally quite broke him up, for it proved, of all the conceivable impressions, the one least suited to his book. He was kept in sight while remaining himself – as regards the essence of his position – sightless, and his only recourse then was in abrupt turns, rapid recoveries of ground. He wheeled about, retracing his steps, as if he might so catch in his face at least the stirred air of some other quick revolution. It was indeed true that his fully dislocalized thought of these manœuvres recalled to him Pantaloon, at the Christmas farce, buffeted and tricked from behind by ubiquitous Harlequin;[8] but it left intact the influence of the conditions themselves each time he was re-exposed to them, so that in fact this association, had he suffered it to become constant, would on a certain side have but ministered to his intenser gravity. He had made, as I have said, to create on the premises the baseless sense of a reprieve, his three absences; and the result of the third was to confirm the after-effect of the second.

On his return, that night – the night succeeding his last intermission – he stood in the hall and looked up the staircase with a certainty more intimate than any he had yet known. 'He's *there*, at the top, and waiting – not, as in general, falling back for disappearance. He's holding his ground, and it's the first time – which is a proof, isn't it? that something has happened for him.' So Brydon argued with his hand on the banister and his foot on the lowest stair; in which position he felt as never before the air chilled by his logic. He himself turned cold in it, for he seemed of a sudden to know what now was involved. 'Harder pressed? – yes, he takes it in, with its thus making clear to him that I've come, as they say, "to stay." He finally doesn't like and can't bear it, in the sense, I mean, that his wrath, his menaced interest, now balances with his dread. I've hunted him till he has "turned": that, up there, is what has happened – he's the fanged or the antlered animal brought at last to bay.' There came to him, as I say – but determined by an influence beyond my notation! – the acuteness of this certainty; under which however the next moment he had broken into a sweat that he would as little have consented to attribute to fear as he would have dared immediately to act upon it for enterprise. It marked none the less a prodigious thrill, a thrill that represented sudden dismay, no doubt, but also represented, and with the selfsame throb, the strangest, the most joyous, possibly the next minute almost the proudest, duplication of consciousness.

'He has been dodging, retreating, hiding, but now, worked up to anger, he'll fight!' – this intense impression made a single mouthful, as it were, of terror and applause. But what was wondrous was that the applause, for the felt fact, was so eager, since, if it was his other self he was running to earth, this ineffable identity was thus in the last resort not unworthy of him. It bristled there – somewhere near at hand, however unseen still – as the hunted thing, even as the trodden worm of the adage *must* at last bristle; and Brydon at this instant tasted probably of a sensation more complex than had ever before found itself consistent with sanity.[9] It was as if it would have shamed him that a character so associated with his own should triumphantly succeed in just skulking, should to the end not risk the open; so that the drop of this danger was, on the spot, a great lift of the whole situation. Yet with another rare shift of the same subtlety he was already trying to measure by how much more he himself might now be in peril of fear; so rejoicing that he could, in another form, actively inspire that fear, and simultaneously quaking for the form in which he might passively know it.

The apprehension of knowing it must after a little have grown in him, and the strangest moment of his adventure perhaps, the most memorable or really most interesting, afterwards, of his crisis, was the lapse of certain instants of concentrated conscious *combat*, the sense of a need to hold on to something, even after the manner of a man slipping and slipping on some awful incline; the vivid impulse, above all, to move, to act, to charge, somehow and upon something – to show himself, in a word, that he wasn't afraid. The state of 'holding-on' was thus the state to which he was momentarily reduced; if there had been anything, in the great vacancy, to seize, he would presently have been aware of having clutched it as he might under a shock at home have clutched the nearest chair-back. He had been surprised at any rate – of this he *was* aware – into something unprecedented since his original appropriation of the place; he had closed his eyes, held them tight, for a long minute, as with that instinct of dismay and that terror of vision. When he opened them the room, the other contiguous rooms, extraordinarily, seemed lighter – so light, almost, that at first he took the change for day. He stood firm, however that might be, just where he had paused; his resistance had helped him – it was as if there were something he had tided over. He knew after a little what this was – it had been in the imminent danger of flight. He had stiffened his will against going; without this he would have made for the stairs, and it seemed to him that, still with his eyes closed, he would have descended them, would have known how, straight and swiftly, to the bottom.

Well, as he had held out, here he was – still at the top, among the more intricate upper rooms and with the gauntlet of the others, of all the rest of the house, still to run when it should be his time to go. He would go at his time – only at his time: didn't he go every night very much at the same hour? He took out his watch – there was light for that: it was scarcely a quarter past one, and he had never withdrawn so soon. He reached his lodgings for the most part at two – with his walk of a quarter of an hour. He would wait for the last quarter – he wouldn't stir till then; and he kept his watch there with his eyes on it, reflecting while he held it that this deliberate wait, a wait with an effort, which he recognized, would serve perfectly for the attestation he desired to make. It would prove his courage – unless indeed the latter might most be proved by his budging at last from his place. What he mainly felt now was that, since he hadn't originally scuttled, he had his dignities – which had never in his life seemed so many – all to preserve and to carry aloft. This was before him in truth as a physical image, an image almost worthy of an age of greater romance. That remark indeed glimmered for him only to glow the next instant with a finer light; since what age of romance, after all, could have matched either the state of his mind or, 'objectively,' as they said, the wonder of his situation? The only difference would have been that, brandishing his dignities over his head as in a parchment scroll, he might then – that is in the heroic time – have proceeded downstairs with a drawn sword in his other grasp.

At present, really, the light he had set down on the mantel of the next room would have to figure his sword; which utensil, in the course of a minute, he had taken the requisite number of steps to possess himself of. The door between the rooms was open, and from the second another door opened to a third. These rooms, as he remembered, gave all three upon a common corridor as well, but there was a fourth, beyond them, without issue save through the preceding. To have moved, to have heard his step again, was appreciably a help; though even in recognizing this he lingered once more a little by the chimney-piece on which his light had rested. When he next moved, just hesitating where to turn, he found himself considering a circumstance that, after his first and comparatively vague apprehension of it, produced in him the start that often attends some pang of recollection, the violent shock of having ceased happily to forget. He had come into sight of the door in which the brief chain of communication ended and which he now surveyed from the nearer threshold, the one not directly facing it. Placed at some distance to the left of this point, it would have admitted him to the last room of the four, the room without other approach or egress, had it not, to his intimate conviction, been closed *since* his former visitation, the matter probably of a quarter of an hour before. He stared with all his eyes at the wonder of the fact, arrested again where he stood and again holding his breath while he sounded its sense. Surely it had been *subsequently* closed – that is it had been on his previous passage indubitably open!

He took it full in the face that something had happened between – that he couldn't not have noticed before (by which he meant on his original tour of all the rooms that evening) that such a barrier had exceptionally presented itself. He had indeed since that moment undergone an agitation so extraordinary that it might have muddled for him any earlier view; and he tried to convince himself that he might perhaps then have gone into the room and, inadvertently, automatically, on coming out, have drawn the door after him. The difficulty was that this exactly was what he never did; it was against his whole policy, as he might have said, the essence of which was to keep vistas clear. He had them from the first, as he was well aware, quite on the brain: the strange apparition, at the far end of one of them, of his baffled 'prey' (which had become by so sharp an irony so little the term now to apply!) was the form of success his imagination had most cherished, projecting into it always a refinement of beauty. He had known fifty times the start of perception that had afterwards dropped; had fifty times gasped to himself 'There!' under some fond brief hallucination. The house, as the case stood, admirably lent itself; he might wonder at the taste, the native architecture of the particular time, which could rejoice so in the multiplication of doors – the opposite extreme to the modern, the actual almost complete proscription of them; but it had fairly contributed to provoke this obsession of the presence encountered telescopically, as he might say, focussed and studied in diminishing perspective and as by a rest for the elbow.

It was with these considerations that his present attention was charged – they perfectly availed to make what he saw portentous. He *couldn't*, by any lapse, have blocked that aperture; and if he hadn't, if it was unthinkable, why what else was clear but that there had been another agent? Another agent? – he had been catching, as he felt, a moment back, the very breath of him; but when had he been so close as in this simple, this logical, this completely personal act? It was so logical, that is, that one might have *taken* it for personal; yet for what did Brydon take it, he asked himself, while, softly panting, he felt his eyes almost leave their sockets. Ah this time at last they *were*, the two, the opposed projections of him, in presence; and this time, as much as one would, the question of danger loomed. With it rose, as not before, the question of courage – for what he knew the blank face of the door to say to him was 'Show us

how much you have!' It stared, it glared back at him with that
challenge; it put to him the two alternatives: should he just
push it open or not? Oh to have this consciousness was to *think*
– and to think, Brydon knew, as he stood there, was, with the
lapsing moments, not to have acted! Not to have acted – that
was the misery and the pang – was even still not to act; was in
fact *all* to feel the thing in another, in a new and terrible way.
How long did he pause and how long did he debate? There was
presently nothing to measure it; for his vibration had already
changed – as just by the effect of its intensity. Shut up there, at
bay, defiant, and with the prodigy of the thing palpably
proveably *done*, thus giving notice like some stark signboard –
under that accession of accent the situation itself had turned;
and Brydon at last remarkably made up his mind on what it
had turned to.

It had turned altogether to a different admonition; to a
supreme hint, for him, of the value of Discretion! This slowly
dawned, no doubt – for it could take its time; so perfectly, on
his threshold, had he been stayed, so little as yet had he either
advanced or retreated. It was the strangest of all things that
now when, by his taking ten steps and applying his hand to a
latch, or even his shoulder and his knee, if necessary, to a panel,
all the hunger of his prime need might have been met, his high
curiosity crowned, his unrest assuaged – it was amazing, but it
was also exquisite and rare, that insistence should have, at a
touch, quite dropped from him. Discretion – he jumped at that;
and yet not, verily, at such a pitch, because it saved his nerves
or his skin, but because, much more valuably, it saved the
situation. When I say he 'jumped' at it I feel the consonance of
this term with the fact that – at the end indeed of I know not
how long – he did move again, he crossed straight to the door.
He wouldn't touch it – it seemed now that he might *if* he would:
he would only just wait there a little, to show, to prove, that he
wouldn't. He had thus another station, close to the thin par-
tition by which revelation was denied him; but with his eyes
bent and his hands held off in a mere intensity of stillness. He
listened as if there had been something to hear, but this attitude,
while it lasted, was his own communication. 'If you won't then
– good: I spare you and I give up. You affect me as by the

appeal positively for pity: you convince me that for reasons rigid and sublime – what do I know? – we both of us should have suffered. I respect them then, and, though moved and privileged as, I believe, it has never been given to man, I retire, I renounce – never, on my honour, to try again. So rest for ever – and let *me*!'

That, for Brydon was the deep sense of this last demonstration – solemn, measured, directed, as he felt it to be. He brought it to a close, he turned away; and now verily he knew how deeply he had been stirred. He retraced his steps, taking up his candle, burnt, he observed, well-nigh to the socket, and marking again, lighten it as he would, the distinctness of his footfall; after which, in a moment, he knew himself at the other side of the house. He did here what he had not yet done at these hours – he opened half a casement, one of those in the front, and let in the air of the night; a thing he would have taken at any time previous for a sharp rupture of his spell. His spell was broken now, and it didn't matter – broken by his concession and his surrender, which made it idle henceforth that he should ever come back. The empty street – its other life so marked even by the great lamplit vacancy – was within call, within touch; he stayed there as to be in it again, high above it though he was still perched; he watched as for some comforting common fact, some vulgar human note, the passage of a scavenger or a thief, some night-bird however base. He would have blessed that sign of life; he would have welcomed positively the slow approach of his friend the policeman, whom he had hitherto only sought to avoid, and was not sure that if the patrol had come into sight he mightn't have felt the impulse to get into relation with it, to hail it, on some pretext, from his fourth floor.

The pretext that wouldn't have been too silly or too compromising, the explanation that would have saved his dignity and kept his name, in such a case, out of the papers, was not definite to him: he was so occupied with the thought of recording his Discretion – as an effect of the vow he had just uttered to his intimate adversary – that the importance of this loomed large and something had overtaken all ironically his sense of proportion. If there had been a ladder applied to the front of the house, even one of the vertiginous perpendiculars employed by painters and roofers and sometimes left standing overnight, he would have managed somehow, astride of the window-sill, to compass by outstretched leg and arm that mode of descent. If there had been some such uncanny thing as he had found in his room at hotels, a workable fire-escape in the form of notched cable or a canvas shoot, he would have availed himself of it as a proof – well, of his present delicacy. He nursed that sentiment, as the question stood, a little in vain, and even – at the end of he scarce knew, once more, how long – found it, as by the action on his mind of the failure of response of the outer world, sinking back to vague anguish. It seemed to him he had waited an age for some stir of the great grim hush; the life of the town was itself under a spell – so unnaturally, up and down the whole prospect of known and rather ugly objects, the blankness and the silence lasted. Had they ever, he asked himself, the hard-faced houses, which had begun to look livid in the dim dawn, had they ever spoken so little to any need of his spirit? Great builded voids, great crowded stillnesses put on, often, in the heart of cities, for the small hours, a sort of sinister mask, and it was of this large collective negation that Brydon presently became conscious – all the more that the break of day was, almost incredibly, now at hand, proving to him what a night he had made of it.

He looked again at his watch, saw what had become of his time-values (he had taken hours for minutes – not, as in other tense situations, minutes for hours) and the strange air of the streets was but the weak, the sullen flush of a dawn in which everything was still locked up. His choked appeal from his own open window had been the sole note of life, and he could but break off at last as for a worse despair. Yet while so deeply demoralized he was capable again of an impulse denoting – at least by his present measure – extraordinary resolution; of retracing his steps to the spot where he had turned cold with the extinction of his last pulse of doubt as to there being in the place another presence than his own. This required an effort strong enough to sicken him; but he had his reason, which overmastered for the moment everything else. There was the whole of the rest of the house to traverse, and how should he screw himself to that if the door he had seen closed were at present open? He could hold to the idea that the closing had practically been for him an act of mercy, a chance offered him to descend, depart, get off the ground and never again profane it. This conception held together, it worked; but what it meant for him depended now clearly on the amount of forbearance his recent action, or rather his recent inaction, had engendered. The image of the 'presence,' whatever it was, waiting there for him to go – this image had not yet been so concrete for his nerves as when he stopped short of the point at which certainty would have come to him. For, with all his resolution, or more exactly with all his dread, he did stop short – he hung back from really seeing. The risk was too great and his fear too definite: it took at this moment an awful specific form.

He knew – yes, as he had never known anything – that, *should* he see the door open, it would all too abjectly be the end of him. It would mean that the agent of his shame – for his shame was the deep abjection – was once more at large and in general possession; and what glared him thus in the face was the act that this would determine for him. It would send him straight about to the window he had left open, and by that window, be long ladder and dangling rope as absent as they would, he saw himself uncontrollably insanely fatally take his way to the street. The hideous chance of this he at least could avert; but he could only avert it by recoiling in time from assurance. He had the whole house to deal with, this fact was still there; only he now knew that uncertainty alone could start him. He stole back from where he had checked himself – merely to do so was suddenly like safety – and, making blindly for the greater staircase, left gaping rooms and sounding passages behind. Here was the top of the stairs, with a fine large dim descent and three spacious landings to mark off. His instinct was all for mildness, but his feet were harsh on the floors, and, strangely, when he had in a couple of minutes become aware of this, it counted somehow for help. He couldn't have spoken, the tone of his voice would have scared him, and the common conceit or resource of 'whistling in the dark' (whether literally or figuratively) have appeared basely vulgar; yet he liked none the less to hear himself go, and when he had reached his first landing – taking it all with no rush, but quite steadily – that stage of success drew from him a gasp of relief.

The house, withal, seemed immense, the scale of space again inordinate; the open rooms, to no one of which his eyes deflected, gloomed in their shuttered state like mouths of caverns; only the high skylight that formed the crown of the deep well created for him a medium in which he could advance, but which might have been, for queerness of colour, some watery under-world. He tried to think of something noble, as that his property was really grand, a splendid possession; but this nobleness took the form too of the clear delight with which he was finally to sacrifice it. They might come in now, the builders, the destroyers – they might come as soon as they would. At the end of two flights he had dropped to another zone, and from the middle of the third, with only one more left, he recognized the influence of the lower windows, of half-drawn blinds, of the occasional gleam of street-lamps, of the glazed spaces of the vestibule. This was the bottom of the sea, which showed an illumination of its own and which he even saw paved – when at a given moment he drew up to sink a long look over the banisters – with the marble squares of his childhood. By that time indubitably he felt, as he might have said in a com-moner cause, better; it had allowed him to stop and draw breath, and the ease increased with the sight of the old black-and-white slabs. But what he most felt was that now surely, with the element of impunity pulling him as by hard firm hands, the case was settled for what he might have seen above had he dared that last look. The closed door, blessedly remote now, was still closed – and he had only in short to reach that of the house.

He came down further, he crossed the passage forming the access to the last flight; and if here again he stopped an instant it was almost for the sharpness of the thrill of assured escape. It made him shut his eyes – which opened again to the straight slope of the remainder of the stairs. Here was impunity still, but impunity almost excessive; inasmuch as the side-lights and the high fan-tracery of the entrance were glimmering straight into the hall; an appearance produced, he the next instant saw, by the fact that the vestibule gaped wide, that the hinged halves of the inner door had been thrown far back. Out of that again the *question* sprang at him, making his eyes, as he felt, half-start from his head, as they had done, at the top of the house, before the sign of the other door. If he had left that one open, hadn't he left this one closed, and wasn't he now in *most* immediate presence of some inconceivable occult activity? It was as sharp, the question, as a knife in his side, but the answer hung fire still and seemed to lose itself in the vague darkness to which the thin admitted dawn, glimmering archwise over the whole outer door, made a semicircular margin, a cold silvery nimbus that seemed to play a little as he looked – to shift and expand and contract.

It was as if there had been something within it, protected by indistinctness and corresponding in extent with the opaque surface behind, the painted panels of the last barrier to his escape, of which the key was in his pocket. The indistinctness mocked him even while he stared, affected him as somehow shrouding or challenging certitude, so that after faltering an instant on his step he let himself go with the sense that here *was* at last something to meet, to touch, to take, to know – something all unnatural and dreadful, but to advance upon which was the condition for him either of liberation or of supreme defeat. The penumbra, dense and dark, was the virtual screen of a figure which stood in it as still as some image erect in a niche or as some black-vizored sentinel guarding a treasure. Brydon was to know afterwards, was to recall and make out, the particular thing he had believed during the rest of his descent. He saw, in its great grey glimmering margin, the central vagueness diminish, and he felt it to be taking the very form toward which, for so many days, the passion of his curiosity had yearned. It gloomed, it loomed, it was something, it was somebody, the prodigy of a personal presence.

Rigid and conscious, spectral yet human, a man of his own substance and stature waited there to measure himself with his power to dismay. This only could it be – this only till he recognized, with his advance, that what made the face dim was the pair of raised hands that covered it and in which, so far from being offered in defiance, it was buried as for dark deprecation. So Brydon, before him, took him in; with every fact of him now, in the higher light, hard and acute – his planted stillness, his vivid truth, his grizzled bent head and white masking hands, his queer actuality of evening-dress, of dangling double eye-glass, of gleaming silk lappet and white linen, of pearl button and gold watch-guard and polished shoe. No portrait by a great modern master could have presented him with more intensity, thrust him out of his frame with more art, as if there had been 'treatment,' of the consummate sort, in his every shade and salience. The revulsion, for our friend, had become, before he knew it, immense – this drop, in the act of apprehension, to the sense of his adversary's inscrutable manœuvre. That meaning at least, while he gaped, it offered him; for he could but gape at his other self in this other anguish, gape as a proof that *he*, standing there for the achieved, the enjoyed, the triumphant life, couldn't be faced in his triumph. Wasn't the proof in the splendid covering hands, strong and completely spread? – so spread and so intentional that, in spite of a special verity that surpassed every other, the fact that one of these hands had lost two fingers, which were reduced to stumps, as if accidentally shot away, the face was effectually guarded and saved.

'Saved,' though, *would* it be? – Brydon breathed his wonder till the very impunity of his attitude and the very insistence of his eyes produced, as he felt, a sudden stir which showed the next instant as a deeper portent, while the head raised itself, the betrayal of a braver purpose. The hands, as he looked, began to move, to open; then, as if deciding in a flash, dropped from the face and left it uncovered and presented. Horror, with the sight, had leaped into Brydon's throat, gasping there in a sound he couldn't utter; for the bared identity was too hideous as *his*, and his glare was the passion of his protest. The face, *that* face, Spencer Brydon's? – he searched it still, but looking away from it in dismay and denial, falling straight from his height of sublimity. It was unknown, inconceivable, awful, disconnected from any possibility –! He had been 'sold,' he inwardly moaned, stalking such game as this: the presence before him was a presence, the horror within him a horror, but the waste of his nights had been only grotesque and the success of his adventure an irony. Such an identity fitted his at *no* point, made its alternative monstrous. A thousand times yes, as it came upon him nearer now – the face was the face of a stranger. It came upon him nearer now, quite as one of those expanding fantastic images projected by the magic lantern of childhood; for the stranger, whoever he might be, evil, odious, blatant, vulgar, had advanced as for aggression, and he knew himself give ground. Then harder pressed still, sick with the force of his shock, and falling back as under the hot breath and the roused passion of a life larger than his own, a rage of personality before which his own collapsed, he felt the whole vision turn to darkness and his very feet give way. His head went round; he was going; he had gone.

III

What had next brought him back, clearly – though after how long? – was Mrs Muldoon's voice, coming to him from quite near, from so near that he seemed presently to see her as kneeling on the ground before him while he lay looking up at her; himself not wholly on the ground, but half-raised and upheld – conscious, yes, of tenderness of support and, more particularly, of a head pillowed in extraordinary softness and fainly refreshing fragrance. He considered, he wondered, his wit but half at his service; then another face intervened, bending more directly over him, and he finally knew that Alice Staverton had made her lap an ample and perfect cushion to him, and that she had to this end seated herself on the lowest degree of the staircase, the rest of his long person remaining stretched on his old black-and-white slabs. They were cold, these marble squares of his youth; but *he* somehow was not, in this rich return of consciousness – the most wonderful hour, little by little, that he had ever known, leaving him, as it did, so gratefully, so abysmally passive, and yet as with a treasure of intelligence waiting all round him for quiet appropriation; dissolved, he might call it, in the air of the place and producing the golden glow of a late autumn afternoon. He had come back, yes – come back from further away than any man but himself had

ever travelled; but it was strange how with this sense what he
had come back *to* seemed really the great thing, and as if his
prodigious journey had been all for the sake of it. Slowly but
surely his consciousness grew, his vision of his state thus completing itself: he had been miraculously *carried* back – lifted
and carefully borne as from where he had been picked up, the
uttermost end of an interminable grey passage. Even with this
he was suffered to rest, and what had now brought him to
knowledge was the break in the long mild motion.

It had brought him to knowledge, to knowledge – yes, this
was the beauty of his state; which came to resemble more and
more that of a man who has gone to sleep on some news of a
great inheritance, and then, after dreaming it away, after pro-
faning it with matters strange to it, has waked up again to
serenity of certitude and has only to lie and watch it grow. This
was the drift of his patience – that he had only to let it shine on
him. He must moreover, with intermissions, still have been
lifted and borne; since why and how else should he have known
himself, later on, with the afternoon glow intenser, no longer
at the foot of his stairs – situated as these now seemed at that
dark other end of his tunnel – but on a deep window-bench of
his high saloon, over which had been spread, couch-fashion, a
mantle of soft stuff lined with grey fur that was familiar to his
eyes and that one of his hands kept fondly feeling as for its
pledge of truth. Mrs Muldoon's face had gone, but the other,
the second he had recognized, hung over him in a way that
showed how he was still propped and pillowed. He took it all
in, and the more he took it the more it seemed to suffice: he
was as much at peace as if he had had food and drink. It was
the two women who had found him, on Mrs Muldoon's having
plied, at her usual hour, her latch-key – and on her having
above all arrived while Miss Staverton still lingered near the
house. She had been turning away, all anxiety, from worrying
the vain bell-handle – her calculation having been of the hour
of the good woman's visit; but the latter, blessedly, had come
up while she was still there, and they had entered together. He
had then lain, beyond the vestibule, very much as he was lying
now – quite, that is, as he appeared to have fallen, but all so
wondrously without bruise or gash; only in a depth of stupor.

What he most took in, however, at present, with the steadier clearance, was that Alice Staverton had for a long unspeakable moment not doubted he was dead.

'It must have been that I *was*.' He made it out as she held him. 'Yes – I can only have died. You brought me literally to life. Only,' he wondered, his eyes rising to her, 'only, in the name of all the benedictions, how?'

It took her but an instant to bend her face and kiss him, and something in the manner of it, and in the way her hands clasped and locked his head while he felt the cool charity and virtue of her lips, something in all this beatitude somehow answered everything. 'And now I keep you,' she said.

'Oh keep me, keep me!' he pleaded while her face still hung over him: in response to which it dropped again and stayed close, clingingly close. It was the seal of their situation – of which he tasted the impress for a long blissful moment in silence. But he came back. 'Yet how did you know –?'

'I was uneasy. You were to have come, you remember – and you had sent no word.'

'Yes, I remember – I was to have gone to you at one to-day.' It caught on to their 'old' life and relation – which were so near and so far. 'I was still out there in my strange darkness – where was it, what was it? I must have stayed there so long.' He could but wonder at the depth and the duration of his swoon.

'Since last night?' she asked with a shade of fear for her possible indiscretion.

'Since this morning – it must have been: the cold dim dawn of to-day. Where have I been,' he vaguely wailed, 'where have I been?' He felt her hold him close, and it was as if this helped him now to make in all security his mild moan. 'What a long dark day!'

All in her tenderness she had waited a moment. 'In the cold dim dawn?' she quavered.

But he had already gone on piecing together the parts of the whole prodigy. 'As I didn't turn up you came straight –?'

She barely cast about. 'I went first to your hotel – where they told me of your absence. You had dined out last evening and hadn't been back since. But they appeared to know you had been at your club.'

'So you had the idea of *this* – ?'

'Of what?' she asked in a moment.

'Well – of what has happened.'

'I believed at least you'd have been here. I've known, all along,' she said, 'that you've been coming.'

' "Known" it – ?'

'Well, I've believed it. I said nothing to you after that talk we had a month ago – but I felt sure. I knew you *would*,' she declared.

'That I'd persist, you mean?'

'That you'd see him.'

'Ah but I didn't!' cried Brydon with his long wail. 'There's somebody – an awful beast; whom I brought, too horribly, to bay. But it's not me.'

At this she bent over him again, and her eyes were in his eyes. 'No – it's not you.' And it was as if, while her face hovered, he might have made out in it, hadn't it been so near, some particular meaning blurred by a smile. 'No, thank heaven,' she repeated – 'it's not you! Of course it wasn't to have been.'

'Ah but it *was*,' he gently insisted. And he stared before him now as he had been staring for so many weeks. 'I was to have known myself.'

'You couldn't!' she returned consolingly. And then reverting, and as if to account further for what she had herself done, 'But it wasn't only *that*, that you hadn't been at home,' she went on. 'I waited till the hour at which we had found Mrs Muldoon that day of my going with you; and she arrived, as I've told you, while, failing to bring any one to the door, I lingered in my despair on the steps. After a little, if she hadn't come, by such a mercy, I should have found means to hunt her up. But it wasn't,' said Alice Staverton, as if once more with her fine intention – 'it wasn't only that.'

His eyes, as he lay, turned back to her. 'What more then?'

She met it, the wonder she had stirred. 'In the cold dim dawn, you say? Well, in the cold dim dawn of this morning I too saw you.'

'Saw *me* – ?'

'Saw *him*,' said Alice Staverton. 'It must have been at the same moment.'

He lay an instant taking it in – as if he wished to be quite reasonable. 'At the same moment?'

'Yes – in my dream again, the same one I've named to you. He came back to me. Then I knew it for a sign. He had come to you.'

At this Brydon raised himself; he had to see her better. She helped him when she understood his movement, and he sat up, steadying himself beside her there on the window-bench and with his right hand grasping her left. '*He* didn't come to me.'

'You came to yourself,' she beautifully smiled.

'Ah I've come to myself now – thanks to you, dearest. But this brute, with his awful face – this brute's a black stranger. He's none of *me*, even as I *might* have been,' Brydon sturdily declared.

But she kept the clearness that was like the breath of infallibility. 'Isn't the whole point that you'd have been different?'

He almost scowled for it. 'As different as *that* – ?'

Her look again was more beautiful to him than the things of this world. 'Haven't you exactly wanted to know *how* different? So this morning,' she said, 'you appeared to me.'

'Like *him*?'

'A black stranger!'

'Then how did you know it was I?'

'Because, as I told you weeks ago, my mind, my imagination, had worked so over what you might, what you mightn't have been – to show you, you see, how I've thought of you. In the midst of that you came to me – that my wonder might be answered. So I knew,' she went on; 'and believed that, since the question held you too so fast, as you told me that day, you too would see for yourself. And when this morning I again saw I knew it would be because you had – and also then, from the first moment, because you somehow wanted me. *He* seemed to tell me of that. So why,' she strangely smiled, 'shouldn't I like him?'

It brought Spencer Brydon to his feet. 'You "like" that horror – ?'

'I *could* have liked him. And to me,' she said, 'he was no horror. I had accepted him.'

' "Accepted" – ?' Brydon oddly sounded.

'Before, for the interest of his difference – yes. And as *I* didn't disown him, as *I* knew him – which you at last, confronted with him in his difference, so cruelly didn't, my dear – well, he must have been, you see, less dreadful to me. And it may have pleased him that I pitied him.'

She was beside him on her feet, but still holding his hand – still with her arm supporting him. But though it all brought for him thus a dim light, 'You "pitied" him?' he grudgingly, resentfully asked.

'He has been unhappy, he has been ravaged,' she said.

'And haven't I been unhappy? Am not I – you've only to look at me! – ravaged?'

'Ah I don't say I like him *better*,' she granted after a thought. 'But he's grim, he's worn – and things have happened to him. He doesn't make shift, for sight, with your charming monocle.'

'No' – it struck Brydon: 'I couldn't have sported mine "downtown." They'd have guyed me there.'

'His great convex pince-nez – I saw it, I recognized the kind – is for his poor ruined sight.[10] And his poor right hand –!'

'Ah!' Brydon winced – whether for his proved identity or for his lost fingers. Then, 'He has a million a year,' he lucidly added. 'But he hasn't you.'

'And he isn't – no, he isn't – *you*!' she murmured as he drew her to his breast.

MARY AUSTIN
The Readjustment

Emma Jeffries had been dead and buried three days. The sister
who had come to the funeral had taken Emma's child away
with her, and the house was swept and aired; then, when it
seemed there was least occasion for it, Emma came back. The
neighbour woman who had nursed her was the first to know
it. It was about seven of the evening in a mellow gloom: the
neighbour woman was sitting on her own stoop with her arms
wrapped in her apron, and all at once she found herself going
along the street under an urgent sense that Emma needed her.
She was half-way down the block before she recollected that
this was impossible, for Mrs Jeffries was dead and buried; but
as soon as she came opposite the house she was aware of what
had happened. It was all open to the summer air; except that it
was a little neater, not otherwise than the rest of the street. It
was quite dark; but the presence of Emma Jeffries streamed
from it and betrayed it more than a candle. It streamed out
steadily across the garden, and even as it reached her, mixed
with the smell of the damp mignonette, the neighbour woman
owned to herself that she had always known Emma would
come back.[1]

'A sight stranger if she wouldn't,' thought the woman
who had nursed her. 'She wasn't ever one to throw off things
easily.'

Emma Jeffries had taken death as she had taken everything
in life, hard. She had met it with the same bright, surface
competency that she had presented to the squalor of the encompassing desertness, to the insuperable commonness of Sim
Jeffries, to the affliction of her crippled child; and the intensity
of her wordless struggle against it had caught the attention of

the townspeople and held it in a shocked curious awe. She was so long a-dying, lying there in that little low house, hearing the abhorred footsteps going about her rooms and the vulgar procedure of the community encroach upon her like the advances of the sand wastes on an unwatered field. For Emma had always wanted things different, wanted them with a fury of intentness that implied offensiveness in things as they were. And the townspeople had taken offence, the more so because she was not to be surprised in any inaptitude for their own kind of success. Do what you could, you could never catch Emma Jeffries in a wrapper after three o'clock in the afternoon.[2] And she would never talk about the child – in a country where so little ever happened that even trouble was a godsend if it gave you something to talk about. It was reported that she did not even talk to Sim. But there the common resentment got back at her. If she had thought to effect anything with Sim Jeffries against the benumbing spirit of the place, the evasive hopefulness, the large sense of leisure that ungirt the loins, if she still hoped somehow to get away with him to some place for which by her dress, by her manner, she seemed forever and unassailably fit, it was foregone that nothing would come of it. They knew Sim Jeffries better than that. Yet so vivid had been the force of her wordless dissatisfaction that when the fever took her and she went down like a pasteboard figure in the damp, the wonder was that nothing toppled with her. And, as if she too had felt herself indispensable, Emma Jeffries had come back.

The neighbour woman crossed the street, and as she passed the far corner of the garden, Jeffries spoke to her. He had been standing, she did not know how long a time, behind the syringa-bush, and moved even with her along the fence until they came to the gate.[3] She could see in the dusk that before speaking he wet his lips with his tongue.

'She's in there,' he said, at last.

'Emma?'

He nodded. 'I been sleeping at the store since – but I thought I'd be more comfortable – as soon as I opened the door there she was.'

'Did you see her?'

'No.'

'How do you know, then?'

'Don't you know?'

The neighbour felt there was nothing to say to that.

'Come in,' he whispered, huskily. They slipped by the rose-tree and the wistaria, and sat down on the porch at the side. A door swung inward behind them. They felt the Presence in the dusk beating like a pulse.

'What do you think she wants?' said Jeffries. 'Do you reckon it's the boy?'

'Like enough.'

'He's better off with his aunt. There was no one here to take care of him like his mother wanted.' He raised his voice unconsciously with a note of justification, addressing the room behind.

'I am sending fifty dollars a month,' he said; 'he can go with the best of them.'

He went on at length to explain all the advantage that was to come to the boy from living at Pasadena, and the neighbour woman bore him out in it.[4]

'He was glad to go,' urged Jeffries to the room. 'He said it was what his mother would have wanted.'

They were silent then a long time, while the Presence seemed to swell upon them and encroached upon the garden.

Finally, 'I gave Ziegler the order for the monument yester-day,' Jeffries threw out, appeasingly. 'It's to cost three hundred and fifty.'

The Presence stirred. The neighbour thought she could fairly see the controlled tolerance with which Emma Jeffries endured the evidence of Sim's ineptitudes.

They sat on helplessly without talking after that until the woman's husband came to the fence and called her.

'Don't go,' begged Sim.

'Hush,' she said. 'Do you want all the town to know? You had naught but good from Emma living, and no call to expect harm from her now. It's natural she should come back – if – if she was lonesome like – in – the place where she's gone to.'

'Emma wouldn't come back to this place,' Jeffries protested, 'without she wanted something.'

'Well, then, you've got to find out,' said the neighbour woman.

All the next day she saw, whenever she passed the house, that Emma was still there. It was shut and barred, but the Presence lurked behind the folded blinds and fumbled at the doors. When it was night and the moths began in the columbine under the windows, it went out and walked in the garden.

Jeffries was waiting at the gate when the neighbour woman came. He sweated with helplessness in the warm dusk, and the Presence brooded upon them like an apprehension that grows by being entertained.

'She wants something,' he appealed, 'but I can't make out what. Emma knows she is welcome to everything I've got. Everybody knows I've been a good provider.'

The neighbour woman remembered suddenly the only time she had ever drawn close to Emma Jeffries touching the boy. They had sat up with it together all one night in some childish ailment, and she had ventured a question. 'What does his father think?' And Emma had turned her a white, hard face of surpassing dreariness.

'I don't know,' she admitted, 'he never says.'

'There's more than providing,' suggested the neighbour woman.

'Yes. There's feeling . . . but she had enough to do to put up with me. I had no call to be troubling her with such.' He left off to mop his forehead, and began again.

'Feelings!' he said, 'there's times a man gets so wore out with feelings he doesn't have them any more.'

He talked, and presently it grew clear to the woman that he was voiding all the stuff of his life, as if he had sickened on it and was now done. It was a little soul knowing itself and not good to see. What was singular was that the Presence left off walking in the garden, came and caught like a gossamer on the ivy-tree, swayed by the breath of his broken sentences. He talked, and the neighbour woman saw him for once as he saw himself and Emma, snared and floundering in an inexplicable unhappiness. He had been disappointed, too. She had never relished the man he was, and it made him ashamed. That was why he had never gone away, lest he should make her ashamed among her own kind. He was her husband, he could not help that though he was sorry for it. But he could keep the offence where least was made of it. And there was a child – she had wanted a child; but even then he had blundered – begotten a cripple upon her. He blamed himself utterly, searched out the roots of his youth for the answer to that, until the neighbour woman flinched to hear him. But the Presence stayed.

He had never talked to his wife about the child. How should he? There was the fact – the advertisement of his incompetence. And she had never talked to him. That was the one blessed and unassailable memory; that she had spread silence like a balm over his hurt. In return for it he had never gone away. He had resisted her that he might save her from showing among her own kind how poor a man he was. With every word of this ran the fact of his love for her – as he had loved her, with all the stripes of clean and uncleanness. He bared himself as a child without knowing; and the Presence stayed. The talk trailed off at last to the commonplaces of consolation between the retchings of his spirit. The Presence lessened and streamed toward them on the wind of the garden. When it touched them like the warm air of noon that lies sometimes in hollow places after nightfall, the neighbour woman rose and went away.

The next night she did not wait for him. When a rod outside the town – it was a very little one – the burrowing owls *whoowhooed*, she hung up her apron and went to talk with Emma Jeffries.[5] The Presence was there, drawn in, lying close. She found the key between the wistaria and the first pillar of the porch, but as soon as she opened the door she felt the chill that might be expected by one intruding on Emma Jeffries in her own house.

'"The Lord is my shepherd,"' said the neighbour woman; it was the first religious phrase that occurred to her; then she said the whole of the psalm and after that a hymn.[6] She had come in through the door and stood with her back to it and her hand upon the knob. Everything was just as Mrs Jeffries had left it, with the waiting air of a room kept for company.

'Em,' she said, boldly, when the chill had abated a little before the sacred words. 'Em Jeffries, I've got something to say to you. And you've got to hear,' she added with firmness, as the white curtains stirred duskily at the window. 'You wouldn't be talked to about your troubles when . . . you were here before; and we humoured you. But now there is Sim to be thought of. I guess you heard what you came for last night, and got good of it. Maybe it would have been better if Sim had said things all along instead of hoarding them in his heart, but any way he has said them now. And what I want to say is, if you was staying on with the hope of hearing it again, you'd be making a mistake. You was an uncommon woman, Emma Jeffries, and there didn't none of us understand you very well, nor do you justice maybe; but Sim is only a common man, and I understand him because I'm that way myself. And if you think he'll be opening his heart to you every night, or be any different from what he's always been on acount of what's happened, that's a mistake too . . . and in a little while, if you stay, it will be as bad as it always was . . . Men are like that . . . You'd better go now while there's understanding between you.' She stood staring into the darkling room that seemed suddenly full of turbulence and denial. It seemed to beat upon her and take her breath, but she held on.

'You've got to go . . . Em . . . and I'm going to stay until you do.' She said this with finality, and then began again.

' "The Lord is nigh unto them that are of a broken heart," ' and repeated the passage to the end.[7] Then as the Presence sank before it, 'You better go, Emma,' persuasively, and again after an interval:

' "He shall deliver thee in six troubles, yea, in seven shall no evil touch thee." '[8]

. . . The Presence gathered itself and was still. She could make out that it stood over against the opposite corner by the gilt easel with the crayon portrait of the child.

. . . ' "For thou shalt forget thy misery. Thou shalt remember it as waters that are past," ' concluded the neighbour woman, as she heard Jeffries on the gravel outside.[9] What the Presence had wrought upon him in the night was visible in his altered mien. He looked more than anything else to be in need of sleep. He had eaten his sorrow, and that was the end of it – as it is with men.

332 MARY AUSTIN

'I came to see if there was anything I could do for you,' said the woman, neighbourly, with her hand upon the door.

'I don't know as there is,' said he; 'I'm much obliged, but I don't know as there is.'

'You see,' whispered the woman over her shoulder, 'not even to me.' She felt the tug of her heart as the Presence swept past her.

The neighbour went out after that and walked in the ragged street, past the school-house, across the creek below the town, out by the fields, over the headgate, and back by the town again. It was full nine of the clock when she passed the Jeffries house. It looked, except for being a little neater, not other than the rest of the street. The door was open and the lamp was lit; she saw Jeffries, black against it. He sat reading in a book, like a man at ease in his own house.

EDITH WHARTON
Afterward

I

'Oh, there *is* one, of course, but you'll never know it.'

The assertion, laughingly flung out six months earlier in a bright June garden, came back to Mary Boyne with a new perception of its significance as she stood, in the December dusk, waiting for the lamps to be brought into the library.

The words had been spoken by their friend Alida Stair, as they sat at tea on her lawn at Pangbourne, in reference to the very house of which the library in question was the central, the pivotal 'feature.'[1] Mary Boyne and her husband, in quest of a country place in one of the southern or southwestern counties, had, on their arrival in England, carried their problem straight to Alida Stair, who had successfully solved it in her own case; but it was not until they had rejected, almost capriciously, several practical and judicious suggestions that she threw out: 'Well, there's Lyng, in Dorsetshire. It belongs to Hugo's cousins, and you can get it for a song.'

The reason she gave for its being obtainable on these terms – its remoteness from a station, its lack of electric light, hot-water pipes, and other vulgar necessities – were exactly those pleading in its favour with two Romantic Americans perversely in search of the economic drawbacks which were associated, in their tradition, with unusual architectural felicities.

'I should never believe I was living in an old house unless I was thoroughly uncomfortable,' Ned Boyne, the more extravagant of the two, had jocosely insisted; 'the least hint of "convenience" would make me think it had been bought out of an exhibition, with the pieces numbered, and set up again.' And they had proceeded to enumerate, with humorous precision, their various doubts and demands, refusing to believe that the house their cousin recommended was *really* Tudor till they learned it had no heating system, or that the village church was literally in the grounds till she assured them of the deplorable uncertainty of the water-supply.

'It's too uncomfortable to be true!' Edward Boyne had continued to exult as the avowal of each disadvantage was successively wrung from her; but he had cut short his rhapsody to ask, with a relapse to distrust: 'And the ghost? You've been concealing from us the fact that there is no ghost!'

Mary, at the moment, had laughed with him, yet almost with her laugh, being possessed of several sets of independent perceptions, had been struck by a note of flatness in Alida's answering hilarity.

'Oh, Dorsetshire's full of ghosts, you know.'

'Yes, yes; but that won't do. I don't want to have to drive ten miles to see somebody else's ghost. I want one of my own on the premises. *Is* there a ghost at Lyng?'

His rejoinder had made Alida laugh again, and it was then that she had flung back tantalisingly: 'Oh, there *is* one, of course, but you'll never know it.'

'Never know it?' Boyne pulled her up. 'But what in the world constitutes a ghost except the fact of its being known for one?'

'I can't say. But that's the story.'

'That there's a ghost, but that nobody knows it's a ghost?'

'Well – not till afterward, at any rate.'

'Till afterward?'

'Not till long long afterward.'

'But if it's once been identified as an unearthly visitant, why hasn't its *signalement* been handed down in the family?[2] How has it managed to preserve its incognito?'

Alida could only shake her head. 'Don't ask me. But it has.'

'And then suddenly –' Mary spoke up as if from cavernous depths of divination – 'suddenly, long afterward, one says to one's self "*That was it?*"'

She was startled at the sepulchral sound with which her question fell on the banter of the other two, and she saw the shadow of the same surprise flit across Alida's pupils. 'I suppose so. One just has to wait.'

'Oh, hang waiting!' Ned broke in. 'Life's too short for a ghost who can only be enjoyed in retrospect. Can't we do better than that, Mary?'

But it turned out that in the event they were not destined to, for within three months of their conversation with Mrs Stair they were settled at Lyng, and the life they had yearned for, to the point of planning it in advance in all its daily details, had actually begun for them.

It was to sit, in the thick December dusk, by just such a wide-hooded fireplace, under just such black oak rafters, with the sense that beyond the mullioned panes the downs were darkened to a deeper solitude: it was for the ultimate indulgence of such sensations that Mary Boyne, abruptly exiled from New York by her husband's business, had endured for nearly four-teen years the soul-deadening ugliness of a Middle Western town, and that Boyne had ground on doggedly at his engineer-ing till, with a suddenness that still made her blink, the pro-digious windfall of the Blue Star Mine had put them at a stroke in possession of life and the leisure to taste it. They had never for a moment meant their new state to be one of idleness; but they meant to give themselves only to harmonious activities. She had her vision of painting and gardening (against a back-ground of grey walls), he dreamed of the production of his long-planned book on the 'Economic Basis of Culture'; and with such absorbing work ahead no existence could be too sequestered: they could not get far enough from the world, or plunge deep enough into the past.

Dorsetshire had attracted them from the first by an air of remoteness out of all proportion to its geographical position. But to the Boynes it was one of the ever-recurring wonders of the whole incredibly compressed island – a nest of counties, as they put it – that for the production of its effects so little of a given quality went so far: that so few miles made a distance, and so short a distance a difference.

'It's that,' Ned had once enthusiastically explained, 'that gives such depth to their effects, such relief to their contrasts. They've been able to lay the butter so thick on every delicious mouthful.'

The butter had certainly been laid on thick at Lyng: the old house hidden under a shoulder of the downs had almost all the finer marks of commerce with a protracted past. The mere fact that it was neither large nor exceptional made it, to the Boynes, abound the more completely in its special charm – the charm of having been for centuries a deep dim reservoir of life. The life had probably not been of the most vivid order: for long periods, no doubt, it had fallen as noiselessly into the past as the quiet drizzle of autumn fell, hour after hour, into the fish-pond between the yews; but these back-waters of existence sometimes breed, in their sluggish depths, strange acuities of emotion, and Mary Boyne had felt from the first the mysterious stir of intenser memories.

The feeling had never been stronger than on this particular afternoon when, waiting in the library for the lamps to come, she rose from her seat and stood among the shadows of the hearth. Her husband had gone off, after luncheon, for one of his long tramps on the downs. She had noticed of late that he preferred to go alone; and, in the tried security of their personal relations, had been driven to conclude that his book was bothering him, and that he needed the afternoons to turn over in solitude the problems left from the morning's work. Certainly the book was not going as smoothly as she had thought it would, and there were lines of perplexity between his eyes such as had never been there in his engineering days. He had often, then, looked fagged to the verge of illness, but the native demon of 'worry' had never branded his brow. Yet the few pages he had so far read to her – the introduction, and a summary of the opening chapter – showed a firm hold on his subject, and an increasing confidence in his powers.

The fact threw her into deeper perplexity, since, now that he had done with 'business' and its disturbing contingencies, the one other possible source of anxiety was eliminated. Unless it were his health, then? But physically he had gained since they had come to Dorsetshire, grown robuster, ruddier and fresher-eyed. It was only within the last week that she had felt in him the undefinable change which made her restless in his absence, and as tongue-tied in his presence as though it were *she* who had a secret to keep from him!

The thought that there *was* a secret somewhere between them struck her with a sudden rap of wonder, and she looked about her down the long room.

'Can it be the house?' she mused.

The room itself might have been full of secrets. They seemed to be piling themselves up, as evening fell, like the layers and layers of velvet shadow dropping from the low ceiling, the rows of books, the smoke-blurred sculpture of the hearth.

'Why, of course – the house is haunted!' she reflected.

The ghost – Alida's imperceptible ghost – after figuring largely in the banter of their first month or two at Lyng, had been gradually left aside as too ineffectual for imaginative use. Mary had, indeed, as became the tenant of a haunted house, made the customary inquiries among her rural neighbours, but, beyond a vague 'They dü say so, Ma'am,' the villagers had nothing to impart.[3] The elusive spectre had apparently never had sufficient identity for a legend to crystallize about it, and after a time the Boynes had set the matter down to their profit-and-loss account, agreeing that Lyng was one of the few houses good enough in itself to dispense with supernatural enhancements.

'And I suppose, poor ineffectual demon, that's why it beats its beautiful wings in vain in the void,' Mary had laughingly concluded.

'Or, rather,' Ned answered in the same strain, 'why, amid so much that's ghostly, it can never affirm its separate existence as *the* ghost.' And thereupon their invisible housemate had finally dropped out of their references, which were numerous enough to make them soon unaware of the loss.

Now, as she stood on the hearth, the subject of their earlier curiosity revived in her with a new sense of its meaning – a sense gradually acquired through daily contact with the scene of the lurking mystery. It was the house itself, of course, that possessed the ghost-seeing faculty, that communed visually but secretly with its own past; if one could only get into close enough communion with the house, one might surprise its secret, and acquire the ghost-sight on one's own account. Perhaps, in his long hours in this very room, where she never trespassed till the afternoon, her husband *had* acquired it already, and was silently carrying about the weight of whatever it had revealed to him. Mary was too well versed in the code of the spectral world not to know that one could not talk about the ghosts one saw: to do so was almost as great a breach of taste as to name a lady in a club. But this explanation did not really satisfy her. 'What, after all, except for the fun of the shudder,' she reflected, 'would he really care for any of their old ghosts?' And thence she was thrown back once more on the fundamental dilemma: the fact that one's greater or less susceptibility to spectral influences had no particular bearing on the case, since, when one *did* see a ghost at Lyng, one did not know it.

'Not till long afterward,' Alida Stair had said. Well, supposing Ned *had* seen one when they first came, and had known only within the last week what had happened to him? More and more under the spell of the hour, she threw back her thoughts to the early days of their tenancy, but at first only to recall a lively confusion of unpacking, settling, arranging of books, and calling to each other from remote corners of the house as, treasure after treasure, it revealed itself to them. It was in this particular connection that she presently recalled a certain soft afternoon of the previous October, when, passing from the first rapturous flurry of exploration to a detailed inspection of the old house, she had pressed (like a novel heroine) a panel that opened on a flight of corkscrew stairs leading to a flat ledge of the roof – the roof which, from below, seemed to slope away on all sides too abruptly for any but practised feet to scale.

The view from this hidden coign was enchanting, and she had flown down to snatch Ned from his papers and give him the freedom of her discovery.[4] She remembered still how, standing at her side, he had passed his arm about her while their gaze flew to the long tossed horizon-line of the downs, and then dropped contentedly back to trace the arabesque of yew hedges about the fish-pond, and the shadow of the cedar on the lawn.

'And now the other way,' he had said, turning her about within his arm; and closely pressed to him, she had absorbed, like some long satisfying draught, the picture of the grey-walled court, the squat lions on the gates, and the lime-avenue reaching up to the highroad under the downs.

It was just then, while they gazed and held each other, that she had felt his arm relax, and heard a sharp 'Hullo!' that made her turn to glance at him.

Distinctly, yes, she now recalled that she had seen, as she glanced, a shadow of anxiety, of perplexity, rather, fall across his face; and, following his eyes, had beheld the figure of a man – a man in loose greyish clothes, as it appeared to her – who was sauntering down the lime-avenue to the court with the doubtful gait of a stranger who seeks his way. Her short-sighted eyes had given her but a blurred impression of slightness and greyishness, with something foreign, or at least unlocal, in the cut of the figure or its dress; but her husband had apparently seen more – seen enough to make him push past her with a hasty 'Wait!' and dash down the stairs without pausing to give her a hand.

A slight tendency to dizziness obliged her, after a provisional clutch at the chimney against which they had been leaning, to follow him first more cautiously; and when she had reached the landing she paused again, for a less definite reason, leaning over the banister to strain her eyes through the silence of the brown sun-flecked depths. She lingered there till, somewhere in those depths, she heard the closing of a door; then, mechanically impelled, she went down the shallow flights of steps till she reached the lower hall.

The front door stood open on the sunlight of the court, and hall and court were empty. The library door was open, too, and after listening in vain for any sound of voices within, she crossed the threshold, and found her husband alone, vaguely fingering the papers on his desk.

He looked up, as if surprised at her entrance, but the shadow of anxiety had passed from his face, leaving it even, as she fancied, a little brighter and clearer than usual.

'What was it? Who was it?' she asked.

'Who?' he repeated, with the surprise still all on his side.

'The man we saw coming toward the house.'

He seemed to reflect. 'The man? Why, I thought I saw Peters; I dashed after him to say a word about the stable drains, but he had disappeared before I could get down.'

'Disappeared? But he seemed to be walking so slowly when we saw him.'

Boyne shrugged his shoulders. 'So I thought; but he must have got up steam in the interval. What do you say to our trying a scramble up Meldon Steep before sunset?'

That was all. At the time the occurrence had been less than nothing, had, indeed, been immediately obliterated by the magic of their first vision from Meldon Steep, a height which they had dreamed of climbing ever since they had first seen its bare spine rising above the roof of Lyng. Doubtless it was the mere fact of the other incident's having occurred on the very day of their ascent to Meldon that had kept it stored away in the fold of memory from which it now emerged; for in itself it had no mark of the portentous. At the moment there could have been nothing more natural than that Ned should dash himself from the roof in the pursuit of dilatory tradesmen. It was the period when they were always on the watch for one or the other of the specialists employed about the place; always lying in wait for them, and rushing out at them with questions, reproaches or reminders. And certainly in the distance the grey figure had looked like Peters.

Yet now, as she reviewed the scene, she felt her husband's explanation of it to have been invalidated by the look of anxiety on his face. Why had the familiar appearance of Peters made him anxious? Why, above all, if it was of such prime necessity to confer with him on the subject of the stable drains, had the failure to find him produced such a look of relief? Mary could not say that any one of these questions had occurred to her at the time, yet, from the promptness with which they now marshalled themselves at her summons, she had a sense that they must all along have been there, waiting their hour.

II

Weary with her thoughts, she moved to the window. The library was now quite dark, and she was surprised to see how much faint light the outer world still held.

As she peered out into it across the court, a figure shaped itself far down the perspective of bare limes: it looked a mere blot of deeper grey in the greyness, and for an instant, as it moved toward her, her heart thumped to the thought 'It's the ghost!'

She had time, in that long instant, to feel suddenly that the man of whom, two months earlier, she had had a distant vision from the roof, was now, at his predestined hour, about to reveal himself as *not* having been Peters; and her spirit sank under the impending fear of the disclosure. But almost with the next tick of the clock the figure, gaining substance and character, showed itself even to her weak sight as her husband's; and she turned to meet him, as he entered, with the confession of her folly.

'It's really too absurd,' she laughed out, 'but I never *can* remember!'

'Remember what?' Boyne questioned as they drew together.

'That when one sees the Lyng ghost one never knows it.'

Her hand was on his sleeve, and he kept it there, but with no response in his gesture or in the lines of his preoccupied face.

'Did you think you'd seen it?' he asked, after an appreciable interval.

'Why, I actually took *you* for it, my dear, in my mad determination to spot it!'

'Me – just now?' His arm dropped away, and he turned from her with a faint echo of her laugh. 'Really, dearest, you'd better give it up, if that's the best you can do.'

'Oh, yes, I give it up. Have *you*?' she asked, turning round on him abruptly.

The parlour-maid had entered with letters and a lamp, and the light struck up into Boyne's face as he bent above the tray she presented.

'Have *you*?' Mary perversely insisted, when the servant had disappeared on her errand of illumination.

'Have I what?' he rejoined absently, the light bringing out the sharp stamp of worry between his brows as he turned over the letters.

'Given up trying to see the ghost.' Her heart beat a little at the experiment she was making.

Her husband, laying his letters aside, moved away into the shadow of the hearth.

'I never tried,' he said, tearing open the wrapper of a newspaper.

'Well, of course,' Mary persisted, 'the exasperating thing is that there's no use trying, since one can't be sure till so long afterward.'

He was unfolding the paper as if he had hardly heard her; but after a pause, during which the sheets rustled spasmodically between his hands, he looked up to ask, 'Have you any idea *how long?*'

Mary had sunk into a low chair beside the fireplace. From her seat she glanced over, startled, at her husband's profile, which was projected against the circle of lamplight.

'No; none. Have *you?*' she retorted, repeating her former phrase with an added stress of intention.

Boyne crumpled the paper into a bunch, and then, inconsequently, turned back with it toward the lamp.

'Lord, no! I only meant,' he explained, with a faint tinge of impatience, 'is there any legend, any tradition, as to that?'

'Not that I know of,' she answered; but the impulse to add 'What makes you ask?' was checked by the reappearance of the parlour-maid, with tea and a second lamp.

With the dispersal of shadows, and the repetition of the daily domestic office, Mary Boyne felt herself less oppressed by that sense of something mutely imminent which had darkened her afternoon. For a few moments she gave herself to the details of her task, and when she looked up from it she was struck to the point of bewilderment by the change in her husband's face. He had seated himself near the farther lamp, and was absorbed in the perusal of his letters; but was it something he had found in them, or merely the shifting of her own point of view, that had restored his features to their normal aspect? The longer she looked the more definitely the change affirmed itself. The lines of tension had vanished, and such traces of fatigue as lingered were of the kind easily attributable to steady mental effort. He glanced up, as if drawn by her gaze, and met her eyes with a smile.

'I'm dying for my tea, you know; and here's a letter for you,' he said.

She took the letter he held out in exchange for the cup she

proffered him, and, returning to her seat, broke the seal with
the languid gesture of the reader whose interests are all enclosed
in the circle of one cherished presence.

Her next conscious motion was that of starting to her feet,
the letter falling to them as she rose, while she held out to her
husband a newspaper clipping.

'Ned! What's this? What does it mean?'

He had risen at the same instant, almost as if hearing her cry
before she uttered it; and for a perceptible space of time he
and she studied each other, like adversaries watching for an
advantage, across the space between her chair and his desk.

'What's what? You fairly made me jump!' Boyne said at
length, moving toward her with a sudden half-exasperated
laugh. The shadow of apprehension was on his face again, not
now a look of fixed foreboding, but a shifting vigilance of lips
and eyes that gave her the sense of his feeling himself invisibly
surrounded.

Her hand shook so that she could hardly give him the clipping.

'This article – from the *Waukesha Sentinel* – that a man
named Elwell has brought suit against you – that there was
something wrong about the Blue Star Mine.[5] I can't understand
more than half.'

They continued to face each other as she spoke, and to her
astonishment she saw that her words had the almost immediate
effect of dissipating the strained watchfulness of his look.

'Oh, *that*!' He glanced down the printed slip, and then folded
it with the gesture of one who handles something harmless and
familiar. 'What's the matter with you this afternoon, Mary?
I thought you'd got bad news.'

She stood before him with her undefinable terror subsiding
slowly under the reassurance of his tone.

'You knew about this, then – it's all right?'

'Certainly I knew about it; and it's all right.'

'But what *is* it? I don't understand. What does this man
accuse you of?'

'Pretty nearly every crime in the calendar.' Boyne had tossed
the clipping down, and thrown himself into an arm-chair near
the fire. 'Do you want to hear the story? It's not particularly
interesting – just a squabble over interests in the Blue Star.'

'But who is this Elwell? I don't know the name.'

'Oh, he's a fellow I put into it – gave him a hand up. I told you all about him at the time.'

'I daresay. I must have forgotten.' Vainly she strained back among her memories. 'But if you helped him, why does he make this return?'

'Probably some shyster lawyer got hold of him and talked him over. It's all rather technical and complicated. I thought that kind of thing bored you.'

His wife felt a sting of compunction. Theoretically, she deprecated the American wife's detachment from her husband's professional interests, but in practice she had always found it difficult to fix her attention on Boyne's report of the transactions in which his varied interests involved him. Besides, she had felt during their years of exile, that, in a community where the amenities of living could be obtained only at the cost of efforts as arduous as her husband's professional labours, such brief leisure as he and she could command should be used as an escape from immediate preoccupations, a flight to the life they always dreamed of living. Once or twice, now that this new life had actually drawn its magic circle about them, she had asked herself if she had done right; but hitherto such conjectures had been no more than the retrospective excursions of an active fancy. Now, for the first time, it startled her a little to find how little she knew of the material foundation on which her happiness was built.

She glanced at her husband, and was again reassured by the composure of his face; yet she felt the need of more definite grounds for her reassurance.

'But doesn't this suit worry you? Why have you never spoken to me about it?'

He answered both questions at once. 'I didn't speak of it at first because it *did* worry me – annoyed me, rather. But it's all ancient history now. Your correspondent must have got hold of a back number of the *Sentinel*.'

She felt a quick thrill of relief. 'You mean it's over? He's lost his case?'

There was a just perceptible delay in Boyne's reply. 'The suit's been withdrawn – that's all.'

But she persisted, as if to exonerate herself from the inward charge of being too easily put off. 'Withdrawn it because he saw he had no chance?'

'Oh, he had no chance,' Boyne answered.

She was still struggling with a dimly felt perplexity at the back of her thoughts.

'How long ago was it withdrawn?'

He paused, as if with a slight return of his former uncertainty. 'I've just had the news now; but I've been expecting it.'

'Just now – in one of your letters?'

'Yes; in one of my letters.'

She made no answer, and was aware only, after a short interval of waiting, that he had risen, and, strolling across the room, had placed himself on the sofa at her side. She felt him, as he did so, pass an arm about her, she felt his hand seek hers and clasp it, and turning slowly, drawn by the warmth of his cheek, she met his smiling eyes.

'It's all right – it's all right?' she questioned, through the flood of her dissolving doubts; and 'I give you my word it was never righter!' he laughed back at her, holding her close.

III

One of the strangest things she was afterward to recall out of all the next day's strangeness was the sudden and complete recovery of her sense of security.

It was in the air when she woke in her low-ceiled, dusky room; it went with her down-stairs to the breakfast-table, flashed out at her from the fire, and re-duplicated itself from the flanks of the urn and the sturdy flutings of the Georgian teapot. It was as if, in some roundabout way, all her diffused fears of the previous day, with their moment of sharp concentration about the newspaper article – as if this dim questioning of the future, and startled return upon the past, had between them liquidated the arrears of some haunting moral obligation. If she had indeed been careless of her husband's affairs, it was, her new state seemed to prove, because her faith in him instinctively justified such carelessness; and his right to her faith had now affirmed itself in the very face of menace and suspicion. She had never seen him more untroubled, more naturally and unconsciously himself, than after the cross-examination to which she had subjected him: it was almost as if he had been aware of her doubts, and had wanted the air cleared as much as she did.

It was as clear, thank Heaven! as the bright outer light that surprised her almost with a touch of summer when she issued from the house for her daily round of the gardens. She had left Boyne at his desk, indulging herself, as she passed the library door, by a last peep at his quiet face, where he bent, pipe in mouth, above his papers; and now she had her own morning's task to perform. The task involved, on such charmed winter days, almost as much happy loitering about the different quarters of her demesne as if spring were already at work there. There were such endless possibilities still before her, such opportunities to bring out the latent graces of the old place, without a single irreverent touch of alteration, that the winter was all too short to plan what spring and autumn executed. And her recovered sense of safety gave, on this particular morning, a peculiar zest to her progress through the sweet still place. She went first to the kitchen-garden, where the espaliered pear-trees drew complicated patterns on the walls, and pigeons were fluttering and preening about the silvery-slated roof of their cot. There was something wrong about the piping of the hot-house, and she was expecting an authority from Dorchester, who was to drive out between trains and make a diagnosis of the boiler.[6] But when she dipped into the damp heat of the greenhouses, among the spiced scents and waxy pinks and reds of old-fashioned exotics – even the flora of Lyng was in the note! – she learned that the great man had not arrived, and, the day being too rare to waste in an artificial atmosphere, she came out again and paced along the springy turf of the bowling-green to the gardens behind the house. At their farther end rose a grass terrace, looking across the fish-pond and yew hedges to the long house-front with its twisted chimney-stacks and blue roof angles all drenched in the pale gold moisture of the air.

Seen thus, across the level tracery of the gardens, it sent her, from open windows and hospitably smoking chimneys, the look of some warm human presence, of a mind slowly ripened on a sunny wall of experience. She had never before had such a sense of her intimacy with it, such a conviction that its secrets were all beneficent, kept, as they said to children, 'for one's good,' such a trust in its power to gather up her life and Ned's into the harmonious pattern of the long long story it sat there weaving in the sun.

She heard steps behind her, and turned, expecting to see the gardener accompanied by the engineer from Dorchester. But only one figure was in sight, that of a youngish slightly built man, who, for reasons she could not on the spot have given, did not remotely resemble her notion of an authority on hot-house boilers. The new-comer, on seeing her, lifted his hat, and paused with the air of a gentleman – perhaps a traveller – who wishes to make it known that his intrusion is involuntary. Lyng occasionally attracted the more cultivated traveller, and Mary half-expected to see the stranger dissemble a camera, or justify his presence by producing it. But he made no gesture of any sort, and after a moment she asked, in a tone responding to the courteous hesitation of his attitude: 'Is there any one you wish to see?'

'I came to see Mr Boyne,' he answered. His intonation, rather than his accent, was faintly American, and Mary, at the note, looked at him more closely. The brim of his soft felt hat cast a shade on his face, which, thus obscured, wore to her short-sighted gaze a look of seriousness, as of a person arriving 'on business,' and civilly but firmly aware of his rights.

Past experience had made her equally sensible to such claims; but she was jealous of her husband's morning hours, and doubtful of his having given any one the right to intrude on them.

'Have you an appointment with my husband?' she asked.

The visitor hesitated, as if unprepared for the question.

'I think he expects me,' he replied.

It was Mary's turn to hesitate. 'You see this is his time for work: he never sees any one in the morning.'

He looked at her a moment without answering; then, as if accepting her decision, he began to move away. As he turned, Mary saw him pause and glance up at the peaceful house-front. Something in his air suggested weariness and disappointment, the dejection of the traveller who has come from far off and whose hours are limited by the time-table. It occurred to her that if this were the case her refusal might have made his errand vain, and a sense of compunction caused her to hasten after him.

'May I ask if you have come a long way?'

He gave her the same grave look. 'Yes – I have come a long way.'

'Then, if you'll go to the house, no doubt my husband will see you now. You'll find him in the library.'

She did not know why she had added the last phrase, except from a vague impulse to atone for her previous inhospitality. The visitor seemed about to express his thanks, but her attention was distracted by the approach of the gardener with a companion who bore all the marks of being the expert from Dorchester.

'This way,' she said, waving the stranger to the house; and an instant later she had forgotten him in the absorption of her meeting with the boiler-maker.

The encounter led to such far-reaching results that the engineer ended by finding it expedient to ignore his train, and Mary was beguiled into spending the remainder of the morning in absorbed confabulation among the flower-pots. When the colloquy ended, she was surprised to find that it was nearly luncheon-time, and she half-expected, as she hurried back to the house, to see her husband coming out to meet her. But she found no one in the court but an under-gardener raking the gravel, and the hall, when she entered it, was so silent that she guessed Boyne to be still at work.

Not wishing to disturb him, she turned into the drawing-room, and there, at her writing-table, lost herself in renewed calculations of the outlay to which the morning's conference had pledged her. The fact that she could permit herself such follies had not yet lost its novelty; and somehow, in contrast to the vague fears of the previous days, it now seemed an element of her recovered security, of the sense that, as Ned had said, things in general had never been 'righter.'

She was still luxuriating in a lavish play of figures when the parlour-maid, from the threshold, roused her with an enquiry as to the expediency of serving luncheon. It was one of their jokes that Trimmle announced luncheon as if she were divulging a state secret, and Mary, intent upon her papers, merely murmured an absent-minded assent.

She felt Trimmle wavering doubtfully on the threshold, as if in rebuke of such unconsidered assent; then her retreating steps sounded down the passage, and Mary, pushing away her papers, crossed the hall and went to the library door. It was still closed, and she wavered in her turn, disliking to disturb her husband, yet anxious that he should not exceed his usual measure of work. As she stood there, balancing her impulses, Trimmle returned with the announcement of luncheon, and Mary, thus impelled, opened the library door.

Boyne was not at his desk, and she peered about her, expecting to discover him before the book-shelves, somewhere down the length of the room; but her call brought no response, and gradually it became clear to her that he was not there.

She turned back to the parlour-maid.

'Mr Boyne must be up-stairs. Please tell him that luncheon is ready.'

Trimmle appeared to hesitate between the obvious duty of obedience and an equally obvious conviction of the foolishness of the injunction laid on her. The struggle resulted in her saying: 'If you please, Madam, Mr Boyne's not up-stairs.'

'Not in his room? Are you sure?'

'I'm sure, Madam.'

Mary consulted the clock. 'Where is he, then?'

'He's gone out,' Trimmle announced, with the superior air of one who has respectfully waited for the question that a well-ordered mind would have put first.

Mary's conjecture had been right, then. Boyne must have gone to the gardens to meet her, and since she had missed him, it was clear that he had taken the shorter way by the south door, instead of going round to the court. She crossed the hall to the French window opening directly on the yew garden, but the parlour-maid, after another moment of inner conflict, decided to bring out: 'Please, Madam, Mr Boyne didn't go that way.'

Mary turned back. 'Where *did* he go? And when?'

'He went out of the front door, up the drive, Madam.' It was a matter of principle with Trimmle never to answer more than one question at a time.

'Up the drive? At this hour?' Mary went to the door herself, and glanced across the court through the tunnel of bare limes. But its perspective was as empty as when she had scanned it on entering.

'Did Mr Boyne leave no message?'

Trimmle seemed to surrender herself to a last struggle with the forces of chaos.

'No, Madam. He just went out with the gentleman.'

'The gentleman? What gentleman?' Mary wheeled about, as if to front this new factor.

'The gentleman who called, Madam,' said Trimmle resignedly.

'When did a gentleman call? Do explain yourself, Trimmle!'

Only the fact that Mary was very hungry, and that she wanted to consult her husband about the greenhouses, would have caused her to lay so unusual an injunction on her attendant; and even now she was detached enough to note in Trimmle's eye the dawning defiance of the respectful subordinate who has been pressed too hard.

'I couldn't exactly say the hour, Madam, because I didn't let the gentleman in,' she replied, with an air of discreetly ignoring the irregularity of her mistress's course.

'You didn't let him in?'

'No, Madam. When the bell rang I was dressing, and Agnes –'

'Go and ask Agnes, then,' said Mary.

Trimmle still wore her look of patient magnanimity. 'Agnes would not know, Madam, for she had unfortunately burnt her hand in trimming the wick of the new lamp from town' – Trimmle, as Mary was aware, had always been opposed to the new lamp – 'and so Mrs Dockett sent the kitchen-maid instead.'

Mary looked again at the clock. 'It's after two! Go and ask the kitchen-maid if Mr Boyne left any word.'

She went into luncheon without waiting, and Trimmle presently brought her there the kitchen-maid's statement that the gentleman had called about eleven o'clock, and that Mr Boyne had gone out with him without leaving any message. The kitchen-maid did not even know the caller's name, for he had written it on a slip of paper, which he had folded and handed to her, with the injunction to deliver it at once to Mr Boyne.

Mary finished her luncheon, still wondering, and when it was over, and Trimmle had brought the coffee to the drawing-room, her wonder had deepened to a first faint tinge of disquietude. It was unlike Boyne to absent himself without explanation at so unwonted an hour, and the difficulty of identifying the visitor whose summons he had apparently obeyed made his disappearance the more unaccountable. Mary Boyne's experience as the wife of a busy engineer, subject to sudden calls and compelled to keep irregular hours, had trained her to the philosophic acceptance of surprises; but since Boyne's withdrawal from business he had adopted a Benedictine regularity of life.[7] As if to make up for the dispersed and agitated years, with their 'stand-up' lunches, and dinners rattled down to the joltings of the dining-cars, he cultivated the last refinements of punctuality and monotony, discouraging his wife's fancy for the unexpected, and declaring that to a delicate taste there were infinite gradations of pleasure in the recurrences of habit.

Still, since no life can completely defend itself from the unforeseen, it was evident that all Boyne's precautions would sooner or later prove unavailable, and Mary concluded that he had cut short a tiresome visit by walking with his caller to the station, or at least accompanying him for part of the way.

This conclusion relieved her from farther preoccupation, and she went out herself to take up her conference with the gardener. Thence she walked to the village post-office, a mile or so away; and when she turned toward home the early twilight was setting in.

She had taken a foot-path across the downs, and as Boyne, meanwhile, had probably returned from the station by the highroad, there was little likelihood of their meeting. She felt sure, however, of his having reached the house before her; so sure that, when she entered it herself, without even pausing to inquire of Trimmle, she made directly for the library. But the library was still empty, and with an unwonted exactness of visual memory she observed that the papers on her husband's desk lay precisely as they had lain when she had gone in to call him to luncheon.

Then of a sudden she was seized by a vague dread of the unknown. She had closed the door behind her on entering, and as she stood alone in the long silent room, her dread seemed to take shape and sound, to be there breathing and lurking among the shadows. Her short-sighted eyes strained through them, half-discerning an actual presence, something aloof, that watched and knew; and in the recoil from that intangible presence she threw herself on the bell-rope and gave it a sharp pull.

The sharp summons brought Trimmle in precipitately with a lamp, and Mary breathed again at this sobering reappearance of the usual.

'You may bring tea if Mr Boyne is in,' she said, to justify her ring.

'Very well, Madam. But Mr Boyne is not in,' said Trimmle, putting down the lamp.

'Not in? You mean he's come back and gone out again?'

'No, Madam. He's never been back.'

The dread stirred again, and Mary knew that now it had her fast.

'Not since he went out with – the gentleman?'

'Not since he went out with the gentleman.'

'But who *was* the gentleman?' Mary insisted, with the shrill note of some one trying to be heard through a confusion of noises.

'That I couldn't say, Madam.' Trimmle, standing there by the lamp, seemed suddenly to grow less round and rosy, as though eclipsed by the same creeping shade of apprehension.

'But the kitchen-maid knows – wasn't it the kitchen-maid who let him in?'

'She doesn't know either, Madam, for he wrote his name on a folded paper.'

Mary, through her agitation, was aware that they were both designating the unknown visitor by a vague pronoun, instead of the conventional formula which, till then, had kept their allusions within the bounds of conformity. And at the same moment her mind caught at the suggestion of the folded paper.

'But he must have a name! Where's the paper?'

She moved to the desk, and began to turn over the documents that littered it. The first that caught her eye was an unfinished letter in her husband's hand, with his pen lying across it, as though dropped there at a sudden summons.

'My dear Parvis' – who was Parvis? – 'I have just received your letter announcing Elwell's death, and while I suppose there is now no farther risk of trouble, it might be safer –'

She tossed the sheet aside, and continued her search; but no folded paper was discoverable among the letters and pages of manuscript which had been swept together in a heap, as if by a hurried or a startled gesture.

'But the kitchen-maid *saw* him. Send her here,' she commanded, wondering at her dulness in not thinking sooner of so simple a solution.

Trimmle vanished in a flash, as if thankful to be out of the room, and when she reappeared, conducting the agitated underling, Mary had regained her self-possession, and had her questions ready.

The gentleman was a stranger, yes – that she understood. But what had he said? And, above all, what had he looked like? The first question was easily enough answered, for the disconcerting reason that he had said so little – had merely asked for Mr Boyne, and, scribbling something on a bit of paper, had requested that it should at once be carried in to him.

'Then you don't know what he wrote? You're not sure it *was* his name?'

The kitchen-maid was not sure, but supposed it was, since he had written it in answer to her inquiry as to whom she should announce.

'And when you carried the paper in to Mr Boyne, what did he say?'

The kitchen-maid did not think that Mr Boyne had said anything, but she could not be sure, for just as she had handed him the paper and he was opening it, she had become aware that the visitor had followed her into the library, and she had slipped out, leaving the two gentlemen together.

'But then, if you left them in the library, how do you know that they went out of the house?'

This question plunged the witness into a momentary inarticulateness, from which she was rescued by Trimmle, who, by means of ingenious circumlocutions, elicited the statement that before she could cross the hall to the back passage she had heard the two gentlemen behind her, and had seen them go out of the front door together.

'Then, if you saw the strange gentleman twice, you must be able to tell me what he looked like.'

But with this final challenge to her powers of expression it became clear that the limit of the kitchen-maid's endurance had been reached. The obligation of going to the front door to 'show in' a visitor was in itself so subversive of the fundamental order of things that it had thrown her faculties into hopeless disarray, and she could only stammer out, after various panting efforts: 'His hat, mum, was different-like, as you might say –'

'Different? How different?' Mary flashed out, her own mind, in the same instant, leaping back to an image left on it that morning, and then lost under layers of subsequent impressions.

'His hat had a wide brim, you mean? and his face was pale – a youngish face?' Mary pressed her, with a white-lipped intensity of interrogation. But if the kitchen-maid found any adequate answer to this challenge, it was swept away for her listener down the rushing current of her own convictions. The stranger – the stranger in the garden! Why had Mary not thought of him before? She needed no one now to tell her that it was he who had called for her husband and gone away with him. But who was he, and why had Boyne obeyed him?

IV

It leaped out at her suddenly, like a grin out of the dark, that they had often called England so little – 'such a confoundedly hard place to get lost in.'

A confoundedly hard place to get lost in! That had been her husband's phrase. And now, with the whole machinery of official investigation sweeping its flash-lights from shore to shore, and across the dividing straits; now, with Boyne's name blazing from the walls of every town and village, his portrait (how that wrung her!) hawked up and down the country like the image of a hunted criminal; now the little compact populous island, so policed, surveyed and administered, revealed itself as a Sphinx-like guardian of abysmal mysteries, staring back into his wife's anguished eyes as if with the wicked joy of knowing something they would never know!

In the fortnight since Boyne's disappearance there had been no word of him, no trace of his movements. Even the usual misleading reports that raise expectancy in tortured bosoms had been few and fleeting. No one but the kitchen-maid had seen Boyne leave the house, and no one else had seen 'the gentleman' who accompanied him. All enquiries in the neighbourhood failed to elicit the memory of a stranger's presence that day in the neighbourhood of Lyng. And no one had met Edward Boyne, either alone or in company, in any of the neighbouring villages, or on the road across the downs, or at either of the local railway-stations. The sunny English noon had swallowed him as completely as if he had gone out into Cimmerian night.[8]

Mary, while every official means of investigation was working at its highest pressure, had ransacked her husband's papers for any trace of antecedent complications, of entanglements or obligations unknown to her, that might throw a ray into the darkness. But if any such had existed in the background of Boyne's life, they had vanished like the slip of paper on which the visitor had written his name. There remained no possible thread of guidance except – if it were indeed an exception – the letter which Boyne had apparently been in the act of writing when he received his mysterious summons. That letter, read and reread by his wife, and submitted by her to the police, yielded little enough to feed conjecture.

'I have just heard of Elwell's death, and while I suppose there is now no farther risk of trouble, it might be safer –' That was all. The 'risk of trouble' was easily explained by the newspaper clipping which had apprised Mary of the suit brought against her husband by one of his associates in the Blue Star enterprise.

The only new information conveyed by the letter was the fact of its showing Boyne, when he wrote it, to be still apprehensive of the results of the suit, though he had told his wife that it had been withdrawn, and though the letter itself proved that the plaintiff was dead. It took several days of cabling to fix the identity of the 'Parvis' to whom the fragment was addressed, but even after these enquiries had shown him to be a Waukesha lawyer, no new facts concerning the Elwell suit were elicited. He appeared to have had no direct concern in it, but to have been conversant with the facts merely as an acquaintance, and possible intermediary; and he declared himself unable to guess with what object Boyne intended to seek his assistance.

This negative information, sole fruit of the first fortnight's search, was not increased by a jot during the slow weeks that followed. Mary knew that the investigations were still being carried on, but she had a vague sense of their gradually slackening, as the actual march of time seemed to slacken. It was as though the days, flying horror-struck from the shrouded image of the one inscrutable day, gained assurance as the distance lengthened, till at last they fell back into their normal gait. And so with the human imaginations at work on the dark event. No doubt it occupied them still, but week by week and hour by hour it grew less absorbing, took up less space, was slowly but inevitably crowded out of the foreground of consciousness by the new problems perpetually bubbling up from the cloudy cauldron of human experience.

Even Mary Boyne's consciousness gradually felt the same lowering of velocity. It still swayed with the incessant oscillations of conjecture; but they were slower, more rhythmical in their beat. There were even moments of weariness when, like the victim of some poison which leaves the brain clear, but holds the body motionless, she saw herself domesticated with the Horror, accepting its perpetual presence as one of the fixed conditions of life.

These moments lengthened into hours and days, till she passed into a phase of stolid acquiescence. She watched the routine of daily life with the incurious eye of a savage on whom the meaningless processes of civilization make but the faintest impression. She had come to regard herself as part of the routine, a spoke of the wheel, revolving with its motion; she felt almost like the furniture of the room in which she sat, an insensate object to be dusted and pushed about with the chairs and tables. And this deepening apathy held her fast at Lyng, in spite of the entreaties of friends and the usual medical recommendation of 'change.' Her friends supposed that her refusal to move was inspired by the belief that her husband would one day return to the spot from which he had vanished, and a beautiful legend grew up about this imaginary state of waiting. But in reality she had no such belief: the depths of anguish enclosing her were no longer lighted by flashes of hope. She was sure that Boyne would never come back, that he had gone out of her sight as completely as if Death itself had waited that day on the threshold. She had even renounced, one by one, the various theories as to his disappearance which had been advanced by the press, the police, and her own agonized imagination. In sheer lassitude her mind turned from these alternatives of horror, and sank back into the blank fact that he was gone.

No, she would never know what had become of him – no one would ever know. But the house *knew*; the library in which she spent her long lonely evenings knew. For it was here that the last scene had been enacted, here that the stranger had come, and spoken the word which had caused Boyne to rise and follow him. The floor she trod had felt his tread; the books on the shelves had seen his face; and there were moments when the intense consciousness of the old dusky walls seemed about to break out into some audible revelation of their secret. But the revelation never came, and she knew it would never come. Lyng was not one of the garrulous old houses that betray the secrets entrusted to them. Its very legend proved that it had always been the mute accomplice, the incorruptible custodian, of the mysteries it had surprised. And Mary Boyne, sitting face to face with its silence, felt the futility of seeking to break it by any human means.

V

'I don't say it *wasn't* straight, and yet I don't say it *was* straight. It was business.'

Mary, at the words, lifted her head with a start, and looked intently at the speaker.

When, half an hour before, a card with 'Mr Parvis' on it had been brought up to her, she had been immediately aware that the name had been a part of her consciousness ever since she had read it at the head of Boyne's unfinished letter. In the library she had found awaiting her a small sallow man with a bald head and gold eye-glasses, and it sent a tremor through her to know that this was the person to whom her husband's last known thought had been directed.

Parvis, civilly, but without vain preamble – in the manner of a man who has his watch in his hand – had set forth the object of his visit. He had 'run over' to England on business, and finding himself in the neighbourhood of Dorchester, had not wished to leave it without paying his respects to Mrs Boyne; and without asking her, if the occasion offered, what she meant to do about Bob Elwell's family.

The words touched the spring of some obscure dread in Mary's bosom. Did her visitor, after all, know what Boyne had meant by his unfinished phrase? She asked for an elucidation of his question, and noticed at once that he seemed surprised at her continued ignorance of the subject. Was it possible that she really knew as little as she said?

'I know nothing – you must tell me,' she faltered out; and her visitor thereupon proceeded to unfold his story. It threw, even to her confused perceptions, and imperfectly initiated vision, a lurid glare on the whole hazy episode of the Blue Star Mine. Her husband had made his money in that brilliant speculation at the cost of 'getting ahead' of some one less alert to seize the chance; and the victim of his ingenuity was young Robert Elwell, who had 'put him on' to the Blue Star scheme.

Parvis, at Mary's first cry, had thrown her a sobering glance through his impartial glasses.

'Bob Elwell wasn't smart enough, that's all; if he had been, he might have turned round and served Boyne the same way. It's the kind of thing that happens every day in business. I guess it's what the scientists call the survival of the fittest – see?' said Mr Parvis, evidently pleased with the aptness of his analogy.

Mary felt a physical shrinking from the next question she tried to frame: it was as though the words on her lips had a taste that nauseated her.

'But then – you accuse my husband of doing something dishonourable?'

Mr Parvis surveyed the question dispassionately. 'Oh, no, I don't. I don't even say it wasn't straight.' He glanced up and down the long lines of books, as if one of them might have supplied him with the definition he sought. 'I don't say it *wasn't* straight, and yet I don't say it *was* straight. It was business.' After all, no definition in his category could be more comprehensive than that.

Mary sat staring at him with a look of terror. He seemed to her like the indifferent emissary of some evil power.

'But Mr Elwell's lawyers apparently did not take your view, since I suppose the suit was withdrawn by their advice.'

'Oh, yes; they knew he hadn't a leg to stand on, technically. It was when they advised him to withdraw the suit that he got desperate. You see, he'd borrowed most of the money he lost in the Blue Star, and he was up a tree. That's why he shot himself when they told him he had no show.'

The horror was sweeping over Mary in great deafening waves.

'He shot himself? He killed himself because of *that*?'

'Well, he didn't kill himself, exactly. He dragged on two months before he died.' Parvis emitted the statement as unemotionally as a gramophone grinding out its 'record.'

'You mean that he tried to kill himself, and failed? And tried again?'

'Oh, he didn't have to *try* again,' said Parvis grimly.

They sat opposite each other in silence, he swinging his eye-glasses thoughtfully about his finger, she, motionless, her arms stretched along her knees in an attitude of rigid tension.

'But if you knew all this,' she began at length, hardly able to force her voice above a whisper, 'how is it that when I wrote you at the time of my husband's disappearance you said you didn't understand his letter?'

Parvis received this without perceptible embarrassment: 'Why, I didn't understand it – strictly speaking. And it wasn't the time to talk about it, if I had. The Elwell business was settled when the suit was withdrawn. Nothing I could have told you would have helped you to find your husband.'

Mary continued to scrutinize him. 'Then why are you telling me now?'

Still Parvis did not hesitate. 'Well, to begin with, I supposed you knew more than you appear to – I mean about the circumstances of Elwell's death. And then people are talking of it now; the whole matter's been raked up again. And I thought if you didn't know you ought to.'

She remained silent, and he continued: 'You see, it's only come out lately what a bad state Elwell's affairs were in. His wife's a proud woman, and she fought on as long as she could, going out to work, and taking sewing at home when she got too sick – something with the heart, I believe. But she had his mother to look after, and the children, and she broke down under it, and finally had to ask for help. That called attention to the case, and the papers took it up, and a subscription was started. Everybody out there liked Bob Elwell, and most of the prominent names in the place are down on the list, and people began to wonder why –'

Parvis broke off to fumble in an inner pocket. 'Here,' he continued, 'here's an account of the whole thing from the *Sentinel* – a little sensational, of course. But I guess you'd better look it over.'

He held out a newspaper to Mary, who unfolded it slowly, remembering, as she did so, the evening when, in that same room, the perusal of a clipping from the *Sentinel* had first shaken the depths of her security.

As she opened the paper, her eyes, shrinking from the glaring headlines, 'Widow of Boyne's Victim Forced to Appeal for Aid,' ran down the column of text to two portraits inserted in it. The first was her husband's taken from a photograph made the year they had come to England. It was the picture of him that she liked best, the one that stood on the writing-table up-stairs in her bedroom. As the eyes in the photograph met hers, she felt it would be impossible to read what was said of him, and closed her lids with the sharpness of the pain.

'I thought if you felt disposed to put your name down –' she heard Parvis continue.

She opened her eyes with an effort, and they fell on the other portrait. It was that of a youngish man, slightly built, with features somewhat blurred by the shadow of a projecting hat-brim. Where had she seen that outline before? She stared at it confusedly, her heart hammering in her ears. Then she gave a cry.

'This is the man – the man who came for my husband!'

She heard Parvis start to his feet, and was dimly aware that she had slipped backward into the corner of the sofa, and that he was bending above her in alarm. She straightened herself, and reached out for the paper, which she had dropped.

'It's the man! I should know him anywhere!' she persisted in a voice that sounded to her own ears like a scream.

Parvis's answer seemed to come to her from far off, down endless fog-muffled windings.

'Mrs Boyne, you're not very well. Shall I call somebody? Shall I get a glass of water?'

'No, no, no!' She threw herself toward him, her hand frantic-ally clutching the newspaper. 'I tell you, it's the man! I *know* him! He spoke to me in the garden!'

Parvis took the journal from her, directing his glasses to the portrait. 'It can't be, Mrs Boyne. It's Robert Elwell.'

'Robert Elwell?' Her white stare seemed to travel into space. 'Then it was Robert Elwell who came for him.'

'Came for Boyne? The day he went away from here?' Parvis's voice dropped as hers rose. He bent over, laying a fraternal hand on her, as if to coax her gently back into her seat. 'Why, Elwell was dead! Don't you remember?'

Mary sat with her eyes fixed on the picture, unconscious of what he was saying.

'Don't you remember Boyne's unfinished letter to me – the one you found on his desk that day? It was written just after he'd heard of Elwell's death.' She noticed an odd shake in Parvis's unemotional voice. 'Surely you remember!' he urged her.

Yes, she remembered: that was the profoundest horror of it. Elwell had died the day before her husband's disappearance; and this was Elwell's portrait; and it was the portrait of the man who had spoken to her in the garden. She lifted her head and looked slowly about the library. The library could have borne witness that it was also the portrait of the man who had come in that day to call Boyne from his unfinished letter. Through the misty surgings of her brain she heard the faint boom of half-forgotten words – words spoken by Alida Stair on the lawn at Pangbourne before Boyne and his wife had ever seen the house at Lyng, or had imagined that they might one day live there.

'This was the man who spoke to me,' she repeated.

She looked again at Parvis. He was trying to conceal his disturbance under what he probably imagined to be an expression of indulgent commiseration; but the edges of his lips were blue. 'He thinks me mad; but I'm not mad,' she reflected; and suddenly there flashed upon her a way of justifying her strange affirmation.

She sat quiet, controlling the quiver of her lips, and waiting till she could trust her voice; then she said, looking straight at Parvis: 'Will you answer me one question, please? When was it that Robert Elwell tried to kill himself?'

'When – when?' Parvis stammered.

'Yes; the date. Please try to remember.'

She saw that he was growing still more afraid of her. 'I have a reason,' she insisted.

'Yes, yes. Only I can't remember. About two months before, I should say.'

'I want the date,' she repeated.

Parvis picked up the newspaper. 'We might see here,' he said, still humouring her. He ran his eyes down the page. 'Here it is. Last October – the –'

She caught the words from him. 'The 20th, wasn't it?' With a sharp look at her, he verified. 'Yes, the 20th. Then you *did* know?'

'I know now.' Her gaze continued to travel past him. 'Sunday, the 20th – that was the day he came first.'

Parvis's voice was almost inaudible. 'Came *here* first?'

'Yes.'

'You saw him twice, then?'

'Yes, twice.' She just breathed it at him. 'He came first on the 20th of October. I remember the date because it was the day we went up Meldon Steep for the first time.' She felt a faint gasp of inward laughter at the thought that but for that she might have forgotten.

Parvis continued to scrutinize her, as if trying to intercept her gaze.

'We saw him from the roof,' she went on. 'He came down the lime-avenue toward the house. He was dressed just as he is in that picture. My husband saw him first. He was frightened, and ran down ahead of me; but there was no one there. He had vanished.'

'Elwell had vanished?' Parvis faltered.

'Yes.' Their two whispers seemed to grope for each other. 'I couldn't think what had happened. I see now. He *tried* to come then; but he wasn't dead enough – he couldn't reach us. He had to wait for two months to die; and then he came back again – and Ned went with him.'

She nodded at Parvis with the look of triumph of a child who has worked out a difficult puzzle. But suddenly she lifted her hands with a desperate gesture, pressing them to her temples.

'Oh, my God! I sent him to Ned – I told him where to go! I sent him to this room!' she screamed.

She felt the walls of books rush toward her, like inward falling ruins; and she heard Parvis, a long way off, through the ruins, crying to her, and struggling to get at her. But she was numb to his touch, she did not know what he was saying. Through the tumult she heard but one clear note, the voice of Alida Stair, speaking on the lawn at Pangbourne.

'You won't know till afterward,' it said. 'You won't know till long, long afterward.'

Glossary of Scots Words

Rather than clogging the text with too many notes, a glossary now follows of the Scots words used in Elizabeth Gaskell's 'The Old Nurse's Story', Amelia B. Edwards's 'The North Mail', Robert Louis Stevenson's 'Thrawn Janet' and Margaret Oliphant's 'The Open Door'. Stevenson uses dialect stringently, while Oliphant tends merely to render accent phonetically. The few words glossed here from 'The Old Nurse's Story' and 'The North Mail' reflect the border country location of these tales. The glossary derives from reference to four sources: *Jamieson's Dictionary of the Scottish Language* (London and Edinburgh: William P. Nimmo, 1877); Charles MacKay's *A Dictionary of Lowland Scotch* (Edinburgh: Ballantyne Press, 1888); the glossary to Barry Menikoff (ed.), *The Complete Stories of Robert Louis Stevenson* (New York: Modern Library, 2002); and the glossary to 'Thrawn Janet' in Michael Hayes (ed.), *The Supernatural Stories of Robert Louis Stevenson* (London: John Calder, 1976).

a' all
aboot about
abune above
ae one
aff off
ahint behind
aik oak
ain own
aince/ance once
alang along
amang among
ane one
arena aren't
askit asked

atween between
auld old
awfu' awful
aye always, still

bairn child
baith both
banes bones
bauldly boldly
begude began
ben inside
bield shelter
bieldy sheltered
birks birches

blythe happy

body a human being, person,
oneself

bogle hobgoblin, ghost; as a
verb, to terrify, enchant,
bewitch

braes sides of a hill

braw fine

brunstane brimstone

brunt burnt

bure bore

burn stream

ca'd called

callant a youth, boy

caller fresh and cool

cam' came

can'le candle

cantrip spell

carline old woman

cauld cold

chafts cheeks

chalmer/cha'mer chamber,
room

chappin' striking (the hour on
a clock)

chittered chattered

clachan a small village with
a parish church (from
the Gaelic, *clach*, a stone,
and *clachan*, stones or
houses)

cla'es clothes

clang clung

clatter noisy and idle chatter

claught snatched at, laid hold
of eagerly

claverin' talking idly,
chattering (from *clavers*, idle
stories, silly calumnies)

collieshangie noisy row, brawl

contrar contrary

corbie craws hooded or

carrion crows; ravens (from
the French, *corbeau*)

cornel colonel

corp corpse

craig throat

cuist cast

cummers female gossips

dae do

daffin' merrily

daur dare

deave deafen

deevil devil

deid dead

deil devil

denners dinners

didna did not

diedly deadly

dirl vibrate; *teeth play dirl*:
teeth chatter; as a noun, a
slight tremulous stroke, a
vibration; applied to the mind,
a twinge of conscience, or what
causes a feeling of remorse

dinna did not

doon/doun down

door dour

drap drop

dreepin' dripping

droun drown

duds clothes

dunt pound; *played dunt*:
pounded

durst dare

dwalled dwelled

dwining wasting away,
declining, waning (also
applied to the moon)

een/e'en eyes

e'en/een evening

eicht eight

eldritch fearful, terrible

fashed bothered

feck plenty, a lot, the greatest part; power, activity, vigour; vigorous, stout (hence *feckless*)

fit foot

fleyed scared

focht fought

forbye besides

forjaskit jaded, fatigued

forrit forward

fower four

fra'/frae from

frichten frighten; *frichtit*: frightened

fu' full

fuff noise of a cat spitting

gab talk

gang go, walk; *gaed*: went; *gaun*: going; *gane*: gone

gangrel outcast

gart cause to

gate way

gey very, amply

gie give; *gied*: gave; *gien*: given

girn grin

glen narrow valley

glisk sidelong glance, glimpse

gloaming/gloamin' twilight

goun gown

gousty stormy, tempestuous; unearthly

gowk fool, half-wit

greet weep, cry, whimper

grue a shudder, curdling of the blood, feeling of horror (hence *gruesome*)

grund ground

gude good; God

guid/guide good

hail/haill whole

hairmed harmed

hame home

hap hop

haud hold

Heeven heaven

heid head

het hot

hinder extreme

hingin' hanging

hirsle to move or creep forward while sitting or reclining, supporting oneself on one's hands and feet; to move, while still in a sitting position, to a nearby seat without absolutely rising; to move with effort, to shuffle, move awkwardly

hoose house

hoots expression of contempt or disbelief

howff haunt, favourite place

hunard/hun'er' hundred

ilka each, every

inower inside, within

ither other

jaloosed suspected

keeked/keekit peeped

keepit kept

ken know; *kens*: knows; *kenned*: knew; *ken't*: known

kilted tucked in

kirk church

kirkyaird churchyard

kye cattle

laigh low

laird lord

lane lone; *your lane*: on your own

lang long

leddy lady; *leddies*: ladies
leed lead
leevin' living
licht light
likit love, delight in
limmer strumpet
lockit locked
lookit looked
lowed flamed, glowed
lown calm, quiet, sheltered
    from the wind
lowp jump, leap
lug ear

mair more
maister master
maned moaned
manse house lived in by a
    minister of the Scottish
    Presbyterian Church
maud plaid worn by shepherds
    in the border country of
    England/Scotland
maun must
meenute minute
micht might
mirk dark
mistrysted disagreed
mony many
moo mouth
muckle great, large, big, a
    great deal of
muir moor
mutch hat, coif (close-fitting
    cap worn under a veil or hood)
mysel myself

na no
nae no, not any, not one
nane none
neist next
neuk nook
nicht night

ony any
onyway anyway
oot out
o't of it
ower over
owercome fragment, scrap
oxter armpit

pairt part
pechin' gasping
pickle bit
pit-mirk pitch-dark
powney pony
projectit/projekit projected
pu'd pulled
puir poor

quo' quoth, said

rairing roaring
reishling rustling
rin run; *rinnin*: running
rumm'led to make a noise or
    a confused sound; to stir
    about

sabbin' sobbing
sae so
saftly softly
sair sore
sang song
sark linen, woollen, silken or
    cotton garment worn next to
    the skin by men and women; a
    shirt or shift
saughs willows (from the
    French, *saule*, and Gaelic,
    seileag)
saul soul
scrieghin' shrieking, screeching
    (a misspelling of *screighing* or
    skreighing)
scunner take an aversion to,

show disgust; as a noun, a
shudder, strong dislike
seelent silent
shaw show
shoon shoes
shoother shoulder
shouers showers
shouldna should not
sib related, of kin by blood or
    marriage (as in *sibling*); bound
    by ties of affection
sic such
siccan such, such kind of
sicht sight
side-lang sidelong
simmer summer
sinsyne since then
sip small spring of water
skelloch scream
skelpt beat
skirled shrieked
skriegh misspelling of
    skreigh or *screigh* – see
    scrieghin'
slockened quenched
sma' small
smoored smothered,
    choked
sodger soldier
soughing sighing
soum swim
spak spoke
spate flood
speerit a spirit
speered asked
spunk a match, spark; spirit
    (hence *spunkie*, fiery,
    high-spirited)
spunkies spirits,
    will-o'-the-wisps
steedy steady
steeked shut
steer stir

stramp tramp, walk
straucht straight
stravaguin' wandering
    aimlessly (from *stravaiging*,
    strolling about, generally with
    bad intent)
suld should
suspeckit suspect, suspected
swat sweat
syne since, ago, then

tap top, height
tauld told
tellt told
thae those
thegether together
thir these
thirled bound; pierced,
    penetrated; caused to vibrate;
    enslaved, subject to,
    enthralled, thrilled
thocht thought
thrapples throats
thrawn as a noun, a *thraw* is a
    twist, one turn of the hand in
    twisting something, a fit of
    ill-humour, a pang, an agony;
    as a verb, *thraw* means to
    wreathe, twist, wrench, as
    well as to oppose, resist;
    hence *thrawn*, twisted,
    contorted, pained, and
    thrawn-gabbit, with a twisted
    or contorted mouth; applied
    metaphorically, *thrawn* means
    a cantankerous, morose
    person who is always
    grumbling; some one who is
    peevish, perverse,
    cross-grained
threep persistently affirm,
    reiterate (more usually spelled
    threap)

thretty thirty
toun town
tummled tumbled
twa two
twal' twelve
tyke small child

unco strange, unknown; a wonder, a strange thing or person
unhalesome unwholesome
unhaly unholy
unstreakit/unstreekit not laid out for burial
upsitten indifferent, lacking in zeal

wa'/wa's wall/s
wad would
wark work, a to-do
wars'lin' wrestling
wast west
waukened awoke

waur worst
wean child
weary sorrowful; *weary fa'*: damn!; the devil take!
wee little
weel well
whammled thumped
wha what
whaten what kind of
wheen number, quantity
whaur where
whiles sometimes
whilk which
wi' with
won went
wrang wrong
wrastlin' wrestling
wud wild, mad
wund wind
wursted worsted

ye you
yett gate

Biographical and Explanatory Notes

Regarding the page references used below for a short story's first publication in book form, very often it was the practice in the nineteenth and early twentieth centuries to begin numbering from the title page of the story. Here, page references start with the first page of the story's text. References within the notes to the *Oxford English Dictionary* are abbreviated '*OED*'.

ELIZABETH GASKELL
The Old Nurse's Story

Elizabeth Cleghorn Gaskell (1810–65) was a novelist and writer of short stories. Her novels are: *Mary Barton* (1848), *Cranford* (1853), *Ruth* (1853), *North and South* (1855), *Sylvia's Lovers* (1863) and the unfinished *Wives and Daughters* (1866). She included Charles Dickens, John Ruskin and Florence Nightingale among her friends, and is the author of a brilliant biography of another good friend, *The Life of Charlotte Brontë* (1857). Gaskell was a committed Unitarian (indeed her husband was a Unitarian minister). She began writing fiction as a means of distracting herself from her grief for a dead son.

'The Old Nurse's Story' was first published in Charles Dickens's weekly periodical *Household Words*, in the 'Extra Christmas Number' (price threepence), 'A Round of Stories by the Christmas Fire' (18 December 1852), pp. 11–20. Other stories in the same volume, by other authors, included 'The Poor Relative's Story', 'The Child's Story' and 'The Host's Story'. It was reprinted in *Lizzie Leigh; and Other Tales* ('by the Author of "Mary Barton," "Ruth," &c.'), 'Cheap Edition' (London: Chapman and Hall, 1855), pp. 69–84. The latter is the copy-text for the version printed here. For explanations of any dialect words in this story (set near the border of England and Scotland), please see the Glossary of Scots Words.

1. *Westmoreland*: a former county in the north-west of England, in the area of the Lake District. In 1974, Westmoreland was merged with the neighbouring country of Cumberland to form Cumbria.

2. *Northumberland*: a county in the north-east of England, on the border with Scotland.

3. *Westmoreland Fells*: the high land and mountains of the Lake District.

4. *Newcastle*: Newcastle-upon-Tyne was the county town of Northumberland and the area's largest city.

5. *andirons and dogs*: andirons – generally used in pairs and also called 'dogs' or 'firedogs' – are horizontal iron bars used for holding logs in an open fireplace. Each andiron is supported on short legs and has an upright guard at one end (the end facing the room), often elaborately ornamented.

6. *beaver . . . stomacher*: though a beaver is a kind of hat, in this context 'beaver' most likely means felted cloth; a 'stomacher' is a waistcoat, or a decorative covering for the chest.

7. *flesh is grass*: a reference to several biblical texts: 'The voice said, Cry. And he said, What shall I cry? All flesh is grass, and all the goodliness thereof is as the flower of the field' (Isaiah 40: 6); 'For all flesh is as grass, and all the glory of man as the flower of grass. The grass withereth, and the flower thereof falleth away' (I Peter 1: 24).

8. *Crosthwaite Church*: the parish church of Keswick, in Westmoreland, the nurse's home county. (The current organ was made in 1837.)

9. *perished*: frozen, near to death with cold.

10. *Doncaster Races*: one of the oldest racecourses in England, dating back to the sixteenth century, is located about one hundred miles to the south of Northumberland at Doncaster, south Yorkshire.

11. *with the army in America*: possibly an indication that this part of the story is set during the American War of Independence (1775–83) but more likely a reference to the war fought between Britain and America from 1812 to 1815.

FITZ-JAMES O'BRIEN

What Was It?

Fitz-James O'Brien (1828–62) was a poet, short-story writer, playwright, critic, Bohemian and wastrel. Born in County Limerick, Ireland, he was the son of a lawyer. He moved to London in 1849, where he rapidly dissipated his inheritance, and so in the early 1850s went to make his fortune in New York. He earned an unstable living as an all-purpose writer, spinning out articles, essays and stories for the periodicals, sometimes flush, and sometimes on the run from creditors. He was brilliant, witty and incorrigible. His greatest successes are his tales of the uncanny, particularly 'What Was It?', 'The Wondersmith' and 'The Diamond Lens' – the two last appearing in the *Atlantic Monthly*. 'The Diamond Lens' tells the story of a strange, human-like creature revealed by a microscope to be living in a drop of water. With the outbreak of the American Civil War in 1861, he enlisted in the New York National Guard; in 1862, he joined the staff of General Lander as a lieutenant. At the Battle of Bloomery Gap, he was wounded in the shoulder, dying of tetanus six weeks later.

'What Was It?' was first printed in *Harper's New Monthly Magazine*, vol. 18 (March 1859), pp. 504–9. The copy-text used here is from *The Poems and Stories of Fitz-James O'Brien* (Boston, MA: Osgood and Co., 1881), pp. 390–407.

1. *balusters*: a baluster is a pillar, one of several supporting a parapet (hence *balustrade*) or, as in this instance, the handrail of a staircase. Balusters are candlestick shaped, slender at the top and base and swelling in the middle; indeed, the word is believed to derive from the Italian *balustra*, 'pomegranate flower', because of the resemblance, in shape, to the half-open flower.

2. *Bleecker Street*: a street some way downtown from 26th Street, running from east to west in Manhattan, two blocks below the southern end of Washington Square, and crossing lower Broadway; its eastern edge ran to the Bowery, a down-at-heel district of pawnshops and dosshouses. Moving uptown to 26th Street would have meant ascending the social scale.

3. *between Seventh and Eighth Avenues*: that is, on the west side of Manhattan.

4. *Weehawken heights*: across the Hudson River, on the Jersey shore, directly opposite Manhattan.

5. *Mrs Crowe's 'Night Side of Nature'*: Catherine Ann Crowe (1790–1872) was a British novelist and writer on the supernatural; her *The Night Side of Nature: Ghosts and Ghost Seers* (1848) was a popular and influential work of non-fiction. Her idea of correspondences between the natural and supernatural realms inspired the French poet Charles Baudelaire (1821–67), though he would also have found the idea in the writings of Emanuel Swedenborg (see note 6 to 'Green Tea'), among others. She suffered from a brief (and public) spell of insanity in 1854, and spent some months in Hanwell Asylum, near London.

6. *opium*: both a common and much-used drug, and a badge of
    entry for nineteenth-century Bohemians; Thomas De Quincey's
    Confessions of an English Opium-Eater (1821) and Samuel
    Taylor Coleridge's poem 'Kubla Khan' (1816), supposedly
    written under the influence of an opium-induced dream, were
    vital in allying the drug with the idea of the unfettered
    imagination.

7. *Shakespeare's 'Tempest' . . . Caliban*: William Shakespeare's play
    The Tempest (1611?) features two non-human characters: Ariel
    is a dainty spirit, androgynous, ethereal, beautiful and playful;
    by contrast Caliban, the product of sex between a witch and a
    demon, is a more comic figure – earthy, gross, sulky and lascivi-
    ous. Ariel is also able to render himself invisible at will.

8. *Like the Guebers . . . faces to the east*: also known as Kebbers,
    Ghebres or Guebres, these are Zoroastrians or Parsees, mem-
    bers of a religious sect popularly thought of as fire-worshippers.
    Zoroastrians pray facing the east in the morning and the west in
    the evening, following the progress of the sun.

9. *port*: bearing.

10. *rana arborea*: a species of tree frog – one not normally found so
    far north as New York.

11. *meerschaums*: pipes with bowls made of the white, clay-like
    material known as meerschaum (from the German, 'sea foam',
    owing to its frothy appearance).

12. *Haroun*: presumably Haroun Al-Rashid (763–809), the Abbasid
    caliph, and a ruler noted for the artistic brilliance that flourished
    during his reign. His court and fictionalized adventures feature
    in a number of stories of *The Arabian Nights*.

13. *afreets . . . from the copper vessel*: in Muslim myth, an afreet
    (also spelled afrit or ifrit) is a powerful demon or jinn. Afreets
    flourished in Romantic verse, appearing in poems by Robert
    Southey (*Thalaba*, 1802) and Lord Byron (*The Giaour*, 1813); in
    her Preface to the 1850 edition of *Wuthering Heights*, Charlotte
    Brontë describes Heathcliff as 'a Ghoul – an Afreet'. The refer-
    ence to an afreet emerging from a copper vessel is clearly a
    reference to 'The Fisherman and the Ifrit' from *The Arabian
    Nights*, where the fisherman releases a spirit from a jar. In his
    footnote to his translation of the story, Sir Richard Burton writes:
    'Not "A-frit," pronounced Aye-frit, as our poets have it. This
    variety of the Jinn, who, as will be shown, are divided into two
    races like mankind, is generally, but not always, a malignant
    being, hostile and injurious to mankind (*Koran*, xxvii. 39).' The
    word 'jinn' – from the Arabic word *janna*, meaning to hide –

implies, among other things, invisibility and concealment. The passage brings together opium dreams (visions arising from the effects of a drug associated with the East), Romantic Orientalism, *The Arabian Nights*, the idea of invisibility, and the demonic.

14. *Brockden Brown's novel . . . Bulwer's 'Zanoni'*: born in Philadelphia, Charles Brockden Brown (1771–1810) was the author of *Wieland* (1798) and other Gothic novels. In this novel, the stranger Carwin ventriloquizes voices in a wood that are heard by Wieland, who mistakes them for the voices of God; deceived by Carwin, Wieland obeys the voices and kills his own family. Edward Bulwer-Lytton (1803–73) was one of the most popular authors of the nineteenth century (see the biographical note on him in 'The Haunted and the Haunters'). His *Zanoni: A Rosicrucian Tale* (1842) is an occultist novel set in the period of the French Revolution; in that novel, the Dweller of the Threshold is a spirit of malice, a dark presence that exists on the boundary between the physical and spiritual realms. The term 'dweller of the threshold' was incorporated in later occultist and mystical texts by contemporary writers on the subject, such as Madame Blavatsky, Rudolf Steiner and Dion Fortune.

15. *a story like Hoffman*: a reference to the tales of Ernst Theodor Amadeus Hoffmann (1776–1822), the brilliant German music critic and writer of uncanny and fantastic fictions.

16. *ghouls*: another Orientalist term (see note 13 above), a 'ghoul' (from the Arabic *ghūl*) is, according to Muslim folklore, an evil spirit that preys on corpses and robs graves.

17. *Goudon's 'History of Monsters'*: I have been unable to trace this work, and infer that it is very likely a fictitious text and a hoax on the reader.

18. *'spirit-circles'*: a reference to the practice of a séance, and to the contemporary vogue for spiritualism, a religious movement concerned with contacting the spirits of the dead. Spiritualism was then particularly strong in the USA, where it had originated in the 1840s.

19. *chloroform*: discovered in the early 1830s, a transparent liquid that could induce unconsciousness; formerly used as an anaesthetic in surgical operations.

20. *Gustave Doré, or Callot, or Tony Johannot*: all illustrators and artists: Gustave Doré (1832–1883) was a Frenchman known for his illustrations of the works of Byron (in 1853), of Dante's *Inferno* (1857) and the Bible (1866); Jacques Callot (1592?–1635) was an engraver from the Duchy of Lorraine best known for a grotesque and violent series of prints called *Les Misères*

de la guerre ('The Miseries of War'); Antoine (Tony) Johannot (1760–1838) was an artist born in Germany, but who lived most of his life in France and who became one of the most celebrated illustrators of the age.

21. *Un Voyage où il vous plaira*: 'A Journey to Wherever You Please' (French); a work by the poet Alfred de Musset (1810–57) and P.-J. Stahl (the pseudonym of Pierre-Jules Hetzel, 1814–86), published in 1843 and illustrated by Johannot (see note 20 above), with sixty-three macabre vignettes.

EDWARD BULWER LYTTON

The Haunted and the Haunters: or, The House and the Brain

Edward George Earle Lytton Bulwer Lytton (or Bulwer-Lytton, and formerly Edward George Earle Lytton Bulwer, 1803–73) was a British aristocrat, first a reforming politician, later an advocate of conservatism, for two years the Secretary for the Colonies, and one of the bestselling novelists of the nineteenth century. His work ranged from a 'fashionable novel' such as *Pelham* (1828) to crime fiction like *Eugene Aram* (1832), from the historical epic *The Last Days of Pompeii* (1834) to the early science fiction of *The Coming Race* (1871). He also wrote volumes of poetry, plays and short stories. Conceited, shy, egotistical, thin-skinned, obsessive, Bulwer Lytton led one of the most public lives of the nineteenth century, his failed marriage a matter of common scandal, and yet he flourished best in privacy. He was deeply interested in occult phenomena, and was something of an adept in its lore. He wrote a number of key works in this field, most notably the Rosicrucian novel *Zanoni* (1842 – see note 14 to 'What Was It?') set in part during the French Revolution, the novel *A Strange Story* (1862), commissioned by Charles Dickens for his magazine *All the Year Round*, and the story included here, 'The Haunters and the Haunted', a classic mid-Victorian ghost story and an initiator of the Victorian 'haunted house' genre.

The copy-text of 'The Haunted and the Haunters' derives from its publication in *A Strange Story; and The Haunted and the Haunters* (London: George Routledge & Sons, 1865), pp. 345–65. According to the title page, this offers a 'New Edition Revised' of the text. This version opens with the following bracketed paragraphs:

This tale first appeared in *Blackwood's Magazine*, August 1859. A portion of it as then published is now suppressed, because encroaching too much on the main plot of the 'Strange Story.' As it stands, however, it may be considered the preliminary outline of that more elaborate attempt to construct an interest akin to that which our forefathers felt in tales of witchcraft and ghostland, out of ideas and beliefs which have crept into fashion in the society of our own day. There has, perhaps, been no age in which certain phenomena have engendered throughout a wider circle a more credulous superstition. But, on the other hand, there has certainly been no age in which persons of critical and inquisitive intellect – seeking to divest what is genuine in these apparent vagaries of Nature from the cheats of venal impostors and the exaggeration of puzzled witnesses – have more soberly endeavoured to render such exceptional thaumaturgia [wonder-workers, workers of miracles] of philosophical use, in enlarging our conjectural knowledge of the complex laws of being – sometimes through physiological, sometimes through metaphysical research. Without discredit, however, to the many able and distinguished speculators on so vague a subject, it must be observed that their explanations as yet have been rather ingenious than satisfactory. Indeed, the first requisites for conclusive theory are at present wanting. The facts are not sufficiently generalized, and the evidences of them have not been sufficiently tested.

It is just when elements of the marvellous are thus struggling between superstition and philosophy, that they fall by right to the domain of Art – the art of poet or tale-teller. They furnish the constructor of imaginative fiction with materials for mysterious terror of a character not exhausted by his predecessors, and not foreign to the notions that float on the surface of his own time; while they allow him to wander freely over that range of conjecture which is favourable to his purposes, precisely because science itself has not yet disenchanted that debateable realm of its haunted shadows and goblin lights.

What Bulwer Lytton describes as the 'portion . . . now suppressed' refers to the longer version of the tale, not highly regarded, in which the magician who initiated the haunting turns out to be still alive, and engaged in occult plots. As Bulwer Lytton mentions at the outset, the story had first appeared in *Blackwood's Magazine*, in vol. 86 (August 1859), pp. 224–45. The previous month's edition of *Blackwood's* had featured George Eliot's classic Gothic tale of telepathy (though that word was first coined in the 1880s) 'The Lifted Veil'. Before its publication in an anthology purely of Bulwer Lytton's work, the story was collected in vol. 10 of the twelve-volume *Tales from 'Blackwood'*, First Series (Edinburgh: Blackwood's Edinburgh Magazine, 1858–61; vol. 10 being published in 1860).

1. *north side of Oxford Street ... dull but respectable thorough-fare*: Oxford Street was then, as it is now, the main shopping street of London, running from east to west, from the junction of Tottenham Court Road and Charing Cross Road, to Marble Arch and the start of Hyde Park. The streets north of Oxford Street could range from the rather smart district between Regent Street and Portland Place in the east to Baker Street in the west, to the vaguer social realms in the vicinity of Marble Arch and Edgware Road, and the decidedly seedy locale of the northern end of Soho, centred around Charlotte Street and Fitzroy Square.

2. *East Indies ... Company*: the East Indies, as opposed to the West Indies, meant Hindustan and the islands of the Indian Ocean, as far as the Malay Archipelago. The East India Company began, in 1600, as a joint-stock company engaged in trade with India. However, by the nineteenth century they had become the effective rulers of the whole sub-continent. In 1858, the year before Bulwer Lytton wrote this story, following the Indian Mutiny of 1857, the Company had been officially displaced as rulers of India by the British government. (The Government of India Act, 1858, established direct rule from London.) The owner of the house returns to England, therefore, at the moment when the Company loses power in India.

3. *Macaulay's Essays*: Thomas Babington Macaulay's *Essays Critical and Historical* (1834) is a book famed both for the clarity of its style and the vapid dogmatism of its arguments. The English historian Lord Acton (1834–1902) remarked of them that they were 'a key to half the prejudices of our age'.

4. *offices*: those parts of the house given over to household work or storage, such as the kitchen, pantry, scullery, cellars and laundry room.

5. *turning-tables*: during the 1850s, an interest in spiritualism and a belief in occult phenomena had become widespread and passionately held by many across Europe and North America. Growing out of mesmerism (see note 10 below), the movement found a first home in Germany, and then in 1848 acquired its first famous case with the Fox sisters and their haunted house in New York. One key feature of early séances was table-turning, in which participants sat around a table with their hands resting on it and waited for the table – supposedly operated by spirits – to move in response to letters of the alphabet being called out. In another sense of the phrase, turning the tables may also form the theme of a story in which a man pursues a ghost.

6. *half-tester*: a bed with a partial canopy (a *tester* being a canopy over a bed, supported by posts or suspended from the ceiling).

7. *Zoological Gardens*: opened in 1828 by the Zoological Society of London, and situated at the northern end of Regent's Park in London, this was the world's first scientific zoo.

8. *fearing that his bite ... madness of hydrophobia*: hydrophobia is the aversion to water symptomatic of rabies – the acute viral disease transmitted by the saliva from the bite of an affected animal and causing madness and convulsions; also another name for the disease.

9. *medium*: the intermediary at a séance between the human attendants and the spirits; in other words, a clairvoyant, a communicator with spirits. The first recorded use of this word in this sense in the *OED* was in America in 1851. Bulwer Lytton had become involved with a number of 'mediums' in the mid 1850s, with whom he had attempted to contact the spirit of his dead daughter, Emily.

10. *mesmerism or electro-biology*: mesmerism – named after its originator, Anton Mesmer (1734–1815), and which he termed 'animal magnetism' – involved inducing a hypnotic trance in a human subject, sometimes for therapeutic ends. Electro-biology originates as a term in the late 1840s and early 1850s. It stands both for the study of electrical phenomena in living organisms, and also as a fashionable offshoot of mesmerism, in which a trance was generated by means of an 'electro-vital force'. In the 1850s, it was practised as an amusement at parties.

11. *Odic*: 'Odic force', a mysterious and dynamic vital force, *od* or *odyle*, believed to inhere in all living bodies, as described by Baron Dr Karl Ludwig Freiherr von Reichenbach (1788–1869), a prominent German chemist.

12. *solar microscope*: a device which uses the sun's rays to project a greatly magnified image of a very small object on to a screen in a darkened room. Displays using a solar microscope were popularized by the late eighteenth-century itinerant lecturer and (self-proclaimed) occultist, freemason and natural philosopher (for *natural philosophy*, see note 3 to 'No. 1 Branch Line: The Signal-man') Gustavus Katterfelto (d. 1799). Other itinerant lecturers, such as John Warltire (1725/6–1810), made similar presentations to the public.

13. *Liverpool*: that he wrote the letter from the port of Liverpool gives away his desire to leave the country, in fact for Melbourne in Australia, as it turns out.

14. *Walworth*: a district of London in Southwark, on the south bank of the Thames.

15. *rapport*: the state of close connection between the mesmerist and the subject, in which the former can act upon the latter. '*En rapport*', a few lines later, derives from the same source (see also note 10 above).

16. *Paracelsus ... Curiosities of Literature*: Paracelsus (Theophrastus Bombastus von Hohenheim, 1493–1541) was a Swiss-born alchemist, astrologer, physician and metaphysician; he exerted a vital influence on the history of occultism, particularly on the Rosicrucian movement. *Curiosities of Literature*, published in six volumes between 1791 and 1823, and much revised thereafter, is an entertaining compilation of biographical anecdotes by Isaac Disraeli (1766–1848), father of the British prime minister Benjamin Disraeli (1804–81).

17. *eidolon*: a Greek word first used in English by Thomas Carlyle in 1828, meaning an insubstantial image, a phantom, a spectre.

18. *volumes of communications ... Bacon ... and Plato*: Bacon could be the English philosopher and essayist Francis Bacon (1561–1626) or possibly Roger Bacon, English philosopher, popularly misremembered as a necromancer (*c*.1214–after 1292); Plato is the Athenian philosopher (*c*.428/7–*c*.348/7). The practice of mediums (see note 9 above) producing posthumous books by famous writers, or posthumous compositions by famous composers, was a feature of nineteenth-century and early twentieth-century publishing. None of these works has ever acquired fame in its own right, partly for the reasons that the narrator of the story describes.

19. *telegraph wires*: the means of communication; the electric telegraph was an invention of the late eighteenth century, but its application on a practical level, with lines across London and on the Great Western Railway, dates from the 1840s. In the late 1850s, attempts were in progress to lay the first transatlantic telegraph wire; these were finally realized in 1866.

20. *pentacle*: a five-pointed star or pentagram used as a magical symbol; the double pentacle referred to three paragraphs later would have consisted of a smaller pentagram superimposed upon a larger pentagram, possibly enclosed within a circle and again used for magical purposes.

21. *vellum*: a kind of parchment originally made from the skin of calves.

22. *anathema*: a curse or denunciation.

MARY ELIZABETH BRADDON
The Cold Embrace

Mary Elizabeth Braddon (1835–1915) was born in Soho, London, the daughter of a solicitor father and journalist mother. Her parents' marriage collapsed due to her father's infidelity. After a spell as an actress, Braddon began a career as a writer of hack fiction, turning out stories of crime and infamy for the 'penny dreadfuls'. However, a more lasting form of literary success came with the serialization of *Lady Audley's Secret* (1861), a key work in the formation of the then new genre of 'the novel of sensation'. A year later, she published *Aurora Floyd* (1862), like its predecessor a novel of bigamy and scheming heroines. Braddon went on to become a prolific novelist, playwright and short-story writer.

The text of 'The Cold Embrace' derives from its initial appearance in book form, in Braddon's first collection of short stories, *Ralph the Bailiff and Other Tales* (London: Ward, Lock and Tyler, 1862), pp. 69–78. The story was first published in the periodical *Welcome Guest* on 29 Sepember 1860. In the book version, Braddon's name does not appear on the title page, but she is identified as 'The Author of *Lady Audley's Secret, Aurora Floyd*, etc. etc. etc.'. Among a number of stories, the volume also includes the famous ghost story 'Eveline's Visitant' and the supernatural tale 'How I Heard My Own Will Read'.

1. *Raphaels, Titians, Guidos, in a gallery at Florence*: sixteenth-century and early seventeenth-century Italian painters: Raphael (Raffaello Sanzio, 1483–1520); Titian (Tiziano Vecelli, 1485–1576); Guido possibly referring to a number of painters, but most likely the baroque painter Guido Reni (1575–1642). All three have paintings on display at the Uffizi Gallery in Florence, Italy.
2. *Brunswick*: or, in German, Braunschweig, a region and town in Lower Saxony, Germany; here the River Oker connects to the Aller and Weser rivers. A German setting for such Gothic tales as this one was traditional.
3. *meerschaum-pipe*: see note 11 to 'What Was It?'.
4. *diligence*: a public stage-coach.
5. *Aix-la-Chapelle*: now more commonly named Aachen, the westernmost city of Germany, close to the border with Belgium and the Netherlands. Traditionally, British people used the French name for the town.
6. *coupé*: a four-wheeled carriage that accommodates two passengers inside and has a seat outside for the driver.

7. *Antwerp ... Rubenses ... Quentin Matsys*: Peter Paul Rubens (1577–1640), the Flemish painter, was resident in Antwerp for much of his life. The city is the place to find many of his greatest paintings, including those held at the Rubenshuis. Quentin Matsys (also spelled Massys, Messys or Metsys, 1466–1530) was an earlier Flemish painter and the founder of the 'Antwerp school'. There are a number of candidates for the 'great picture' by Matsys at Antwerp, including *Jesus Chasing the Merchants from the Temple* or the *St John Altarpiece*, both on show at the Koninklijk Museum voor Schone Kunsten (Royal Museum of Fine Arts).

8. *Newfoundland*: a very large, generally black dog.

9. *Carnival*: a yearly celebration in February before the advent of Lent (see also note 11 below).

10. *domino*: a loose, hooded cloak worn with an eye mask as a costume at masquerades.

11. *Débardeuse*: a young woman dressed as a *débardeur*, a docker or stevedore, employed to unload produce from ships (French); the *débardeuse* was a typical character at the Paris Carnival (see note 9 above), immortalized by the French caricaturist Paul Gavarni (1801/4–66), who specialized in illustrating the Carnival.

12. *salle*: a hall, or room (French).

13. *polka*: a polka is a lively dance tune, originating in what is now the Czech Republic, and invented in commemoration of the Polish Uprising of 1830–31.

14. *gendarmes*: soldiers employed on police duties (French).

AMELIA B. EDWARDS

The North Mail

Amelia Ann Blanford Edwards (1831–92) was a novelist, poet, children's author, writer of short stories, translator from the French, an ardent supporter of women's suffrage and a well-respected expert on Egyptology. She was also a travel writer, producing the bestselling *A Thousand Miles Up the Nile* (1876) after a voyage along the river. Although she had written and published short stories from her teenage years, her first published book was the novel *My Brother's Wife* (1855). She often wrote stories for Dickens's *Household Words* and *All the Year Round*, especially for the Christmas editions. In addition to 'The North Mail', her other most celebrated piece of ghost fiction is *Monsieur Maurice* (1873), a 'novelette'.

'The North Mail' first appeared in *Miss Carew* (London: Hurst and

Blackett, 1865), vol. 2, pp. 197–230. That is the copy-text used here. The tale is often anthologized under the title 'The Phantom Coach'. For explanations of the occasional Scots words used within this story, please see the Glossary of Scots Words.

1. *the grouse season*: this traditionally lasts from 12 August (known as the 'Glorious Twelfth') to 10 December.

2. *Dwolding*: this appears to be a fictitious place name; however, there is a village named Wyke in west Yorkshire, south of Bradford, mentioned three lines later. The servant's accent and a later use of a Gaelic word by his master might suggest that the story is supposed to take place still further north.

3. *now't*: nothing (northern English).

4. *flitches*: sides of bacon.

5. *speculum*: in this instance, a glass or metallic mirror used as part of a reflecting telescope.

6. *optician*: formerly, someone who studied optics.

7. *galvanic battery*: an apparatus employed since the very beginning of the nineteenth century for the production of galvanic electricity (electricity from a chemical source), and often used for medical purposes. The name derives from the discoverer of the process, Luigi Galvani (1737–98). Galvani had famously investigated electrical processes in the body, using static electricity to stimulate (hence *galvanize*) dead frogs' legs. His nephew Giovanni Aldini (1762–1834) animated human corpses in the same way.

8. *Louis von Beethoven*: the German composer Ludwig van Beethoven (1770–1827). This French version of Beethoven's name was common in nineteenth-century France, and therefore, to a lesser extent, in Britain. The passage possibly alludes to the nineteenth-century pseudo-science of phrenology: that is, the belief originating in the writings of Franz Joseph Gall (1758–1828) and Johann Caspar Spurzheim (1776–1832) that the character and mental powers of a person have specific locations in the brain, the bones of the skull adapting to accommodate these areas. The popular version of this belief therefore involved the reading of character through attention to a person's physiognomy and bumps on the head. Beethoven was a favourite subject for such enquiries.

9. *Watts to Mesmer . . . the Magi and Mystics of the East*: Henry Watts (1815–84) was a notable Victorian chemist; his *A Dictionary of Chemistry and the Allied Branches of Other Sciences* had begun to be published in 1863. However, given that the action of the tale is set twenty years earlier (the story being published

in 1865), this identification is untenable. In that case, it might be that Watts is a slip for James Watt (1736–1819), the pioneer of the steam engine, and member of the Lunar Society, the Birmingham-based club for natural philosophers (for *natural philosophy*, see note 3 to 'No. 1 Branch Line: The Signal-man'). For Mesmer and Reichenbach, see notes 10 and 11 to 'The Haunted and the Haunters'; for Swedenborg, see note 6 to 'Green Tea'; for Plato, see note 18 to 'The Haunted and the Haunters'. The other names in the list are: Étienne Bonnot, Abbé de Condillac (1715–80), French philosopher particularly interested in sensation, and the origin and development of consciousness and language; René Descartes (1596–1650), French mathematician and philosopher concerned with scepticism; George Berkeley (1685–1753), Irish philosopher and bishop, whose idealist philosophy (partly prompted by the desire to counter the scepticism of Descartes and English philosopher John Locke) suggested that human beings can only know sensations and perceptions, and that therefore the world might be thought only to exist in the perceiving subject; Aristotle (384–322 BC), Greek philosopher. The Magi refers vaguely to the philosophers of the ancient Near East; the 'Mystics of the East' may refer to Indian or Chinese, Buddhist, Hindu or Taoist philosophers. The roll-call of great thinkers signals a move from science to pseudo-science, from electricity to philosophy, from the present to the past. All the thinkers mentioned are concerned with (and provide various answers to) questions concerning the nature of life, reality and consciousness. The first-named authors are particularly pertinent in relationship to ghosts, in so far as they all seem to have been fascinated by the vital principle of life. However, such specific interests become somewhat blurred as the names go on to become merely a list.

10. *usquebaugh*: a word (pronounced 'us-quee-bar') derived from the Scottish and Irish Gaelic term (*uisge/uisce beatha*) for 'water of life' or 'whisky'.

11. *recal*: by the 1860s an old-fashioned but nonetheless correct spelling for 'recall'.

CHARLES DICKENS

No. 1 Branch Line: The Signal-man

Charles John Huffam Dickens (1812–70) was, of course, one of the greatest and most successful Victorian novelists. He uses elements of the supernatural in a number of his novels and stories, most particularly in the inset narratives included in *The Pickwick Papers* (April 1836–November 1837) and in the Christmas books *A Christmas Carol* (1843) and *The Haunted Man* (1848). In addition he wrote a handful of short ghost stories other than 'No. 1 Branch Line: The Signal-man', notably 'To Be Read at Dusk' (1852) and 'To Be Taken With a Grain of Salt' (1865).

The copy-text of 'The Signal-man' is from its first publication in his own weekly journal *All the Year Round*, vol. 16, no. 400, pp. 20–25, in the Christmas edition of 1866. Although this once very popular magazine was by then already launched on its lingering decline, such Christmas editions were hugely successful, on occasion selling up to 300,000 copies. The story is printed in double columns. In the contents list and throughout the story, 'signalman' is so spelled, whereas in the heading it is hyphenated, 'signal-man'; the inconsistency has been retained in this edition. Under the general title 'Mugby Junction', the story is one of eight in that edition, of which four are by Dickens and one (the last) by Amelia B. Edwards. All the stories use Mugby Junction and the railway as a narrative focus.

1. *The Signal-man*: a man employed to signal to trains whether the line is clear; a word coined, and an occupation established, in this context, in the late 1830s and early 1840s (the OED gives the earliest usage as 1840).
2. *recal*: see note 11 to 'The North Mail'.
3. *natural philosophy*: like the old-fashioned spelling of 'recal' (see note 2 above), in the 1860s a slightly outmoded term, meaning the study of the natural sciences, or what was by then already more commonly named physics.
4. *perspective-glass*: a telescope; in another context, this could be a device that uses mirrors to produce a distorted visual effect.

SHERIDAN LE FANU

Green Tea

Joseph Thomas Sheridan Le Fanu (1814–73) was born in Dublin, a privileged member of the Anglo-Irish elite, and spent the greater part of his writing life in that city, where he made his name as a bestselling novelist, short-story writer, journalist and newspaper proprietor and editor. He studied at Trinity College, Dublin, and though he qualified as a barrister, he never practised the law. He began writing ghost stories in the 1840s, and over the next thirty years established himself as one of the greatest practitioners of the genre. Most of the best of his ghost stories were collected in two books: *Ghost Stories and Tales of Mystery* (1851) and *In a Glass Darkly* (see below). After his death, a number of uncollected stories appeared in *The Purcell Papers*, edited by the poet Alfred Perceval Graves (1880), *The Watcher and Other Weird Stories* (1894) and, most significantly, *Madam Crowl's Ghost and Other Tales of Mystery*, edited by M. R. James (1923). James's championing of Le Fanu led to a revival of interest in the author; he also remained a significant figure to Irish writers, notably W. B. Yeats, James Joyce and Elizabeth Bowen. In addition to his short stories, he wrote a number of novels, including a trio of mid-Victorian sensation masterpieces, blending realism and the supernatural: *The House by the Churchyard* (1861–3), *Wylder's Hand* (1864) and *Uncle Silas* (1864).

The copy-text of 'Green Tea' derives from *In a Glass Darkly* (London: R. Bentley & Son, 1872), vol. 1, pp. 3–95. This book, a classic of supernatural fiction, consists of three volumes, comprising five tales in total: 'Green Tea', 'The Familiar' and 'Mr Justice Harbottle' (vol. 1); 'The Room in the Dragon Volant' (vols. 2 and 3); and 'Carmilla' (vol. 3). 'Green Tea' first appeared in Dickens's *All the Year Round* (23 October–13 November 1869), Le Fanu benefiting from Dickens's interest in the genre both as writer and editor.

1.   *Professor Van Loo of Leyden*: the professor is, of course, a fictional character; Leiden, or Leyden, is a town in the Netherlands, famous for its university (founded in 1575), which was, from the seventeenth to the late eighteenth century the foremost institution in the world for the study of botany, theology, law, natural philosophy (see note 3 to 'No. 1 Branch Line: The Signalman') and, more pertinently, medicine.

2.   *the funds*: government bonds; a safe and secure investment.

3.   *Warwickshire*: a county in the north-west Midlands.

4.   *Kenlis*: there is no such village in Warwickshire; however, the name has Irish connections, being the old name for Kells in County Meath.

5.   *Dawlbridge*: this appears to be a fictional place.

6.   *Swedenborg's Arcana Cælestia ... pure vellum ... carmine edges*: Emanuel Swedenborg (né Swedberg, 1688–1772) was a Swedish philosopher and mystic. He died in London, and is buried in Shadwell. Originally a natural philosopher (for *natural philosophy*, see note 3 to 'No. 1 Branch Line: The Signal-man'), Swedenborg began writing his mystical works in the 1740s, after a period of hallucinatory or visionary experiences, in which he saw and conversed with God and angels. The meanings of these

visions were promulgated in a number of books. After his death, his beliefs were fostered by the New Church and other Sweden- borgian societies and communities; the poet and artist William Blake (1757–1827) was briefly an adherent of Swedenborgian- ism. Swedenborgian beliefs also feature strongly in Le Fanu's novel *Uncle Silas* (1864). The *Arcana Coelestia* ('Heavenly Secrets' or 'The Mysteries of Heaven') was originally published in Latin in eight volumes (1749–56). It sets out Swedenborg's version of Christianity through a series of numbered interpret- ations and responses to the biblical texts of Genesis and Exodus. The work was translated into English by clergyman John Clowes (1743–1831) in twelve volumes (1774–1806); a new translation appeared from 1857 to 1860. For *vellum*, see note 21 to 'The Haunted and the Haunters'; carmine refers to the crimson colour derived from cochineal (made from crushed beetles).

7. *'When man's interior . . . bodily sight'*: this quotation is a transla- tion of *Arcana*, 1619.

8. *'By the internal sight . . . and so on'*: this quotes *Arcana*, 994.

9. *'There are . . . evil spirits'*: this passage does not seem to refer to any particular paragraph from the *Arcana*, but expresses an idea found often in Swedenborg's writings.

10. *'With wicked genii . . . within it'*: a paraphrased translation of *Arcana*, 1760.

11. *'The evil spirits . . . their former state'*: a translation of *Arcana*, 5852. The quotation omits to translate the middle part of the paragraph, which asserts, among other things, that good spirits are also with man. In his book *Elegant Nightmares: The English Ghost Story from Le Fanu to Blackwood* (Athens, OH: Ohio University Press, 1978), Jack Sullivan correctly points out that Le Fanu's use of Swedenborg involves 'a distortion, or at least a darkening of the original' (p. 22).

12. *'If evil spirits . . . good of faith'*: these two paragraphs are from one paragraph in the *Arcana* – number 5863.

13. *'Nothing is more . . . destroy him'*: in his excellent notes to the Oxford World's Classics edition of *In a Glass Darkly* (1993), Robert Tracy suggests that the source for this quotation may not derive directly from the *Arcana*, though he finds a similar statement in *Arcana*, 292.

14. *'The delight of hell . . . eternal ruin'*: from *Arcana*, 5864. The quotation omits the first half of the sentence, which proclaims that the delight and bliss of heaven is to do good to human beings.

15. *'representatives' and 'correspondents'*: in Swedenborg's

philosophy, spirits are manifested to sight by 'representatives' (representations) or 'correspondents' (correspondences) which embody them, taking the form of natural objects.

16. *bestial forms*: there does not seem to be precisely such a paragraph in the *Arcana*. Swedenborg talks about beasts in *Arcana*, 3646, but there merely intends to show the distinction between beasts and men, in so far as only human beings have spiritual loves and ends, whereas beasts are confined to the earthly.

17. *Dr Harley ... practised in England*: possibly an allusion to Harley Street in London, the famous locale of the city's physicians; some critics have suggested that this could be instead a reference to the prominent Victorian physician Dr George Hartley (1829–1896), though the story's setting, around the year 1805, and the range of Hartley's interests (jaundice, histology – the science of organic tissues – and poisons) make this somewhat unlikely.

18. *hippish*: hypochondriacal, low in spirits.

19. *London season*: coinciding with the sittings of the Houses of Parliament, and the terms of colleges and law-courts, the period from just after Christmas to mid-June when balls and dinners were held and there were trips to the opera. At the close of the season, aristocrats and the well-to-do would retreat to the sea or to country estates.

20. *triste*: sad (French).

21. *portrait of Schalken's ... background of darkness*: Godfried (or Gottfried) Schalken (1643–1706) was a Dutch painter, known in particular for his portraits of people set in shadow and candlelight. The reference also alludes to Le Fanu's early story 'Strange Event in the Life of Schalken the Painter' (1839).

22. *Paganism ... nemesis sure*: it is not clear why the study of paganism need be fatal; clearly it involves close acquaintance with the pre-Christian past and that may threaten the clergyman's faith. Also possible is that the unity of religion, art and manners might refer to a freer attitude towards sex, perhaps including sex between men; *A Problem in Greek Ethics* (1883) by John Addington Symonds (1840–93), an early advocate of male homosexuality, was only fifteen years away.

23. *skance*: oblique, sidelong.

24. *affections*: physical afflictions, diseases.

25. *the 'paries'*: the wall of a hollow organ or cavity within the body.

26. *Shropshire ... the country near the Dee*: Shropshire is an English county on the border with Wales; the River Dee flows from Wales into England, and also forms part of that same border.

27. *delirium tremens . . . cerebral heart*: delirium tremens is an anach-
ronistic term (within the context of the story) meaning that
species of delirium produced by excessive alcohol consumption,
and characterized by trembling and delusions. The phrase was
coined in 1813 by Thomas Sutton (1767?–1835); he had studied
medicine, at London, Edinburgh and, in a link to Dr Van Loo,
Hesselius's correspondent, at Leiden. Sutton used the expression
when describing how the condition is rendered worse by bleeding
the patient, but improved by administering opium. Later writers
limited the term to refer to the effects of alcohol. 'Cerebral heart'
appears to refer back two paragraphs in the text to the idea that
the brain is the heart of a system of circulation of spiritual fluid.

HARRIET BEECHER STOWE

The Ghost in the Cap'n Brown House

Harriet Beecher Stowe (1811–96) was a bestselling novelist and a
humanitarian campaigner against slavery. She grew up in Connecticut,
and her New England background provides the setting for 'The Ghost
in the Cap'n Brown House'. Her father, Lyman Beecher, was himself
a committed opponent of slavery. He was also a Calvinist pastor while
she herself was subject to religious doubts, though late in life she
attended an Episcopalian church, and also became interested in spiritualism. In 1836, she married the biblical scholar Calvin Stowe. Her
novel *Uncle Tom's Cabin* (1851–2) was a publishing phenomenon,
and a work of vital importance in the fight for the abolition of slavery
in the USA; Abraham Lincoln is supposed to have greeted her as the
little lady who had begun this big war. The collection of tales in
Oldtown Fireside Stories (1871) follows on from her novel *Oldtown
Folks* (1869), apparently set in a fictional version of Natick, Massachusetts. The stories are supposed to be told by Sam Lawson to a listening
audience of children. Stowe's interest in spiritualism had its commercial aspects: while working on *Oldtown Folks*, she had contemplated
writing an article on the planchette, a form of ouija board, and there
is a suggestion that in that novel (and perhaps in the stories that
followed) she consciously targeted America's 'four & five million of
spiritualists' as a suitable market given the supernatural aspects of her
book (see Joan D. Hedrick, *Harriet Beecher Stowe: A Life* (Oxford:
Oxford University Press, 1994), p. 346).

The text of 'The Ghost in the Cap'n Brown House' used here is from
its first printed appearance, in Britain, in *Oldtown Fireside Stories*
(London: Sampson, Low, Marston, Low & Searle, 1871), pp. 201–28.

In 1872, the first American edition was published in Boston by J. R. Osgood. The contents page of the British edition gives the story's title as 'The Ghost in Capt'n Brown House'; the title page and heading of the story have 'The Ghost in the Cap'n Brown House'; while the running heading of the story has 'The Ghost in Cap'n Brown House'. The collection was also known and published as *Sam Lawson's Oldtown Fireside Stories*.

1. *Sam*: this is Sam Lawson, the narrator of this and other tales in the collection (which was also published under the title *Sam Lawson's Oldtown Fireside Stories* – see the biographical note above).
2. *Cotton Mather's 'Magnalia'*: Cotton Mather (1663–1728) was a New England Presbyterian divine, the author of *Magnalia Christi Americana* ('The Great Works of Christ in America'; 1702), a first-hand history of religious life in New England. It includes an account of the Salem witch trials of 1692–3, in which details of supernatural happenings are given.
3. *Charles River*: named after England's King Charles I, this river flows through eastern Massachusetts before entering the sea at Boston Harbor.
4. *Oldtown*: a fictional place, though partly derived from Harriet Beecher Stowe's husband's memories of Natick, Massachusetts. However, geographically, Oldtown does not fully resemble Natick, which is not built on the Charles River (see note 3 above), which in the story flows a little to the south of the town.
5. *massy*: mercy.
6. *Guinea*: a country in West Africa well known in the nineteenth century as a long-established centre for the slave trade. The story is set at some point before 1808, the year when Congress banned the importation of slaves to America (though the institution of slavery itself remained in force until 1865).
7. *crookneck-squashes*: an American variety of squash (gourd), the neck, or base, of which is bent backwards.
8. *John Bull*: the personification of Englishness, usually taken to mean someone hearty, stout, bluff, rough and no-nonsense.
9. *Sherburne . . . manty-makin'*: Like Natick, Sherburne is a town in Middlesex County, Massachusetts, on the Charles and Sudbury rivers; 'manty-making' means 'dressmaking'.
10. *her goose and her press-board*: a goose is an iron, named after the supposed resemblance of its handle to a goose's neck, and a press-board is an ironing-board.
11. *Ammonites, and Perresites, and Jebusites*: Ammonites and Jebusites are tribes mentioned in the Bible. The former are referred to

in Deuteronomy 23: 3, for instance: 'An Ammonite or Moabite shall not enter into the congregation of the Lord; even to their tenth generation shall they not enter into the congregation of the Lord for ever'; while the Jebusites are a Canaanite people listed in the table of nations (Genesis 10: 16). 'Ammonite', which may also evoke the extinct group of sea-animals often found in fossilized form, could be a misremembered version of 'Amorite', another Semitic tribe. Similarly, 'Perresites' is very likely a mistake for another biblical tribe, the Perizzites (Genesis 13: 7), though perhaps Stowe also intends a malapropism for 'Parisians', 'Persians' or even 'parasites'. In Exodus 3: 8, 'Amorites', 'Perizzites' and 'Jebusites' are mentioned together as possessors of Canaan, 'a land flowing with milk and honey', in the context of the Israelites escaping from Egyptian bondage. In the USA, this text was often adapted to express the hopes for freedom among African-American slaves.

12. *flip*: a hot drink consisting of beer and spirits and sweetened with sugar, sometimes also mixed with beaten egg.

13. *Needham and Sherburne*: Needham is another Massachusetts town, to the east of Natick, significantly closer to Boston. For Sherburne, see note 9 above.

14. *Sadducees*: members of a Jewish religious sect that flourished between the second century BC and the first century AD, who stressed the centrality of the written Law, and denied the supernatural elements of Judaism, such as the reality of angels, the immortality of the soul and the resurrection of the dead.

15. *Jamaiky*: Jamaican rum.

ROBERT LOUIS STEVENSON

Thrawn Janet

Robert Louis Stevenson (né Robert Lewis Balfour Stevenson, 1850–94) passed a childhood in Edinburgh, the town of his birth, confined by sickness and terrified by the hellfire imagination of his devoted nurse. He avoided following his father's profession of engineer (his father was famously responsible for great improvements in lighthouse building), and instead embarked, after a detour into the law, on a career as writer. He also rejected the harsher implications of his father's Protestant faith, though imaginatively he remained engaged with a vision of sin and moral duplicity. He was a regular contributor to the *Cornhill* (see below) and *London* magazines, as well as to *Temple Bar*, *Longman's Magazine* and *Unwin's Annual*. It was in these periodicals, and others, that his essays and short stories first appeared. Afflicted with tuberculosis, Stevenson was obliged to travel to warmer climates for his health; characteristically, this medical necessity was interwoven with his own taste for adventure. His short life came to an end in Valima, Samoa. Stevenson was an inspiring figure, the centre of a personality cult among writers of the 1880s and 1890s; an extravagant dandy and a celebrator of heroic exploits; a Romantic dreamer and psychological explorer; a dynamic fellow and a vulnerable invalid. The contradictions of his personality are mirrored in the themes of duality and ethical complexity that run through his fiction. His great works of the supernatural and fantastic include: 'The Body Snatcher' (1884); 'Olalla' (1885); 'Markheim' (1886); *The Strange Case of Dr Jekyll and Mr Hyde* (1886); and 'The Bottle Imp' and 'The Isle of Voices', collected in *Island Nights' Entertainments* (1893).

The copy-text of 'Thrawn Janet' comes from its first book publication in *The Merry Men and Other Tales and Fables* (London: Chatto & Windus, 1887), pp. 137–51. The volume contains a number of other supernatural fictions, including 'Will o' the Mill', 'Markheim' and 'Olalla'. The story originally appeared, under the signature 'R.L.S.', in Leslie Stephen's *Cornhill Magazine*, vol. 44 (October 1881), pp. 436–43. Stevenson wrote often for the *Cornhill*; many of his early essays for the magazine were collected in *Virginibus Puerisque* (1881) and *Familiar Studies of Men and Books* (1882) and his early supernatural story 'Will o' the Mill' had appeared there in January 1878. For explanations of the dialect words that abound in 'Thrawn Janet', please see the Glossary of Scots Words.

1. *Balweary . . . Dule*: Balweary is a fictional place, which Stevenson was to refer to again in his unfinished novel *The Weir of Hermiston* (1894). 'Dule' is a Scottish word meaning sorrow, grief; the 'weary' in 'Balweary' does similar work of setting a disconsolate mood.

2. *1st Peter, v and 8th . . . seventeenth of August*: a reference to the biblical text 1 Peter 5: 8: 'Be sober, be vigilant; because your adversary the devil, as a roaring lion, walketh about, seeking whom he may devour.' The date of the Reverend Soulis's darkest sermons, on the Sunday following 17 August, commemorates the date of the crisis of Stevenson's tale. It also possesses other significances. Regarding the liturgical calendar, 15 August is the date of the Assumption of Mary, though this is a date unlikely to be celebrated by the Scottish Protestants of the tale; nonetheless it is distinctly possible that there may be some parodic reference to

the raising (by hanging) of Janet, or to her ultimate disappearance by an act of God. However, more likely, Stevenson refers to the date's commemoration of 17 August 1560, when, led by the example of John Knox (1514–72), the Scottish parliament ratified the Scots Confession, a markedly Calvinist document, symbolizing the official break with the Roman Catholic Church. Less likely is that the date also commemorates 17 August 1643, when Scotland officially joined the Parliamentary side against Charles I, on condition that the English should effectively accept Presbyterianism.

3. *those hints that Hamlet deprecated*: a reference to William Shakespeare's *Hamlet*, I. v. 172–80:

> That you, at such times seeing me, never shall,
> With arms encumbered thus, or this head-shake,
> Or by pronouncing of some doubtful phrase,
> As 'Well, well, we know', or 'We could, an if we would',
> Or 'If we list to speak', or 'There be, an if they might',
> Or such an ambiguous giving out, to note
> That you know aught of me – this do swear,
> So grace and mercy at your most need help you.

Probably not coincidentally, these lines occur at the end of the scene where Hamlet has encountered his father's ghost, and in the same speech, where Hamlet tells his friend: 'There are more things in heaven and earth, Horatio, / Than are dreamt of in your philosophy' (ll. 166–7).

4. *moderates*: Presbyterian clergymen who, in opposition to the more traditionalist Evangelicals, held liberal views on doctrine and church discipline; the Moderates gained power in the Church of Scotland in 1712, when congregations lost the right to elect their pastors. The name continued to be applied until the mid nineteenth century.

5. *witch of Endor*: a seer consulted in secret by King Saul, who had fallen out of favour with God; at Saul's command, the woman calls up the ghost of the prophet Samuel so that the king can ask his advice, but the ghost merely predicts Saul's downfall (1 Samuel 28: 3–25).

6. *glebe*: piece of land.

7. *Law's Memorials: Memorials: or the Memorial Things That Fell Out Within the Island of Britain, Nov 1638 to 1684* (first published in 1818) is a work by a Presbyterian clergyman, Robert Law (d. c.1686), with much emphasis on the supernatural, the

demonic and the apparition of spectres. The Introduction by
Charles Kirkpatrick Sharpe (1781–1851) to the first edition of
that work provides a definitive history of Scottish witchcraft.

8. *Accuser of the Brethren*: a reference to Revelations 12: 10: 'And
I heard a loud voice saying in heaven, Now is come salvation,
and strength, and the kingdom of our God, and the power of his
Christ: for the accuser of our brethren is cast down, which
accused them before our God day and night.' The Hebrew word
'Satan' can mean either 'adversary' or 'accuser'.

9. *grogram*: a coarse material made from silk, mohair and wool
(from the French *gros grain*, 'coarse grain').

10. *change-house at Knockdow . . . Kilmackerlie*: a change-house
was an inn, where travellers could rest and change their horses.
While Kilmackerlie is a fictional place, Knockdow is a real Scottish town, in the western lowlands of Scotland, near the Isle of
Bute and Greenock, in the Firth of Clyde.

MARGARET OLIPHANT

The Open Door

Margaret Oliphant (née Wilson, 1828–98) was born at Wallyford,
Midlothian, and spent her childhood there and at Lasswade, Glasgow,
Everton and Birkenhead. This peripatetic upbringing was the result of
her father's haphazard career as a clerk. Margaret was educated by
her mother, also named Margaret Oliphant. Launched on a career as
a novelist, in 1852, young Margaret Wilson married her cousin Francis
Oliphant, a painter and a designer of stained glass. Within five years
of the wedding, she had endured the descent into alcoholism of her
brother, and the deaths of one of her five children, her beloved mother
and her husband. Although her literary career was highly successful,
she often struggled financially. She was a regular contributor to *Blackwood's Magazine*, a sympathetic biographer and a talented novelist –
as well as a prolific one, producing nearly one hundred novels (including several that she gave to her brother to be published under his
name). She was a Christian writer, with a taste for mysticism, and
a shrewd analyst of family relationships. Her supernatural fiction
represents some of the finest work she did, and some of the best stories
in the genre are hers: *A Beleaguered City* (1879) is a profoundly
moving short novel, and, among her short stories, 'The Land of Darkness', 'The Lady's Walk' and 'The Open Door' are outstanding. M. R.
James thought her the master of the 'religious ghost story' and
remarked of 'The Open Door' that it was one of the very few ghost

stories 'wherein the elements of beauty and pity dominate terror';
'there are moments of horror; but ... we end by saying with Hamlet:
"Alas, poor ghost!"' (from his article 'Ghosts – Treat Them Gently!'
in the *Evening News*, 17 April 1931).

'The Open Door' was first published in book form in *Two Stories
of the Seen and Unseen*, the other story being 'Old Lady Mary' (Edinburgh and London: William Blackwood and Sons, 1885), pp. 3–84.
This supplies the copy-text used here. The story had first appeared in
Blackwood's Magazine, vol. 131 (January 1882), pp. 1–30, just missing the traditional Christmas publication. Oliphant was a frequent
contributor of stories, essays and reviews to *Blackwood's*. For explanations of the dialect words used in the story, please see the Glossary
of Scots Words.

1. *Brentwood*: a fictional village, but in her edition of Oliphant's
    stories, *A Beleaguered City and Other Tales of the Seen and the
    Unseen* (Edinburgh: Canongate, 2000), Jenni Calder suggests
    that it is modelled on Lasswade, a village on the River North
    Esk, about nine miles south of the centre of Edinburgh, where
    Oliphant had lived for a time during her childhood.
2. *Simla*: the summer capital of the British Raj, a place for colonial
    bureaucrats and their families to escape from the heat of the
    plains. Now called Shimla, the town lies in the north-west Hima-
    layas, in the Indian state of Himachal Pradesh.
3. *no little Eton at Fettes*: Eton College is one of the oldest and
    most prestigious English public schools. With money left by
    Sir William Fettes (1750–1836), the independent school Fettes
    College, at Comely Bank, Edinburgh, in the town's northern
    suburbs, was opened in 1870. This dates the story as occurring
    before that year.
4. *Pentland Hills and the Firth*: a range of hills to the south and
    south-west of Edinburgh; the Firth of Forth is the estuary of the
    River Forth. The land in between is the old county of Midlothian,
    with the Pentland Hills running down its western side, and the
    city of Edinburgh and the Firth of Forth directly north.
5. *the Castle and the Calton Hill ... Arthur's Seat*: Edinburgh
    Castle dominates the city from the height of Castle Rock; Calton
    Hill lies in the centre of Edinburgh, to the east of the New Town,
    with the Dugald Stewart Monument, Nelson's Monument and
    the National Monument to the dead of the Napoleonic wars, all
    then prominently visible; Arthur's Seat is the highest peak in a
    group of hills in Holyrood Park, a wild and unbuilt-on place
    right in the centre of the city.

6.   *grimy with paper-making*: in the nineteenth century, industrial paper mills were common along the River North Esk.

7.   *accidenté*: uneven or broken ground (French).

8.   *'the offices'*: see note 4 to 'The Haunted and the Haunters'.

9.   *In this transitory life … Prayer-book … going to happen*: the 'Prayer-book' is the Book of Common Prayer; the passage may be referring generally to passages such as these words of the burial service: 'in the midst of life we are in death.' However, it is more likely that the narrator quotes directly the words of the prayer of intercession at the communion service: 'And we most humbly beseech thee of thy goodness, O Lord, to comfort and succour all them, who in this transitory life are in trouble, sorrow, need, sickness, or any other adversity.'

10. *brougham*: a closed, horse-drawn carriage, originally with two wheels but usually, by the end of the nineteenth century, with four.

11. *refracted sound*: the deflection, or bending, of sound waves as they enter a medium where their speed is changed; refraction in particular can bend sound waves downwards, contributing to and thereby amplifying the overall sound heard by the listener.

12. *phonetic disturbance*: a disturbance of speech but here referring to an auditory disturbance.

13. *mediums*: see note 9 to 'The Haunted and the Haunters'.

14. *fine as Burns … in no kirk*: the writings of the Scottish poet Robert Burns (1759–96) are marked by their compassion towards those who rarely receive it. Therefore this comment could allude to a number of poems, but, given the context, most likely it refers to the last stanza of 'Address to the Devil' (1786), in which the poet expresses the hope that the Devil himself might be saved if he could only feel sympathy for human beings.

15. *the 'Children's Record'*: there are a number of periodicals with similar titles, but the most likely to be meant here is *The Children's Record of the Free Church of Scotland*, a pious mid-Victorian publication, still appearing in the 1860s.

16. *ventriloquism*: the art of throwing one's voice so that it sounds as though it originates in another person or object; though the word (derived from Latin and meaning 'to speak from the stomach') dates from the late eighteenth century, the practice dates back to (at least as far as) the ancient Greeks, who called it gastromancy (from *gaster*, 'belly', and *manteia*, 'prophecy') and used it for divination in the belief that noises of the stomach were the voices of the dead and could be interpreted by the gastromancer to foretell the future. In the nineteenth

century, spurious ghosts were often found to be faked using ventriloquism.

17. *apostolical benediction*: the blessing given by the priest at the conclusion of a service.

18. *prodigal*: a reference to the Parable of the Prodigal Son, in Luke 15: 11–32.

RUDYARD KIPLING

At the End of the Passage

Rudyard Kipling (1865–1936) was born in Bombay. He left for England in 1871, where he was educated, and then in 1882 returned to India. Here he worked as a journalist and writer, achieving literary fame young. In 1889, he returned to London and three years later married an American, Carrie Balestier. They lived together first in Vermont, USA, and then in England, eventually settling in Sussex. Kipling is one of the greatest short-story writers in the English language, a memorable poet, and a writer of some marvellous children's books. His works include: *The Jungle Book* (1894), *The Second Jungle Book* (1895), *Stalky and Co.* (1899), *Kim* (1901), *Just So Stories* (1902), *Puck of Pook's Hill* (1906), *Rewards and Fairies* (1910) and his autobiography, *Something of Myself* (1937). Kipling wrote a number of excellent supernatural and uncanny tales, most notably 'The Mark of the Beast' (collected, along with 'At the End of the Passage', in *Life's Handicap* – see below) and 'They' (collected in *Traffics and Discoveries*, 1904). The following notes draw in part upon the Kipling Society's notes to the tale prepared by John McGivering and Dr Gillian Sheehan, and available online at www.kipling.org.uk.

The copy-text of 'At the End of the Passage' is based on its first book publication in *Life's Handicap: Being Stories of Mine Own People* (London and New York: Macmillan and Co., 1891), pp. 159–84. The story first appeared in the USA in the *Boston Herald* (20 July 1890) and in the United Kingdom in *Lippincott's Magazine* (August 1890).

1. *The sky is lead . . . Himalayan*: the opening poem is by Kipling.

2. *'life, liberty, and the pursuit of happiness'*: Kipling quotes the words of the American Declaration of Independence (1776).

3. *punkah*: a large swinging fan, suspended from the ceiling and operated manually, in this case by an unnamed servant, also known as a 'punkah-wallah' or 'punkah-coolie' (for *coolies*, see note 6 below).

4.   *apoplexy*: a seizure caused by an obstruction in or bursting of an artery, cutting off the supply of blood to the brain and leading to a loss of consciousness or the inability to move or speak.

5.   *Gaudhari State line*: a fictional place, but perhaps based on the district of Ajmere-Merwara, which lies 250 miles south-west of Delhi.

6.   *Indian Survey . . . coolies*: the Indian Survey was a government agency responsible for the mapping of India. The term 'coolie' – possibly derived from the Tamil word *kūli*, meaning to 'to hire' – was used by European colonists to refer to a native hired worker.

7.   *Pilsener*: a pale lager, originally from Pilzen in the Czech Republic. The OED records the earliest instances of its use in English as dating from the last quarter of the nineteenth century.

8.   *bumblepuppy*: originally a form of the game bagatelle played outdoors, it became an expression used for 'whist played unscientifically' (OED).

9.   *Gazette of India*: a newspaper published by the imperial government used for making official announcements.

10. *drag*: a four-horse coach.

11. *King's Peg . . . Heidsieck*: King's Peg is a mixture of brandy and champagne; Heidsieck is a brand of champagne.

12. *Rao of Jubela*: 'rao' is a title given to an Indian chief or prince; Jubela is a fictional Indian state.

13. *Pathan*: a Pashto-speaking inhabitant of the region where, at the time of this story, Afghanistan and India met.

14. *Chlorodyne, opium pill . . . nitre, bricks to the feet . . . burning-ghat*: Spurstow describes the usual course of cholera and its treatment: the drug cholorodyne, composed of chloroform, morphia and prussic acid, was used in the second half of the nineteenth century to induce sleep and to stop diarrhoea; opium would also act as a sedative and also apparently prevent diarrhoea; nitre means, in this instance, potassium nitrate, used as a diuretic; bricks were applied to the feet to warm the patient's extremities; a 'burning-ghat' is a funeral pyre, a place by a riverside where Hindus cremate their dead.

15. *Graphic*: a British illustrated magazine – edited at the time of Kipling's story by Edwin Locker – that printed pictures, articles and fiction. The *Graphic* serialized the work of some distinguished writers, including, in 1891, *Tess of the D'Urbervilles* by Thomas Hardy (1840–1928).

16. *Chucks*: the would-be genteel boatswain in the novel *Peter Simple* (1834) by Captain Frederick Marryat (1792–1848).

17. *babu*: originally a Hindu term of respect, equivalent to 'mister',

the word was in time applied by British colonists in a derogatory way to a Hindu, or especially Bengali, clerk who supposedly spoke an overly ornate, florid and mangled English.

18. *Job*: a reference to the central character in the Book of Job from the Bible; a good man condemned to extreme and unwarranted suffering.

19. *gold mohur on the rub*: the mohur was at that time the Indian coin with the highest value; a 'rub' is a rubber or series of card games.

20. *'Grasshopper's Polka' . . . prestissimo*: for *polka*, see note 13 to 'The Cold Embrace'; this particular polka was composed by Ernest Bucalossi (1859–1933). The term *prestissimo* is a musical direction meaning 'very quickly'.

21. *'Glory to thee . . . Or powers of darkness me molest'*: the text is a slightly misquoted version of the 'Evening Hymn' by Bishop Thomas Ken (1637–1711).

22. *cockchafer*: a large flying beetle, also known as a maybug, common in England and elsewhere in Europe.

23. *Well done, David!*: a reference to I Samuel 16: 23: 'And it came to pass, when the evil spirit from God was upon Saul, that David took an harp, and played with his hand: so Saul was refreshed, and was well, and the evil spirit departed from him.'

24. *the blessed Jorrocks . . . I sleeps*: Jorrocks is the Cockney grocer and Master of Foxhounds in novels by Robert Smith Surtees (1805–64). The quote is a reference to Chapter 7 of *Handley Cross* (1843): 'where the M. F. H. [Master of Foxhounds] dines he sleeps, and where the M. F. H. sleeps he breakfasts.'

25. *heat-apoplexy*: a late nineteenth-century medical term for sunstroke (for *apoplexy*, see note 4 above).

26. *spiking your guns*: rendering guns unusable, originally by forcing a spike into the touch-hole (the aperture in the breech of a gun through which the charge is ignited). This was a practice employed by artillery crews to prevent their weapons being used by the enemy in the event of their being captured. Applied metaphorically, the phrase means to frustrate someone's plans or stop someone doing something.

27. *twelve-bore rifle, an express, and a revolver*: a twelve-bore gun would be a large shotgun, firing a bullet weighing just over an ounce (about 40g); an Express is a quick-firing hunting rifle; a revolver is a pistol in which the bullets are contained in a revolving cylinder.

28. *nipples . . . lever*: attached to the breech, or back of the gun behind the bore, the nipple is a small, perforated piece of metal

on which the percussion cap ignites; the lever is the part of a gun by which the barrel of a breech-loader opens.

29. *doll-head bolt*: a doll's head in a rifle (not usually in a revolver – see note 27 above) is 'a top extension fitting into the mortice in the top of the standing-breech' (*OED*).

30. *rowelled*: to 'rowel' is to press the spiked star-shaped wheel at the extremity of a spur against the flesh (usually of a horse), on occasion (and certainly here) breaking the skin; in his novel *The Light That Failed* (1891), Kipling writes: 'He was rummaging through his new campaign-kit and rowelling his hands with the spurs.'

31. *A blind face*: an allusion to stanza 7 of Kipling's poem 'La Nuit Blanche' (a French expression meaning a 'sleepless night'), a poem which first appeared under the title 'Natural Phenomena' in the *Civil and Military Gazette* (7 June 1887):

> Then a Face came, blind and weeping,
>   And It couldn't wipe its eyes
> And It muttered I was keeping
>   Back the moonlight from the skies;
> So I patted it for pity,
>   But it whistled shrill with wrath,
> And a huge black Devil City
>   Poured its peoples on my path.

32. *the Rains*: the Monsoon season of heavy rains following the heat of April and May, typically beginning in early June.

33. *Simla*: see note 2 to 'The Open Door'.

34. *My great Scott!*: an exclamation of astonishment, supposed originally to refer to the popular American general Winfield Scott (1786–1866), a national hero in the USA after his successful campaign in the Mexican–American War (1846–8).

35. *Sahib*: a term of respect used by Indians when addressing a British colonist or European; the word originally derives from the Arabic for 'friend'.

36. *Kodak camera*: the brand name for this well-known make of camera was coined by the American George Eastman (1854–1932) and registered as a trademark in 1888. Eastman Dry Plate Company (from 1892, the Eastman Kodak Company) produced the first cameras manufactured for non-expert use; very soon the word 'Kodak' became synonymous with 'camera'.

37. *'There may be Heaven ... We-ell?'*: the last two lines of 'Time's Revenges', a poem by Robert Browning (1812–89) first collected

in *Dramatic Romances and Lyrics* (1845), seventh volume in the series 'Bells and Pomegranates'. Kipling has slightly (and in the case of the last word very likely deliberately) misquoted: 'There may be heaven; there must be hell; / Meantime, there is our earth here – well!'

LAFCADIO HEARN

Nightmare-Touch

Patrick Lafcadio Hearn (1850–1904) was a journalist, translator, and writer of stories. His life was incorrigibly Bohemian, endlessly adventurous. Born of an Irish father and Greek mother in the Ionian Islands, he moved to Dublin at the age of six. Educated in Yorkshire, he slipped off, as soon as he could, for Paris. From there, he went to America, roughed it in New York and finally went to pick up a small annuity in Cincinnati. He established his career in journalism through a taste for the macabre and dangerous (his first notable article was the detailed description of a half-burnt murder victim). After some years in disreputable New Orleans, he wrote books of reportage on a tidal wave in the Gulf of Mississippi and on life in the West Indies. The messiness of his life makes an odd contrast with the polished precision of his writing. In 1890, he finally found his true subject when he went to Japan, initially as a newspaper correspondent. He stayed there for the rest of his life, marrying a Japanese woman from a Samurai family, having four children, becoming a Japanese citizen (with the name Koizumi Yakumo) and holding down a job as Chair of English Literature at Tokyo University. A number of his Japanese stories have supernatural themes; before he left for Japan, he had already published a volume of Chinese ghost stories. 'Nightmare-Touch' occupies a mysterious ground, somewhere between essay, memoir and short story.

The copy-text of the story comes from its first book publication in *Shadowings* (London: Sampson, Low, Marston & Co., 1900), pp. 235–46, where it is included in a section entitled 'Fantasies'. There are a number of other uncanny tales in the book, including 'The Corpse-Rider'.

1. *Orfila's Traité des Exhumés*: a reference to *Traité des Exhumations juridiques et considérations sur les changemens physiques que les cadavres éprouvent en se pourrisant* ('Treatise on Judicial Exhumations and Thoughts on the Physical Changes that Corpses Experience in Decomposing'; 1831) by Mathieu Orfila (1787–1853), a typically macabre choice of reading for Hearn.

Born in Spain, Orfila was the founder of toxicology and a pioneer of forensic science.

2. *anamorphosis*: in art, a distorted or deformed image that is designed to become clear either when viewed from a particular angle or by using a mirror.

3. *transom*: in American English, a fanlight window above the lintel of a door.

W. W. JACOBS

The Monkey's Paw

William Waymark Jacobs (1863–1943) was a Londoner, growing up by the docks in Wapping in a state of teetering respectability; his father was manager of the South Devon wharf, with a wavering income and a large family to support. Educated at private school and then at Birkbeck College, he became a clerk in the civil service – a position he retained until 1899, when he gave up his job to become a full-time writer. He began writing in the mid 1880s, and went on to achieve success and popularity, particularly in the period from the late 1890s until the outbreak of the First World War. He specialized in comic tales, stories of sailors, and supernatural fictions. 'The Monkey's Paw' is by far the best known of all his tales, and has become the basis for a stage play (by L. N. (Louis Napoleon) Parker, Jacobs's sometime collaborator), several films, radio plays, television adaptations and an opera.

The copy-text of 'The Monkey's Paw' derives from its first book publication in the short-story collection *The Lady of the Barge* (London and New York: Harper & Brothers, 1902), pp. 29–53. The book contains several other supernatural masterpieces, including 'The Well' and 'In the Library'. 'The Monkey's Paw' had first appeared earlier that year in *Harper's New Monthly Magazine*, vol. 105, no. 627 (September 1902), pp. 634–9. Both in the magazine version and book form, the story contains one illustration by Maurice William Greiffenhagen (1862–1931), with the caption ' "What's that?" cried the woman', and showing the startled old couple in their bedroom. The book features other illustrations by Greiffenhagen and also by J. F. Sullivan (1852–1936).

1. *fakirs*: a fakir is strictly a beggar, from the Arab word for a poor man, but the word was applied more specifically to, first, Muslim and then later also Hindu mendicants and ascetics.

2. *the Arabian Nights*: the collection of fables, folk tales, comic and fantastic stories also known as *The Book of One Thousand and*

One Nights. As in other folk tales, the theme of wishing appears often in this collection. However, the choice of *The Arabian Nights* rather than the collections of fairy tales by the Brothers Grimm or Charles Perrault alludes to the fact that the paw comes from the East, a mysterious place of magic, where desire turns out to be an entrapment.

3. *bibulous*: originally the word meant 'absorbent of moisture', then by extension came to mean 'addicted to drink', though without the harsher overtones of 'alcoholic'.

MARY WILKINS FREEMAN
The Wind in the Rose-Bush

Mary Eleanor Wilkins (1852–1930) was born in Randolph, Massachusetts, the daughter of a carpenter and (later) a small shopkeeper in Brattleboro, Vermont. In 1883, following the death of her parents, she returned to Massachusetts. She lived there until her marriage to Dr Charles M. Freeman in 1902, when she moved to New Jersey. The marriage appears to have been an unhappy one. Her writings focus on New England rural life, its meanness, constrictions and repressions. Although she wrote several novels, her talent was for brevity. Her first two story collections were also perhaps her finest – *A Humble Romance* (1887) and *A New England Nun* (1891) – though there is much that is good in a late work such as *Edgewater People* (1918).

The copy-text of 'The Wind in the Rose-Bush' comes from its first publication in *The Wind in the Rose-Bush, and Other Stories of the Supernatural* (New York: Doubleday, Page & Co., 1903), pp. 3–37. The volume contains eight illustrations by Peter Sheaf Hersey Newell (1862–1924), the celebrated turn-of-the-century children's book illustrator. The illustration that accompanies 'The Wind in the Rose-Bush' has the caption ' "What makes that rose-bush blow so when there isn't any wind?" ' and forms the frontispiece to the volume. The book itself is a classic collection of ghost stories, including the notable vampire tale 'Luella Miller'.

1. *Porter's Falls*: despite Mary Wilkins Freeman's reputation as a storyteller of New England, the only actual Porters Falls is in West Virginia; however, as there is no Ford Village in the vicinity, a fictional setting is equally likely. However, see note 7 below.

2. *froward*: perverse, unreasonable, hard to please.

3. *dormer windows ... piazzaless*: a dormer window forms an extension from the sloping roof of a house, with the glass for

the window set vertically within it; a piazza, in this context, is a veranda or porch, as so named in New England.

4.   *hydrangeas and cannas*: respectively, a shrub native to America and a lily-like tropical American plant with large, attractive leaves and bright flowers.

5.   *Brussels carpets*: carpets with a linen backing and a woollen upper surface.

6.   *duds*: clothes.

7.   *Lincoln*: there is indeed a town named Lincoln in West Virginia, at some distance from Porters Falls, being around 160 miles away.

8.   *'The Maiden's Prayer'*: a short piece for piano by Tekla Bdarzew-ska-Baranowska (1834–61), an appropriately short-lived Polish composer who wrote the piece when she was only twenty-two years old. 'The Maiden's Prayer' was one of the bestselling piano pieces of the nineteenth century.

9.   *cupola*: picking up the Italianate resonances of 'piazza' (see note 3 above), a cupola is a domed roof.

M. R. JAMES

'Oh, Whistle, and I'll Come to You, My Lad'

Montague Rhodes James (1862–1936) was a highly talented palaeographer, an important medievalist (or, as he put it, 'Christian archaeologist'), a solid biblical scholar, a prodigious archivist and antiquarian, a prolific bibliographer, a capable editor, a distinguished Provost of King's College, Cambridge, and of Eton College, and, incidentally, the greatest of all ghost-story writers. He is unique in this volume in being the only writer represented who was not a professional author. As a result, perhaps, he published only thirty or so stories, elegant and endlessly intriguing tales. These were collected in *Ghost Stories of an Antiquary* (see below), *More Ghost Stories of an Antiquary* (1911), *A Thin Ghost and Other Stories* (1919), *A Warning to the Curious* (1925) and *Collected Ghost Stories* (1931). Three other stories were published in periodicals after 1931. Many of the stories in the first two collections (including ' "Oh, Whistle . . ." ') were written for the yearly Christmas celebrations at King's College, Cambridge, where James was a don; he was apparently a brilliant and theatrical reader of his own work. He also translated the fairy stories of Hans Christian Andersen (1930) and wrote a fantasy children's book, *The Five Jars* (1922).

The text of ' "Oh, Whistle . . ." ' is based on its first publication, in *Ghost Stories of an Antiquary* (London: Edward Arnold, 1904), pp. 183–225, where it is the seventh story out of the eight collected in the volume. The story was very likely first read out loud during the Christmas 1903 festivities at King's. The published volume itself came out in time for Christmas 1904, priced at six shillings (the typical, and relatively expensive, price for a single volume in the Edwardian period). On the title page, the author's name is given as 'Montague Rhodes James, Litt.D., Fellow of King's College, Cambridge'; like the title of the volume, this assertion of James's official and academic life strikes the same erudite tone as the stories themselves. The volume is illustrated by James McBryde (1874–1904), a close friend of the author who had recently and unexpectedly died. Two of his four illustrations belong to the present story: one shows the dream figure of the hunted man sprawling by a groyne, and is captioned 'Looking up in an attitude of painful anxiety'; the other depicts the confrontation of the Professor with the figure of the bed-clothes, and carries the caption 'He leapt towards him upon the instant'. The Professor in the latter illustration, at odds with the text, appears as an elderly man, though perhaps his terror has aged him. (The other two illustrations are for 'Canon Alberic's Scrap-Book'.)

1. *'Oh, Whistle, and I'll Come to You, My Lad'*: The title and refrain of a poem by Robert Burns (1759–96), in which a young woman sings of her fidelity to her secret lover. The poem was likewise quoted in Chapter 9 of *Redgauntlet* (1824), the novel by Sir Walter Scott (1771–32) and the source for one of the best and most influential nineteenth-century ghost stories, 'Wandering Willie's Tale'.

2. *Professor of Ontography . . . St James's College*: the word 'ontography' – literally, 'writing about being' or the description of things as they are – was coined in 1902 by the American geographer William Morris Davis (1850–1934) to refer to that part of geography which describes the human response to the natural environment. The Professor's college is fictitious; however, given the author's name the use of St James is intriguing.

3. *East Coast – in point of fact to Burnstow*: the East Coast might mean either Norfolk or Suffolk, the 'East Anglian' counties famous for the flatness of their landscape, and the width of their beaches at low tide. Although Burnstow is a fictional village, in his introduction to *The Collected Ghost Stories* (1931), M. R. James himself identified it with Felixstowe, Suffolk, a popular Victorian seaside resort that the author had visited in 1893 and 1897–8.

4. *Templars' preceptory*: the Knights Templar (the 'Poor Knights of Christ and the Temple of Solomon') were a military and religious order founded in 1118 and suppressed by Pope Clement in 1312. They were particularly associated with the Crusades and with the protection of pilgrims to Jerusalem. Templar buildings and communities were spread all over Europe and the Middle East. Due to rumours of secret initation rites and to the blackening of their name at the time of the order's dissolution, the Templars were sometimes seen as blasphemous or occultist. This reputation led to a prolonged interest in them that acquired new force with the foundation of freemasonry and, later, among turn-of-the-century occult writers. A preceptory was a name given to a subordinate Templar community, or otherwise to the buildings inhabited by the community.

5. *the Long*: the summer vacation traditionally taken by law-courts and Cambridge and Oxford universities.

6. *a double-bedded one*: now this would be a room with a single double-bed, but in the early 1900s the phrase could also mean, as here, a room with two single beds.

7. *'Dombey and Son'*: Dr Blimber is the headmaster of Dotheboys Hall, the Brighton school where young Paul Dombey is sent in Charles Dickens's *Dombey and Son* (1846–8). Blimber's academy is famous for forcing its pupils to take in what they are not yet able to learn. Parkins's ignorance of Dickens might be taken as one of the indications that he is 'destitute . . . of the sense of humour'. As Rogers misquotes Dr Blimber, it proves hard to locate the original quote. However, there is a scene in Chapter 12 of *Dombey and Son* in which Blimber grabs the attention of his pupils so peremptorily while they are eating that one of them nearly chokes on his drink.

8. *apple-pie order*: perfect neatness.

9. *ancien militaire*: old soldier (French).

10. *inclinations towards a picturesque ritual . . . deference to East Anglian tradition*: the Vicar would appear to have Anglo-Catholic or 'High Church' leanings: that is, he conducts services that retain some of the rituals and doctrines associated with Roman Catholicism. Traditionally, East Anglia was a stronghold of Dissenting and 'Low Church' beliefs; these are clearly shared by the Colonel. They were also, in a modified and more urbane form, shared by M. R. James himself; his father had been an Evangelical clergyman with a living in Great Livermere, Suffolk.

11. *incarnadined*: reddened.

12. *Disney*: the Disney Professorship of Archaeology was estab-

lished by John Disney, an English barrister and antiquarian, in 1851.

13. *circular form*: the Templars (see note 4 above) used round buildings in imitation of the Church of the Holy Sepulchre in Jerusalem, said to be built on the site of both the crucifixion and the resurrection of Christ.

14. *ferae naturae*: wild in nature (Latin).

15. *martello tower . . . black wooden groynings*: a Martello tower is a circular tower first established in the Napoleonic Wars for use in coastal defence and named after a tower of this construction at Mortella Point in Corsica. There are several Martello towers at Felixstowe, as elsewhere along the East Anglian coast. A groyning, or 'groyne', is a wall that extends from the beach into the water and acts as a barrier against the sea, controlling erosion.

16. *'Now I saw in my dream . . . to meet him'*: a reference to the Puritan classic *The Pilgrim's Progress* (1678) by John Bunyan (1628–88). In the scene referred to, the Pilgrim confronts Apollyon, the Destroyer, angel of the bottomless pit. M. R. James misquotes the passage, which should read: 'But now, in this Valley of Humiliation, poor *Christian* was hard put to it; for he had gone but a little way before he espied a foul *Fiend* coming over the field to meet him; his name is *Apollyon*.'

17. *boots*: a servant employed in hotels to clean the guests' shoes.

18. *the writing on the wall to Belshazzar*: Daniel 5: 1–4 describes the feast held by Belshazzar, King of Babylon, who sees a hand writing a message on the wall in front of him. Only Daniel can interpret the message, which prophesies the destruction of Belshazzar's kingdom.

19. *fur . . . venit*: this is a much-disputed message. The opening words might be read as 'furbis, flabis, flebis', though opinions differ on the order in which they should be set. 'Furbis' is either cod Latin for 'you will steal' (from 'fur' for *furis*, meaning 'thief') or proper Latin for 'you will be mad' (from *furere*); 'flabis' means 'you will blow' (as in *flatus*, 'blowing', 'breathing', *flabellum*, 'a small fan', or *flabilis*, 'airy'); and 'flebis' means 'you will be sorry' (as in *flere*, to 'weep for', 'bewail', 'lament'). These words could also be read as 'fur, flabis, flebis'. In his annotations to M. R. James's *Casting the Runes and Other Ghost Stories* (Oxford: Oxford University Press, 1987), Michael Cox remarks: 'H. E. Luxmore, MRJ's former Eton tutor, recorded hearing [M. R. James saying] what he called "Fur Flebis" (i.e. " 'Oh, Whistle' ") . . . That would strongly suggest this second reading of the phrase is the correct one. That would render the phrase as "Thief,

you'll blow, you'll be sorry".' The second Latin phrase Parkins translates for himself. The swastikas on either side of the words bear, of course, no direct relationship to their subsequent use by the German Nazi Party. In the later nineteenth century in Britain, there was renewed interest in the symbol. This was partly as a result of finding swastikas during archaeological excavation of early human settlements in Europe, and partly owing to imperial contact with Indian cultures, where the swastika remained a religious symbol for Hindus, Buddhists and Jains. It therefore represented a point of cultural connection between pre-Christian Europe and modern India. At its simplest, its use in India designated good luck, and it was in this spirit that in the early twentieth century Rudyard Kipling used the symbol to adorn his books.

20. *Experto crede*: I have experienced this, so believe me, I know (Latin).

21. *like some great bourdon in a minster tower*: in this context, a bourdon is the lowest bell in a peal of bells, here heard ringing from the tower of a collegiate or cathedral church. I have been unable to find any English poem that contains this or a strikingly similar phrase.

22. *little better than a Sadducee*: see note 14 to 'The Ghost in the Cap'n Brown House'. The inclusion of this reference in more than one tale suggests the importance, in some ghost stories of the period, placed upon embarrassment of the religious sceptic.

23. *Sadducees . . . Old Testament*: there is indeed no mention of the Sadducees (see note 22 above) in the Old Testament.

24. *cleek*: an iron-headed golf club.

25. *enormities of the Vicar . . . Feast of St Thomas the Apostle*: this saint's day now takes place on 3 July; however, in the early twentieth century it was celebrated, as here, on 21 December (often the shortest day of the year). (The Episcopalian Church still marks the saint's day on that date.) It clearly fits Parkins's scepticism that St Thomas should be the doubting disciple. Celebrating this day is an 'enormity', in the view of the Colonel, as Low Church Christians or Evangelicals would have regarded the recognition of saints' days as Papist, that is, Roman Catholic.

26. *wive*: i.e. wave; the boy's accent would seem more cockney than East Anglian. For those who see the story as exploring Parkins's repressed sexuality, this error of pronunciation is clearly a significant one. James often uses a Suffolk or cockney accent in his tales; he was a talented mimic – his friend Gwendolyn McBryde remarked that he would 'sometimes personate some countryman

or cockney' (quoted in Julia Briggs, *Night Visitors* (London: Faber & Faber, 1977), p. 127).

27. *sixpence . . . shilling*: a shilling consisted of twelve pence. The Colonel is surprised into being more generous than he at first intended.

28. *railway-rug*: a blanket or rug for keeping railway passengers warm. Parkins has after all been travelling by train in December.

29. *delirium tremens*: see note 27 to 'Green Tea'.

30. *surplice*: a loose gown of white linen worn by clerics and choristers during church services; the garment was frowned on by some Puritans, Evangelicals and Low Church Christians, and serves perhaps, therefore, as a vague reminder of the Colonel's distaste for High Church paraphernalia.

AMBROSE BIERCE

The Moonlit Road

Ambrose Gwinnett Bierce (1842–1914?) was an American journalist and short-story writer. He was born in a log cabin in Horse Cave Creek, Ohio, and fought in the American Civil War on the side of the Union, rising to the rank of major in the cavalry. With the end of the war in 1865, Bierce moved to San Francisco where he soon established himself, with Bret Harte, Mark Twain and Joaquin Miller, as a leading member of a new Western literary elite. Following his marriage to Mary Day, he moved to England, where he lived from 1872 to 1876. His failure to achieve there the level of success he had enjoyed in California prompted his return to the USA. He was a brilliant journalist, who nevertheless rather looked down on the profession. Bierce was an infamously mordant and cynical writer: his nickname was 'Bitter Bierce'. A disillusioned irony informs his best work; he himself thought of it, in fun, as devilish: Satan was his supposed collaborator on *The Fiend's Delight* (1872). His other most notable works are: the macabre and dark short stories contained in *Tales of Soldiers and Civilians* (1891); *The Monk and the Hangman's Daughter* (1892), a full-length romance translated from German; a collection of uncanny tales, *Can Such Things Be?* (1893 – see below); and *The Cynic's Word Book* (1906), republished as *The Devil's Dictionary* (1911), a compendium of sourly sarcastic definitions. The date and manner of Bierce's death remains unknown, as, in 1913, motivated by weariness with his own life, he departed for Mexico, in the middle of its own civil war, where he vanished, very likely finding the 'euthanasia' or happy death that he sought there.

The copy-text of 'The Moonlit Road' derives from *Can Such Things Be?*, vol. 3 of *The Collected Works of Ambrose Bierce* (New York and Washington: Neale Publishing Company, 1910), pp. 62–80. An earlier version of *Can Such Things Be?* had appeared in 1893, as a book of twenty-five tales, containing such classics as 'The Death of Halpin Frayser' and ' "The Isle of Pines" '. When the book was reissued in the *Collected Works*, a number of stories were cut, and many more, including 'The Moonlit Road' (which had first appeared in an edition of *Cosmopolitan* in January 1907), added. The *Collected Works* were published in twelve volumes between 1909 and 1912, and as an economic venture were a failure, apparently helping to bankrupt the publishers.

1. *Yale*: with Harvard and William and Mary, one of the three oldest universities in the USA; founded in the 1640s and located, far from Nashville, in the north-east of the United States at New Haven, Connecticut.

2. *Youth is Gilead, in which is balm for every wound*: in Genesis 37: 25, when Joseph's brothers conspire against him, they sell him to Ishmaelites 'bearing spicery and balm and myrrh' from Gilead (the mountainous region east of the River Jordan). Proverbially this balm, a resinous gum, also known as 'balsam of Mecca', has powerful healing properties: 'Is there no balm in Gilead; is there no physician there? why then is not the health of the daughter of my people recovered?' (Jeremiah 8: 22); 'Go up into Gilead, and take balm, O virgin, the daughter of Egypt: in vain shalt thou use many medicines; for thou shalt not be cured' (Jeremiah 46: 11). The African-American spiritual 'There is a Balm in Gilead' talks of the balm (taking it as a form of the redemption offered by Jesus) as something that will make the wounded whole. The balm is also referred to in Edgar Allan Poe's poem 'The Raven' (1845) – 'Is there – is there balm in Gilead? – tell me – tell me, I implore' (line 89) – and in Chapter 12 of Mark Twain's *The Adventures of Tom Sawyer* (1876).

3. *katydids*: small green insects of the family Tettigonniidae, related to the cricket. The sound produced by the males of the genus *Pterophylla* ('winged leaf') is supposed to resemble the reiterated phrase 'Katy did, Katy didn't'.

4. *Caspar Grattan*: it might be that the name 'Caspar' is an allusion to Caspar Hauser (died 1833), a young man discovered wandering in Nuremburg in 1828, after having been supposedly kept in a locked room in solitary confinement for the first eighteen years of his life. 'Caspar Grattan's' sense of disassociation regard-

ing his identity, and the feeling that he has entered life as a full-grown adult may be meant to evoke Caspar Hauser's predicament. The Hauser story was again current in the 1890s following the publication of Elizabeth Evans's *The Story of Kaspar Hauser from Authentic Records* (1892), the Duchess of Cleveland's *The True Story of Kaspar Hauser from Official Documents* (1893) and Andrew Lang's *The True Story Book* (1893). 'Grattan' might suggest reference to a number of Irish writers and politicians.

5. *potter's field*: place of burial for unknown or indigent people.

6. *Remote, unfriended, melancholy, slow*: the opening line of the poem *The Traveller, or a Prospect of Society* (1764) by Oliver Goldsmith (1730?–74).

7. *via dolorosa*: 'way of sorrow' (Latin); the route supposed to have been taken by Jesus Christ as he went from Pilate's judgement hall to Calvary, the place of crucifixion.

8. *'the captain of my soul'*: this quotes the last line of a poem, 'Invictus' ('Unconquered' in Latin), by William Ernest Henley (1849–1903): 'I am the master of my fate: / I am captain of my soul.'

9. *the medium Bayrolles*: this character turns up in another story by Bierce, 'An Inhabitant of Carcosa' (collected, along with 'The Moonlit Road', in *Can Such Things Be?*, 1910). In a footnote at its close, this tale is revealed as having been communicated by the spirit Hoseib Alar Robardin to the medium Bayrolles. The story went on to influence Howard Phillips Lovecraft (1890–1937) in his creation of the 'Cthullu Mythos', a fictional cycle in which inhabitants of modern New England glimpse or come into contact with the remnants of an ancient and malevolent civilization. Bayrolles might be a pun on the French word *paroles*, meaning 'words' (see also the Introduction, pp. xxxi–xxxiii). For *medium*, see note 9 to 'The Haunted and the Haunters'.

10. *Valley of the Shadow*: an allusion to Psalm 23: 4: 'Yea, though I walk through the valley of the shadow of death, I will fear no evil.'

HENRY JAMES

The Jolly Corner

Henry James (1843–1916) was born in New York and educated there, as well as in London, Paris, Geneva and Harvard. From 1875, after two long prior visits to Europe, he became an expatriate, living for a year in Paris, for over twenty years in London, and from 1898 in Rye, in Sussex. He also spent significant periods of his life in Italy. He was naturalized as a British subject in 1915. Henry James devoted his life to literature. He was (in his own words) an 'unsaleable' author, and yet also one of the most significant novelists, critics and short-story writers of the late nineteenth and early twentieth centuries. Among his greatest novels are *The Portrait of a Lady* (1881), *The Bostonians* (1886), *What Maisie Knew* (1897) and *The Wings of the Dove* (1902). His many volumes of short stories include: *The Lesson of the Master* (1892), *The Real Thing* (1893), *Terminations* (1895), *The Soft Side* (1900) and *The Better Sort* (1903). James wrote some of the finest ever ghost stories, most notably his classic short novel *The Turn of the Screw* (first serialized in *Collier's Weekly*, 1898, and published in book form in *The Two Magics* that same year).

'The Jolly Corner' was first published in the first number of the *English Review* (December 1908). It was placed in very distinguished company, between a poem by Thomas Hardy ('A Sunday Morning Tragedy') and a short memoir ('Some Reminiscences') by Joseph Conrad. The copy-text used here is based on its first book publication in *The Altar of the Dead, The Beast in the Jungle, The Birthplace and Other Tales*, vol. 17 of the *New York Edition* (London: Macmillan and Co., 1909), pp. 435–85. 'The Jolly Corner' is the ninth of ten tales, coming directly after a sequence of other classic stories of the supernatural: 'Owen Wingrave', 'The Friends of the Friends', 'Sir Edmund Orme' and 'The Real Right Thing'.

1.   *Irving Place*: a Manhattan street, running from East 14th Street northwards to Gramercy Park, east of Union Square and Park Avenue South.

2.   *the inventor of the sky-scraper*: the first skyscraper, the Home Insurance Building in Chicago (constructed 1884–5), was designed by William Le Baron Jenney (1832–1907). He used a load-bearing steel frame to carry the weight of the building. The term 'sky-scraper' had been in use since the late eighteenth century to mean the uppermost sail in a sailing ship; over the next hundred years, the phrase was adopted for high-standing horses, tall men, tall hats, high-hit balls in baseball games, and tall stories. In his book *The American Scene* (London: Chapman & Hall, 1907), written on a return journey to the USA undertaken from August 1904 to July 1905, James had written (on p. 77) with fascination and dismay about what then seemed the specifically American phenomenon of the skyscraper:

Crowned not only with no history, but with no credible possibility of time for history, and consecrated by no uses save the commercial at any cost, they are simply the most piercing notes in that concert of the expensively provisional into which your supreme sense of New York resolves itself. They never begin to speak to you, in the manner of the builded majesties of the world as we have heretofore known such – towers or temples or fortresses or palaces – with the authority of things of permanence or even of things of long duration. One story is good only till another is told, and sky-scrapers are the last word of economic ingenuity only till another word be written.

He was speaking particularly of the area south of 23rd Street, which is precisely the locale of Spencer Brydon's New York.

3. *Mrs Muldoon's broomstick*: as her accent later makes clear, Mrs Muldoon is Irish. Following the large-scale emigration from Ireland to America from the 1840s onwards, precipitated in great part by the Irish Famine, the Irish housekeeper and female servant was a cliché of New York life and a staple figure in later nineteenth- and early twentieth-century literature.

4. *pour deux sous*: for two cents (French), or, in former French currency, ten centimes; in other words, a small amount.

5. *worshipped strange gods*: a biblical echo; see, for example: 'And they forsook the Lord God of their fathers, which brought them out of Egypt, and followed other gods, of the gods of the people that were round about them, and bowed themselves unto them, and provoked the Lord to anger' (Judges 2: 12); 'They provoked him to jealousy with strange gods, with abominations provoked they him to anger. They sacrificed unto devils, not to God; to gods whom they knew not, to new gods that came newly up, whom your fathers feared not' (Deuteronomy 32: 16–17).

6. *ombres chinoises*: a shadow-puppet show (French – literally, 'Chinese shadows').

7. *rapprochement*: a connection or comparison (French).

8. *Pantaloon ... Christmas farce ... Harlequin*: Pantaloon and Harlequin are both stock figures from the Italian *commedia dell'arte*. Pantaloon was traditionally an elderly figure of authority, the guardian, or elderly suitor, of the beautiful heroine (Columbine) and mocked by the Clown. Harlequin is himself clown-like, a rival for the affections of Columbine; being mute, he relies on dumbshow. The Christmas farce refers to the English harlequinade, a form of pantomime.

9. *the trodden worm of the adage*: 'the smallest worm will turn,

being trodden on'; most likely this adage originated in William Shakespeare's *King Henry VI, Part Three*, II. ii. 17.

10. *pince-nez*: a pair of glasses that perch on the nose, unattached to the ears (French).

MARY AUSTIN

The Readjustment

Mary Austin (née Hunter, 1868–1934) was born in Carlinville, Illinois. After graduating from Blackburn University, she moved with her family to California. In 1891, she married Stafford Wallace Austin. The couple lived in the Owens River Valley, where Mary Austin wrote and taught. Their first child, Ruth, born in 1892, was mentally disabled; she was given first of all to the care of another family, and then moved to an institution, where she lived until her death in 1918. Mary Austin separated from her husband in 1905. Three years later, she moved to Italy, where she studied with a religious order known as the Blue Nuns. She spent some time in Paris and London, before returning to the USA, where she divided her time between Carmel and New York. Her views were socialist, feminist and mystical; her writings celebrated the desert life of the American west and Native American culture. Her work includes: idiosyncratic religious writings (such as *The Man Jesus*, 1915); fiction (including the book of short stories *The Basket Woman*, 1904, and the novel *A Woman of Genius*, 1912); children's books (*The Trail Book*, 1918); poetry (*Children Sing in the Far West*, 1928); plays (such as *The Arrow Maker*, 1911); books on nature (such as *The Land of Little Rain*, 1903); and an autobiography (*Earth Horizon*, 1932).

The copy-text of 'The Readjustment' comes from its first publication in book form in the volume of short stories *Lost Borders* (New York and London: Harper & Brothers, 1909), pp. 154–65.

1. *mignonette*: a small but fragrant herbaceous plant with yellowish-white flowers.

2. *wrapper after three o'clock in the afternoon*: a wrapper was an outer garment used for household work. It was sometimes known as a 'morning wrapper', and there are indications that this was a garment mainly worn early on in the day. The implication here presumably is that Emma Jeffries has finished all her housework by three o'clock, and that this is evidence of impeccable respectability. To wear one after that hour would look slovenly.

3. *syringa-bush*: lilac.

4. *Pasadena*: then a small town in the vicinity of Los Angeles,

California, and in the 1900s famed for the clear quality of its warm, dry air and therefore as a winter resort for wealthy Easterners, and a healthy locale for the sick.

5. *rod*: a measure of distance equal to five and a half yards (six metres).

6. *'The Lord is my shepherd'*: the opening words of Psalm 23.

7. *'The Lord is nigh . . . broken heart'*: from Psalm 38: 18. The verse continues: 'and saveth such as be of a contrite spirit'.

8. *'He shall . . . evil touch thee'*: from Job 5: 19.

9. *'For thou shalt . . . waters that are past'*: slightly misquoted version of Zophar's rebuke in Job 11: 16: 'Because thou shalt forget thy misery, and remember it as waters that pass away.'

EDITH WHARTON

Afterward

Edith (Newbold Jones) Wharton (1862–1937) was an American novelist and short-story writer, an analyst of the opulent New York of the late nineteenth and early twentieth centuries, and an explorer of the relations between America and Europe. She grew up in an atmosphere of distinguished privilege, educated at home, moving between New York, her birthplace, and the family's summer house at Newport, Rhode Island. In 1885, she married Edward Wharton; his ill-health prompted travel to Europe, where they settled in Paris. The couple divorced in 1913. Her greatest novels include: *The House of Mirth* (1905); *Ethan Frome* (1911), a tragic account of New England life; *The Custom of the Country* (1913); and the Pulitzer Prize-winning *The Age of Innocence* (1920). Her autobiography is *A Backward Glance* (1934). As a ghost-story writer, she is indebted to the example of her friend Henry James, though in fact her stories are more given than his to the shocking dénouement.

The copy-text of 'Afterward' is from *Tales of Men and Ghosts* (London: Macmillan and Co., 1910), pp. 323–73. The story was first published in the January 1910 issue of *Century Magazine*.

1. *Pangbourne*: there is no Pangbourne in the English west-country county of Dorset, though there is a Pangbourne, many miles east, in Berkshire, on the Thames north-west of Reading.

2. *signalement*: the description of a person for a passport, or of a wanted criminal (French).

3. *dü*: in a manner standard at the time, Wharton attempts to render the West Country accent.

4. *coign*: a vantage point for observation.

5. *Waukesha*: Waukesha, then a small town, in Wisconsin, in the upper Midwest of the USA, is 'the soul-deadening' and ugly place where the couple have spent their marriage. The New World place name (wrongly supposed to derive from the Algonquin word for 'little foxes') forms a linguistic contrast to the old English names of Dorset.

6. *Dorchester*: a market town in southern central Dorset.

7. *Benedictine*: the order of monks (known as the 'Black Monks' due to the colour of their habits) founded by St Benedict around 529. The Benedictine Rule set out the highly regulated, ascetic and organized life of the monastery, bound by strict rules of punctuality and the orderly division of the day.

8. *Cimmerian night*: from the opening passage of Book 11 of Homer's *Odyssey*, the Cimmerians were a people fabled to live in perpetual darkness at the entrance to Hades, land of the dead.

PENGUIN CLASSICS

THE MOONSTONE
WILKIE COLLINS

> 'When you looked down into the stone, you looked into a yellow deep that drew
> your eyes into it so that they saw nothing else'

The Moonstone, a yellow diamond looted from an Indian temple and believed to
bring bad luck to its owner, is bequeathed to Rachel Verinder on her eighteenth
birthday. That very night the priceless stone is stolen again and when Sergeant
Cuff is brought in to investigate the crime, he soon realizes that no one in Rachel's
household is above suspicion. Hailed by T. S. Eliot as 'the first, the longest, and
the best of modern English detective novels', *The Moonstone* is a marvellously taut
and intricate tale of mystery, in which facts and memory can prove treacherous and
not everyone is as they first appear.

Sandra Kemp's introduction examines *The Moonstone* as a work of Victorian
sensation fiction and an early example of the detective genre, and discusses the
technique of multiple narrators, the role of opium, and Collins's sources and
autobiographical references.

'Enthralling and believable ... evokes in vivid language the spirit of a place' P. D.
James, *Sunday Times*

Edited with an introduction and notes by Sandra Kemp

PENGUIN CLASSICS

DEAD SOULS
NIKOLAI GOGOL

> 'It's not a question of the living. I've nothing to do with them.
> I'm asking for the dead'

Chichikov, a mysterious stranger, arrives in the provincial town of 'N', visiting
a succession of landowners and making each a strange offer. He proposes to buy
the names of dead serfs still registered on the census, saving their owners from
paying tax on them, and to use these 'souls' as collateral to re-invent himself as
a gentleman. In this ebullient masterpiece, Gogol created a grotesque gallery of
human types, from the bear-like Sobakevich to the insubstantial fool Manilov, and,
above all, the devilish conman Chichikov. *Dead Souls*, Russia's first major novel,
is one of the most unusual works of nineteenth-century fiction and a devastating
satire on social hypocrisy.

David Magarshack's introduction discusses Gogol's plan for a novel in three
parts, tracing Chichikov's progress from sin to redemption, and tells how Gogol
destroyed part of the manuscript in the grip of madness. The surviving sections,
volume one and a fragment of volume two, are translated here.

'Gogol was a strange creature, but then genius is always strange'
Vladimir Nabokov

Translated with an introduction by David Magarshack

THE STORY OF PENGUIN CLASSICS

Before 1946 ... 'Classics' are mainly the domain of academics and students; readable editions for everyone else are almost unheard of. This all changes when a little-known classicist, E. V. Rieu, presents Penguin founder Allen Lane with the translation of Homer's *Odyssey* that he has been working on in his spare time.

1946 Penguin Classics debuts with *The Odyssey*, which promptly sells three million copies. Suddenly, classics are no longer for the privileged few.

1950s Rieu, now series editor, turns to professional writers for the best modern, readable translations, including Dorothy L. Sayers's *Inferno* and Robert Graves's unexpurgated *Twelve Caesars*.

1960s The Classics are given the distinctive black covers that have remained a constant throughout the life of the series. Rieu retires in 1964, hailing the Penguin Classics list as 'the greatest educative force of the twentieth century.'

1970s A new generation of translators swells the Penguin Classics ranks, introducing readers of English to classics of world literature from more than twenty languages. The list grows to encompass more history, philosophy, science, religion and politics.

1980s The Penguin American Library launches with titles such as *Uncle Tom's Cabin*, and joins forces with Penguin Classics to provide the most comprehensive library of world literature available from any paperback publisher.

1990s The launch of Penguin Audiobooks brings the classics to a listening audience for the first time, and in 1999 the worldwide launch of the Penguin Classics website extends their reach to the global online community.

The 21st Century Penguin Classics are completely redesigned for the first time in nearly twenty years. This world-famous series now consists of more than 1300 titles, making the widest range of the best books ever written available to millions – and constantly redefining what makes a 'classic'.

The Odyssey continues ...

The best books ever written

PENGUIN (🐧) CLASSICS

SINCE 1946

Find out more at www.penguinclassics.com